THE HORRORS THAT CREATED US

ELUDING DESTINY

BOOK TWO

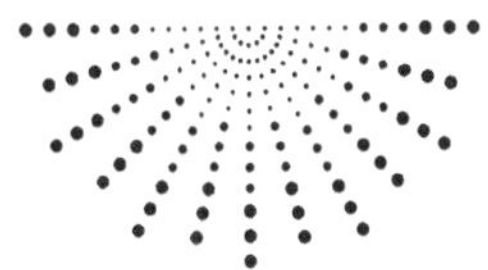

CHARLIE NOTTINGHAM

LIQUID MIND PUBLISHING

THE ELUDING DESTINEY SERIES

Eluding Destiny

The Horrors That Created Us

Aftershocks

The Precipice

Land of Light

The Quiet Army

Sacred Sins

Flash Back

The Shift

Lost to Time

Gods Among Us

The Cover Up

Blank Slate

Sign up for Charlie's newsletter and receive a free copy of the Eluding Destiny prequel, Blood Bar:

https://liquidmind.media/eluding-destiny-prequel/

CONTENT WARNING

This story is intended only for mature audiences.
It contains adult language, drug and alcohol abuse,
violence, sexual assault, and other sensitive material.
Please read at your own discretion.
If you're a survivor and need someone to talk to,
call 1-800-654-4673
If you're struggling with addiction and need someone to talk to,
call 844-534-1996
You aren't alone.

*This one's for all the women and girls out there.
The ones that support other women, the ones that have busted their asses for everything they have, the ones working day in and day out to make their dreams come true, the ones that get back up each time the world beats them down.
We and the women that came before us have spent far too long fighting for things we should have had since the beginning of time.
It's our time to shine.
I got your back.*

CHAPTER ONE

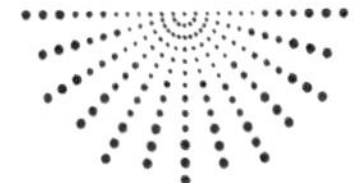

JANUARY 8TH, 2019 - JEREMY - THE TRIAL

The rumors did the place justice. The Elders Hall was older than anyone who stood within it that day. The winged babies painted on the domed ceiling saw more people led to their deaths than I'd ever want to acknowledge. Everything was trimmed in gold paint and intricate woodwork above the white marble floors.

The eyes of the many statues situated around the pews seemed to stare at me anywhere I sat. I didn't see any books laying around, but somehow, that's what it smelled like. A library. It even had the same chill in the air. The whispers around the room were just as quiet.

From an outside perspective, it just looked pretentious. Rich and fancy, not scary. But something about that place chilled me to my core.

"I don't know what the point to this is," I muttered to Laila. "They don't give a shit. This is a child's problem."

"Moe's murder is a child's problem? What she had Ally do to you. That was a child's problem?"

"Not to me, not to you. But to them." I glanced up at the twelve old men and women situated around the semicircular table murmuring amongst themselves. "Yeah, baby. We don't matter. The only reason we got this hearing at all is because we have connections to Angels that rank higher than her."

She ran her tongue along her teeth. "Well, let's just hope they're as wise as they claim to be. That bitch doesn't deserve to have wings after what she did."

I licked my lips and gave a nod. She wasn't wrong, Mary did some fucked up shit.

What happened last year tore me up more than I'd ever be able to admit aloud. But I knew that didn't matter to them. Mary would walk. And truthfully, I didn't want her to get kicked out of Heaven either.

I wanted to understand why she did it. I wanted to understand what I did that made her hate me. But I didn't want her to lose the one thing that she loved about herself.

"Ladies and gentlemen, please have a seat," the woman in a white robe at the center of the large wraparound desk said. "Would the accused please come to the stand?"

The whispers of the small audience—primarily made up of my family members—fell silent. We turned and watched as Mary stood from the front row. She walked in silent humbleness to the center of the semicircle before the Elders.

"State your name, age, race, occupation, and accused crime for the court, if you would," the woman at the center seat said.

"My name is Mary. I have no surname." She held her hands folded together in front of her hips as she spoke. "My exact date of birth is unknown, but I believe it's somewhere over two thousand years in the Earth realm. I'm an Angel for the Skoulda Guardian clan, or was, rather, before these events ensued. I stand accused of the murder of a Siren named Allisia from the Atlantic coast of the Americas."

"Pleasure to see you again, Mary." The woman smiled. Mary gave a civil nod as Laila scoffed beside me.

"They know each other? And she gets a say in all of this?" She spoke in a low whisper.

"She probably knows every one of them up there," Leah murmured beside Laila.

"That's bullshit," Laila said.

Not that I disagreed but I expected nothing less. Mary was well known and well liked. My family? Well known, certainly. But never well liked. At least, not my generation of it.

"And how do you plead, Mary?" the woman asked.

"Guilty, your honor. I did it. I killed that girl."

The woman leaned back in her chair and sucked her teeth. "Care to explain why you felt it necessary to kill an endangered creature?"

"Ally wanted to inform one of my children that I was her mother. It was only a matter of time before she did or before one of the many psychics close to my daughter would have figured it out."

"Well, that's a crock of shit," Laila blurted.

"Excuse me?" the woman at the table said.

"Laila." I put my finger over my lips. But she was already standing.

"I said that's a crock of shit." Laila put her hands at her hips.

I rubbed my tense forehead. The love of my life. The defiant, obnoxious, out-spoken love of my life.

"And who are you?" the woman said.

"Laila." She gestured toward Mary. "Her daughter. Can I get called to the stand here? Because—"

"When you learn to talk like a lady, I may allow you to speak in this court."

Laila curled her lip in disgust. I wanted to laugh but I bit it back. 'Acting like a lady' was never Laila's strong suit. And I understood her frustrations, but in this court, our frustrations meant nothing. Gender meant a whole hell of a lot. Our opinions though? Practically useless.

"No, I'm curious," a man said a few seats down from the first woman. "What did Mary say that was 'a crock of shit?'"

"The Siren wasn't telling us anything and Mary knew that," Laila said. "We weren't questioning Ally because we wanted to know who my birth mother was. We were questioning her to figure out who gave her legs in exchange for raping my boyfriend. And to see if she knew who tried to kill him. Just so happened that Mary was responsible for both."

"Is your boyfriend in the court today?" the man asked.

She turned to me. I awkwardly ran my hand along my mouth as I stood. "That's me."

"Is that what happened?" he asked.

Mary looked at me over her shoulder. Her brows were pulled together, her throat bobbed with a swallow. She felt guilty. And for some reason, it hurt to see her that way. I should've been as angry as Laila was, but I wasn't. I was just... hurt.

But I cleared my throat. "Yeah. Yeah, that's what happened."

"*You* were raped." One of the women laughed. "How does that work exactly?"

I didn't care for the word either. Technically, that was what had happened. But I didn't want to talk about it. I didn't want to explain it, especially not to them. It made me feel gross and violated, and I hated even thinking about it. But what did it matter now? Ally was dead. She couldn't do it to anyone else. I had no recollection of the event. The only reason I was even there was because it *might've* helped Laila get justice for Moe's murder.

"Um, well, if you use your powers to get someone in bed, that's not exactly consent," Laila said.

"Did you say no?" the man asked.

"She did something to my head. I don't really remember it."

"So, you didn't say no then?" another voice from the table said.

"Well, I didn't say yes."

"And I take it she didn't drug you to..." She glanced toward my pelvis. "So, there must have been some attraction on your end."

"Is that so?" the first woman said. "Were you drugged?"

I turned my gaze to the marble floor. "No. I wasn't drugged."

I knew this was what they'd say. I knew that in their minds, I had no right to feel the way I did. To them, I was a man who'd gotten my dick wet. It didn't matter that I was forced. It didn't matter that I hadn't wanted it. It didn't matter that it was assaulted, because I was a man. What did they care? I didn't remember it anyway.

Although, having expected this, no matter how much the reminder ached in my chest and made my skin crawl, the fact remained. This was the reaction I'd anticipated. Which was why I'd hoped Mary trying to kill me would warrant some sort of punishment.

"Were you tied down? Was there a knife at your throat?" the woman asked.

"You're kidding, right?" Laila said. "A Siren's primary ability is to sing a song that makes people want to take their clothes off and—"

"Only if there is attraction," the man said. "So. Were you attracted to her?"

I licked my teeth and moved my shoulders in something of a shrug. "I didn't find her unattractive."

"That settles that part then," the woman said.

"What?" Laila said. "But she—"

"He has no recollection of the events and it was at least somewhat mutual, or something wouldn't have worked." The man shrugged. "This is irrelevant."

The outcome I'd expected.

"Are you serious right now? You *condone* this?" Laila's voice was filled with disgust.

The woman turned to Mary. "Did you try to kill this boy?"

"No." Mary looked at me over her shoulder again with that same guilty expression. "No, I would never do that. I love Jeremy, I watched him grow from a child to the man standing here today. What Laila is referencing was a misunderstanding. I did accidentally hurt him, that is true. But I did not try to kill him. I was just trying to slow him down to give me more time to get to the Siren. I put morion inside of his car and caused an accident. The intent was only to halt his arrival at the Siren's home. The morion made it so that he couldn't teleport the vehicle when he started to crash. When I saw how bad the accident was, I started to help but then Laila arrived with Jeremy's brother. They took him back to his sister to be healed and all was well."

"You arrived." The woman made a face at Laila. "How did you know he was in an accident?"

"He's my par animo. I felt it."

The Elders looked between us. "Is that so?"

"It is."

"They're right, your honors," Mary agreed. "Chamuel confirmed it about three years ago."

The woman in the middle leaned back and crossed her arms against her chest. "I see."

"But ultimately, Mary," another Elder said, "you did these things to keep your identity confidential as you swore an oath to do before this child was even conceived."

"I did," Mary murmured. "Above all else, I am loyal to Heaven and our father, the one true God. Although I do agree that many of my methods were less than humane, I was following orders."

"And who are we to argue with the lord himself?" The woman in the center smiled. She glanced at Laila and I with an expression I had a hard time placing. Contempt, perhaps.

"We are not," another Elder said.

"You've done as you were told, and you will not be punished for doing so," the woman in the center said.

A deep breath fell from my nose.

Was I surprised at the way this was heading? No, it was exactly what I'd anticipated. I also hadn't want to see Mary die for this, nor did I want her to get kicked from Heaven, but I wanted her to to face *some* form of punishment. At the very least, a slap on the wrist. But it looked like she was going to get off completely free.

"Are you serious?" Laila blurted with a darting gaze. "This woman stabbed an old man more than a dozen times for the purpose of—"

"Protecting her identity, no?" one of the men said. "Moses Baker, I presume is who you're referencing."

Her teeth gritted to a line. "And that's just okay with you people? That she murdered someone in cold blood to protect a secret I figured out anyway?"

"Moses Baker had no place on this land," the woman said. "He had no rights the moment he crossed to this realm. I certainly won't condemn a loyal servant of God for an alien."

"Then you're a cunt," Laila snapped.

My heart palpitated and my eyes shot open.

I'd been a part of this world my entire life. And from the moment I could remember hearing my Dad talk about the Elders with a terrified gaze in his eyes, I feared ever standing within that room with those men and women. They worked directly with the Archangels and God himself. They had more power than anyone. Killing the love of my life would be like swatting a fly to them.

Mary turned to me with the same expression.

"Talk to me that way again and I'll have your tongue, little girl," the woman said with a piercing gaze.

"Oh, fu—"

I leaned over and put my hand over her mouth. She swatted it away. I widened my eyes further.

"Mind your woman there, boy," the first man to speak said.

"Before someone does it for you," another man blurted.

Laila scoffed. "I don't know what time period you're living in but—"

"Stop." I turned to her with eyes bigger than the ocean and shook my head.

I almost never told her what to do. But I wasn't about to end up in a blood bath with some of the oldest, most powerful leaders in the supernatural world. I'd rather her be mad at me than end up without a tongue. Or worse, not walk out of that hall at all.

"Are you done now?" the woman in the center asked. "Or do you need a little time out?"

Laila glared.

"Let's just go," I murmured with a hand on her back.

She clamped her teeth together. She took my hand. I looked to my siblings in the pew beside us. We all teleported back home in pairs.

———

"No, that was bullshit." Laila's nostrils flared. "They made it out like what Ally did to you was perfectly acceptable."

"I'm a man. Kinda figured they would," I muttered, raising a paint brush to the corner of the baseboard. "Don't know if you noticed but gender equality is pretty irrelevant to them."

"No shit." She lowered herself to the floor beside me and picked up another brush. "I just... I thought that something would happen to her.

Some form of punishment. In the human world, she'd get at least twenty years."

"She'll get hers. What goes around comes around." I took the brush from her hand and met her gaze. "But you shouldn't be in here. All these fumes are bad for the baby."

"It's a little paint." She rolled her eyes and snatched it back. "The baby's fine."

"If you say so," I said.

Gliding the brush along the window frame, Laila said, "Just sucks that he's never going to get justice."

Ever since Moe died, all she'd talked about was Mary getting what she deserved for killing him. And I understood. Mary told her that she killed Moe so that Laila would inherit his business, and that burden weighed heavy on her shoulders. In her eyes, she was responsible for his death. I knew that she wasn't. I was sure that Moe, wherever he was, knew the same. But that was a heavy cross to carry.

"Is that what you want? Justice?" I sat the brush down and touched her cheek. "Or is this about the blame game you've been playing?"

Her voice was soft, a bit sad. "I just want to go back in time and keep it from happening."

"It'd be nice if it worked like that. But do you think Moe would want you to hold onto all this resentment? Because I knew Moe too and he wasn't the vengeance type. He was the live and let live type."

"Well, I'm not."

I smiled and touched her hip. "Well. I think that if Moe were here, he'd tell you to be happy and not to worry about something you can't change."

"I think he'd tell me to find a man who knows how to paint." She squinted at the top of the windowsill. "We just stained these and here you go painting all over it."

I looked to the speck of green on the cherry wood. "Are you talking about that little, tiny drop smaller than a pinhead?"

"It's bigger than a pinhead." She pulled away and brought herself to the tips of her toes. I looked over the little bump starting to protrude from her flat stomach and smiled.

Even though we'd lost in court that day, I was so happy. *We* were so happy.

I had her, she had me, we had our diner, and nothing else mattered. Life was better than it'd ever been. I was ready to shut the door on what happened a few months before, the paranormal bullshit helping Angels track down rogue supernaturals, and move onto better days. Maybe that was why my reaction wasn't as volatile as Laila's. She wanted all of the wrongs made right regardless of how we both knew the hierarchies in our world operated.

I wasn't naive enough to expect anything more than what we'd gotten, but I was *done.*

I wouldn't waste another second fighting for them. If all of this had shown me anything, it was how little I mattered to the facilities I'd given years of my life to.

My trauma, Laila's trauma, meant nothing to them.

That was the catalyst I needed to leave that life behind.

The Chambers, the Council, the Angels... all of that shit was my past.

This was my future.

As awful as the path that led us there was, we finally had what we wanted. We were done taking orders. We were focusing on ourselves and what *we* wanted.

A family. A good one, not like the one I'd had. With a mom and a dad more in love than anyone else. Full of love, and passion, and peace. The two of us and our child, living happily ever after with a simple, human existence. Not that we'd forget what we were, but to leave the past in the past. To stop worrying about Demons and vamps that didn't matter to us anyway.

They were all that mattered. They were all I wanted. A happily ever after with my family.

"Now you're just nit picking." I smiled.

"No, you're just messy." She licked her thumb and began scrubbing.

I ran my tongue along my smiling lips and lifted the brush from the can. I reached around her and brushed a streak of green paint across her creamy cheek.

She gasped before she turned to me, mouth open as wide as her eyes.

"Oh, geez, I'm sorry." I grinned. "I'm just so messy, I don't know how that happened."

"Oh yeah?" Her mouth curved into an unwilling smile. I took a step back and held my grin as she leaned down to grab the other paint brush. "Come here."

"No." I laughed and took another step back.

She lunged forward on her tip toes, sliding the brush from my forehead to my chin. "Oh, geez, I'm sorry."

"That's it." I leaned down and stuck my hand into the bucket of paint.

"Don't you dare. If you fling that across this baby's room—"

"Fling it?" I asked. "Who said anything about flinging it?"

I teleported in front of her and pressed my lips to hers. I raised my hand to her cheek and slid my dripping hand to her neck.

"There ya go." I smiled, moving my hand to her hip. "No drips or anything."

She tried to force down her smiling lips before she reached up and wiped her cheek. She leaned forward and slid it along my chest.

"Do you want to take this outside?"

Laila grinned. I laugh, grabbed ahold of her hips, and tugged her into me. She laughed and rested her head against my chest. "I love you, ya know that?"

"I do know that." I kissed her hair and tightened my arms around her waist. "And I love you too."

Happy. We were *so* happy.

CHAPTER TWO

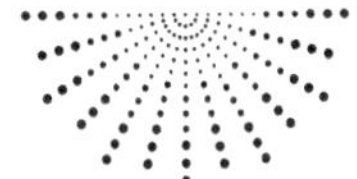

JANUARY 21, 2019 - LAILA

KAI CALLIDY, CELENA JONES, ADALYN

Three names printed in the back of Moe's Journal. My brother, and my two sisters.

On the other side of the glass pane stood one of them. Unfortunately, the one with a last name. The one I likely would've been able to track down on my own.

Her long blond hair dangled before her tired blue eyes. A red flush warmed her round cheeks. She held her strong shoulders high, proud, but I knew the weight she was carrying all too well.

We'd gotten a call this morning from one of Jeremy's friends. Wyatt Braxton. Although we'd left the Chambers behind, if a loved one was in need, we helped however we could.

That call had been about her. Celena Nicole Jones.

She was bitten by a Werewolf, and her cousin saw Celena's first shift. The girl didn't want knowledge of the supernatural world, so I'd just wiped her memories.

Looking at Celena on the other side of the glass pane though, I wished I could make her forget too.

That wasn't possible. Not really. Becoming a Werewolf was irreversible. She had no choice; she had to accept what she was.

But fuck, I wished I could take this pain away. Showing her that page in Moe's journal, explaining my theory that we were related, certainly hadn't made this any easier.

Jeremy's fingers found mine, dragging my attention to his gaze. "You got her blood?"

I thumbed the vial in my pocket, giving a nod. With her permission, I was taking it to the underground hospital to run some tests. Obviously to confirm if she was the girl Moe cited in that book, but also to see if she had any other dormant powers we didn't know about.

He frowned. "You okay?"

I was in better shape than she was, that was for certain. But my chest was tight, and my hands were shaky.

Maybe I was worried for her. Maybe I felt bad for making her bad day worse with my theories. Maybe I felt like shit because I knew how it felt to be roped into this world and feel like your entire life was a lie.

"Yeah, I'm alright."

He gave a smile. "Good, because we're gonna be late if we don't leave now."

The strong smell from the car air freshener wafted to my nose and made my stomach spin. Gazing out the passenger side window, I watched the snow-covered trees whoosh past in a blur of gray and white. The tips of my fingers coasted over the bump of my belly that had just started to appear a few weeks prior.

Jeremy pulled our hands to his lips and kissed my knuckles. I turned to meet his gaze and gave a smile. "What?"

"What's going on up there?" He pointed toward my head with a grin. "You've barely said a word since we left."

I thought it was obvious.

My mind was on the barely eighteen year old girl who'd just been turned into a Werewolf against her will. She was just immersed in a world she never knew existed, she was scared, and I wanted to help her.

Aside from that, the pack who'd turned her was a barbaric one. I'd had many interactions with Werewolves, and for the most part, I liked them. But these fuckers were beasts, and I was scared for her safety.

"I'm just worried about her."

"Celena?" he asked. I nodded, and he shrugged. "I wouldn't be. She's smart. So is Wyatt. They're tough kids, they can handle themselves."

That wasn't just it. Maybe they were big kids, maybe they could handle things on their own. But she was my sister. I felt connected to her. And even if she wasn't my sister—although I was fairly certain she was—I had a bad feeling about this. She needed me. And I needed to be there for her.

"Wyatt's just a wolf though. And Celena has no idea how to use her powers. They don't seem to be connected to anger and fear like they are for me. She doesn't know what her powers are yet, she can't protect herself," I said. "I don't know. I just feel like I have to do something. I have to help her."

"If they ask for it, we'll do what we can. But it isn't our battle."

"We're supposed to protect people, aren't we? Isn't that the point in having all of these powers?"

"I know how hard it is for you to see someone who needs help. I know you want to dive in and fix it. I get that you want to go in guns blazing and right wrongs and save people but you're pregnant, Lai. Just relax for now. Enjoy the peace while we have it."

"I'm pregnant, Jeremy. I'm not defenseless. I'm more powerful now than I've ever been and—"

"Do you have any idea what that alpha did to Wyatt's girlfriend because he told her what he was?" Jeremy met my gaze with furrowed brows. He looked back to the road. "Damon's smart. He knows the rules. The Council and the North American Monarch know about what they did, and they let him get away with it because he said he was preventing exposure. They would do the same to you, if not worse. Any shitty creature in our world would do just about anything to see you dead. They keep their distance but only because we stick to ourselves. Killing a couple rogues is one thing. But you can't go up against a pack that's been around for hundreds of years and has hundreds of wolves to back them up," he said. "Not while you're carrying our baby, Laila. You just can't."

"Oh. So you're putting your foot down? Is that it?"

He rolled his eyes. "You make your own choices, you know that. But I think we both know you wouldn't forgive yourself if something happened to this baby because you rushed into something you weren't ready for."

"She's my sister, Jeremy. You would do just about anything to keep your sister safe, wouldn't you?"

"You literally just met her, Laila."

My already defensive gaze grew raged. He was right, I didn't know Celena yet. But that didn't matter.

I felt how scared she was. I could see how alone she felt.

"What's that supposed to mean? I should just let her die?"

"She's not going to die," he muttered with a shake of his head. "Trust me, they want her alive. She was turned by one of them, she's a part of their pack. And she was a hybrid before she was turned. She's a commodity, they aren't killing her."

"It's those two against everyone else and she has no idea how to control her powers," I said. "They can't do this on their own."

"I'm not saying we won't help them, Laila. But even with all of us combined, it's not enough to take them on. For us to win against them, she needs to figure out how to use her powers. Even then, I still don't know. With as big as their pack is, not to mention their mates... We'd lose. There's no way in hell we wouldn't. And who knows how many of us would go down in the process. Plus, are you ready to slaughter families? Because that's what we'd be doing. We'd be pillaging an entire community, not just a few wolves who don't want to stay in line."

I turned my gaze out the window. I saw the point he was making. In Jeremy's eyes, we'd left the Chambers, and none of this was our concern anymore. But if Celena was my sister, it *was* my business.

Although, I supposed he was right. I wasn't one for slaughtering villages.

"If she needs my help, I'm not going to turn my back on her," I said.

"I never said that we would. But we're not going on a suicide mission either. If they want to take the pack down, it'll be planned. We're not walking blindly into a battle we can't win. Especially a battle that isn't ours."

"I guess you're right." My fingers ran along my firm stomach. "I just want to make sure she's going to be okay. I was in her head; I saw how dark her life's been. She's so gloomy and jaded. She has a lot to heal from, you know?"

"If she's your family, she's my family." He turned and met my gaze as we came to a stop light. "I'll make sure nothing happens to her. But I don't want you to get involved with this pack shit. Not while you're pregnant. I'm not trying to be controlling. I just need you to be safe. I need our baby to be safe. I'd do anything to protect you guys, and if that means I'm being a dick, or controlling, I'm sorry. But at least the two of you'll be safe."

"That doesn't make you a dick." A slow exhale left my lips. I watched the snowflakes hit the windshield and melt to little water droplets for a long, quiet moment. "You're right. The baby comes first."

His tone softened, smile coming to his lips. "Let's not argue, okay? Today's supposed to be a good day."

"We might not find out the sex today, ya know." I smiled as I turned toward him. "And what does it matter anyway? They can be a boy, they can be a girl, I don't care. You can't put so much emphasis on gender. That just fills kids heads with sexist and outdated linear views of sexuality and gender identity."

"It's not that I really care. I just have a feeling he's a boy. And I want to win the poll." He gave an excited grin, hand moving to my belly.

I chuckled, looked down, and held either side of the baby bump. "They're already betting on you, kid."

Jeremy had been the perfect parent since I told him I was pregnant. I never saw him as excited as he was to be a father. He'd already read four books on pregnancy and one on birth. He spent hours on parenting blogs reading everything from whether or not I should eat my placenta to caring for my nipples while breast feeding.

He recently took over most of my duties that I couldn't do from my desk at Moe's. He obsessed over the nursery as we remodeled. He made sure to use stains and polishes on the hardwood floors that had the least numbers of carcinogens possible. He painted with the mildest paints, bolted furniture to the walls, and baby proofed every sharp edge and cabinet door that he could. He even put a lock on the toilet seat— which got to be a real pain in the ass with how often I was pissing those days.

I always wanted to be a mom, but I think Jeremy wanted to be a dad even more. Considering he lost his parents when he was young, I understood why he was so obsessed with doing it right. I'd never thought Jeremy would be the PTA sort of guy, but that parental instinct that'd kicked in only made me fall for him harder.

CHAPTER THREE

LAILA

I stared up at the little blob on the ultrasound as the cool gel on my belly grew warm with my body heat. The room was dark aside from the light of the machine. It reeked of hospital. I never quite understood what that smell actually was. Old people, maybe? Chemicals? I didn't know. Best to just label it as hospital.

"Can you tell the sex yet?" Jeremy squeezed my hand, squinting hard at the image.

The technician chuckled. "It's a little early but I do have a good idea. You can't take it with too much merit though because it might look like one now and look completely different in a couple weeks."

"But if you had to guess?" Jeremy turned to meet her gaze.

She chuckled and gestured to the screen. "Alright, so right here, that's the head, and here are the legs." She ran her finger along the circle I found to resemble a tadpole far more than a baby. She moved the tool lower down to my pelvis and pushed in a bit. "And if you look right here..." I squinted at the image, now appearing to look a bit like a rotisserie chicken. "You can see a—"

"It's a boy!" Jeremy quickly stood and excitedly pumped his fist into the air like his favorite team just landed the touch down at the Super Bowl. I smiled at his expression of sheer joy.

The technician laughed. "If I had to guess, I'd say it's a boy."

He leaned down quickly, took my face in his hands, and kissed me. He met my gaze, holding my cheeks. "I told you. I told you it was a boy." He pulled away and turned back to the screen.

"You did." I smiled as the technician pulled the tool from my stomach and wiped it with a cloth.

She clicked a few more buttons and the printer began to hum. "I don't think I need to ask if you guys want pictures."

"Is he okay?" Jeremy asked. "Is he healthy and everything?"

"The doctor has to view the images to be sure, but between you and me, everything looks exactly like it's supposed to." She smiled. "Your little boy looks perfect."

My lips pulled up in a soft smile at the frozen image of my baby on the ultrasound. There he was. Small and resembling something between a tadpole and a chicken, but still the cutest tadpole-chicken I ever did see.

CHAPTER FOUR

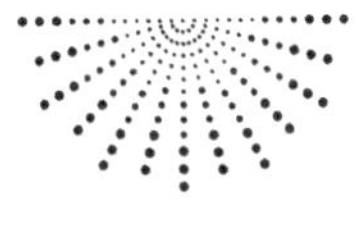

LAILA

"You have to keep them closed," Jeremy urged, his hands over my eyes from behind.

"Yeah, yeah. I know the routine."

We stood in our messy, partially remodeled living room waiting for him to teleport. He insisted I wear a dress—code that he was taking me somewhere warm but thought he was sly by saying dress instead of shorts.

"No peeking."

"I know, baby. Let's just go because I'm starving."

He chuckled and we swirled through space. We landed somewhere hot and humid. The salty smell of the ocean wisped to my nose. I heard music in the distance, too far for me to make out the instruments over the roaring waves slapping the shore, but soft and beautiful all the same.

"Okay, so I'm going to let go of your eyes, but you have to keep them closed," he murmured at my ear before kissing my neck.

"Alright." I smiled, fingers grazing his. "But I don't smell any food. I thought that's why we were going out."

"Don't worry, there's food." He placed his arm around my waist, guiding me forward, taking slow steps. Warm sand settled between my toes.

"Where are we?" I asked. "Is there going to be food I like or is it going to be snails again?"

"You're pregnant, you shouldn't eat escargot right now. And I learned my lesson last time. Snails aren't your thing."

"Neither is squid for future reference."

"Okay, so stand here for a second." He released my waist. I heard the shuffling of his pant legs for a moment. "Alright, now open your eyes."

As I did, my gaze caught on a small circular table placed in the sand with two chairs covered in a dainty white cloth. It sat about fifty yards from the peaceful, white foamed shore. A set of dinnerware laid in front of each chair with white cloth napkins and sparkling silverware.

A neat globe of white lilies rested between two taper candles on either side. Fire flickered at their tips. Hues of pink and orange from the dusking sun illuminated the quiet, seemingly private beach.

Jeremy stood beside the table. His black hair was pulled back into a neat ponytail at the nape of his neck. His smile stretched so far up his cheeks that the corners of his lips nearly met his eyes on his diamond shaped face. His pastel cerulean button up brought out the electric blue of his eyes against mine. I should've known something was up— he was always in ripped T-shirts and bleach-stained jeans.

I couldn't help but grin like a little girl. We'd been together for just over three years and every time I looked at that smile, my belly still danced with butterflies. Yet, even in those sweet and innocent moments, I still wanted to sit on his face.

"Baby, you didn't have to do all of this. I just wanted Chipotle or something."

He laughed and pulled my chair out. "Just enjoy it."

I smiled again, kissing him before I sat. He moved around the table and lowered himself on his chair.

"You're the best boyfriend a girl could ask for, you know." I reached across the table to take his hand.

He shrugged, still smiling. "I try."

"So, what are we celebrating?" I gestured around. "It isn't our anniversary."

"Can't I just do something nice for you?" He held that sweet grin, squeezing my hand.

"This isn't just nice, baby, this is a whole hell of a lot."

He tried to press down his smiling lips. "I just love you."

I smiled. "I love you too. Thank you, this is beautiful."

And it was. I was abundantly grateful. But I was promised dinner.

His smile heightened. "But there's no food?"

"But there's no food." I grinned.

He laughed and pulled out his phone. He typed for a moment. Then three men in white shirts and black slacks appeared a few hundred feet away. They made their way from a small walkway in the brush below the tiered cliff side that must have led to civilization. They headed toward us carrying dishes covered with silver lids.

"Babe, this is extra as fuck."

"Just shut up and have fun." He sent me a playful smile.

—

I covered my laughing lips as I ate my last bite of lamb. "Stop making me laugh, I'm gonna choke."

Jeremy laughed. "But seriously, what if you poop on the table? That's a really common thing with birth—"

"You have to stop telling me all these disgusting birth facts while I'm eating." I wiped my mouth and leaned back in my chair.

"But you're always eating." He smiled. He blinked a few times, smile falling. "That sounded like I was calling you fat, didn't it? Because you're not. You're perfect. You just snack a lot—"

I laughed. "Shut up and kiss me."

He smiled, stood, and walked around the table. Joy sparkled in his gaze as he helped me to my feet, hand sliding around my waist. The other traced up my side until it found my neck and then cupped my cheek.

The music I heard in the distance earlier grew louder. I pulled away and looked past Jeremy to a small band playing on a low terrace. There was a mandolin, an accordion and a few other instruments I'd never seen before. The peaceful, gentle sounds echoed perfectly from the hillside.

I gazed up at them and back to Jeremy. "You really planned this out, didn't you?"

He smiled and pulled away, but extended his hand to mine. "Dance with me."

"You know I can't dance." I laughed.

"I'll lead." He playfully wiggled his fingertips.

Letting out an exasperated sigh, smiling, I accepted. He tugged me into his chest and stabilized me against his chest. We swayed for a moment, then he stepped back and held up his palm, gesturing for me to spin.

After an awkward little turn, I stumbled back into his torso. Laughing, we both got the message not to attempt that one again.

I lay my head against his heart, listening to the soft thumps, relaxing into his warm embrace.

Moments like these reminded me why I loved this man. I was not the romantic type, but Jeremy was. If he knew I had the day off, he'd tell me to pack a bag, he'd cover my eyes, and then poof. We'd go on a weekend getaway to one of the seven wonders of the world, or he'd do this. Find us a private beach and dance with me until the sun set.

It was the simplest of moments, but it was one of the sweetest too.

"I love you more than anything," Jeremy said quietly. He leaned back to meet my gaze, sweet smile still wide across his lips.

I smiled back. "I love you too."

"You're the most kind-hearted, courageous person I've ever met, and I don't know how I lived before I met you. You have this love for life and this amazing soulful glow that makes me feel alive just being around you." He softly cupped my face in his hand. Unease crept into his joyous eyes. "There isn't a day that goes by that I don't wonder what I did to deserve you. We've been through so much together, and despite all of the bullshit, we always come out stronger. We always bounce back further than we fell and it's because we make the perfect team. Now we're going to have a baby and start this little family…" His smile widened as he raised his hand from my cheek to push hair behind my ear. "I never thought that I could love anyone as much as I love you. I never thought I'd be this lucky. I thank God every day that I met you because you are the best thing that's ever happened to me, Laila."

I laughed. "I know, baby. I feel the same way. You mean the world to me."

He smiled. He swallowed hard and pulled away. He reached into his pocket and lowered himself to his knee.

"I want to be with you forever, Laila. Will you marry me?"

Oh. So that's what all the hoopla was about.

CHAPTER FIVE

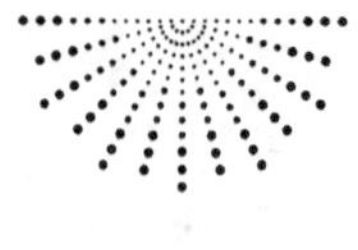

LAILA

I guess I should have realized what he was doing. But taking me away to some foreign country for a romantic date or fancy dinner wasn't out of the ordinary for Jeremy. He had always been a sappy, over-the-top kind of guy.

"Oh, my god." I cupped my hand over my mouth.

He stared up at me holding a black box with a beautiful antique engagement ring. One I recognized, and one I knew his little sister had had her eyes on for as long as I'd known them. His big blue eyes gazed up at me like a happy puppy, waiting for my response.

My stomach sunk. I hated the idea of marriage. To me, it was an ancient ceremony that danced around the concept of ownership. I knew what I was about to say was going to break his heart and I hoped it wouldn't leave me without my best friend.

"Baby." I began lowering myself to the sand beside him. As I got closer to the ground, his grin gradually receded.

"Oh," he murmured. "Well, shit."

"You caught me off guard. I..." I reached forward and lifted his chin to pull his gaze to mine. "I love you more than anything. You know that."

"But you don't want to marry me," he muttered. He pulled his other knee from its angle until he sat cross legged.

"I want to spend every day with you for the rest of my life."

His sad eyes moved between mine. "But?"

"But I'm pregnant." I laughed. "And I'm not even twenty-one yet."

"What difference does it make?" he said quietly. "If you want to be with me for the rest of your life, why don't you want to make it official?"

Touching his neck, I smiled and pulled him in for a kiss. "It is official," I murmured. "Why do we need a ring and piece of paper to prove that? You have me and I have you. That's more than enough. We don't need the piece of paper to tell us what we already know. We love each other and we're going to be together until the day we die. We'll find each other again in the next life and spend every day for the rest of that one together too."

"But I want to be your husband. I want you to be my wife." He grazed my cheek, eyes searching mine. "I want our son to know that we're happy and in love. I want him to grow up seeing you and me as partners."

"Baby, I don't want a shotgun wedding," I said. "Our son is going to know how much we love each other by seeing us together. We're Laila and Jeremy, we're us. We're adorable. Kids don't notice something as arbitrary as a ring and a certificate."

"Then just say yes." He gave a hopeful smile. "We can be engaged for a decade for all I care. We don't have to rush into things, we can wait."

"Jeremy—"

"I want to stand in front of all the people we care about and show everyone how much I love you. I want to vow to be your partner for now and forever. I want to dance with you in front of all of our friends and family and sing along to some cheesy love song. I want to celebrate our love. I want to—"

I cut him off by pressing my lips to his. I lifted my knees around his thighs. My hands locked around his neck as his moved to my waist.

I loved him. I'd always loved him. And I wanted him to know that. I just didn't want a ceremony to prove it.

After a moment, he pulled his lips back and rested his forehead to mine. "I just want to marry you."

"I want to spend the rest of my life with you," I whispered. "I just don't want to get married."

His sad eyes shifted between mine for another moment. "We should probably go eat that dessert before the bugs get to it. It was a hundred bucks apiece."

CHAPTER SIX

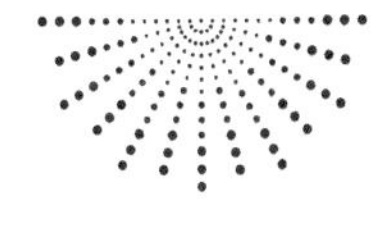

LAILA

Jeremy's bare chest rested against my naked back. He played with strands of hair that laid against my shoulder. The smell of his citrus cologne mixing with the slightest hint of salty sweat touched my nostrils. I watched the moon outside the window and traced my fingertip along the stray hairs on his slender pectorals.

He breathed out a slow, sad sigh. I rolled over to meet his gaze, giving a smile. "What is it?"

He forced a smile. His head shook against the blue satin pillowcase, twirling my hair around his finger. "I'm fine."

"You're upset I said no," I murmured.

"I'm not upset. I just wish you would have said yes."

I chomped on my lower lip. It wasn't that I'd said no to hurt him. Marriage just wasn't my thing. He should have picked up on that by now.

"Why is it so important to you?" I pushed long black waves behind his ear.

"Why are you so against it?"

My shoulder lifted in a shrug. "Marriage was used as a business transaction for thousands of years. Women were traded like cattle to the highest bidder so that her family could become wealthier."

"But that's not what marriage is today," he said. "Marriage is the living personification of love. It's how we show the world how much we love our partners. It's how children know their parents are going to be together forever."

My forehead scrunched up. "Is that what this is about?" I ran my thumb against his jaw. "You think couples have to be married to raise their kids right?"

"No. But I don't want our kids to go to school and have to explain why we have different last names. I don't want to have to keep calling you my girlfriend like you're some short-term fling. You're my partner, you're my world. I want to be able to say 'she's my wife' instead of 'she's my girlfriend' when people ask how we know each other. You're literally my soulmate, Laila. We've been together for three years. We live together, we work together, we run a business together. Hell, you bought me a car."

"It's *our* car." I smiled. "And just so you could get around until the Charger's up and running again. And even once it is, we needed something safe for the baby."

"Exactly. This is *our* home. It's *our* car. It's *our* money. It's *our* life. We share everything. We do *everything* as a couple. Nothing is mine, nothing is yours; it's all *ours*. Wouldn't the next logical step be to make it all *officially* ours?"

I chuckled. To me, this was official. The whole certificate, government tracking us as a union rather than two individuals wasn't for me.

But clearly, it was for him.

I met his serious gaze. When he didn't smile back, I cocked my head to the side. "It's really that important to you."

He lifted his shoulder in a shrug. "I know you think it's just a piece of paper, but it's so much more than that to me. It shows everyone else what we already know."

I chewed the inside of my jaw and thought for a moment. I didn't give a damn about the paper. I couldn't care less about a ring. But he looked so hurt. And in a lot of ways, he was right. At least if we were married, I wouldn't have to keep paying workman's comp on him for the diner.

"Fine."

He furrowed his brows and sat up. "What?"

I let out a teasing, exasperated sigh. "I guess I'll marry you."

The widest, most excited grin I'd ever seen came to his lips. His eyes opened a little wider. "Are you serious?"

Seeing his smile made me do the same. "Look, I don't care about marriage. The whole concept is bizarre and weird to me but you're right. We're basically married already, all that's missing is the stupid piece of paper. It doesn't matter to me but if it's important to you, we'll get the damn paper."

He leaned down and excitedly pressed his lips to mine. His hand found my neck to pull my face closer to his. "Really?"

"Don't get too excited, I have some conditions."

His smile stayed firm on his lips. "Whatever it is, it's yours. I'll sign a prenup if you want. I know this is your business and I would never try to take it from you—"

"Don't be stupid." I laughed. "I don't want a prenup. You won't try to take Moe's. You know how much this place means to me."

"What are your conditions then?" He played with some hair that rested against my collar bone.

"Well, I'm not getting married while I'm pregnant. I don't want to look back at pictures for the rest of my life and see this little shit making me the size of a walrus. I'd rather he be there in a cute little tux carrying our rings down the aisle."

"You're not a walrus, but fair enough." His thumb gently drifted along my jaw.

"And I don't want some massive party. We can have our close friends and family, but I don't want to have a multitude of people whose names I won't remember in fifty years. I don't want to spend tens of thousands of dollars on some party. I don't want to throw away our savings on some dress I'll wear once and food we probably won't have time to eat."

"You could wear a garbage bag and we could eat McDonald's for all I care."

I knew he wasn't going to like my last condition. "And I don't want your mom's ring."

"But it's a family heirloom."

"I know, and it's beautiful. But you have four other siblings, and they don't have the money that we do. Hannah loves that ring. And if her and Kai stay together, he'll never be able to afford something so nice."

"She said it was okay—"

"I'm sure she did, baby, but I still don't want to take that from her."

He frowned. "I want you to have an amazing ring and I don't have the money to buy you one as nice though."

"Sure you do." I smiled and pushed hair from his face. "We have over five hundred grand in the bank."

"But I don't want you to buy your own ring—"

"I won't be buying it, we will. It's *our* money, remember?"

"But I wanted to surprise you."

I laughed. "When it comes to jewelry, we both know it's better if I choose what I get. If you got me something hideous, I wouldn't have the heart to tell you and I'd walk around wearing something that I hate for the rest of my life."

"Hey, I have good taste. You loved that necklace I got you for your birthday last year."

I shrugged and pressed my lips to a line, trying to hide my look of disgust. My mind traveled to that atrocious, gawky purple amulet on a gold chain he'd been so excited to fasten around my neck.

He smiled. "You hate it?"

"Hate's a strong word."

That I would definitely use to describe that necklace.

"Why didn't you say anything? We could have exchanged it." He held his smile. "But you said you loved it."

I shrugged slightly. "Have you ever seen me wear it?"

"I just thought you didn't want anything to happen to it," he muttered.

"Oh, love." A quiet laugh left my lips as I touched his cool cheek. "I wanted to throw it in the garbage disposal. I wanted to Titanic that bitch into the ocean. I wanted to drop it into a volcano."

"Ouch." He laughed. "It's your birth stone, it even has your name engraved on it."

"And it was the sweetest thing anyone has ever bought me. But it's hideous."

"Message received; we'll pick your ring out together."

"And one more thing I don't think you're gonna like," I murmured.

"Uh-huh?"

"I want to stay a Callidy." I expected his brows to fall but they didn't move. "I get why you don't want our kids to explain why we have different last names, but it isn't uncommon for women to keep their last name anymore. And I love my name. It's the only thing I have left of my dad, and it's a strong, Fae surname. People know what I am when they hear it and I like it that way."

"I get it." He chewed his lip, nodding slightly. "But what about my son?"

"He can be a Skoulda." I smiled. "That name means a lot in the supernatural world, more than mine. I want people to know where he comes from and who they're fucking with if they come near him."

His smile heightened. "Deal."

I smiled. "So, you agree to my terms?"

"I'll do whatever you want if it means I get to marry you."

Rolling beneath the sheets, he slid on top of me and pressed his lips to mine. I smiled against them, butterflies dancing in my stomach. His lips lowered to my jaw, and then to my neck. The warm hand at my hip drifted toward my leg. Then his knee nudged them open.

My belly did somersaults as he traced a teasing path to my opening. Still lubricated from a few minutes before, he gently pushed himself inside of me. I gasped, tightening my arms around his back.

He smiled down at me as he massaged my G-spot, thumb caressing my clit, eyes full of joy. He kissed me once more, whispering at my lips, "I love you."

I smiled and kissed him back. "I love you, too."

Smiling still, he kissed down my jaw to my neck. His lips were a gentle brush as they made their way down my chest, across my belly, onto my pelvis. When he made it to my vulva, his lips parted, and his tongue snuck through.

A deep breath of bliss fell from me, eyes closing, body arching toward him. It was the gentlest of touches, but it was enough to make me crave when he'd go deeper. When he'd plunge into me, and...

He kissed instead, trailing to my inner thigh.

I laughed, opening my eyes and meeting his gaze. "Jeremy."

He grinned. "What? You can tease me with marriage, but I can't tease you with an orgasm?"

"You know what, I can still retract my offer."

Smirking, his mouth went back to my pussy. Before I had time to say a word, his lips made a circle around my clit, and he flicked his tongue up and down at an impeccable speed.

Sudden, intense pleasure overtook me. Completely encompassed by the sensation, my body rolled closer into him, unable to bring in an even breath as he massaged and licked those magnificent spots.

How's that feel, baby? His voice said into my thoughts.

"So good," I whispered. "So fucking good."

His shoulders lifted with a chuckle.

As he slowed, bringing the tip of his tongue to that most sensitive spot at the top of my clit, I gasped, unable to stop my body from bucking toward him. Squirming beneath him, near scream leaving my lips, he pinned my thigh to the bed.

I was already sensitive from the last orgasm, but now, whatever he was doing was pure magic. I rolled and writhed, aching for more, aching to finish. It was overstimulating, but it felt so good, and I wanted nothing more than to satisfy that yearn for finish that coiled deep within my belly.

Look at me, his voice was a seductive whisper in my mind.

I opened my eyes and turned down. Those glistening blue eyes were practically smiling, watching me writhe and tremble for him.

"Jeremy," I moaned.

He smiled, tongue moving just as fast and fingers massaging the perfect place. *Come for me, baby.*

Jesus Christ, I don't know what it was about a man saying that that made me gush liquid between my thighs, but it did the trick every time. I swore it was a super power of his.

Cusping that peak of exaltation, my vision blurred around the edges, but I kept my eyes on his. He didn't slow his rhythm, touching with just the right amount of pressure and speed. His gaze was practically all that I could see, and it was all I needed. The comfort of those gorgeous eyes, the smile they shined, the pride he radiated from pleasuring me alone.

When the contractions slowed, he finally stopped pulsing inside of me. He kissed his way back up my body.

"See? Marriage won't be so bad." He craned over me. "You'll get this every day."

I laughed, lifting my hand to his cheek. "Every day, huh?"

"Twice a day if you're lucky." He grinned.

Laughing, I said, "Oh, really?"

"I mean, as long as you don't threaten to retract your offer again."

I laughed. "Shut up and kiss me."

With a smile, he leaned down and did so once more. He cupped my face in his hand, leaning back to meet my gaze. "Thank you."

"Thank *you*." I smirked. "Do you want to go again? I think the tally's uneven now."

"Two orgasms was enough for one day." His eyes still shined with joy, flittering slowly between mine. "But I can't wait for you to be my wife."

I smiled and kissed him one more time.

Still, I viewed marriage as a way for the government to keep tabs on us and to flaunt our partners to the world like a trophy. But it mattered to him, and making him happy mattered to me.

As long as I got that man's magic tongue for the rest of my life, I didn't have much to complain about.

CHAPTER SEVEN

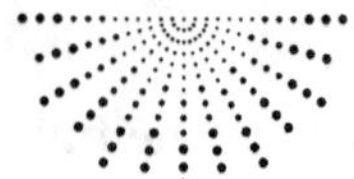

JANUARY 22, 2019 - LAILA

I pushed the big front door open and kicked off my shoes. The familiar smell of warm apple candles touched my nose. Heat blowing from the vents invited me in, pushing long black hair into my face.

"Leah!" I called. "Where are you?"

"In here," she yelled from the sunroom.

I dropped my bag on the table and started toward the back of the house. "Thank God we got an all-wheel drive car, or I wouldn't have made it up your guy's road. Is your plow broke or something?"

"Nah, I've just been busy," she murmured. She sat on the couch leaned toward her laptop on the coffee table. Her lavender hair was pulled into a messy bun at the top of her head above her big black glasses.

She hadn't been herself lately. She was never very focused on her appearance but recently she'd completely drowned herself in research. It seemed that every waking moment, she was staring at that screen. Mostly coming back with dead ends.

Last October when everything in my life turned upside down, a detective approached me after catching my abilities on a security camera. He wanted my help to find his missing wife and daughter who were both part Fae. Leah agreed after a bit of battling and cast a simple location spell.

But the results didn't show a location, not for Ramirez's family. Nor did it show a location for the lost Skoulda brother we'd believed was dead for the last seven or so years. The spell worked for every other person we could think of. But not the three of them. All three were declared dead, but none of their bodies ever found.

It put Leah into something of a manic spiral. She was filled with guilt after realizing she'd spent the last seven years thinking that her brother was dead when she should have been looking for him. Out of all the Skoulda kids, Leah and Chris were always the closest. They were only a few years apart, so it made sense. When he disappeared without a trace—aside from a shit ton of blood—she was sure he was dead. But now, we had evidence that he wasn't. And she thought we had the power to bring him home.

I was worried about her. But I understood. Hell, Celena was going through my mind like a broken record and we'd only just met.

"Have you found anything new recently?" I asked as I plopped onto the couch beside her.

"Maybe." She turned her computer to me. "I found this article. It's from a little town in Washington State."

I leaned forward to read the by line.

Kidnapped Boy Escapes Captivity: Father Still Missing

I lifted the laptop to my thighs and read silently. Leah chewed her thumb nail and read over my shoulder.

Local business owner Richard Flynn contacted the police after his employee Derek Stevenson failed to show up for work and respond to his messages for three consecutive days.

When police arrived to do a welfare check on the family, obvious signs of forced entry were found. The home was discovered to have over 7 liters of blood throughout and no victims. DNA later confirmed that the blood found inside the home belonged to both Derek Stevenson and his three-year-old son, Cage Stevenson. No other DNA or fingerprints were found at the home.

Four days later, a little boy in torn, dirty clothes walked into a fast-food restaurant crying and begging for help. When law enforcement arrived, they quickly identified the boy as Cage Stevenson.

The boy wasn't discovered to have any obvious signs of blood loss and appeared entirely healthy aside from a few scratches and bruises.

Upon investigation, the child refused to talk. The only thing he said to police was that "Daddy saved him."

With no living relatives remaining, the boy has been turned over to child services and will be placed into foster care.

7/18/18 09:43:17

Definitely sounded familiar.

I looked up and met her gaze. "Do you know who took the kid in?"

She took the laptop and clicked a few buttons. "That's where it gets interesting. I hacked into the police database Ramirez uses and was able to find his adoptive parents."

"He was adopted that quick?" I asked.

A cunning grin came to her lips, head bobbing in a nod. "But the weird part isn't that he was adopted, but *who* adopted him." She turned the screen to face me. "Janis and Elijah Wilson."

"Is that name supposed to mean something to me?"

"I know them." She clicked a few more times. "I mean, not personally. But they're Guardians, they live in upstate Idaho. They're kind of famous in our world. They're on the Chambers and everything."

The Chambers ranked just below the Council and Elders. They were leaders within the supernatural world. Monarchs of the wolf packs, incredibly old Vampires, High Priestesses in important Covens, and the most well renowned Guardian clan leaders. Including Jeremy's grandparents, Raphael and Adele Skoulda.

"Upstate Idaho," I murmured. "That's where Mary was going to send the kids when your uncle died."

"Yeah. They operate a home for orphaned supernaturals."

I thought for a moment. "So, Cage Stevenson, he's one of us."

"Yeah. The MO is exactly what happened to Ramirez's kid."

"And Chris."

She smiled. Her gaze stayed locked on the screen. "And Chris."

CHAPTER EIGHT

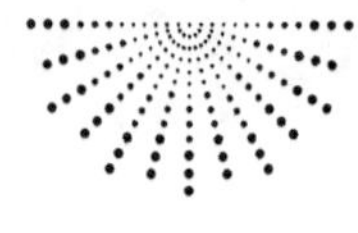

LAILA

I spun the red chili in the metal pot before me. Warm, aromatic scents drifted toward my nose. The sun peeked in from the French doors to the patio, brighter than ever against the blanket of white in the yard.

"So, you said no." Leah gestured to my hand on the ladle.

"At first."

"Why?" she asked. "I thought you'd say yes."

"I don't know. I just don't like the concept of marriage. Women were forced to get married because it was their only means of survival for centuries. We had no purpose in life besides becoming a wife and popping out babies. Now there's no reason to marry unless you're religious, which Jeremy and I obviously aren't."

She huffed. "As someone who has only had the right to marry the gender that I'm attracted to for four and a half years, I have to say that I completely disagree."

"Eh, fair enough," I said.

I lifted the spoon and took a slurp. The hot liquid touched my tongue. Not too bad but missing something. Too bland. I grabbed the salt and sprinkled some to the pot.

She smiled. "But you ultimately said yes?"

I laughed quietly. "Yeah. He got emotional about it, saying we're basically married already, and he loves me and wants to show his love to the world, blah, blah, blah." I spooned another scoop to my lips. They curved in a smile. Just the right combination of flavor. Leah dipped her finger in the pot, eyes meeting mine for more information on the proposal. "I figured why not. If it means that much to him, I'll just do it."

"Fair enough." She gestured to my hand. "Why aren't you wearing the ring?"

I shrugged again. "Because I know Hannah wants it."

She laughed, smile pulling up her lips. "Yeah, she told Jeremy she was fine with it, but she was pissed."

I'd figured as much. Hannah wasn't one to tell anyone no, let alone her big brother. I smiled back. "I couldn't take that from her."

"Good call." She walked to the fridge licking her finger. "Speak of the devil."

Not even a second later, Hannah came down the steps wearing a big grin. Her long black waves bounced as she rushed toward me. She grasped my palm in her dainty hand. Immediately, her wide smile fell to a frown. Those big, electric blue eyes grew dewy. "You said no?"

I laughed and took my hand back. "I said no to your mom's ring."

Her face lit back up. "Oh, thank God. I wanted it so bad."

"And that's why I said no."

"Have you set a date? And I'm going to be a bridesmaid, right? Of course I am, duh. What color scheme were you thinking? I think blue would be great, blue looks great with Jeremy's complexion. And mine since I'm basically the female version of him. But it's your day, of course."

"Oh, of course." I smiled. Leah rolled her eyes but held her smile. "We're not planning anything right now. I'm fat and pregnant and I want to pop this baby out before I start trying on dresses and stressing about caterers and flowers and all that dumb shit."

"So you're gonna let my little nephew" —she moved her hands to my stomach as if to cover the baby's ears— "be a bastard?"

I smacked her hand away. "Ew. That's an ancient mindset."

Leah took a sip of her scotch. "You do realize that you're the only person in this room that *isn't* a bastard, right, Hannah?"

"Oh, you know what I mean," Hannah said. "If you're gonna get married anyway, why not just do it before the baby comes? You can just have a quick ceremony before he's born and then a bigger one later down the line."

"All I want is a quick ceremony, Han. I don't want anything fancy."

Her mouth fell open. "But you have all that money. You can go all out."

"Or I could have a quiet little ceremony in the yard, just invite the people that mean the most to us and walk away spending a couple grand. I don't want to waste all the money Moe made sure I'd have to live on and keep his business afloat for some silly party."

"A wedding is not some silly party." Hannah raised her hand to her chest. "It's the most important day of your life."

Leah laughed. "We aren't all hopeless romantics like you and your brother."

"Hey, you!" Adam jogged down the maid steps. His big eyes stretched as far open as his mouth was wide. He darted across the kitchen, grabbed my hand, and squinted down at it. "You said no?" He looked up quickly with creased brows. "Why'd you say no?"

I chuckled and pulled away. "I didn't want your mom's ring."

A big smile lifted his lips. He wrapped his arms around my shoulders, lifted me into the air, and spun me in a circle. "You're finally going to be my sister."

I laughed again as he sat me down. "I guess I am."

"This is awesome. My best friend that isn't related to me is officially going to be a part of the family. I mean, you've always been like family, but now you're actually going to *be* family."

"Wow, congratulations," I heard from the steps. I turned to meet Brody's gaze. He adjusted the collar of his beige polo and forced a smile. "That's great. I'd say let's pop a bottle of champagne, but Jeremy doesn't drink and you're pregnant."

"Yeah, I wish I could have some champagne right now." I smiled back, trying to lighten the mood. I figured the news was hard on him and didn't want to rub his nose in it. "But thank you." I turned back to Adam and Hannah. "All of you guys."

"We're just glad you aren't a cunt," Leah said. "Or human."

"Well, that's racist," Adam said.

"Hey, we've both been with humans and we know how that ends." Leah shrugged and took another sip from her glass. "Tell me I'm wrong, bro."

CHAPTER NINE

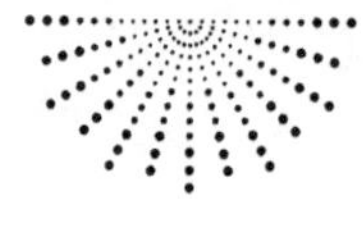

LAILA

The arm of the cushy couch pillowed my body. My feet rested in Jeremy's lap. The sun illuminated against the hardwoods behind him, shining warmth into the room. The taste of red sauce popped on my tongue.

"So we can come by tonight then?" Leah said into her phone. She sat in the armchair beside me, still hunched over that laptop and scribbling in a notebook.

Jeremy ran his tongue over his teeth. Cocking his head to the side, he swallowed. "Is that cumin?"

"Just a little bit." I took a bite of mine.

He lifted another spoonful to his lips. With a mouthful, he said, "I dig it."

"Yeah, it's not overpowering but it hits the back of your tongue really nicely."

"The flavor is there but you taste everything else too. It doesn't take over, you know?"

"I think I'm gonna do that from now on," I said. "Mom'll kill me for changing her recipe."

"Just use hers when she comes over for dinner." He grinned.

"Hey, Jeremy, can you give me a lift?" Leah set her phone in her lap and pushed up her glasses.

"Yeah, sure. Where to?"

The faintest hint of hope glimmered in her eyes. "I found a lead on Ray's kid and Chris. I was thinking maybe I should bring him along. Let him see what we're seeing."

"Isn't it all the way in Idaho?" I sat forward. "Because Ray hates teleporting. He'd be sick as shit if he went that far."

"Maybe. But it's for his family. I think he'd want to be there."

"Did you let him know you have a lead?" I asked.

She stood. "No, I'll go call him now. You fill Jeremy in."

I nodded as she wandered up the stairs.

"What'd she find?" He laid his ceramic bowl to the coffee table.

I sat up and spun my legs to the ground. I summed it all up, he listened, then teleported out to grab Ray.

We stood at the base of a fifteen-foot-wide stone stairway tucked deep in the woods. The dewy scent of rain touched my nostrils, wind blowing a cool chill down my spine. I always thought Jeremy's house was huge, but it didn't touch this place. The near castle towered high above the ground like a skyscraper. But maybe it just looked so high from the bottom of the practically never-ending staircase. It was built from large rocks a million shades of brown and gray as if it had been assembled from the rocky bed of a river. Large ferns sat on either end of the large mahogany door.

Brightly colored curtains shined from inside the windows. Smiling children played behind them. Some were pink with butterflies while others were decorated with baseballs and basketballs or superheroes or Hello Kitty. Others were simple vivid shades of pink or blue. The vibrance pulled away from the ominous appearance of the old mansion.

The front door slowly creaked open. Without much thought, I

started up the steps. We were here for a reason and I was ready to have some answers. Or, at the very least, some hints at where to look next.

"That's not creepy at all," Ray muttered.

Leah rolled her eyes. Brushing past me, she said, "Just because we can do things that you can't doesn't mean it's creepy."

"Sorry," he muttered close behind me.

"Just keep your fear of us to yourself when you're here," Jeremy said. "They're just kids. Most of them have been raised believing that their powers are gifts. They don't realize that people like you are afraid of them."

"Yeah. Right, right. I'm sorry."

"Don't apologize," I said as we made it to the porch. "Just don't treat them like they're monsters. In another life, it could be your daughter in a place like this."

"Right. Of course."

As we made it to the door, Leah knocked on the frame. "Knock-knock." When no one responded, she walked inside.

I followed close behind, stepping onto the orange and blue Aztec print rug. My lips curved into a smile as I took in the décor. If I had to put a label on it, I'd say it fell somewhere between a classic and a boho-chic sort of feel. The hardwoods were stained a light cedar color and the walls were painted a peaceful shade of yellow. The baseboards trimmed the room the same light cedar as the floors. Ominous outside, hippy-dippy inside. My kinda style.

A white wolf with blue eyes meandered into the hallway ahead. She approached slowly. Leah extended her hand like a peace offering. "An Angel told me I could come tonight and talk to your parents. Do you know where they are?"

She drew closer and sniffed Leah's hand. She took a few steps toward the rest of us, nose wiggling. When she made it to Ramirez, the hair on her back began to stand. Snarls left her bared teeth.

"It's okay," Ramirez said. "I'm a friend of theirs." As he reached down, she lunged forward and snipped. I laughed quietly. The wolf stepped back and howled. Ray fell backward into Jeremy. He narrowed his gaze a bit but helped Ray steady his balance.

To my left, a woman trotted down the brightly lit cedar steps. She toted a baby on her hip. "Oh, relax, Cassie. He's allowed here."

I was sure she couldn't be Janis. This woman couldn't have been more than thirty-five.

She moved messy red curls from her pale white face. A smile eased up her wide, bright red lips. Her eyes glistened a peaceful shade of blue so light they were nearly gray. They rolled as the wolf howled.

"Yes, I know he's human. But it's okay." The wolf howled again as she made her way to the landing. "Don't you talk to me like that, little girl. I'm the parent, I get to make the decisions." She howled again and the woman wiggled her finger at her. "You need to go shift any way. Dinner will be done any minute."

The wolf huffed and bared her teeth at Ray once more. She brushed past the woman and up the steps.

"I'm sorry about that. Teenagers, what can I say? They're a different breed." She smiled and extended her free hand to Leah. "I'm Janis. You must be Leah."

"And this is—"

"Laila Callidy and Jeremy Skoulda." Janis turned to us with a smile. "I know who you are." She took my hand and gave it a firm shake in her cold fingertips. "It's a pleasure to meet the living legends."

"Oh, I wouldn't say we're legends." I laughed.

"Don't be modest." She smiled wider. "You're the first of your kind to be seen in ages. I remember the last time a bond like yours was rumored. That feels like forever ago. Eight hundred years or so?"

My eyes widened. "Wow, I thought that you were Guardians."

"We are, dear. But no one mentioned we were Vampires?"

The first I'd met that wasn't a purebred. Perhaps the kindest thus far. In fact, one of the few hybrids I'd met at all outside of my brother and sister. That brought an unusual level of comfort.

"No, I don't think they did." My gaze shifted to Leah and Jeremy. They smiled.

"Don't worry, sweetie. I won't bite." She chuckled. "Let me set this baby in his chair and call the kids down for dinner. Are you hungry? You're welcome to join us."

"We just ate, but please enjoy your meal," Leah said.

"Well, at least have dessert. I made this chocolate lasagna with pudding and homemade whipped cream and squished up Oreos. It's amazing, you have to try it."

"I'll eat whatever they don't want." I raised my hand.

Oreos had been my biggest craving so far. Chili, and Oreos. Which probably accounted for the five pounds I'd put on in addition to the typical pregnancy weight gain.

"Great." She smiled. "Alright, follow me to the table, you can make yourself a plate."

CHAPTER TEN

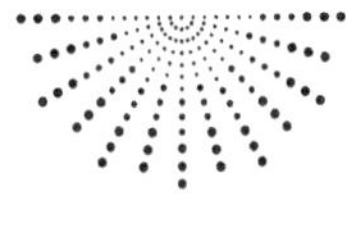

LAILA

I gazed out over the group of rowdy children at the dining table from my perch in the sitting room. At least fifteen kids, maybe even more, sat around the table so big, I thought it belonged in the board room of some executive building. I took a bite of my dessert and glanced at each child. They were all so different. From their skin color, to their body types, to their abilities; no two were close to the same.

It was obvious what some of them were. Like the little girl who waved her hand and livened up the wilting roses in the center of the table. Or the teenage boy who put a flame over the green bean casserole to crisp the onions at the tops.

There were a lot of Fae. Our homeland was littered with war. I didn't know much about it—only what I'd heard from my brother, Kai, and read in Moe's journal. But I knew that many of them fought with their lives to make it to Earth. Even if they could only send their children.

Despite my momentary grief, they looked so content. They laughed and played, pushing each other's shoulders as they joked. Some of them were more solemn than others but they still looked grateful. Happy, even.

"Do you want a glass of wine?" Janis asked, pouring herself one. She laughed. "Oh my, I'm sorry. I almost forgot you were pregnant."

"I didn't realize it was so obvious already," I muttered, giving a smile.

"Oh, no. I wouldn't have known just by looking at you." She sat at a chair across from me. "But everyone's talking about this baby."

"Really?"

"Something to do with the par animarum. Apparently, you're carrying one very powerful child."

"Huh," I murmured. "I didn't realize it was that big of a deal."

"It's a very big deal." She smiled. "So how do you feel? About becoming a parent, I mean."

"I'm excited. Not as excited as Jeremy, but I'm just a go-with-the-flow kind of person. It'll be a good time."

Janis chuckled. She sipped her wine, glancing over the children. "It's the most amazing thing anyone can ever experience. Such a mundane thing, really. Almost everyone has children, you wouldn't think it's all that special. And yet, it's the most extraordinary thing imaginable."

I saw it the same way. Children were a beautiful thing. A simple thing, though. That was how I viewed my pregnancy as well. Ordinary, mundane—just like the billions of other women who came before me. Of course, motherhood seemed exciting. But it didn't seem as extravagant to me as it did to my fiancé.

"Are they all yours?" I gestured to them.

"I don't like to think of it that way. They're all their own people. They call me Mom, or Janis, or Mrs. Wilson." She shrugged. "I'm not in the business of replacing their families. I'm just here to help them live until they feel ready to live on their own."

I smiled, looking at Jeremy. He kneeled beside a little boy with a smile. He made a coin disappear behind his ear. The boy's mouth dropped, and Jeremy grinned.

"I like that philosophy. How long have you been doing this?"

She sipped her wine and chuckled. "God, I don't know. Maybe a few decades after I was changed."

I huffed. "You've been raising kids for a thousand years?"

"It may sound hard, but…" With a shake of her head, she smiled over the children. "It has been at times. But this. This is the easy part. Watching them grow old and disappear…" She frowned. "That's what's hard."

My hand moved to my belly. I couldn't imagine how hard it must have been to lose a child. Let alone hundreds or thousands.

"That must've been awful," I murmured.

"Some of them, I turned when they were old enough to ask me to. But most of them want to live and die a natural death." She raised her glass to her lips and took a big gulp. "Not that I blame them, of course. I wouldn't have chosen this either."

"No?" I cocked my head to the side. Generally, vamps were changed on their own accord. She was the first I'd met that hadn't been, in fact.

Janis looked up from the kids and met my gaze. "No one told you anything about me, did they?"

"Not really. I knew your name. Jeremy mentioned your family taking him and his siblings in when he talked about his parents dying but it never really passed that."

"Well, I'm sure you know that most of our kind… Or your kind, I suppose, don't like Vampires. I don't like most of them either. But my husband and I, we were Guardians first. That's how we got changed. We were hunting a nest, we underestimated their size," —she stifled a yawn— " and they changed us. It was revenge of sorts."

"That's horrible," I said. "A friend of mine was just changed against her will. It's an awful thing to experience."

"It certainly didn't go as planned. But when you're immortal, you have to find something to live for. Elijah and I, we had been trying to get pregnant long before we were turned. It didn't seem to be in the cards for us, even then. We tried to find something to keep us busy, but life was just… Lonely, I suppose. Our friends lived and then they died. Our family lived and then they died. People didn't live as long as they do now, of course."

"God, I can't even imagine," I murmured.

She raised her glass and took a sip. "The network of supernaturals wasn't as complex as it is now either. When a child with abilities was orphaned, they were often placed with human families that didn't understand them. Many were executed for what they were. Others retreated to the woods and lived on their own. It was devastating." She was quiet for a moment. "I didn't know that these things were happening then. But once I did, I knew I'd found my calling. So we just started taking them in. It started with one, and then two, and then ten. At one point, we had fifty-eight children at once."

My eyes widened. I couldn't fathom having two, let alone almost sixty. "Wow. You really had your hands full."

She laughed. "Well, when you don't need sleep to survive and you can move as fast as the speed of light, parenting that many kids isn't as much of a challenge."

"But eating. That must be difficult at times," I muttered.

"Sometimes. We have friends. We drink animal blood if we don't have other options. We need a lot more of it, but it does get the job done. Overall though, thirst isn't the issue for us that it once was."

"Well, at least you don't kill people."

"I'm a protector of humanity." She smiled. "It'd be a bit hypocritical, don't you think?"

CHAPTER ELEVEN

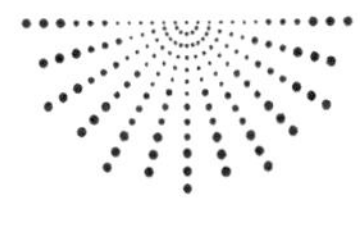

LAILA

"Cage." Janis crouched next to a young boy with dark skin and curly black hair, glancing up at us then back to him. "Sweetie, these are friends of mine. You know what Katie can do, right?"

He nodded, bashfully glancing up at us.

"Well, this lady" —she gestured to Leah— "she can do that too."

"That's cool," he muttered.

"She'd like to talk with you, if you're okay with that."

He turned up to Leah. "Why is your hair purple?"

I smiled. That was what amused me about kids in our world. They had no objection to their mind being probed, but aside from that were as normal as every other human child.

Leah laughed as she lowered herself to the ground. She crossed her legs in a lotus position. "Well, purple is my favorite color. So I made my hair purple."

He looked up at Janis. "Can I make my hair green?"

She laughed. "We'll talk about it in a couple years. But you don't mind talking with them?"

"I'm okay. Go, Mama."

She put her hands up in surrender and laughed. "Alright, I'll go check on Kaley. Let me know if you need anything."

Janis stood and started to the doorway. She glanced at me with a smile, gave a small wave and started up the steps.

I stepped toward them and crouched on the floor. My lips lifted in a smile, extending my hand. "My name's Laila."

He shook my hand. "I'm Cage." He lifted a toy car into the air, spun it around without touching it, then let it fall back to the ground. He met my gaze. "What can you do?"

"Oh, all kinds of things."

"Are you the one they talk about?" he asked.

A quiet laugh. "That depends, what do they say?"

"That you can do anything."

I laughed again and shook my head. "I wouldn't say I can do *anything*. But I can do a lot."

"Can you show me?" I pulled a flame to the tip of my finger. He waved his hand, completely unimpressed. "Lots of us can do that."

I laughed again as he turned back to his toys. "What else can you do?"

He lifted the car to his hand and blew on it. Suddenly, a coating of ice encased it.

I gave a modest smile "Yeah, that's way cooler."

He grinned. He turned back to his toys on the race-car rug.

"That's awesome." Leah smiled. "You're a really cool kid, you know." He nodded with a proud grin. "Can I be honest with you, Cage?" He looked up and met her gaze. "We're here because we need your help."

"You need *my* help?" he asked.

She smiled. "I do."

"I'm a kid." He scrunched down his eyebrows. "What can *I* do?"

"Well, my brother…" She paused unsure of how to go on. I thought about taking the reins. I knew how hard it was for her to talk about Chris. But she continued before I had the chance. "My brother was taken a few years ago. I believe the people who took him are the same people who took you and your dad last summer."

He looked down. "I don't like talking about that."

"That's okay. You don't have to say a word. My power is seeing what's inside people's minds." She tapped on her head. "If you let me hold your hands for just a few minutes, I can see what happened. You don't have to think about it or anything."

He looked up. "You just want to hold my hands?"

"That's it. It'll only take a couple of minutes."

He still looked nervous, but nodded. "Okay."

She set her palms over his and gently wrapped them around his chubby fingers. Her eyes closed as Cage looked around the room.

CHAPTER TWELVE

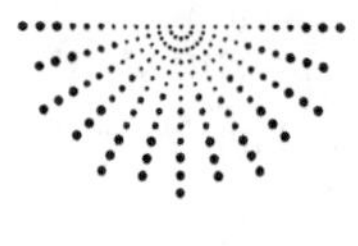

LAILA

"Thank you so much for having us, Janis," Leah said as she pulled her jacket over her shoulders.

"Of course, sweetie," she said. "I hope we were able to help."

Leah smiled. "It's more than we had this morning."

"I'm glad. I hope you find them. And please, know that you're welcome here any time. These kids can always use some guidance from the outside world. Especially the teens."

"Thank you, Janis." Jeremy smiled. "Sorry we missed Elijah. Maybe we'll catch him next time."

"Of course. It was a pleasure meeting you all. And please, send me an invitation if you have a baby shower."

I laughed quietly. What kind of gift would a thousand-year-old Vampire bring to one of those? "I'm pretty sure it'll be in the daylight hours."

She grinned. "I can work something out."

Jeremy gave one last smile. We all appeared in the living room of the Skoulda home.

"Oh, God." Ramirez struggled to stand. His hand cupped over his mouth. He ran to the powder room.

As Leah and I sat on the couch, I asked, "So what did you see?"

"Not much. They were in their living room reading a book and these people swarmed the front door. They were wearing white hazmat style jumpsuits that covered them head to toe. Cage coated them in ice, but it didn't freeze them. That must have been why they were wearing them." She chewed her lip, head shaking slightly. "Then they shot his dad in the stomach and picked up Cage. He fought them, obviously, and they just..." She swallowed hard in an attempt to maintain her composure. "They started beating him. They beat him until he passed out."

A child. These people hit a *child* until he was unconscious.

"Jesus Christ," I murmured.

"They shot him?" Jeremy asked.

"Yeah," Leah murmured. "I think they were human."

Jeremy narrowed his gaze. "What would humans want with a Guardian and his kid?"

Unease swirled in my stomach. Humans knowing about us at all was terrifying. But humans having the equipment and knowledge of how to subdue us sent a shudder through the room. Exposure was a nightmare for good reason. Of course, certain high-up governing entities were aware of our kinds. They worked hand in hand with the Chambers. But we held strict alliances with them. We stayed out of their way and they stayed out of ours. In exchange, they kept their mouths shut about what they knew. They also got a lot of funding from the Chambers for their silence.

But it was always the little guys that concerned us. Local police departments, FBI, religious groups, private organizations known for racism against their own kind—let alone entire other species that operated behind closed doors.

"I wish I knew," Leah said. "Then they were in the back of a van. It was set up kind of... I don't know how to describe it. There were computers all over the walls. And medical equipment. Blood bags, syringes, sterile equipment, the works."

"Like an ambulance?" I asked.

"I don't know. Not really but kind of. It was super clean. Everything was really modernized. Like, if I hadn't felt the swaying of the vehicle, I wouldn't have known it was a car if that makes any sense."

"What happened after that?" I asked.

"His dad was lying face down on some type of gurney. They were doing some sort of surgery or something on him. Maybe to repair the bullet wound? He was belted down, and he was screaming and..." She took in a slow, deep breath. "Then Cage started screaming too. I guess his dad realized he was awake, and the back door flew open. Derek screamed 'run' and Cage flew out of the door. He landed on the road and darted into the woods. The car stopped and came back but Cage kept running. He ran through the woods for days before he ended up at that McDonald's."

I slid my hand over my belly, chest growing stiff. It must have been an awful thing for that child to experience. But the idea of how many others it could have happened to made my stomach hurt. "That's terrifying."

Jeremy sat on the corner of the coffee table. He gritted his teeth to a hard line. "Do you think they're experimenting on us?"

A thick lump condensed in my throat as Leah nodded. "It looks like it. But I asked Janis, and she's certain it isn't any government. Apparently, they talked about it at the last Chambers meeting. Your grandpa brought up that we were looking into Chris's disappearance. And with all that, I can't help but wonder how. Even I would've been able to use my abilities to get out of a situation like that. Chris definitely would have been able to."

Jeremy 's tongue ran along his lips, gaze turned to the floor. He rubbed his hand against his clean shaved mouth and chin. "I don't know."

Leah was quiet for a moment. "I need a drink."

A few months ago, that'd have been me too. I always was one to pour some whiskey in times of stress. But these days, stress just made me tired. Stifling a yawn, I said, "And I need sleep."

"Yeah, me too," Jeremy said. "I'll take Ray home and we'll go."

"Alright. Can you drive? I'm beat."

"Yeah, I'll drive."

CHAPTER THIRTEEN

LAILA

The Forester bounced through the potholes. Crisp, snow scented wind blew in from the cracked window. I gazed up at the night sky through the glass. The stars twinkled above us like a million diamonds in the dark blue abyss. It was a clear night, a rarity in Pennsylvania, especially at this time of year. The moon shined down against the snow like a spotlight reflecting against each sparkling crystal of ice.

As I watched them flutter through the atmosphere, my lips pulled down in sadness. How long had it been since Chris had seen the moon? How long had it been since Ray's daughter, Lydia, had caught snowflakes on her tongue? How long since they smelled that cool snow I cursed at earlier that morning when I struggled my way up the Skoulda driveway?

"You alright, baby?" Jeremy squeezed my hand.

I turned his way and forced a smile. "Yeah, I'm fine."

"But?" He squeezed my hand again, glancing from the road to meet my gaze.

"A lot of people disappear in our world. They run off and start new lives or they turn up missing and we crack it up to some old Demon looking for vengeance. All this... It just makes me wonder how many of us these people have, ya know? And what it's been like for them wherever they are."

"Yeah," he said. "Yeah. Chris has been gone for seven years in May. Hundreds of us, and that's at the least, have died mysteriously or went missing since then. If they paced out their abductions for a decade, they could have thousands of us. And they've got to be pretty damn smart to hold that many of our people against their will."

The car fell silent. We knew they were alive, at least Chris and Ray's wife and child. But if they'd managed to hold them for that long, who would they even be after all this time?

I was quiet for a moment. "And if by some slim chance we do find them, what are they gonna be coming home to?"

He blew out a deep exhale. "Yeah, I've been thinking about that too."

I turned to get a better look at him. The circles beneath his eyes were as dark as the woods around us. His breaths were slow and heavy.

"What about you, baby? Are you okay?" I touched his thigh.

He laughed quietly. "Not really."

I leaned across the center console and snuggled up against his arm. He delicately wrapped his hand around my shoulder. "What's on your mind?"

He was quiet for a moment. But I waited. Jeremy had no problem when it came to talking about how he felt. Unless guilt played a part. While he had no choice in what had happened to Chris, he also had no hope that he was alive until recently. And I knew that weighed heavy on his conscience.

"My brother has been gone for almost seven years," he murmured. "Seven. And so much has happened. I was only sixteen when he disappeared. I became a drug addict, I got clean. Leah's girlfriend died. Adam's girlfriend died. *His* girlfriend died. Annie died. So many of us died." He tapped the steering wheel as a sad, ironic chuckle left his lips.

"Not only did I fall in love with you, but we're soulmates. He'd get a kick out of that." He paused for a moment, and his voice softened. "We're having a baby. And we're engaged. Hannah's going to college in the fall. And... God, I don't know. Chris wouldn't even recognize this life."

I wrapped my arm around his chest as best I could to listen. "I wasted all those years mourning someone who isn't dead. I buried myself in drugs to block out a loss I never should have felt. And I never even looked for him. I never even tried. That was my brother. He... he was my idol. And I didn't even look for him."

"But all that blood, baby," I murmured. "Why would you?"

"We never found a body." His voice was soft, sad. "We shouldn't have stopped looking until we found a body."

Suddenly I wished I hadn't brought it up. All of this was eating away at him and I wished I could take that pain away. Desperate to see him smile, I turned my head up to face him. "What was he like?"

He glanced down and then back to the road. A soft smile lifted his lips. "He was smart. Like, really smart. He had a free ride to Columbia, you know."

I gave a gentle smile back. "No, I didn't."

"Yeah. On an academic scholarship."

"Wow," I murmured.

That didn't surprise me, all the Skouldas were smart. Adam the least thereof, but still not dumb. Jeremy was a genius too; he just didn't go to school. When I asked why, he always said because he didn't know what he wanted to do. And that he loved working with me at Moe's anyway.

"And he was an artist." His smiled stretched higher at the memories. "A really good artist, I'll have to show you his paintings the next time we go over. He couldn't sing but we played guitar like a boss. He's the one who taught me. Kinda outshined him in that department though." He laughed quietly, smile growing so genuine that my heart hurt.

Learning that Chris was alive was the hardest thing he had to experience so far. I prayed that we could find him, but I feared that we wouldn't. Then his heart would break all over again. And I prayed that if that day came, he didn't go down the road he did last time he lost his big brother.

"Really?" I asked.

"Yeah. God, you would have loved him. He was an all-out humanitarian. He'd teleport into any natural and international disaster he saw on the news. Remember the earthquake in Haiti?" I nodded, and he continued. His pace picked up, tone growing confident and nostalgic. "We went. I mean, I didn't do much. I wish I would have done more but Chris was just amazing. He teleported into all these little nooks and crannies and flashed people to safety. I was more scared than he was. I thought someone would see us. I'm sure a lot of people did and just chalked it up to being traumatized, but Chris didn't care. He just wanted to save them all. We stayed up for three days straight teleporting people out of the wreckage. He just wouldn't stop. But then news crews started coming in and we had to leave. He would have stayed if he could've though."

I smiled. "He sounds like an amazing person."

His smile grew a little somber. "He was a saint."

"I wonder what he would have thought of us." I smiled up at him, trying to bring his smile back. "Like, as a couple and everything."

"He would have loved you." He let out a huff of a laugh, glancing down at me with a grin. "I mean, he probably would have called you a dumb ass for being with me but."

"Oh, shut up. You're amazing."

He kissed my hair. "I'm alright."

Just as I sat up to jokingly smack him, I jolted forward against the seat belt. Jeremy's arm quickly lifted back to the steering wheel in attempt to swerve as he slammed the breaks. But it was too late.

A little, navy blue figure slammed against our front end. It flew against the windshield. Then plummeted to the ground in a spray of crimson. A reflexive screech left my lips. I grasped my racing heart.

"Holy shit." Jeremy slammed the car into park. His wide eyes came to mine. "Are you okay?"

I nodded and reached for the door handle. We jumped from the car, not wasting a second. Loud, violent screams pierced our ears.

I ran to the front. My vision was still adjusting, I couldn't see much.

But that sound wasn't of an injured animal. That would have made my heart hurt too, but it was so much worse.

The screams of a child.

My knees collapsed to the cold, hard ground. All that I could see was navy speckled with red. He was so small. But the cries leaving his blood coated lips were so loud. I couldn't make out much of what he looked like in the blinding headlights, but he couldn't have been older than ten. My heart hammered at my ribs, stomach aching.

"Just breathe," I whispered. I reached down to touch his face. "It's okay, buddy. It's alright, we're gonna help you."

As my skin met his, a shock of electricity ran up my arm. The connection was so strong that it sent me stumbling backward.

"Duele!" he said. "Duele!" *It hurts.*

"I'm so sorry." Jeremy dropped behind him. "I'm so sorry."

He reached down to touch the boy, but he squirmed away. "No me lastimes! Por favor, no me lastimes. Por favor!" *Don't hurt me! Please don't hurt me. Please!*

"No te lastimaré," Jeremy said quietly. "Por favor, mi amigo. Deja que te ayude. Por favor." *I won't hurt you. Please, my friend. Let me help you. Please.*

Still crying, the little boy nodded. Jeremy gave a warm, gentle smile. He lifted him to his arms. I stumbled to my feet. As he walked to the back seat, he looked to me and said, "Call Adam. Tell him to bring Kai to our house right now. This wound's too big for you to heal."

He slid into the car and disappeared.

CHAPTER FOURTEEN

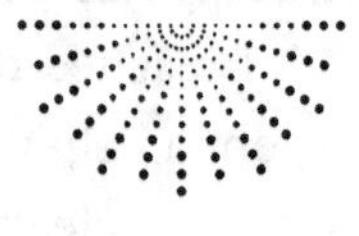

LAILA

"Sé que duele, lo sé." Jeremy soothed the little boy's sweaty hair while he screamed. "Pronto terminará. Lo siento mucho. Lo siento mucho." *I know it hurts. I know. It'll be over soon. I'm sorry. I'm sorry.*

My chest was tight at the image before me. A child covered in blood, writhing against my fiancé's hands. My brother pouring healing, yet agonizing, energy into his body.

Kai pulled away. "Are ye sure I ought to keep going? The lad's beggin' me to stop."

"Just fucking finish," Jeremy nearly yelled. "He's gonna bleed out."

Kai took in a deep breath. "It'll be over soon, little lad." He put his hands over the little boy's body, sending white light from his palms into the boy's skin.

The boy screamed again, louder that time. Jeremy struggled to soothe him in Spanish. His little back arched. Jeremy gripped his shoulders firm to the blanket covered sofa. He was doing the right thing, but if I didn't know it, I'd have thought he was torturing the kid.

I had to turn around. Just watching it made me nauseous. I'd felt that pain, and although it was lifesaving, I wouldn't wish it on my worst enemy. It was the most excruciating thing imaginable. In the moment that it happened, I would have rather been dead than experience that kind of agony.

Hannah stood beside me with her hand cupped over her mouth. Tears beaded down her cheeks. I handed her a tissue. While she wiped, I grabbed her elbow. "Come downstairs with me. He's going to be hungry when they're done."

Hannah lowered herself to the barstool at the counter. I walked into the kitchen. I needed food. I couldn't drink or smoke my anxiety away, I had to bury it with food.

"Is the pain really that bad?" Hannah asked. "Being healed, I mean."

"It's indescribable."

Silence settled between us for a moment. I cut into a coffee cake Max had prepared earlier, trying desperately to ignore the screams echoing from upstairs.

"He just keeps begging them to stop," Hannah murmured. "He keeps saying 'don't hurt me.'"

"He'll be alright in a few minutes."

Even though I knew that rationally, it didn't make the reality any more comfortable. Someone out there didn't know where their baby was or what was happening to him. Because he was being held down on my couch. Probably experiencing the worst pain he ever had.

"Have you called Ramirez?" she asked.

"You mean, did I wake up the man we just took home that has to be at work in four hours to tell him Jeremy ran a kid over with our car?" I called to the front.

"Right," she muttered. "I'm sorry."

"No. No, I'm sorry." I grabbed the sliced cake, a gallon of milk, and made my way to the serving area. "I'm just a little overwhelmed right now."

"I can imagine. He's going to be okay though, right?"

"Yeah, he'll be alright. Traumatized, but he'll live."

"Lo siento mucho," Jeremy said to the little boy. He crouched in the corner behind the couch. "Lo siento mucho. Pero ahora estás un o. Ahora estas bein amigo." *I'm sorry. I'm sorry. But now you're better. Now you're well, friend.*

His brows were pulled together, his lips curved down in a frown. The poor kid hated Jeremy right about then. Not that I blamed him, I hated Jeremy when he held me down for his sister to heal me too. But I was a neutral party so far. The kid may not have trusted me yet, but he didn't hate me.

"Give me a minute with him, alright?" My fingertips grazed Jeremy's shoulder.

He turned his concerned gaze back to me. He straightened up. "Do you speak Spanish?"

"No hablo Espanol mucho, no hablo Espanol bien. Pero si," I said. "Go get changed. I'm gonna get him cleaned up."

He was quiet for a moment. "He's really scared."

"We'll be okay."

He looked over the boy once more. He pecked my cheek, walked toward the bedroom, and pulled off his bloody shirt. I lowered myself to the ground beside the boy with a smile. That was when I got my first good look at him.

His skin was a milky umber color. He had dark brown hair and big chocolate brown eyes stretched wide in fear. His nose was large on his little face, though I was sure he'd grow into it. His cheeks hollowed slightly into his mouth. His lips were small but plump on his round face. He wore a bloodied navy scrub-like outfit. It hung as loosely on his body as a Barbie doll in a child's clothing. He was skinny, abnormally skinny. His clavicle bone protruded beneath his skin more than a super model's in a strapless dress.

"Me llamo Laila." I smiled as I brought myself into a cross-legged position. "Cuál es un ombre?" *My name's Laila. What's your name?* He said nothing, just gazed at me in fear. "Habla usted ingles?" *Do you speak English?*

He held up his thumb and forefinger as if to say, "a little bit."

My smile stayed in place. I reached to the coffee table to grab the cake and glass of milk. I held it out in front of him. "Are you hungry?"

He snatched it from my hands and began pawing into it with full fists. "We have more, buddy. Take your time."

He continued scooping it into his mouth with his bare hands. Crumbs flew like rain, landing on the ground around us in puddles. Once he'd finished it, he began picking up the broken pieces off the floor and carefully placing them onto his tongue.

I passed him the glass of milk. He took it in his bony hands, leaned his head back, and guzzled. It spilled from the corners of his lips down his face. It pooled in the crevice of his clavicle at his collar.

My bloated stomach ached with guilt as I watched him scarf it down. He clearly hadn't eaten in an awfully long time. He was covered in mud and blood. His eyes were more bloodshot than my fiancé's after a night toking with his brothers.

I couldn't wrap my mind around how anyone could allow a child to reach that state.

Once he finished, his begging gaze met mine. He said, "Mâs, por favor." *More, please.*

I planted my smile back on. I stood and walked to the half-remodeled kitchen. I grabbed a few cookies from the glass jar and a miniature bottle of orange juice from the fridge. I started back to the couch, kneeled next to him, placed the cookies on the plate and the juice beside it.

As he lifted it to his lips, he began furiously nibbling the cookie the way he had the cake. "Hay mâs, hay mâs." *There's more.*

He met my gaze and pulled the cookie from his mouth. His mouth moved in slow chews for a moment. He took another bite.

I smiled. "Beuno, beuno." *Good, good.*

He continued eating the cookies as I grabbed the remote off of the coffee table. I turned it on and changed the station to Nickelodeon. *SpongeBob* played. His eyes widened with excitement. He shifted onto his bottom, pulled his knees up against his chest, and scooted against the wall.

"Quédate aquí." *Stay here.* I smiled as I brought myself to my feet. While I walked to the bedroom, I looked over my shoulder at him. For the first time, I saw that sweet little boy smile. He ate his cookies and drank his juice with the purest, most grateful expression I'd ever seen on a child. For the simplest of pleasures.

I walked through the threshold into my room. Jeremy sat on the bed. He wore only his boxers, resting his dismal face against his palm. His arms were caked with dried blood against his white skin. I noted a few smears of red pasted against his cheeks as he turned up to look at me.

"Any progress?" he asked.

"He ate a piece of coffee cake and he's munching on some cookies now," I said. "So some, I guess."

He bit his lip, moving his head up and down quickly as he stood. "Good. That's good."

"I was wondering if you could run to Walmart and get some clothes while I give him a bath. I have baby clothes but nothing his size."

Jeremy grabbed a wet rag off the dresser he'd been using to wipe himself up. He looked at himself in the mirror, scrubbing the blood off of his cheek. "Yeah, I can do that. Do you know what size he is?" Before I could respond, he shook his head. "Of course, you don't. Whatever that thing he's wearing is doesn't have a size on it."

Clearly, we were on the same page about that boy. He'd come from somewhere awful. The only question was where.

"If I had to guess, I'd say a six or seven in kids. You can grab a few different sizes. He seems to like SpongeBob, so if they have anything with his face on it or something."

"SpongeBob, gotcha. I think I'll grab a couple toys or something too. Maybe he'll hate me less if I give him something he likes."

I frowned. "He's just scared."

"Yeah, well, torturing him probably didn't help." He licked his lips and rubbed his head. "I've never seen it done on a kid."

"Neither have I," I muttered. "It was hard to watch."

Silence followed. He wiped the rest of the blood from his arms and tossed the rag into the laundry bin. He pulled a pair of sweatpants and a T-shirt from his dresser, threw them on and slid his wallet into his pocket. He gave me a quick kiss goodbye before disappearing.

I was far from a trauma counselor. What was I supposed to say to this kid? He didn't know me. All he knew was that we hit him with our car, tortured him, then filled him with goodies. Like a reversed Hansel and Gretel. Well, not quite but close enough.

I turned back to the door and walked into the living room. The boy had moved a little further from the corner, now sitting slightly in front of the couch instead of beside it. He glanced at me with hesitation. I smiled. When I sat beside him, he looked back to the screen.

For a few minutes, I watched him watch the TV. My gaze shifted over his bony, diminutive body. I didn't know why this child was alone, barefoot in thirty-degree weather and nearly naked in the middle of the road at midnight. I didn't know why he was running through the woods by himself. I didn't know why his parents weren't looking for him.

But after looking at his frail, malnourished little body a moment longer, I knew that whoever let this abuse and neglect go on as long as it had didn't deserve him. They deserved a punishment worse than death.

As it cut to the commercial, he turned to me and pointed to the plate. "More, por favor."

Ah, my opportunity. Bribery. Fucked up to bribe a kid for food, but I needed to know what the fuck happened to him and where the hell he came from.

"How about I make you a deal?" His sweet brown eyes stared up at me. "Tell me your name and I'll get you another cookie."

His quiet, soprano voice said, "Daniel."

Not much but a start.

My lips lifted to a smile. I stood. "That's a beautiful name." I extended my hand for him to take. He gazed at it for a moment. He accepted it and stood beside me. His tiny fingers tightly grasped mine.

I led him to the kitchen. After flicking on the light, I reached into the cookie jar and pulled one out. "You can have this one, but if you want another, you have to do something else for me."

He grabbed ahold of the cookie and chomped into it. "Hmm?"

My eyes shifted over him. The mud on his bare feet, the crusted red on his cheeks. "You have to get a bath."

"Bath?"

"Bañera," I said. "Bath."

He thought about it for a long moment. "Si, bañera."

CHAPTER FIFTEEN

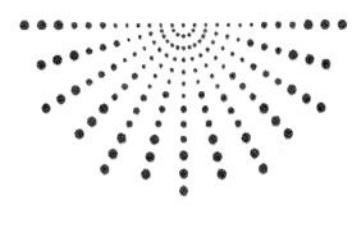

LAILA

The lavender-scented baby wash danced to my nose from the cast iron tub. I swooshed the warm water around, so bubbles formed. I'd been stocking up on baby supplies since I told Jeremy I was pregnant. I had plenty of hygiene items. Most of them were tailored for someone much younger than Daniel but it'd do the trick.

Daniel sat patiently on the toilet. I grabbed a washcloth off the shelf and threw it into the tub. "Stay here," I said as I stood.

I hurried into the baby's room to grab a green towel with a frog's face as a hood and the mesh bag of baby toys. They were definitely for a baby, not someone Daniel's age, but I figured that any toys were better than none.

I returned to the bathroom and rested the hood of the towel on the doorknob. "Rana!" he shouted, pointing to the towel. "Rana!"

I turned to him with a smile. "Si, rana. Frog."

Annunciating just as I had, he said, "Frog."

I gestured for him to get down and lowered myself to the rim of the bathtub. He moved to the floor and scratched his back, yawn leaving his little lips. I grabbed ahold of the navy pants and pulled them down.

I noted a series of scars over his legs and feet that appeared surgical. Brushing it off, I helped his shirt up over his shoulders.

Nothing could have prepared me for what I was about to see.

Tens, if not close to a hundred, more scars over his chest. They weren't little ones like a little boy who played hard would have. No.

They were large, thick white cicatrices. Some were an inch long, others even longer. But they didn't look carelessly placed. Some were crooked and jagged, but most of them were even slits, as if inflicted by a scalpel. Straight, surgically positioned lines.

The marks descended to his ankles. They covered nearly every inch of his body that clothes would touch. It was only then that I noticed the one just above his collar bone at the base of his neck. It wasn't until the mud and blood were washed from his body that I saw them descending his arms as well.

My expression must have changed because Daniel said. "Que pasa?" *What happened?*

I turned my gaze up to look at his face. I moved my finger to the scars. "Who did this? Quien hizo esto?" I asked with furrowed brows.

"Doctores," he said quietly.

"A doctor? A doctor did this to you?"

"Si."

Maybe Jeremy was right. Maybe they were experimenting on our people. That thought sent a heavier chill down my spine than the scars themselves.

I forced a smile. "Let's get you cleaned up." I gestured to the tub. "Vamos a limpiarte."

He started to walk to the tub. As he turned, I moved my hand to cover my mouth. I struggled not to gasp, utterly flabbergasted by the marks on his back.

There were at least a hundred. Maybe even more. I couldn't tell because they overlapped. They were long and skinny, as if inflicted by a whip, yet so many clumped together that I couldn't tell where one stopped, and another began. They strayed in every direction, even onto his bottom. There were smaller scars too, like the ones on his chest, but they were overshadowed by the long, lumpy cicatrices. They protruded off of his skin like some kind of diseased rash. But they weren't. They were scars thicker than the width of the boy's fingers, even thicker than mine, bulging like some type of cancerous growth.

My stomach tightened and swirled. I watched his feeble legs climb over the side of the tub into the soapy, bubbly water.

He wasn't just abused or neglected. He was meticulously tortured, like a prisoner of war.

Daniel couldn't have been more than eight years old. And his skin was scarred worse than any warrior I'd ever seen.

I gazed at Daniel's frail little body curled up on the couch. He had the plush SpongeBob Jeremy bought him tucked under his chin. His head rested on the white throw pillow as his eyes fluttered back and forth beneath their lids. He was tucked in a blue, fuzzy snowflake blanket I left out on the couch for decoration.

I hugged my knees. Watching him dream, my heart ached. When was the last time he slept so peacefully?

He looked like any other kid lying there. Holding his stuffed toy, head gently resting on the pillow five times its size. His little face looked so content, so tranquil. But he was far from peace.

Most importantly, why the hell was he here? And why only a few hours after we met another little boy who'd been kidnapped? There was no way in hell there was no correlation there.

Jeremy's hand grazed my shoulder. I jumped and sparks flew from the tips of my fingers.

"Sorry," he murmured. "I didn't mean to scare you."

Clutching my chest, I stood, whispering, "It's okay. Let's go talk."

We tiptoed to the bedroom. He carefully closed the door behind us. I sat on the bed chewing my inner jaw and running my fingers through my hair.

Jeremy leaned against the dresser across from the foot of the bed. "Did you get anything out of him?"

I nodded slow. "His name's Daniel."

"Daniel," he murmured.

I chewed my trembling lip as tears puddled in the corners of my eyes. I wiped them away. Jeremy walked to the bed and took my face in his hands. "What's the matter?"

I was quiet for a moment. "I think they're fucking with us."

He squinted and sat beside me. "What do you mean? Who?"

"Whoever had Cage. Whoever has Chris and Ray's family."

His head turned to the side. "What? What do you mean?"

"When I leaned down to help Daniel after the accident, he shocked me. And not just a little static electricity. It was strong, like when you use your energy. It almost knocked me off my feet."

"He's one of us?" Jeremy asked.

"I think so. It can't be a coincidence that we just went and met Cage tonight and we hit this kid with our car. This little boy who barely speaks any English appears out of nowhere in our incredibly white town. Just shows up in the middle of a road almost no one drives at midnight? He's clearly been abused and neglected for years," I said. "No, it can't just be a fluke. If I've learned anything in the past year, it's that if it looks too coincidental to be a coincidence, it probably isn't a coincidence. It looks like a duck, quacks like a duck, it's probably a duck and all that."

"Abused," he puzzled. "How do you know he was abused?"

"When I was getting him in the bathtub, I pulled his shirt off, and he's just... He's completely covered in scars. He's... It's harder to find the skin than the scars."

Jeremy was quiet for a moment. "It's really that bad?"

I swallowed the stiff lump in my throat. "I've never seen anything like it in my life. It's like he was... Like he was tortured."

He clenched his hands to fists as they began to glow blue light. Sparks flew from his closed palms like a sparkler on the fourth of July. It wasn't common for Jeremy to grow so angry that he couldn't control his powers. In fact, I'd never seen it until that moment.

Hurting kids always lit a fire under our asses that nothing else was capable of.

CHAPTER SIXTEEN

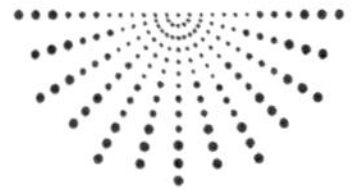

JANUARY 23, 2019 - LAILA

"I bet it was a warning." Leah glanced at Daniel playing with some of the boys' old action figures in the sunroom. "They know we're getting closer. We're gathering information, they're getting scared. Telling us to back off."

"Maybe," Jeremy muttered.

"But by letting us find him, we have more information. We have more to go on," I said. "It would've made more sense to keep him hostage. That's how they cover their tracks, they don't leave a shred of evidence behind. Even Cage, he didn't see anything. Not really. He didn't get to wherever they were planning on taking him. All he saw was the back of their truck and some guys in hazmat suits. That's not much of a loose end. But Daniel, they had to have had him for years. The scars have scars, that's how bad it is. The tissue is harder than a rock. They've had him held captive for at least half of his life. Maybe even more. Everything he must have seen, everything he must know tucked away in that little head of his... That's a thread they can't want pulled."

"Maybe they're just throwing a dog a bone," Brody said. "A peace offering of sorts."

Jeremy rubbed his chin. "I don't know. But I have a really bad feeling about all of this. Maybe it's just because I ran him over. But I don't know. Something isn't adding up. Like Laila said, they're experts at covering their tracks. They leave *nothing* behind. They go so far as to fake their captive's deaths. And then they just drop this kid practically on our doorstep?" He shook his head. "No. We're missing something."

"I think it's a warning," Leah said. "Like, back off. Or this will be you."

"We should call Ray." Adam poured a cup of coffee. "He might be able to check missing persons and see when and where the kid went missing from."

"Do you have any idea how many Mexican kids are missing in the U.S.?" Leah asked. "Thousands. Do you know how common of a name Daniel is? We don't even know the kids' age. It'd be like looking for a needle in a haystack. And even if that weren't the case, Daniel's death was probably faked just like Chris's and Ray's family. And if he's from Mexico, which I'd say is probably the case from his accent, the chances of finding any evidence are even more slim. Crime rates are astronomical there."

Adam said, "Either way, we should talk to Ray. He needs to know what's happening here."

"Didn't you hear Laila? His back?" Brody said. "Can you imagine what that's going to do to his head?"

"Yeah, Brody, I can," Adam snapped. "They have our brother. They're doing those horrible things to him as we speak. But at least I know."

"Well, maybe it's better if we didn't."

Adam teleported in front of him and stiffened his shoulders. Brody laughed at his tough guy persona and Adam drew closer. "Why the fuck would it be better?"

"Because there's nothing we can do. We have nothing to go on."

"We have Daniel." Adam pointed to the sunroom and took a step forward.

"Even if we get something from him, he's a kid. He's not going to know where he was being kept. He didn't speak their language; his memories of their conversations won't be clear. He didn't escape, he was set free. They didn't just reveal themselves to us or something. We know close to nothing about these people. We aren't going to find him, at least not because of this. We don't have enough. They wouldn't have turned him over to us if he had information we needed. They're smart, dude."

I saw both points. Brody was right, we knew next to nothing. All we knew for certain was that our people were being tortured by people faking their deaths.

Chris and Amy, Ray's wife, were white. Lydia was half Latina, half white and Daniel was evidently Latino. Cage and Derek Stevenson were both black. No particular pattern, no MO aside from the fact that they were all supernaturally inclined.

By offering up Daniel, they were telling us one thing though. This went beyond borders.

Still, that was hardly anything. We only knew what they were allowing us to know. Daniel may have been a lead but not a concrete one. However, I did agree with Adam. Ray had to know. If for nothing aside from helping us establish rights to hold him until his parents were found.

Adam gritted his teeth to a hard line as he took a step closer, so close that their chests nearly touched. I saw Adam's hand tighten and interjected.

"Alright, boys." I stepped between them and put a hand on each of their chests to push them apart. "We aren't fighting each other. This is bigger than us."

Adam gritted his teeth but walked back to the kitchen counter.

"Laila's right. This is huge," Leah said.

"We now know for a fact that they have, or have had at one point, at least six of our people. They probably have a lot more."

"And they're using magic," Leah said. "That's the only way they could shield their location from us. Either they have a really powerful Witch working for them or they're being forced. One way or another, we aren't just up against an enemy. We might be up against our own too."

We all let out some sort of sign of frustration. I sighed, Jeremy rubbed his eyes, Brody bit his lip, Adam shook his head, Leah poured some scotch into her coffee. It wasn't going to be easy.

Before everyone went on with their days, I took a moment to talk to Adam. I asked him if he would answer the calls on my emergency phone because I didn't want to have to rush away and leave Daniel. He rolled his eyes but took it.

"I think we should take him to the hospital." Jeremy looked at Daniel napping on the love seat to our left.

"Why? He's not hurt."

"I don't know. Maybe they can look at his scars and see what they're from."

"I think it's pretty obvious what they're from," I muttered.

"Well, yeah, some of them were definitely torture," he said. "But the ones on his chest and limbs, they were done with a scalpel. They must have done something to him. And we have no idea what he's vaccinated for. He should have a titer test done."

"I don't think that'll go over well. He said that doctors did that to him. He's going to be terrified as soon as he sees them. He's been through enough already."

Jeremy shrugged. "I could see if Olivia could take a look at him."

I turned to him with a narrowed gaze. "Your ex-girlfriend?"

He laughed, studying my expression. "I just want the kid to be seen by a professional."

"She's not even a doctor."

"She's a PA." He gave a half smile. "What? Are you jealous or something?"

"Am I jealous of your ex-girlfriend? The girl who wears blue eye shadow with red lipstick and nothing else?" I laughed as I sat forward. "Yeah, babe. I'm full of envy."

"Why don't you want me to ask her then?" he asked.

"I just don't like her," I said.

"You've only met her twice."

"Yeah, two times too many." I shrugged and walked to the kitchen to get another cup of coffee.

"What's your problem with her?" He trailed behind me. "She was nice the last time we ran into her. She didn't say anything rude to you or anything."

I laughed. "You're really that dense, aren't you?"

He leaned over the island to meet my gaze as I poured creamer into my coffee cup. "What do you mean?"

A huff left my lips. "That's just it. She didn't say anything rude to me the last time we saw her because she didn't say *anything* to me."

"Nuh-uh. She said hi," he said.

I laughed. "No, she said, 'Oh, hi, Jeremy!' and hugged you. She acted like I wasn't even there."

"Maybe she didn't know what to say."

"She touched your arm."

He raised his hand to his chest in mock shock. "Oh my God, how heinous. That slut."

My gaze narrowed. "You know what I mean. It wasn't just a friendly hello. She slid her hand down to yours. It was weird."

A chuckle left his lips. "You're paranoid."

I rolled my eyes. "And you don't understand women."

"You're just jumping to conclusions."

"No, I just know bitches. And it's obvious to anyone with eyes that the bitch still has a thing for you."

He scoffed. When my gaze remained steady, he laughed. "We dated when we were in high school, that's ancient history for both of us."

I grabbed the coffee pot and poured my cup. Gazing at him over my mug as I took a sip, I muttered, "*We* started dating when I was in high school."

His eyes narrowed. "We're different."

In fairness though, he didn't know I was in high school until I was almost out. When we met, I was careful to avoid mentioning what I did between seven and two Monday through Friday. Since my friend who'd introduced us was nineteen, and I worked full time, he assumed I was the same age as her.

He wasn't exactly happy when he realized I was eighteen. But nothing had happened until I was of age, it wasn't even a three year age gap, and he was already in love with me by the time he realized.

"Either way. I still know when a bitch wants my man, and that bitch wants my man."

He flashed a boyish grin. "So you *are* jealous."

"I'm not jealous." I laughed. "I just want to punch her stupid face."

Okay, maybe I was a little jealous. Rationally, I knew I didn't have a reason to be. Jeremy never acted on her advances. But Olivia liked every single thing he shared on Facebook. Except for the pictures that had me in them. The bitch was all about sharing his memes but didn't even say congratulations on our baby announcement. And she didn't like the ultrasound photos of him. Maybe that was a childish thing to be mad about, but my little rotisserie chicken was adorable. And I was offended.

He laughed. He disappeared and reappeared behind me. His arms wrapped around my waist. He kissed my neck. "Well, lucky for you, I'm not interested in her stupid face."

"No?" I smiled as his lips traveled to my collar bone.

"No." His long black hair brushed my cheek. "Just your stupid face."

I laughed and smacked him away. I turned to look at him. "You sure know how to make a girl feel special."

"Ah, well" —he grinned— "What can I say, I'm a real lady's man."

I laughed again. I leaned onto my tip toes and pressed my lips to his. "You're an ass." I pulled away but he grabbed my hips and lifted me to the counter. He kissed me again. I giggled at his lips.

"But you love me."

"That, I do."

He kissed me again and cupped the side of my neck in his hand. I lifted my arms around his head. My fingers interlocked behind his neck, warmth and comfort settling between us.

CHAPTER SEVENTEEN

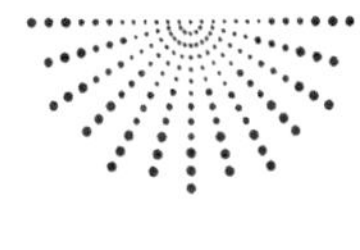

LAILA

I'd conceded a little while later. Whether I liked Olivia or not, Jeremy was right. Daniel needed to be seen by a professional. He called her and she answered before the third ring. Then sweetly agreed to be there just as soon as her shift ended. Jeremy *loved* the eye roll I gave him at that.

Nonetheless, there were some things that needed done at Moe's before she arrived. Jeremy left to handle them. Part of me hoped he wouldn't be back by the time she came so I wouldn't have to deal with her incessant flirting. The other half of me hoped he would so his presence would keep me from saying something less than kind.

But a friend from the underground hospital dropped her off before he got back.

As Olivia set her bag on the breakfast nook table, I gave her a polite smile. "Thank you for coming."

"It's no problem." She avoided my gaze as she unpacked her medical supplies.

She *was* pretty. I could see her and Jeremy having been a cute couple once, as much as that thought made me want to hurl. At barely five one though, the height difference must have been really weird. I only stood a couple inches taller and even we looked a little silly.

Though tied into a messy bun, her golden waves complimented her lightly tanned skin. I knew from their pictures together in her cheerleading uniform that she wasn't always as dorky as the thick glasses she wore now made her appear. But she did pull it off. She had a tiny button nose between her widespread eyes, which admittedly, wouldn't have looked so cute without the glasses.

Her tits were huge though. Lucky bitch. I couldn't help but notice how well the tight V-neck showed them off. Joke was on her though, Jeremy was always an ass guy. However, she beat me in that department too.

"Did Jeremy tell you anything about Daniel?" I asked from my perch on a stool at the island.

"Yeah. Enough, anyway," she muttered.

"So you know that he's terrified of doctors?" I asked.

"That's why I changed out of my scrubs." She laid a series of syringes out on the table.

Oh, yeah. That's definitely why.

"I think it would stand to reason that he's also afraid of needles."

"Well, I'm going to need a needle to get a blood sample."

I bit my lip as if it were the urge to punch her stupid face. "Do you plan on holding him down to get that?"

"If I have to." She laid her stethoscope next to the syringe.

I chuckled, amused at the thought of Daniel zapping her onto her ass.

"Is that a problem?"

I bit my smiling lip. "Not for me."

She looked back to her equipment. Footsteps peddled down the maid stairs into the kitchen. Olivia and I both turned to see Hannah carrying her backpack. She forced a smile. "Oh, hey, Liv."

"Wow, you look great, Hannah." Olivia smiled. "You're all grown up now."

"Yeah, I guess puberty does that to you. You look nice too."

"Thanks," Olivia said.

Hannah walked to me and put her hand on my belly. "Any kicks yet, little man?"

"I promise, you will be the first one I call when he does." I chuckled, running my hand over my stomach.

"You should probably be feeling some movement by now." Olivia gestured toward my belly. "How far along are you?"

"Right around fourteen weeks."

"Oh, wow. I guess not then. Sorry, I thought you were further along," Olivia said.

Little jabs like that were why I didn't like her. She was caddy and juvenile. The girl had to have weighed at least twenty pounds more than I did yet still had the nerve to comment on my weight.

In all honesty, it didn't offend me. I knew I'd put on a few pounds since I'd gotten pregnant, but I didn't care. But those types of comments aimed at someone with lower self-esteem could be detrimental to their mental health. Olivia worked in healthcare, she had to have known that. And that's why I couldn't like her. She knowingly hurt other people with her words like some pathetic teenager and wasn't willing to grow up.

Hannah met my gaze and rolled her eyes. "So when are you and Jeremy going ring shopping?"

I smiled, seeing exactly what my soon to be sister-in-law was doing. We had quite the friendship. Nothing ever got between us. I knew her loyalty lied with me over the girl who cheated on her brother in high school. "I'm not sure yet. We were hoping to go today, but everything with Daniel... I don't know. We'll see."

"Oh, you're getting married?" Olivia asked.

"That's the plan."

"Well, at least something was planned." She gave a phony smile.

That bitch. Damn, I hated her.

Hannah gritted her teeth to a hard line, gaze shifting from me and then to Olivia.

"Oh, good, you made it." Jeremy smiled as he came into the kitchen. "Thanks for coming."

Olivia's smile widened. "Of course. Happy to help."

"I'm sure you are," Hannah muttered under her breath, digging in the fridge.

"Hey, beautiful." Jeremy gave me a quick kiss. He walked to the coffee pot. "Sorry I'm late. It was crazy at Moe's."

"What do you mean? What happened?" I asked.

"Just an issue with the whole sellers."

"Let me guess. The produce guys brought us half of our order again."

"Yup. And Insisted that it was the exact order they received."

"And you showed them the receipt, right? Because last time, I ended up having to give them a bank statement of how much we paid to even look into the order."

I knew we didn't need to waste time about a work conversation at that moment. But I can't say I didn't enjoy the fact that Olivia saw us talking about our normal, human partnership.

He poured his coffee and took a sip. "Oh, yeah. I showed them the receipt. I told them we wouldn't renew our contract at the end of February when it's up if these problems weren't resolved."

"And?"

Jeremy grinned. "And they're making an extra trip tomorrow to drop off the missing half of our order. And took fifty percent off of next month's order. Which I placed today."

"You're the best." I smiled back.

"Either way, I don't think we should renew the contract when it's up. They've been dicking us around for months."

"Yeah, I don't know why Moe kept them. I think they were friends a few decades ago or something. But yeah, I agree."

"We should ask around for recommendations from the other restaurants in town. Somebody has to have a good produce guy."

"I'll ask Beverly at the bakery down the road."

"Good idea."

"I hate to interrupt, but I do have somewhere to be later," Olivia interjected.

"Oh, of course." Jeremy set his coffee down. "I'll go get Daniel."

"No, that's okay." I stood. "He hates you enough after last night. I'll handle this one."

"Maybe we should go somewhere a bit more isolated anyway,"

Olivia said. "If he's scared already, doing an exam in the middle of the kitchen might make things worse."

"Yeah, I agree. We'll go to Jeremy's old bedroom upstairs. It's up the steps—"

"Third door on the right." She put her tools back into her bag. She turned her gaze up to meet mine. "I remember."

My gaze involuntarily narrowed.

Oh, cool, you remember where you fucked my fiancé in your teenage years. Whoop di do. Too bad you'll never fuck him again.

Jeremy pressed his lips to a line. "Let's go get Daniel." He put his hand on my shoulder to guide me toward the front.

As we made it into the living room, I looked up at him and laughed. "Yeah, I'm definitely just paranoid."

He tried to crease down the corners of his flattered smile. "Fine, you were right."

"Mhm." I lowered myself to Daniel who stared intently at Peppa Pig. "Hey, buddy."

"Hola," he muttered. His gaze glued to the TV, chin resting in the palm of his hand.

"Can I talk to you?" I asked.

He turned to look at me. "Que pasa?"

"I'm worried about you." I reached forward and pushed hair behind his ear.

Jeremy said, "Quiero asegurarme de que estás bien." *I want to make sure you're okay.*

"Estoy bien. Estoy bien," he insisted. *I'm okay. I'm okay.*

"I know, buddy. Lo sé. Pero quiero estar romet de que no estás enfermo," I said. *But I want to make sure you're not sick.*

He grabbed my hand. His voice moved quickly as his eyes filled with fear. "No estoy enfermo. Por favor, no rometo. Me lastiman. No me gustan, son malos. Por favor, Laila. No dejes que me hagan daño. No dejes que me hagan daño."

"He's talking too fast, what is he saying?" I looked up at Jeremy.

Jeremy frowned. "He says he isn't sick. He's begging you not to let them hurt him. He thinks the doctor's going to take him again."

"Oh, no, buddy. No one's going to take you anywhere. Nadie te va a llevar. Te mantendré a salvo, lo rometon." I soothingly squeezed his hands and ran my thumb along the back of his. "Lo rometon." *I promise.* He gazed at me trustingly for a moment. "I won't let them hurt you again. But can we please check you out? Just to be sure you're okay?"

He looked up at Jeremy and then back to me. "You stay?"

"Yeah, buddy. I'll stay with you the whole time."

CHAPTER EIGHTEEN

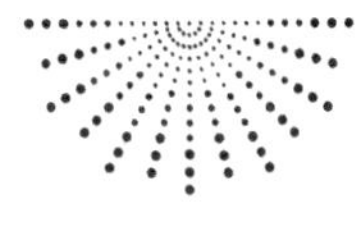

LAILA

Daniel sat on my lap patiently letting Olivia examine his back. "I'm really concerned with what these will do as he grows. The scarring is so severe I'm worried that they're going to put pressure on nerves and cause some pain," she murmured. "Especially through puberty. Aside from that, he'll probably be extremely uncomfortable to go shirtless in public. I'd like to have him seen by a plastic surgeon once he adjusts to normal life a bit. They might be able to cover these or at least flatten them. But his lungs sound pretty good. Something sounds a little off, but I wouldn't be too concerned."

She scooted her chair around to the front of us. "Can I look at your belly now?"

"Muéstrale tu barriga, amigo," Jeremy said from the bed, smiling gently.

He leaned back for Olivia to examine his stomach. She slid her gloved finger along his scars. "That's weird." Her finger grazed a cicatrix slightly to the side of his left rib.

"What is it?" I asked.

Her breaths were suddenly panting in and out harder and faster. "This scar is from a thoracotomy."

Jeremy squinted, leaning forward. "Why would they cut into his lung?"

"My guess without doing a chest X-ray? With the obvious systematic abuse found all over his body, I would think that at one point, he probably had a fractured rib that pierced it. They probably had to do a lobectomy which explains why something doesn't sound right. And this scar here is probably where the drainage tube connected to the bag."

I wrapped my arms around him tighter. Who could beat a child so badly that they had to have a portion of their lung removed? Whoever these people were, I was really beginning to wonder if they were human. Humans couldn't be that cruel.

She went on gently feeling his skin. "There's a lot of scar tissue here. But other than the thoracotomy, none of these seem medically necessary for any possible reason. It's like they did it just for the hell of it."

My heart grew heavy, and I thought I'd be sick. At that point, I thought I'd seen a lot of horrible things. I guess I had. More than most people do in a lifetime. Of course, a different type of horror than most.

I knew that evil existed. I'd seen Werewolves, Sirens, Vampires and Demons. I'd seen true evil. But never had I seen anything *that* evil. Years of ongoing, consistent, methodical abuse on a child. No, it wasn't even abuse. Abuse didn't touch this. It was agonizing torture.

Olivia pulled back and looked him over. "Considering the situation, I don't think it would hurt to do an MRI and CT either. I think we should run any and every test on him imaginable. Whoever did this to him... Some of these scars are huge and I can't even begin to imagine why. God only knows what they were doing under his skin."

"I'm not running a thousand tests on him right now," I murmured with a shake of my head. "He needs some time to heal."

"Suit yourself." She reached into her bag. "The longer you wait for the tests, the longer until you know what's happened to him. The longer until you have more clues as to *why* this happened to him."

She turned back to us with a syringe. Daniel shook his head vigorously. His gaze of terror turned from the needle to me. "No, por favor. Por favor, Laila! Por favor!"

"It's okay," I murmured. "Solo dolerá por un segundo."

Tears raced down his face. He started to hyperventilate, body quivering in fear. "Por favor, Laila! Por favor! Por favor!"

Olivia grabbed his arm and pulled it out to face her. His lip quivered and his eyes flooded with tears. He could barely breathe, and she hadn't even put on the tourniquet.

Without thought, I decided.

"We aren't going to do this right now."

She furrowed her brows. "I'm already here. I might as well take a quick sample."

"No, we're going to wait."

"That's ridiculous. He's been used as a science project for years. We need to at least check his platelets and electrolyte levels."

"And we will. But he has been traumatized enough in the past twelve hours." I put my hand around his arm that Olivia still tightly gripped. "Thank you for everything. But we're holding off on the blood work for now."

She released him. "You have no idea what is going on inside of his body."

"Maybe not but I know what's going on inside of his mind," I said. He gripped me tight, burrowing his head into my chest. "He's been through enough. Let's give him some time to heal."

She turned to Jeremy. "Don't you think we need to run these tests?"

"Yeah, definitely. But Laila's right. The kid's terrified. And considering what you just saw all over him, I'd think you'd understand why now wouldn't be the best time to force him to give a blood sample."

"For all you guys know, he could have HIV or hepatitis." Her eyes shifted from Jeremy to me quickly. "You have no medical history, you don't know where he's from, you don't know who his parents are. You're taking a huge risk here."

"Well, if my risk helps a child that's experienced more suffering than all of the people in this room combined feel just a little bit better" —Jeremy shrugged— "it's worth it."

CHAPTER NINETEEN

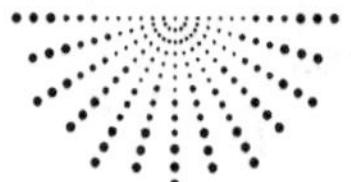

JANUARY 31, 2019 - LAILA

Things were odd after finding Daniel. Ramirez filed a report and tried to find his parents, but as Leah said, it was close to impossible. He pulled some strings and managed to find a way for Jeremy and me to keep him in our physical custody for either ninety days or until the parents were found, whichever came first. The courts didn't particularly want to dump him into the foster system considering the clear abuse that took place.

I didn't particularly want to take Daniel in. I was pregnant with my first child. I didn't have room for another one at that time.

But I had to make sure he was safe. I hoped that after he adjusted a bit to the real world, maybe he could go live with Janis and Elijah. I gave her a call and she said she'd try to figure out somewhere to put him if it came to that. I found the chances of locating his mother or father unlikely, so it seemed like the most reasonable option.

Jeremy and I purchased our rings the week prior and we were waiting for them to be resized and engraved. I actually started to get excited. After trying on my simple, yet beautiful solitaire styled ring, my finger felt empty. I found myself glancing at it from time to time, thinking about how plain my finger looked. Before, I'd thought about an engagement ring as a sort of collar and the wedding band as a leash, but I began to see it as a symbol of intricate connection rather than a simple tether.

Adam and Jeremy told me that a lot had been going on with Celena. Admittedly, it seemed like they struggled to keep the details from me. In all fairness, I didn't ask for them.

Truth be told, I was pretty overwhelmed with Daniel. Nearly every waking moment of my life had been engulfed by him. Not that I minded, I enjoyed seeing him so happy.

I found it peculiar how quickly I grew to love that child. Maybe it was the pregnancy hormones, or maybe it was because I was so terrified of the people who tortured him. Like keeping him safe gave me some false sense of control over the situation.

Leah hadn't found any new information on them yet. Every time I looked at Daniel's back, I was reminded of how horrible the people behind all of this were and I was terrified. I guess it didn't seem real until Daniel.

I'd heard the stories about Chris. Nearly all that Ray talked about was Amy and Lydia. But I guess I never really thought about what was *happening* to them. Yet, when Daniel happily splashed around in the tub, all I could think about were those scars. How much pain he felt at the crack of each whip and how agonized he must have been at each slice on his stomach.

Slamming on the front door of Moe's pulled me from my dreams. I sat forward in bed wiping my eyes and glanced at the clock. It was four in the morning. Surely it wasn't an angry customer yet.

I tapped Jeremy's chest. "Baby. Baby, do you hear that?"

"Huh?" He turned to the other side and dozed back to sleep.

I rolled my eyes and stood. I grumbled, "If that's a murderer, you will have no one to blame for my death except for yourself."

He didn't budge. Never did.

I stepped into my slippers and pulled on my robe as the bangs continued. When I made it through the hallway, into the living room and out my apartment door, the sounds became clearer. Still couldn't quite place who they were coming from, but when someone banged on my door in the middle of the night, that was never a good thing.

"Laila!" I heard. "Laila!"

I hurried down the steps taking two at a time. I rushed through the kitchen into the dining area. I couldn't make much out through the blinds, but her voice became clear.

After slamming the lock off and ripping the door open, I found Celena standing on the doorstep. Her blood speckled blond hair was pulled into a falling ponytail. From the tip of her head to the soles of her black shoes, nearly every inch of her was at least splashed with red. Thick trails of black mascara trickled down her cheeks all the way to her chest. Her crimson covered hands trembled like a tree in a thunderstorm.

"It's Wyatt." She gestured to her haphazardly parked Land Rover a few yards away. "I-I can't heal him. I'm trying, but I just can't—"

"Go through the kitchen door, all the way to the end, up the steps, and call Jeremy's name. Tell him I need him." I brushed past her to the car. She took off. I bolted to the passenger side and pulled the door open.

Wyatt lay motionless, half on the seat, half on the center console. I shook him with vigor, but he wouldn't budge. Blood oozed from an opening in his abdomen. I lifted his head to steady his face and meet his gaze. But he couldn't look at me if he wanted to.

His eyes were as vacant as an abandoned building. He wasn't just unconscious; he physically couldn't move his eyes. I touched his wrist to feel for a pulse. It thumped slow against my fingertips. I could barely feel it. But it was there.

I went into his mind, hoping that he was just poisoned. But there was nothing there. He wasn't dreaming. He wasn't even thinking. He was nearly at death's door.

It was exactly what I'd been afraid of. I knew something would go wrong. The two of them didn't stand a chance against that pack, not yet. Jeremy and I were going to have one hell of an argument once Wyatt and Celena were taken care of.

Jeremy ran toward us in a full sprint sporting his boxers and nothing else. "I'll send Brody to bring you guys over and watch Daniel." He laid his hand on Wyatt and disappeared.

Celena fell to the ground at the doorsteps. Her bloody hands quaked violently. Fast breaths heaved in and out of her chest. "It's all because of me," she whispered. "This is all my fault."

I walked to her and squatted to meet her gaze. "He's going to be okay, sweetie. I promise, he's going to be back to normal before you know it."

"You don't understand," she murmured. .

That expression sent a shiver down my spine. I knew it all too well. When someone was trying to catch their breath, then they tell you that you don't understand, that means someone's dead. But I couldn't think about that. My sister was a wreck. All I needed to focus on was bringing her back down.

"Go inside, okay? I'm going to move your car. Just sit down, alright?"

CHAPTER TWENTY

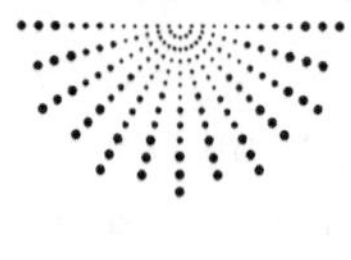

LAILA

I helped Celena into the shower and got her a change of clothes. After I closed the bathroom door, I checked on Daniel in the baby's room. He lay asleep, face turned away from the flashing light of the TV. Thankfully. I had no clue how I'd explain those screams if he'd woken.

I made my way to the kitchen and put on a pot of coffee. As the warm aroma filled my nostrils, my thoughts started to wander.

I wasn't sure if I was cursed or simply blessed with the ability to help. Even when things in my life were going well, everyone else's life seemed to fall apart.

What must've been going through Celena's head when she was on her way here? Just a month ago, she was a normal kid. Her life was kind of a mess, but *she* was normal. Or at least, she didn't know she *wasn't* normal. But now, her life had been turned upside down. I knew what that felt like and I wouldn't wish it on my worst enemy.

I blamed myself for Moe's death for a while. I guess I still do at times, even after all of these years. But somewhere along the way, I realized that it couldn't have been my fault.

I didn't want him dead. I didn't put that blade in his chest. I loved him.

Still, it was hard to let go of the blame when I remembered Mary telling me that I needed the life insurance money to start over. That I needed to move away. That I needed to leave Jeremy and abort my baby.

I turned to the sink and rinsed some coffee grounds down the drain. Brody appeared in the living room.

"Hey." I turned off the water and dried my hands.

"Hey, you." Brody sat at the bar stool.

I gestured to Celena in the bathroom. "So do you know anything about all this?"

His lips pressed together. He scratched the side of his head. "Yeah, soo... Nobody wanted you to get involved."

"Because I'm carrying the family miracle baby, right?"

He chuckled. "Nobody wants you to get hurt either."

I sat at the bar beside him. "I know I have precious cargo here and all, but someone could at least tell me when something crazy is happening. She is my sister, you know."

"Well, I guess I have to now."

"Looks like it."

He rubbed his hand down his mouth. "They're in pretty deep. Over their heads deep. I don't know what happened tonight. But last week, Celena's aunt was killed by the pack. And from what I understand, pretty gruesomely. They beat her up pretty bad too from what Adam said. She called your phone, so he went and picked her up. I guess she was in real bad shape. Leah went down and healed her. Then the other day, Wyatt calls Jeremy. He said he needed help with something but wouldn't really talk about it. So Jeremy went down for a little while and talked to him. I guess he started presenting with powers out of nowhere."

Wyatt was the first Werewolf I'd met, and he'd left a good impression of them in my mind. He was respectful, kind, and usually the smile that lit up a room—an all around good kid.

I couldn't say that we were the best of friends, but he was one of Jeremy's, and that held some merit.

Still, to my knowledge, Werewolves didn't have abilities outside of shifting.

"But he's a wolf, isn't he?"

Brody said, "Well, yeah, but a hybrid. Apparently, anyway. Ashley bound his powers when he was a baby like your dad did to you."

My head cocked to the side. "But why would powers just show up like that? That isn't normal. Celena's were activated by the change but Wyatt went through the change years ago."

"Yeah, that's why Jeremy went. But it turns out that Wyatt got his powers the same way you got yours."

"What do you mean?" He gave an awkward half shrug. "You mean, he has a par animo, too?"

He gestured toward the bathroom.

My brow arched. "Celena?"

"That's what Jeremy said."

"That's insane," I muttered. So far, Jeremy and I were the only two that had met one another. The reality of the par animarum at all was a stretch to any supernatural creature's imagination. But two pairs in less than four years? That had to mean something. Maybe that war the myth mentioned, and the one Moe talked about in his journal had some truth to it after all. "It's even weirder that she's my sister."

"I was thinking that too," he said.

I took in a deep breath. I found myself doing that on a regular basis those days. I heard the shower turn off and stood. "How was Wyatt when you left?"

"Not great. He's healing, but really slowly. The weird thing is that he doesn't even seem to be in pain."

"They shot him up with a lot of ketamine," Celena said from the bathroom door. She came down the hallway rubbing her hair between two sides of a white towel. "He's probably too fucked up to scream if he wanted to. Sorry, I wasn't eavesdropping. Wolf's hearing."

"Yeah, I gotcha," I said. "Do you wanna talk about what happened over breakfast?"

"No, that's okay. I'm a little nauseous to be honest. I'd love a cup of coffee though."

"Sure." I smiled. Brody glanced at her and then back to me with a squint. "Oh, sorry. Celena, this is Brody. Brody, this is Celena."

"Nice to meet you." He extended his hand.

"Likewise." She shook it. "Wyatt's mentioned you a couple of times. It's nice to put a name to a face."

"Yeah, same here."

He gazed at her for a moment. She wiped the back of her hand against her cheek. "Did I miss some blood or something?"

Coming out of his trance, he cleared his throat. "No. No, I'm sorry. It's just weird how you all look alike. I mean, it makes sense. You're siblings so you're expected to look alike. I just knew Mary for so long and I never knew she had kids, and now I see all of you as adults, and none of you are much younger than she looks, so it's just... Kind of bizarre."

"Mary?" she asked.

"Our biological mom," I said.

"Oh." She gave an awkward, uncomfortable expression. "Thanks, I guess."

"Trust me, it's a compliment," I muttered.

Brody turned to me with a 'fuck you' gaze. I chuckled. "Brody, will you take us to the house? She and I can talk while they work on Wyatt."

"Yeah, sure."

CHAPTER TWENTY-ONE

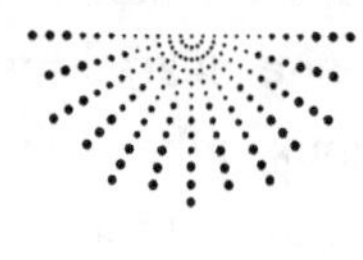

LAILA

"So what happened?" I lowered myself to the breakfast nook across from Celena.

"I knew something was going to go down after the funeral." It got quiet for a second or two. She looked for a way to go on but seemed unsure of where to start. After a moment of spinning her spoon in her mug, she looked up and met my gaze with tears in her eyes. "They killed Wyatt's mom."

I felt my eyes widen as my hand made its way to cover my mouth. My eyes filled with salty water and my chest grew tight. "Oh my God."

I didn't know Ashley all that well. She was more of a friendly acquaintance than anything. The news hurt though. Not even so much for myself, but for Wyatt. I knew they were close.

"I got my mom out of town because I knew that after the funeral it would all pick back up. And my uncle, and my cousin and her boyfriend," she murmured, voice shaky. "I didn't think that they would do that to her. Or maybe I did, and I just knew she wasn't going to leave, or that she'd be easy to find if she did." She used the back of her hand to wipe her eyes.

"But after my mom and everyone left, Wyatt came over. We were watching TV, and just, I don't know. Just chilling, I guess. He dozed off. He started talking in his sleep, and crying, and then screaming. When he woke up, he was panicking. He told me I had to get dressed and we had to go. He said he had a premonition and we had to get out of town, or we were going to die. Or at least, him and Ashley would. They were going to take me and initiate me into the pack. So I did and we went to his house to get Ashley, but they were already there.

"I can't remember what everyone said, but they were all arguing. And this guy tried to inject Wyatt with ketamine and wolfsbane, so I stabbed him in the eye with an umbrella."

I couldn't help the giggle that left me. She said it so matter of fact and nonchalant as if stabbing someone in the head with an umbrella was a normal means of self-defense.

She tried to fight her smile. "It's not funny, Laila."

"No. No, of course not. I'm sorry. That's just quite a way to go."

She laughed. Her face got serious again. "But after I killed him, the rest of them were really mad."

"Makes sense."

She took a slow sip from her coffee. "They came toward us and Wyatt killed one of them with the energy thing he can do now, and then..." She paused. "Then Drew just slit Ashley's throat. Another one stabbed him while he was distracted and shot him up with all that ketamine and wolfsbane. And I tried fighting the last one, but he was like a brick wall and he had me by my throat, and Brendon, he knocked Drew out and then the guy who held me by my throat dropped me. He fought with Brendon for a minute while I crawled over to Wyatt. And then Brendon killed him and helped me get Wyatt to the car. I tried healing him while we were driving but I don't have a clue what I'm doing. I have no idea how I did it last week. And I tried calling you guys, but I think Wyatt's powers were fucking with the phones or something. I just typed Moe's Diner western PA into the car's GPS, and it took me to you. I can't believe how fast I got here; I was sure he wasn't going to make it."

It got quiet for a moment. And I was fuming, but I maintained my composure. Yeah, I was busy with Daniel, but had I known this was going to happen, I would have fucking been there. And I'd have killed those bastards myself.

I smiled. "Well, it looks like he did."

A genuine smile pulled at her lips. "I guess he did."

"That's because of you." I reached across the table and squeezed her hand. "He's alive because of you."

She pulled it away. Duly noted, she was not a fan of physical touch. "None of this would have happened at all if it weren't for me."

"You didn't choose to be turned, Celena. And from what I understand, Wyatt chose to involve himself in the situation, right? You didn't ask for his help?"

"But he didn't know this would happen. I'm sure he wouldn't have helped me that day if he did."

"You know about what happened to Farrah?" She gave a nod. I went on, "Then you know as much as I do that Wyatt knew what he was getting himself into. He may be young, Celena, but he's not stupid. He was looking for a reason to fight them. And the fact that they hurt you, even if he didn't know who you were to him yet, letting them take you and do those awful things when he had the ability to intervene would have been damn near impossible."

"What do you mean?"

I shrugged. "The way you felt when they tried to hurt him, and you stabbed that guy with the umbrella. You were unable to think, right? Your body just did whatever it had to do to protect him. He probably felt the same way when Drew was assaulting you. He didn't want to stop it, he had to." I wrapped my hands around my warm mug. "I know the bond is weird. Believe me, no one knows that as much as me. But it's a bigger picture. Our sole purpose in life is to protect our mate. I know it sounds stupid and tacky and I guess in a way, it kind of is. But it's uncontrollable. We put them above anything else because once we've found them, it's nearly impossible to be without them. We feed each other with life. We're literally one soul split in half. We couldn't watch our par animo in pain and do nothing to stop it. It's involuntary."

While that was true, part of me was considering stabbing Jeremy with an umbrella for not telling me about all of this. If it were his sibling and I didn't tell him, all hell would break loose. But god forbid anything happen to his baby.

She raised her cup to her lips and took a sip. "It's not just him. My aunt is dead because of me. Now Ashley... I'm just wondering who'll be next."

"Our experiences may not have been identical, but I lost someone because of what I was. I didn't kill him either, but I still felt like it was my fault. I still do sometimes. But at some point, I had to let go of the blame." She gazed down at her cup as I studied her. "Who do you blame for the death of Romeo and Juliet?"

She shrugged. "I don't know. Both of their dumb asses."

I bit back my laugh and maintained my serious expression. "It was everyone's and no one's fault," I said. "You could say it was their parents for letting the feud go on for so long. Or Mercutio because he took Romeo to the ball and that's where he met Juliet. Or the apothecary that made the poison for Juliet. Or Friar Lawrence for knowing about the affair and not bringing it into the public eye or for not getting the letter to Juliet in time. Or even the nurse for trying to persuade Juliet to marry Paris." I paused for a moment. She held my gaze, waiting for me to continue. "You could argue who was to blame for hours. But ultimately, they're dead and they aren't coming back. No guilt trip is going to change that."

She turned her gaze back down to her coffee. "Well, that's encouraging."

"Hey," I heard from the doorway. I turned to see Jeremy and Kai walking into the kitchen.

"Is he okay?" Celena hurried to her feet.

Kai wiped blood on his harem pants. "He's all right, love."

"Just in a really deep K hole," Jeremy said. "How long ago did they dose him?"

"About two and a half hours now. Maybe even three. Is that normal?"

He shrugged. "His body works a lot different than a human's. Did they give him a lot?"

"Oh yeah. Like, three vials."

"Well, he didn't OD, so I think he'll be okay. It might take some time to get out of his system though. He's there mentally, he just can't move. We brought him upstairs to my old room. I'm sure he'd love some company."

She hurried toward the steps. "Thank you so much."

"You're welcome," Kai muttered as he watched her race past him.

"Third door on the—" I began.

"It's okay. I smell him," she called.

Kai turned to meet my gaze. "Why does she look so familiar?"

"Probably because she's our sister."

His eyes widened. "The hell d'ya mean?"

"Mary's her mother. She gave her up as a baby like she did with us," I said.

He smiled wider. "We've got another sister?"

I smiled back. Don't get me wrong, I was ecstatic to have another sibling. Especially a little sister because the one I had already loved to throw in my face how she was older and wiser. But having more siblings meant far more to Kai than it did to me. Family was the absolute world to him.

"Looks like it," I said.

CHAPTER TWENTY-TWO

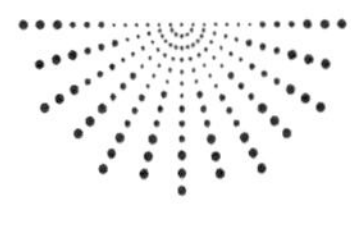

LAILA

"You told me not to worry about them, Jeremy." I wagged my finger at him. I yanked off my pajamas and tossed them in the hamper. "What did you say again? 'They're tough kids. They can handle themselves. Blah, blah, blah.'"

Jeremy sighed. He stepped into a pair of jeans and brought himself to his feet. "You're going to wake up Daniel."

"I'm waking him up in a minute any way. Why did you keep all of this from me? We're supposed to be partners, Jeremy. We're supposed to be equals. We don't keep things from each other, especially not when it's about family."

His gaze met mine. "First of all, you gave Adam your phone to take your emergencies. It seemed like you wanted to focus on Daniel—"

"Of course I did. But I could have at least been *told* what was going on."

"You would have jumped headfirst into the middle of their war, Laila." His tone harshened. "I want to help them, but we have shit going on too. We can't just jump into a war right now, especially a war that isn't ours. You *especially* can't."

"So yet again, I'm left out of the discussion because I'm pregnant?"

I asked. He rolled his eyes and turned to his feet. "I'm strong, Jeremy, I can help."

His tone was just as firm, but his expression softened. Barely. "You were left out of the conversation because you're reckless. I'm sorry. But it's true."

I scoffed. "You're ridiculous."

"You died, Laila," Jeremy snapped. His firm gaze met mine. "You fucking died. Your heart stopped beating. If it weren't for Leah getting there just in time, you'd be gone. I know you're powerful but you're not unstoppable. You only know how to control a few of your powers. One day, maybe you'll be invincible. But right now, you aren't. Everyone has told you time and time again how strong you are and I'm not saying that you aren't, but your ego has you convinced that nothing will take you down. And something will if you don't use your head instead of your heart for once." His eyes shifted quickly between mine. "Until you can teleport and master healing and air and water and earth, and whatever your Guardian powers are, whatever other Angel powers you have, you aren't unconquerable. You are mortal. You can die. And you will if you aren't careful. If you just dive into their war, you aren't going to make it out alive. You need to learn what battles you can and can't win. And the reality is, we can't take on Damon. He's backed by the North American Monarch, he has an army behind him, and there aren't even ten of us. The rest of us understand this but you don't and that's why no one told you."

He was right. He was *so* right, and I should have listened. I was barely grown. I may have had my shit together, but my confidence was my biggest downfall. Rationally, I knew why Damon got away with the shit he did. He knew how to bend the rules to his will. But I was angry. A friend was dead, and it could have been my sister.

The words rolled out of my mouth almost involuntarily. "I may not be immortal, but if she could have told me what was happening, Ashley wouldn't be dead. She would still be here."

"How, Laila?" he barked. "They could have called on their way to Wyatt's, but their phones didn't work. So what? Are you just going to follow her around every second of every day?"

I narrowed my gaze and pulled my hoodie over my T-shirt. He was right and I didn't have a good argument. So I said, "Fuck you."

He sucked his teeth, gaze holding mine for a moment. He looked down and pulled his tennis shoes on. "Whatever, Laila. Be pissed at me. But at least you and our baby are alive."

"Long time no see, man." Brody wrapped his arms around Wyatt in a hug. I set Daniel down and murmured for him to go play in the sunroom. "How long has it been?"

Wyatt laughed and squeezed his shoulders. A big smile brightened his dismal face. "At least two years now, I think."

"Damn, you got huge." Brody pulled away. "Do you even work out? Or is it just a side effect of the wolf thing?"

Wyatt was shorter than Brody, probably around five nine, but far wider. His biceps had to have been twice the size of mine, and his broad chest harder than stone.

He had a strong jaw dusted in a thin beard that made him look at least half a decade older than the eighteen years he was. His eyes were a warm brown with sparkles of honey throughout, contrasting beautifully on his sepia colored skin.

"I don't really work out, so I guess."

He huffed. "That's some bullshit."

"Is that...?" I heard Hannah say from the steps. "Wyatt!" she yelled.

She sprinted down the stairs. Her arms wrapped around him. He laughed and lifted her into the air, spinning her in a quick circle.

Celena glanced at them awkwardly. Not necessarily in a jealous way but it clearly made her uncomfortable. I probably would have felt the same way in her shoes. But the Skouldas were an affectionate bunch. They were French, after all.

"Wow." Hannah smiled as he set her down. She squeezed either of his biceps. "When did you get so big?"

"I don't know, when did you ditch the braces and glasses?" Wyatt smirked.

"Oh, let's see. I think it was right around the time you stopped coming around." She pushed his chest. "What the fuck, man? You could at least reply to an old friend's texts once in a while."

He held his smile, shrugging. "Sorry, things have just been pretty crazy lately."

"They always are." She turned to Celena. "Oh God, I'm so rude. I'm sorry, I'm Hannah."

Celena forced a smile and shook her hand. "Celena."

"Oh, shit, I'm sorry, darlin'." Wyatt moved his hand around her waist. "Celena, this is my childhood best friend, Hannah. And Hannah, this is my girlfriend, Celena."

"Wow, okay. I'm sorry for that whole running hug thing. That might've looked a little weird from where you're standing. It was completely platonic, we're basically siblings," Hannah said. "And you're Laila's sister, right?"

"Um..." She glanced at me. "I think that's the consensus."

"Oh, well, I'm dating your brother." She smiled. "So, ya know. Nothing weird goin' on here."

The stiffness in Celena's gaze softened, a look of relief washing over her. She smiled and shook her hand. "No worries."

"We were all really close growing up," Wyatt said. "My mom worked with their mom on cases together before she passed."

"Yeah, they used to make Leah and Chris watch us when we ran around outside. Wyatt and I were always close because everyone else had powers and we didn't." She glared at her brothers. "We actually had to follow the rules."

"You could've kept up if you played smarter instead of harder." Adam shrugged from the stove.

"So how's your mom? I haven't seen her in forever," Hannah said with a big smile.

The room fell silent. It'd only been a few hours since they arrived. Word hadn't spread to everyone just yet. Wyatt cleared his throat. "She died last night."

Hannah's brows pulled together. Her mouth fell open. "Oh, Wyatt. I am so sorry. I had no idea."

"You were asleep when they got in." Leah came down the steps, Kai close at her tail.

"Have you guys met Kai yet?" I gestured towards the stairs. It wasn't much but anything to change the subject.

"No, I don't think we have. Heard of you though," Wyatt said.

"I think I did last night," Celena said.

I made my way across the kitchen. "Kai, this is Wyatt, he's an old friend of... Well, everyone here."

Kai smiled. He extended his hand to Wyatt. "Pleasure to meet ye."

"And Celena, this is Kai." I smiled. "My twin brother." I turned to Kai. "And Kai, this is Celena." His smile widened. He withdrew his handshake and wrapped his arms around her.

She awkwardly patted his back. "Oh, another hugger."

He pulled away with a grin. "Are you Elite as well?"

"Am I..." Her face screwed up in confusion. "I don't know, I just found out I had powers like—what? A week ago?"

"Oh, no. Ye've got to learn then. Did ye do that test ye did on me?" he asked me.

He clasped Celena's hands out in front of him. The look on Celena's face told me to beg him to release them, but she'd have to get used to this. Kai was as lovey dovey as they come.

"DNA, you mean?" I asked. He nodded. "Yes, but I haven't had the chance to discuss them with her. Do you want to talk in private?"

"That's okay, I'm dying to know. What did you find out?" Celena turned to meet my gaze.

"Well, you're definitely our sister." I put my hands on my hips. "We have the same mother. But we have different dads, which I was expecting. It looks like your dad was all Fae though."

"What bloodline?" Kai asked.

"I'm getting there." I turned back to Celena. "You aren't Elite, but you're pretty damn close. It looks like you can control water, spirit, fire and air."

"Everything but earth," Kai muttered. "That's all right. Earth's the most boring anyway. All ye can do with it is grow a pretty garden."

Her eyes widened slightly. "Wow, that's a lot."

"It's a good thing," I said, looking between Wyatt and Celena. "With your combined power, once you get it under control, you two should be able to take the pack down. Then you can go off and live your lives without looking over your shoulder. Especially if you can figure out how to tap into your Angel abilities. But it's going to take some time. You need to perfect the ones you've used in addition to the ones you didn't know existed yet. The ones you haven't used are probably going to be better in terms of war than the ones you currently use. Either way, it won't be easy." I glanced at Jeremy over my shoulder. He rolled his eyes. "And you won't be able to do it alone."

"I can't help with the Angel abilities, but I've mastered all five elements. I can show ye everything ye need to know." Kai nearly bounced with excitement.

"And I'll help Wyatt work on the energy manipulation," Jeremy said from the breakfast nook. He glared at me for a split second. He looked back to Wyatt as if to prove that he was helping. "We can start later today when Laila's done with her shift and can take Daniel."

"I can work with Celena while Hannah's at school," Kai said.

Leah said, "Okay, so training is covered. Now we have to figure out where you two are gonna stay because you clearly can't go home."

Wyatt sighed. "Yeah, not an option."

"They could stay in the old cabin." Brody nibbled on a piece of bacon. "It isn't a palace, but it'd be enough for the two of you."

"That sounds good to me." Wyatt turned to Celena. "Is that okay with you, darlin'?"

"Yeah, just one little thing that might be an issue. I told my uncle I'd take care of my aunt's dogs. Would it be okay if I brought them here?"

"Never." Leah smirked. "Of course you can bring the dogs. There'll be two in there already, what's a few more."

Wyatt chuckled. "We'll need to get clothes too so if someone could take us there later, that'd be great."

"Yeah, I can," Adam said.

"I'll probably need to file a missing person's report on Mom," Wyatt muttered. "I'm sure they took the body but if I don't report her missing, I'll be the first one they blame."

"Yeah, of course, hon," Leah said.

"I'll need to get my transcripts too," Wyatt said. "So I can enroll in the high school here."

"We're going to go to school together!" Hannah exclaimed with a smile.

"Probably not," he said. "If they have a cyber program, I'll just do that. I'm gonna have to get a job now."

"I could use some servers down at the diner. I've had a few move on to bigger things," I said.

He turned to meet my gaze. "That's very nice of you, Laila. I would really appreciate it."

I gave a smile. "Least I can do."

CHAPTER TWENTY-THREE

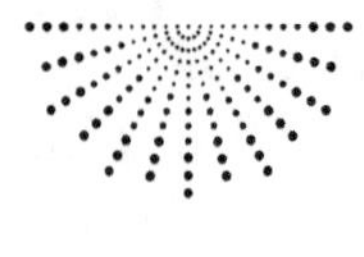

LAILA

Soft rock moved into my ears from the speakers above. The smell of burgers and grease from the fryer wafted to my nose. I took a sip from my warm coffee. A sweet, middle-aged couple approached the register. I pulled on a smile and set it back down.

"Did you enjoy your meal with us today?" I asked.

They handed me their check and two twenties. "Oh, yes. It was wonderful. We love what you've done with the place, by the way," the woman said. "We've been eating here for thirty years and it's needed a good remodel for the past twenty."

"Aww, thank you." I smiled, eyes shifting around. We really hadn't changed much. A fresh coat of white on the walls, some reupholstering on the ripped red cushions. Moe's was an iconic place, I wanted to leave it as it'd been. "I didn't want to take away from all of its character, so I basically just looked for a newer version of everything. We got real ceramic tile instead of that old linoleum but kept the checkers. And the bar stools and booths are all the same frames, I just had them redone. Now all that's left is this ugly counter." I tapped the Formica with my open palm. I opened the drawer to cash them out.

"So you're the new owner?" the man asked.

"Yes, sir." I smiled, handing them their change. "Moe was a close family friend. He didn't have many friends left and he knew how much I loved this place." I shrugged and took another look around. "I'm just glad it didn't get bought out by some chain, you know?"

"So are we." The man smiled. "Nothing has changed. I mean, I guess the amenities have improved a bit, but the service is still great and so is the food."

"We learned from the best. If you don't mind, please give us a review on Yelp. It really helps small businesses like us."

"We'll have to ask our grandson to show us how to do that, but we definitely will," the woman said. "You take care."

"You too." I waved. "And thank you for your business." They smiled as they headed out the door, little bell ringing above their heads.

I felt an arm catch my waist and rolled my eyes. I sighed. Jeremy rested his head on my shoulder. "Don't be cute. I'm mad at you."

"C'mon, you can't stay mad at me forever." I turned to face him. He held a small bouquet of lilies. His lips lifted in a sweet smile. "I'm sorry." Messy black hair swung into his face. "I don't want to fight."

It's not like I *wanted* to fight either. But damn it, he hid something big from me. Still, I grabbed the flowers and held them to my nose. "You were mean."

"So were you." I made a face, and he quickly chimed back in. "But I know. And I'm sorry," he muttered. "Can we go talk in the office for a minute?"

I turned to Sophie. She filled some cups with pop beside the coffee maker. "Could you take whatever tables walk in? My last one just left."

A smile moved up her dark round cheeks to her big brown eyes. She was used to me and Jeremy's banter. She was also used to taking over when we went to 'talk' in the office. "Oh, yeah. No problem."

"Let's go, butt head," I muttered to Jeremy. We pushed our way past the stainless-steel door, yelling "right behind you," as we hurried to the office. Jeremy shut the door. I sat at the chair in front of the desk. He lowered himself next to me, leaning forward to take my hand.

"I'm sorry I was a dick this morning. I shouldn't have gotten so angry. I just heard about Ashley." His gaze softened. "You know she was always like family to me, so I wasn't in a good state of mind. But I shouldn't have taken that out on you and I'm sorry."

Still, I believed that had I known what was happening, Ashley may still be alive. But I shouldn't have said what I did. "I'm sorry I said fuck you. And for what I said about her. That wasn't fair. I really am sorry for your loss. I know that must've been hard."

"I deserved it."

"No. No, you didn't. It's not fair to talk to you like that."

"But I shouldn't have lied to you," he murmured. "I mean, I guess I didn't lie, but regardless, I should have been more honest with you than I was."

While calling me reckless hurt my feelings, he didn't have much to apologize for. I knew that he was right. "I'm not happy that you did it, but I understand. You love me and you love this baby. I know how scared you are of losing us and I know it must be terrifying when I go off on my tangents about helping people. I get excited and I just—"

He caught my cheek and turned my face to his. "That's what I love about you, Lai. Don't apologize for that."

"I'm not apologizing for *that*," I murmured. "I just know it can drive you crazy and I don't blame you. I know it comes from a place of love. Just please talk to me about it next time, okay? Don't assume I can't rationalize a situation. I know I get a little overbearing but just tell me. I might be upset at first, but if you give me some time, I'll see your perspective. I just don't like being told what I can and can't do."

"Don't I know," he muttered. My gaze narrowed a bit. He laughed quietly. "And I'm not trying to control you. I just want you to be safe. Neither of us would forgive ourselves if something happened to this baby."

Fair enough. "Yeah, you're right. I love this little turd even if he is giving me stretch marks."

He laughed. His palm gently grasped my cheek. He kissed me. "You're beautiful with or without the stretch marks."

I huffed. "You're just saying that because you love me."

He pulled me into him and grabbed my hip. "I do love you, but that has nothing to do with why you're so beautiful."

That's what I loved about that man. When I'd mention something like not liking my body, he'd go the extra mile

to prove that he did.

I smiled and kissed him again. After a moment, I pulled back. "I need to get back to work."

"You don't have a couple minutes?" His hand on my hip gently slid down. He brushed beneath the edge of my skirt to my bare thigh.

I laughed. "You need to get back to Daniel."

His lips moved to my neck. My eyes closed, goosebumps raising over my skin. He gently kissed down my chest. My stomach flipped. "He's back at the house with Leah and Brody." His fingers skimmed along my thigh, leaving a trail of shivers that quaked into my belly. "We should really try to use the time we have when there aren't any kids around carefully. It won't be long, and we'll never be alone again."

Just that tease was enough to make my belly flip with anticipation. When his calloused fingers traced from my jaw to the back of my head, gently grasping a fistful of my hair, a helpless breath fell from my lips.

It was a scarce occasion that I turned down sex, especially here. I'd always gotten a thrill out of fucking when there was a crowd a few doors over. Having to stay quiet, knowing anyone could walk through inside... "I guess I can spare a *couple* minutes."

His gaze met mine, smile brightening his face. "I'll make it work."

As I laughed, he grabbed my hips and hoisted me onto the desk.

Kissing passionately, he hiked up my skirt while I unbuckled his jeans and tugged them to the ground. He hauled me to the edge of the desk, and our chests touched. Each beat of his now slamming heart thudded against mine as he pushed himself inside me.

A gasp of satisfaction escaped me, basking in the sting of my opening stretching around him.

"Fuck," Jeremy groaned, voice a raspy whisper. He rested his forehead on mine, holding my hair tighter. His free hand slid up my thigh, and his thumb found my clit. The warmth of his breath on my cheeks brought chills to my skin, and that passion in his eyes only enhanced my pleasure. "Why's the sex so much better after we scream at each other?"

I wanted to laugh, but a moan fell from my lips instead. He wasn't wrong; there was something incredibly thrilling about make up sex.

Maybe it was the adrenaline, maybe it was because Jeremy railing me as I scratched my nails into his back was the closest we'd get to violence against one another.

I didn't know, and I didn't care. All that mattered in this moment was the pleasure.

"Harder," I whispered, sneaking a hand up the back of his shirt and digging my nails into his skin. "Fuck me harder."

His mouth fell slightly open, half smile coming to his lips. He tightened his fingers at my scalp, yanking my head back slightly, exposing my neck.

My breath hitched as he brought his lips to my throat. He kissed softly, but when he thrusted in again, slamming against some magnificent spot deep inside me, a helpless moan left me.

Chuckling, he did it again, and my moan loudened, grasping him tighter for stability as the pressure building deep within my belly intensified.

"*Shh-sh.*" His lips trailed to my ear, teeth catching on the lobe. "You're gonna get us caught."

That only deepened my desire and forced the moan that escaped me to grow louder.

He laughed again, kissing just below my ear, sucking my skin gently. Releasing my hair, his hand drifted to my face instead. As he cupped his palm over my lips, he thrusted in, harder than the last.

I was already seeing stars, but his thumb gained speed on my clit. Involuntarily, my legs quivered. That hand over my lips was the only thing that kept the rest of the diner from hearing my screams, and for whatever reason, that only turned me on more.

Little trembles coursed through my core, and Jeremy let out a soft groan of his own. "Fuck, stay right there, baby. Just like that."

His voice at my ear was like its own erogenous zone. It was so soft and melodic, yet so deep and raspy at the same time. His breath vibrating at my neck, the pleasure that tickled his voice... It alone was almost enough to make me come.

You feel so fucking good, I whispered to his thoughts.

He laughed, lips coming back to mine. Thrusting in again, his mouth muffled my moan. *You're gonna scare off our customers, woman.*

The thought of someone hearing turned me on more, but I did my best to lower my volume. *It's your fault for fucking me like a god.*

He laughed again, hand lifting back to my lips. I wasn't sure why I loved that as much as I did, but it was always a telltale that he was about to do something utterly fucking amazing.

And he did.

He thrusted in so deep, so hard, that it almost hurt. I groaned into his fingers, and he clenched them tighter around my cheeks. His thumb on my clit quickened, moving so fast that it practically became a vibrator.

Every pore over my body felt electric, quaking with desire and exaltation. "Tighten your legs around my hips," he whispered, voice deep and sultry, "because I want to be as deep inside you as I can get when you come around my cock—"

It was like magic. Jeremy spoke in that seductive voice, whispering little mantras of pleasure, and my body collapsed around him. He squeezed tighter over my lips as I screamed out in bliss, and that look in his eyes only made it better.

A groan of his own escaped, eyes flicking between mine, washing over me like I was the most amazing thing he'd ever laid eyes on. I held him tighter, bringing him as close to me as space allowed, doing everything in my power to make sure his climax was as good as mine.

As my contractions slowed, so did his thrusts.

Smiling, he released my face, circled his arms around my back, and pulled me as close to him as we could get.

Breathing in the smell of his cologne, overtaken by joy, and pleasure, collapsing into his comforting embrace, I closed my eyes.

I fucking love this man.

He laughed, kissing my neck. "I love you more."

I hadn't intended for him to hear that, but I laughed too, burying my face into his chest.

"You know what though?" he asked.

"Hmm?" I murmured, unable to make out much else.

"I'm gonna miss when you aren't pregnant, and I have to start pulling out again."

I patted his back. "You were never very good at it anyway, baby."

Our son was proof of that.

CHAPTER TWENTY-FOUR

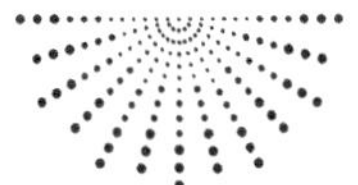

MARCH 10, 2019 - LAILA

Nearly six weeks passed since Celena and Wyatt arrived. Things had been pretty docile in that time. We hadn't run over any children, no one had gone missing, and no one was murdered. That may sound like a simple occurrence but in our way of life, that was a big deal. Things were going smoothly for once.

Celena and I had started to form a friendship of sorts. We weren't incredibly close, at least not yet, but we were becoming fast friends. She was kind but mostly pretty quiet. When she did talk, her words were articulated carefully. She'd throw a witty comment in here and there, but she was near silent most of the time.

If I didn't know she was eighteen, I would have thought she was much older. She was very mature for her age. I didn't see that yet, but I would soon enough. She had a particularly good understanding of where she was in this world. She knew what she was capable of. More importantly, she knew what she wasn't. She knew when to run rather than fight.

Wyatt started school at Hannah's high school cyber program and Celena continued on with the school she was enrolled in in West Virginia. Celena was reluctant to continue her education. But she agreed it would be a waste of the last twelve years if she didn't graduate. I think once she realized she'd be alive for at least a few hundred years, she figured a few more months couldn't be too bad. The two of them also started working at the diner. It was clear that neither of them had worked a day in their life, but as the weeks went on, they learned the ropes and did a half-decent job.

Wyatt had started to get a good handle on his powers and Celena's were coming along slowly but surely. She had managed to nearly master water, and was working on spirit, but no one had been injured for her to heal so she wasn't getting much practice. She fixed up a few daily scrapes and burns that occurred in day-to-day life within the family but that was about the extent. She hadn't managed to manipulate air or fire even once, but I couldn't blame her.

After all, I hadn't used water or earth at that point either. I had learned to heal in the past few months by practicing on animals at shelters when no staff were on shift though. I was beginning to have more luck with air than I had a few months ago. I hadn't perfected it, but I was able to use it at my beck and call without being scared for my life. I suppose she was making more progress than I had after only a few weeks of having abilities.

I was twenty weeks pregnant then. Two weeks prior, I felt the baby kick for the first time. I expected it to be some magical sensation. And the first time, it was. Maybe even the second and third. But as he grew, he started doing this thing where he would wrap his toes around my lowest rib on the left side. It was cool at first. But I was growing sick of it. It was like we were arguing. He would do it and I would tap my abdomen and he'd move away for a second, then do it again a moment later. It became something of a game we played. Needless to say, he usually won.

Jeremy was as sweet and doting as ever. He began to pick up more of my shifts at the diner. I felt a bit anti-feminist letting him take care of me as I rubbed my swollen ankles and carted Daniel around. At some point though, I realized that it made him happy to feel like he was providing for us. And I was a lot less stressed.

I was still working; I was just primarily doing paperwork. Pay roll, preparing tax information, writing checks, making phone calls, basically all the boring stuff. I genuinely hated the paperwork. But I was doing it before I got pregnant along with a minimal forty-hour work week. Granted, it was still my least favorite part of the job. But it was also a lot less physical work than I had to do before.

Daniel adjusted to things pretty well. He gained about fifteen pounds and was starting to appear like a normal happy little boy aside from the scars. The two of us were trying to help one another learn the other's language too. We made a good bit of progress. Daniel started to primarily speak broken English.

Still, I wasn't sure of his age. I bought a bunch of those workbooks at Walmart for different age groups starting at kindergarten and working up to fourth grade. I thought about getting fifth grade as well, but I was sure that Daniel couldn't be that old.

He was doing math problems at a first-grade level which would have led me to believe he was around six, but he was way too big to be that young. I concluded that was most likely the age he was abducted. We believed him to be around eight years old. Of course, he was reading at a preschooler's level in English, so I got children books in Spanish. He seemed to be reading at a kindergarten level.

I hadn't managed to get him to the hospital to run tests yet. I dilly-dallied around with the idea of dosing him with a sedative in order to perform the tests. But the more I thought about it, the more I realized I couldn't do that. The child had been tortured and drugged for God only knew how long. He had PTSD. I couldn't destroy his trust in me by forcing him to undergo tests that terrified him.

Honestly, I didn't know what I was doing. I was kind of just winging it. I didn't know much of anything about how to raise a kid and I certainly didn't know anything about raising a torture victim. I didn't know if I should enroll him in school or if he wasn't ready. I didn't know if I should turn him over to Janis and Elijah, or if that would be too traumatizing.

I didn't know what to do about any of it. But I just kept rolling with the punches.

CHAPTER TWENTY-FIVE

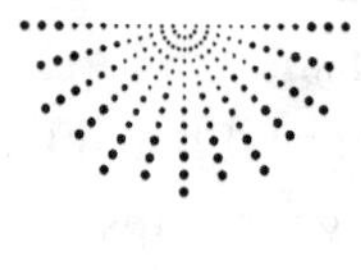

LAILA

"Good morning, beautiful." Jeremy kissed cheek, pulling me from my sleep. I rolled over to the bright sun shining in through the curtains. A yawn escaped my lips. I rubbed against my eyes and stretched my arms above my head.

"Good morning," I muttered. I glanced at the clock reading 10:36. I gasped and hurried to my feet. "Jesus, how'd I sleep through my alarm?"

He grasped my hand, laughing, and pulled me back to the bed. "Because I turned it off."

"What? Why?"

"You were up late with Daniel and you needed a full night's sleep." He flashed a sweet smile. "I took care of the morning rush. Daniel ate breakfast. We went for a walk down to the corner store because we were out of toothpaste and we stopped at the park on our way home."

"But I had to place next month's orders this morning—"

"I handled it." His smile widened. He played gently with a lock of my hair. "And I called the plumber about the leaky sink in the basement bathroom. They're coming by in a couple hours to take care of it. I thought it was just a few loose bolts, but I tightened everything and it's still dripping so they're gonna have to handle it. Oh, and I got a quote for the spring landscaping."

"Wow, really?" I smiled, leaning back onto the pillows.

He smiled wider. "I know you've had a lot on your plate. I wanted to help."

I gave a smile back. "Baby, you don't have to do everything. I'm not incapacitated, you know. I'm just pregnant."

As much as I appreciated everything he was doing, it was a little overbearing. Sure, I loved help. But he wasn't just helping, he'd taken over a lot of my favorite things about owning the diner. And it was so sweet, and I loved him for it. But aside from taking care of Daniel, it was like I had nothing to do.

"Yeah, I know. But I wanted to handle some stuff so you could enjoy yourself today."

"What do you mean?"

His smiled got so big that it reached his bright blue eyes. "The jeweler called this morning. We can pick up our rings this afternoon. It kinda timed out perfectly because Hannah's off school for an in-service day. I figured you guys could go get your nails done or whatever. Then go out for dinner or something while I go pick up the rings."

That shifted my mindset pretty quick. He hadn't handled everything because I couldn't, he wanted today to be special for me. A warm sensation settled over my body. Butterflies danced in my stomach and my smile wouldn't come down.

He really was the sweetest man in the world.

I smiled. "You don't have to do all that, babe. I don't need to—"

"You don't need to, but you were bitching about your nails. And this way, they'll look all fancy with your ring and shit." He cupped my cheek and smiled down at me. "I'll watch Daniel while you're out and then you guys can take him with you to dinner. You've been talking about how you can't really reach your toes that well for the past few weeks and it just seemed like a good opportunity for you to enjoy some time to yourself. Oh, and your mom called. She wants you to send her a picture of the ring as soon as you get it. She was going to stop by, but she picked up an extra shift and isn't going to have time today."

I grasped his chin and pulled his lips to mine. "I don't know how I got so lucky with you."

"I could say the same." He gave a sweet, boyish grin.

"Oh, hush. You do so much more for me than I do for you."

"That's not even close to true. We're partners. Sometimes, I put in a little more than you. Sometimes, you put in a little more than me. That's the way it's supposed to work."

"Yeah, but you don't have to do everything, baby." I laughed quietly. "I don't want you to get overwhelmed either."

"I'm not overwhelmed." He gave a sweet, happy smile. "I don't mind. It's nice actually. Getting all this stuff taken care of around Moe's, I mean. It makes me feel accomplished and a lot less guilty for not having a job."

"That's silly. You're practically the manager here. I should probably put your name on the books, huh? If you get hurt behind the counter, you could sue me." I smirked.

He chuckled. "Well, once we're married, you wouldn't have to pay workman's comp on me anyway. So you might as well just wait to put my name on anything."

I stood. "This is true."

"Speaking of which, have you thought about that at all?" he asked. "The wedding, I mean."

The wedding wasn't a top priority at the moment. We'd just become foster parents to a little boy, I had pregnancy brain, I was trying to get to know my new sister, and life was just too hectic. I did feel bad though. He was so ready to take that next step and I just kept procrastinating.

I tugged off my T-shirt and pushed my sweatpants to my ankles. "Not really."

"Not even a date?"

"Probably at some point in the future." I smirked.

"Like, this year? Next year?"

"I don't know. Maybe next year. I haven't given it much thought." I turned to meet his sad gaze as I pulled a blouse over my head. "I'm sorry, baby. I know it's important to you. I just figured since I'm pregnant and we're waiting until after the baby is born that we had plenty of time."

"Yeah, I know. But you're past the halfway mark now. I thought maybe you'd started thinking about it a little more."

I walked to the bed where he sat and lifted my knees around either side of his lap. His hands found my hips. Mine went around his neck. I pressed my lips to his and kissed him slow. "I'll make you a deal. Next week, I'll get somebody to baby sit. You and I will go out to dinner and we'll set a date. We'll decide on colors, and the food, and the theme. I promise. We'll start making plans.

CHAPTER TWENTY-SIX

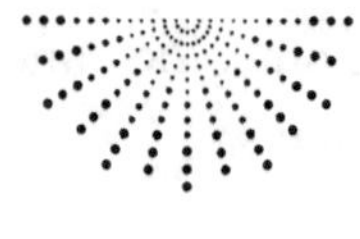

LAILA

I lifted my hand to block the sunset that blinded me on the highway. Warm spring air whooshed in from the open window. It was early yet, but it was starting to smell like summer. A little humid but not quite hot yet. Just that perfect touch of spring. Aside from the drip I sniffled to my nose from allergies, I was just beginning to enjoy my favorite season.

"Damn it. I should have gone with the black too." Hannah looked at my hand. "This green is hideous."

"It's festive. Very luck of the Irish." I pulled it back to the steering wheel. "I like it."

"You're a liar. It looks like I have gangrene."

I laughed. "Do you even know what gangrene is?"

"It's like, dead tissue. It turns green, right?"

"No, dumb ass. It's just dying flesh. If anything, it's black."

"Huh," she muttered. "Why do they call it gangrene then?"

I shrugged. "I don't know, look it up."

"That's stupid." She pulled a joint from her purse. "Am I allowed to smoke in here or is that a no go?"

"You're good. Jeremy does it all the time." I rolled down the windows.

"You don't want to hit it, do you?"

"I wish." I laughed. "I can't wait until this little guy is out of me. I'm gonna drink the biggest margarita. And smoke the biggest blunt. Literally as soon as he's out. The cord won't even be cut yet."

She laughed. "I bet Jeremy would love that."

I propped my elbow against the door, resting my face in my palm. "Okay, so I'm not imagining it. He's being a little weird, right?"

"Like super overprotective? And clingy?"

"Yeah, he won't let me do anything," I said. "He shut off my alarm so I could sleep in. He made all my phone calls. He ran all my errands. He just wants to like... I don't know. He wants me to put my feet up and relax. All the damn time. And it was sweet at first, and it's still sweet, but..."

"He's smothering you?" Hannah asked.

"Little bit." I laughed. "He should have been the one to get pregnant."

Chuckling, Hannah said, "When summer comes, and the baby's born, all those caveman protective instincts will go straight to protecting the little man, and you'll have your life back."

"Just gotta stick it out 'til then, huh?"

***

"Hey, kiddo," I called to Daniel. He darted past Jeremy to me and Hannah at my old beat-up beetle. His smile was as wide as the warm blue sky. I'll never forget that smile.

"Look, look." He handed me a drawing on a piece of printer paper. "Me, and Laila, and Hannah in the bug!" He pointed to each of us in his picture and then between us in real life.

"Wow, that is beautiful, buddy. Is it for me?"

He nodded with a big smile, pushing wavy brown hair from his eyes. "You keep."

"I'll keep it forever. Go ahead and hop in."

"Are you sure you want to take the bug?" Jeremy called as he got closer. "The Forester is safer. I don't mind—"

"Baby. I'm fine." I grinned. "I know it's a piece of shit, but I got around in it just fine for years before we got the Subie. Don't worry so much, okay?"

I was only driving a few miles out of town; he was going all the way to Pittsburgh. The Subaru was better on gas. It just made sense for me to take the bug.

"Alright, alright. Whatever you say."

I smiled and took a few steps forward. I leaned to the tips of my toes to kiss him. He kissed me back, wrapping his arms around me in a tight hug. After a moment, I pulled back. "Do you want me to get you anything? I think we're going to Olive Garden."

"Yeah, just get me whatever you're having."

I handed him the car key. "Alright, will do."

"Be careful," he said. "I love you."

"I always am." Smiling, I slid into the driver's seat, grabbed his shirt, and tugged his mouth to mine. I held his cheek, basking in the citrusy smell of his cologne. The taste on his lips flooded my senses, and my heart skipped a beat. When he touched my waist, tugging me closer to him, my belly flipped. Leaning back, his hair a curtain between us, my smile widened. "I love you too."

He huffed. "Gonna leave me all high and dry like that?"

I laughed. "You're not opening tomorrow. So when I get home, we'll get Daniel to bed, and then we have all night to ourselves."

"All night, huh?" Jeremy smirked.

"*All* night—"

"Could you two get a room?" Hannah mumbled under her breath. "You're gross."

I laughed, and so did Jeremy. He leaned in, kissed me one more time, and shut my door.

CHAPTER TWENTY-SEVEN

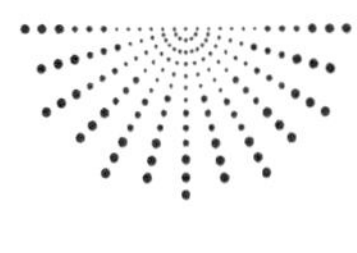

LAILA

My fingers slipped to the button of my jeans to yank them open. I had five too many bowls of salad and way too much endless pasta. An involuntary burp moved up my esophagus followed by a baby barf that sent me reaching for my water bottle. It stunk too. I cranked my window down for some fresh air.

I flicked on my high beams to see better on the dark road. Though spring, we hadn't made it to daylight savings yet. A humid fog was setting in that made it nearly impossible to see. I squinted though, keeping my eyes on the distance ahead.

"Is it just me or were the bread sticks less garlicy than usual?" Hannah said. She reclined in her seat and rubbed her bloated stomach.

"I thought they were pretty damn good," I said. I glanced at Daniel in the rearview. "What do you think, Daniel? Did you like the bread sticks?"

"Si." He smiled wide.

"Maybe I'm just picky," Hannah muttered. "So are you excited to get your ring?"

I smiled. "Yeah. Yeah, I am actually."

"God, I can't wait to see it," Hannah said. "Why didn't you take a picture when you picked it out?"

"My finger looked fat as hell. It was three sizes too small."

"That's stupid. I want to see the ring. I don't care about your finger."

"Well, you'll see it when we get home."

"True." Hannah gave an awkward, excited little squeal. She clapped her hands like a preschooler getting to go outside for recess. "I'm so excited! I can't wait. I love weddings. He better get down on one knee."

"He already did that," I retorted.

"Yeah, but you said no."

"And I retracted my no."

"Exactly, so he has to do it again."

"That's stupid." I laughed.

In my rear-view mirror, I saw headlights nearing my fender. I stepped on the gas a little harder, knowing that I had a habit of being a snail when there was a kid in my car. And then they got closer, so close I was surprised they didn't hit me.

"Alright, buddy. I'm already going ten over the speed limit here," I muttered.

They cut the wheel and slammed into the other side of the two-way road. Then they flew past me. They swerved back into my lane ahead of me. I was a slow driver in the bug, so I was used to people cutting me off.

"What the fuck is this dude's problem?" Hannah made an angry wave at the dashboard.

"Beats me." I gently touched my breaks to keep a good distance between us.

I couldn't make out much through the fog and darkness. Once they were in front of me though, I could tell it was some type of larger vehicle. But it was too far ahead for me to make out any details.

"What a tool," Hannah said.

I chuckled.

Suddenly, they slammed onto their breaks. I was a good distance behind, at least a few car lengths. But we were going about fifty miles per hour. And my old bug didn't have the best breaking capabilities.

I instinctively put my hand in front of Hannah, the Mom seat belt I'd always called it.

I hit those breaks *hard.* But not hard enough for an old, solid metal tank on wheels. Had I been in the Subaru, I may have been able to break in enough time.

My front end met the tow hitch at the rear of their car, sending us forward into our seatbelts.

My heart pounded against my chest, but I wasn't hurt. My belly wasn't pushed too hard against the belt, my head didn't hit the steering wheel. I was fine. Just shaken.

"Oh my God, are you guys okay?" I asked with a quick look to Hannah and Daniel.

"Fuck." Hannah rubbed her head. "Shit, am I bleeding?"

I flicked the overhead light on and gazed at her forehead. Just above her right temple was a deep cut about an inch long. Blood trickled from her forehead along the bone of her cheek. "Yeah, something got you pretty good." I turned to Daniel. "You alright, buddy?"

He nodded quickly. "Si. I okay."

"Alright." I put the car in reverse and inched back slightly. I shifted the car into park. Following the procedure for an accident, I reached into the glove compartment, took out my insurance information, grabbed my phone from the cup holder to take photos, and headed outside. "I'll be right back."

As I stepped from my car, the driver from the car I hit stepped from his. He turned and met my gaze. "Geez, oh man. Is everyone alright? That damn deer just ran right out in front of me," he said as we started toward one another. "I know they say, 'just hit the deer,' but you don't think like that in the moment, you know?"

"Yeah, we're all good back here." I gave a friendly smile. "Do you have your insurance information handy?"

"Yeah, of course." He drew closer, probably about two or three yards from me. Then the back of his van door pushed open. But it was dark inside, and I didn't give it much thought at first. Perhaps my bump had damaged the mechanism.

As I got closer to him, I quickly realized it wasn't paperwork in his hand.

It was a small black handgun.

That's when it clicked.

The van-like vehicle. The gun. The dark deserted road.

I dropped my papers to the ground. "What are you doing?" Sparks flew from the tips of my fingers.

A half chuckle, one I should have remembered. "Just get in the car, Laila."

"How do you know my name? Who are you?"

In the dim headlights, I saw a devilish grin pull up his lips. "I guess you wouldn't know, huh?"

I brought a ball of fire to my hand. "You're the people that had Daniel," I said. "You're the people that tortured him."

"Not me personally."

"What the fuck are you doing?! Get off of me!" I heard Hannah yell behind me.

"No! No! Por favor!" Daniel screamed. "Laila!"

I turned quickly. Two large men pulled them by their hair from my car. I didn't even know how they got to them; it didn't make sense. The back door had opened but no one stepped out.

I started toward them but then the man in front of me said, "Uh-uh."

The gun clicked. I stopped. I gazed at Hannah. The man who held her put a knife to her throat. Daniel kicked and screamed, trying to escape the second man's grasp.

I wasn't nearly as scared as I should have been. My heart raced. My blood boiled beneath my sweaty palms. But I tried to remain calm.

In human existence, it's important to stay calm in situations like those. But that was always my problem. I resisted the emotions that ruled my abilities. Fury fed my fire and I fought it. I tried to remain calm, cool and collected because I was afraid of what I could do.

The only illumination came from my headlights and the small interior light inside the beetle. I couldn't make out every detail, but

Hannah's expression was clear in the pale blue moonlight. She was petrified.

My jaw tightened as my arms went up in flames. "Let them go," I said. They walked Hannah and Daniel a few feet toward the front of the Beetle.

"Look, you put up a fight, people are going to die. But not if you get into the car," the driver said. "Just get inside and they live."

"Don't fucking do it, Laila," Hannah yelled. She grasped the hand that rested at her throat. She tried to shove it away, but he pushed the blade further into her skin.

"If you fucking hurt them." I held a ball of fire in each hand and extended it toward the driver and the man who held Hannah.

Daniel cried and screamed, some in Spanish and some in English. I couldn't make out most of it. He was talking too fast. Or crying, rather. He flailed and yelled as gallons of water exploded from his eyes.

I'll never get that image out of my head. The heaving sobs that made their way from his little lungs as he cried out my name. The way his blood shot brown eyes dumped tears as he kicked and threw his fists around. The outright terror all over his little body.

"When you get in this car," he said. "You throw that at me, they kill them. You throw that at me, you kill your fiancé's little sister and the kid. Just get in the car, Laila. Keep the blood off your hands."

"I swear to God, Laila," Hannah yelled. She stomped her feet. "You get in that god damned car and Jeremy will never forgive me. Fucking kill them. Kill them!"

"I'd kill you too," I said. I looked between Hannah and Daniel and then the driver. A lump formed in my throat as I murmured, "This can't be happening."

"Kill me then!" Hannah screamed. "You have my nephew in your stomach. I swear to God, just fucking kill them. Kill them!"

I looked at them and then the driver again. "How do I know you won't kill them when I get in the car?"

"We don't want them." He shrugged. "We want you. Always did."

"No!" Hannah screamed. She violently shook her head. "Just fucking kill them!"

He gestured towards the guys. They lowered the knives but just slightly. "They'll get in your car right after you get in ours."

Hannah was my best friend. All of the Skouldas were. They were my family. We were a team.

I was responsible for Adrian's death and I still hadn't forgiven myself for it. In fact, I never would.

I was responsible for Moe's death too. Some part of me would never forgive myself for that either.

I couldn't let another person I loved die because of me. Especially not Hannah.

I could get on the inside. I could save them all. I could save Chris, and Amy, and Lydia. I could save them all. They were human. They didn't know what Jeremy and I were; they didn't know about our bond.

Jeremy could find me through our bond. I was sure of it.

I chewed my lip that strived to quiver. But I held my composure. The flames retreated closer into my skin until my arms pulsed a warm, orange glow. "If you hurt them, I'll fucking kill you."

He laughed. "I believe you."

"Don't do it, Laila. Please don't."

"You tell Jeremy I love him, okay?" I swallowed the knot forming in my throat, forcing a smile Hannah's way. "And my mom, and my sister. Tell them I'll be okay."

"You're being a fucking idiot, Laila," she yelled. "You can't do this!"

I'll get an inside look of what they're doing, Hannah, I projected into her mind. *I can find them. I'll bring everyone home. Me and Jeremy's bond, he'll find me. And he'll find everyone else.*

"Tell them I'm sorry." Tears burned across my eyes then. "Tell Jeremy I'm sorry."

"Jeremy's never going to forgive me, Laila. Please don't do this," she begged. "Don't go."

"I love you guys." I took a step closer to the van. As I backed into it, I turned to the driver. "Let them go."

He gave the guys a nod. They both dropped the knives. Hannah lunged toward me and the guy grabbed her by her shoulders. Effortlessly, he tossed her to the ground.

The driver shoved me into the back of the van. As I fell to my ass and the door shut, I saw Hannah screaming and scurrying to her feet through the tinted back window.

Daniel breathed a sigh of relief as the knife fell to the ground. Sadness washed over him when the door slammed. But he was okay. He'd be okay, I'd done as they asked.

Then, the guy who held him grabbed him by the back of the neck. He shifted it to the side. He snapped upward.

I'll never forget the look on Daniel's face. It was quick, he didn't suffer, but the moment those hands touched his neck again, he froze in petrification.

Those big brown eyes wide in fear, mouth open in terror. The rise in his brows as the edges of his eyes crinkled. The flare of his nostrils just before tears formed in his irises in the moment that he realized.

"No! You fucking liars!" My flaming hands slammed into the door. Tears gushed down my cheeks. My throat grew so thick it was hard to breathe. My stomach ached and my tense muscles trembled.

His small, frail little body collapsed to the ground.

The driver laughed. The rest of them rushed into the front of the car. I saw Hannah collapse beside Daniel as she cried over his dead body.

"I'll fucking kill you!" I screamed between sobs. "I'll fucking kill you all!"

CHAPTER TWENTY-EIGHT

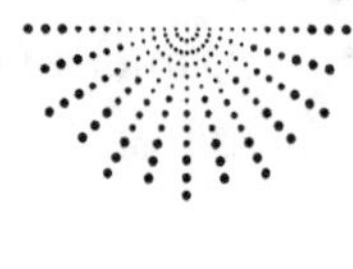

JEREMY

I was the happiest I'd ever been.

Maybe that sounded melodramatic, but as I made small talk with the jeweler, as I rolled the windows down and took in the humid spring air, as I reversed from my parking spot, I couldn't stop smiling. I probably looked like an idiot to anyone who drove past me on the highway, but I just couldn't stop smiling.

For the first time in my life, I had everything I wanted.

I had the most beautiful fiancé in the world. I was about to be the center of the biggest dream I ever had. Consciously, I wasn't aware of how deeply I craved parenthood until Laila showed me that sonogram a few months before. But from the moment I realized I was going to be a dad, my outlook did a complete one-eighty.

Being a husband and father meant more to me than anything. Honestly, I think the reason I loved Laila so irrationally at that time was because of my overwhelming infatuation with a normal life. That's what she was to me, normal.

That's how we met. She was human. I thought that she was simple. She wanted to live a simple life in our simple town. She came from a normal family. She wasn't a tortured soul filled with trauma and personal demons yet, and I was so grateful we'd left the Chambers before she saw how dark this world could get.

The sound of the wind whirled in from the cracked window as I drove down the highway. I sang along to the newest Blue October album as I flicked my joint into the ashtray and gazed out at the cloudy evening sky. There was a Cinnabon off of the exit just outside of Pittsburgh, and we rarely went out that way, so I stopped and grabbed a few. Laila bitched continuously about how we didn't have any nearby and I thought it'd make her night.

I drove to the diner after I pulled off the turnpike. That's where Laila said she would be, but her car wasn't parked out back. I assumed she was still with Hannah, so I headed toward the house.

When I pulled into the driveway, I didn't pay much mind to the bug parked haphazardly in its usual spot. I just assumed she'd be waiting inside like she always was.

"Laila," I called. Pulling off my Chuck's, I noted the silence and stillness of the usually chaotic, hustle-bustle household. "Baby," I yelled up the steps as I made my way through the foyer.

"Hey, Jeremy," Leah murmured, coming in from the kitchen.

"Hey, where's Laila? I thought she'd be at home, but her car wasn't there so I came here. Is she upstairs?" I grabbed the handrail and started up the first step.

"Let's go sit down." Leah placed her hand on my arm. Her green eyes were bloodshot, and her cheeks looked a little flushed.

I furrowed my brows and chuckled. "In a minute. I want to get her these before they get cold."

"Just come have a seat, okay?"

Her expression was... unusual. It was soft. Leah was many things, but far from soft. And the last time I'd seen her eyes so red—aside from some long nights with a four-foot bong—was at Annie's funeral.

"What's wrong?"

"Let's just sit, okay?"

My breath caught. "What's going on, Leah? Where is she?"

She licked her lips before chewing the bottom one. "Something's happened. C'mon, sit down. Let me explain."

"Where is she?" I asked again, heart picking up speed. "Is she okay?"

Leah paused, slowly shaking her head. Her already dreary gaze grew even more sad. "I don't know."

"What do you mean you don't know?" I raised my voice a little. "Her car's outside."

"Just sit down for a minute—" She touched my arm again.

I flung it away. "I'm not gonna sit down. What the hell is going on?" I glanced around, blinking fast. My gaze fell on Celena and Wyatt sitting on the couch. The skin beneath their eyes was damp. Celena swallowed hard and quickly looked away. I looked back to Leah. "Where's Daniel?"

My heart sunk to my stomach as a knot formed in my throat. Wyatt hung his head low, stroking the black scruff along his jaw.

"Before I tell you this, I need you to prepare yourself. We're going to figure it out. Just like we always do, okay?" Leah said.

"Quit beating around the bush," I snapped. "What's going on?"

She was quiet for a moment. "Hannah and Laila were on their way back from dinner. They got into a little fender bender—"

"What? Are they okay?" My mind immediately went to the ambulance that barreled past me on the highway. Was that them? Was she on her way to the hospital? No, she couldn't be, the bug was out front.

"No one was hurt in the accident. But it wasn't *just* an accident."

My forehead creased. "What do you mean?"

"Laila got out to exchange insurance information, and..." She paused. Her eyes shifted between mine for a second, brows pulling together slightly. She quickly straightened them out to a confident façade. "It was a trap. It was the people who had Daniel."

I blinked quickly as my heart rate became erratic. My vision started to get a little disoriented and nearly blue around the edges. For a second, I told myself to wake up. It couldn't be real. I just saw her.

"Where are they? Where's Hannah?"

"They pulled her and Daniel out of the car," Leah continued with a soft, sad gaze in the gentlest tone I'd ever heard leave her lips. "They had knives to their throats. They used them as collateral against Laila because they knew she wouldn't let anything happen to them."

"Collateral—what do you mean collateral?" I said quickly.

My hand that held the pastries and our wedding rings began to tremble. The beating in my chest picked up speed. My stomach clenched. Anxious sweat puddled along my forehead.

"Sit down, Jeremy." Leah gently grabbed ahold of my bicep as my legs began to shake. I felt her in my head attempting to calm my racing heart but pushed her back.

"Damn it, Leah, just fucking tell me."

She was quiet for a moment. "They were going to kill them if Laila didn't get in their car."

"No." I shook my head. "No, Laila wouldn't. She wouldn't put our baby at risk. She—she's too powerful. There's no way."

"They cut Hannah's throat—"

My stomach gurgled. "What? Is she—"

"She's fine. She's okay." Leah gave a gentle nod. "But Laila knew they weren't fucking around."

I shook my head again. My lip began to quiver. My heart hammered inside of my ribcage. I blinked hard, trying to make sure that it wasn't a bad dream I had to wake up from. The room was practically spinning.

"No. No, they don't... Laila wouldn't. She wouldn't let them get her. She's powerful," I said. "They—they couldn't have taken her, she's too powerful."

"She gave herself over," Leah said quietly.

"No." I stepped off the stairs. "No, she didn't. She wouldn't do that, she's pregnant. She's about to have a baby. She—she wouldn't let anything happen to our baby. She wouldn't, she loves him. She—"

"She wasn't going to let Hannah die." Leah placed her hand on my arm again. "But we're going to get her back. We're going to bring her home, Jeremy."

"This can't be happening," I murmured. Still blinking hard, I took in heavy breaths. Then they stopped entirely. "Where's Daniel? Did they take him too?"

Leah's eyes softened. She gave a slow shake of her head. A thin layer of water formed over her irises. "No, they didn't take him."

"Where is he then?" I asked.

"He didn't make it," she whispered.

I violently shook my head as I took a step back. My quaking palm grasped the handrail to steady me. A lump the size of a basketball formed in my throat. Wyatt started toward me with a concerned expression.

"No. No, no, no. This isn't real," I said. "This isn't happening."

"We're gonna bring her back, Jeremy," Leah said.

For a moment, I made a trying attempt to focus on her energy. Going into her mind was as easy as wanting to hear her voice and magically doing so. It was hard to explain, yet so incredibly simple. But when I thought of her, all I could see were our million memories together.

She wasn't there. It was like a picture frozen in time. I couldn't access where she currently was.

"I can't feel her." I squeezed my hands around my head. I felt the color drain from my face. "Why can't I feel her? I—I can't reach her mind. How is that possible, Leah? I'm supposed to feel her anywhere. How is this possible?" I released the sides of my head. "Where did it happen? Maybe—Maybe I can follow her energy. I've teleported a trail before, maybe it would work now—"

"That's what Adam and Brody are doing right now." She gently touched her hands to mine. "Hannah is at the police station with Ramirez. He's putting out an APB on her right now. We got the license plate, Jeremy. We're tracking them. We're going to find her, okay?"

"I—I just got our rings." My erratic breaths grew into hyperventilating. I looked down at the bag in my hand, blinking hard in attempt to see straight.

"We—we're going to start—" Tears overflowed my burning eyes. "We're going to plan the wedding. I—I need to talk to her mom. Oh my God, she's going to lose it. I—I have to go."

I quickly spun around and stumbled. Wyatt rushed to me. He placed his hands on my shoulders to keep me from falling.

"You need to breathe, bud." Wyatt's eyes locked with mine. "She's going to be okay, but she needs you. You have to stay strong."

"I have to find her. I have to go get her. I have to bring her home."

Wyatt's honey-colored eyes held mine carefully. "You will, man. You will, but you can't do that if you aren't breathing. Come sit down."

Biting my lip, I gave a slow nod. Wyatt kept a brotherly hand on my shoulder as we started toward the couch.

Still holding the jewelry and Cinnabon bag, my head fell to my hands. Tears spilled between the cracks of my fingers like a leaking roof in a rainstorm. Wyatt wrapped his arm around my shoulder as Leah sat on the other side of me. She gently placed her hand on my upper back and moved it up and down.

I didn't know what to do. I didn't know what to say. All that I could do was cry.

Because I knew. These people had tortured a compliant child for years. And my fiancé... she was far from docile. I couldn't begin to imagine what they'd do to her.

CHAPTER TWENTY-NINE

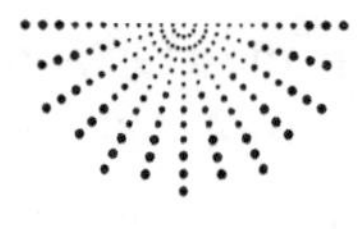

LAILA

My head pounded against my crown, ripping me from a sleep I didn't remember falling into. I blinked a few times, trying to see through my heavy eyelids. My back ached like I'd sat in a movie theater seat for the entirety of Braveheart.

The smell of bleach and rubbing alcohol filled my nostrils. The air smelled clean. Too clean, really, like a chemical kind of clean.

Like hospital.

There was no noise. Not a single hum of a heater or a chirping cricket outside the window. I could hear a pin drop from a mile away. Maybe it was just the thudding in my head, but the silence was so loud that it hurt.

I rubbed my shivering arms as I sat forward. It was so dark that I could barely see my hand in front of me. Moon light shined in from a window behind me and a dim, bluish light shined in from the wall in front of me.

I reached around for something to grab, some way to see which way I was heading. My hands found the surface I'd lain on, feeling cold metal against the tips of my fingers. It was so cold it almost stung.

I started to my feet, still grasping the table I was sleeping on for stability. My toes touched the cool ground and sent shivers up my spine. I started toward the light coming in from the window ahead. I struggled onto my tip toes to look out. I hoped to see something notable. Something helpful in some way or another.

But I didn't. It was just a dimly lit hallway with similar windows on similar metal doors across, beside and diagonal from me. There was a glowing keypad on the only door without a window to the far left.

I struggled to avoid the claustrophobia that was slowly setting in.

Cold metal met my fingers as I slid them down the frame, but that was all I felt. Smooth, cold metal.

No knob.

There was no knob.

As that realization smacked through me, my stomach dropped.

Practically involuntarily, my fists slammed against the pane, screaming, "Where the fuck am I?"

"Shut the fuck up," a female voice called.

My heart skipped. "Is somebody there?"

"Yeah, there's a lot of fucking somebodies here and we're all trying to get some damn sleep. So shut the fuck up."

"Jesus, Haley," a man's voice called. "She's a newbie, she's scared. Cut her some slack."

"Fuck off," the woman I assumed to be Haley said.

"She's a cunt, you'll get used to it," the man said. "What's your name?"

"Laila." I gazed around to determine which direction his voice came from. "I'm Laila."

"Well, Laila. Welcome to hell."

I stumbled back to the table I'd soon realize was my bed. "I don't remember getting here."

Hell or not, it was gonna be okay. Jeremy was gonna find me, I was sure of it. Nothing could get between our bond. Nothing.

"They either knock you out or drug you when they pick you up."

It was all something of a blur. Like a dream so intense you wake up to a sweat soaked bed, remembering only the sensation of fear, but having no clue what you were afraid of. "I don't know."

"You gotta speak up, dude. My ears are pretty good but it's still hard to hear through these." He hit the wall behind me enough that it vibrated the bed.

"I said I don't remember." I raised my voice a bit. "Do you know where we are?"

"Somewhere that gets a lot of rain and has all four seasons," he said. "Haley smelled the ocean on her clothes when she got here. Maybe Washington? Or Canada? I don't know, some of the guards have an accent. But it doesn't matter. They're smart. No one's coming for us."

"My fiancé will." I nodded. "He's probably looking for me right now."

Haley laughed. "He might be looking but he won't find you."

"He will. You'll see."

She laughed again. "God, I wonder if you look as dumb as you sound."

The guy laughed. "I've been here for years. We all have. Hate to break it to you, but your fiancé thinks you're dead. He's probably planning your funeral."

It slowly started to come back. The fog, the blinding headlights, the handgun. Hannah screaming that I was a fucking idiot.

"No, you don't understand. He knows I'm not. They all do. My friend, my fiancé's sister. She saw me get taken. I'm sure she got the plates. We've been looking for them. For all of you, I guess," I said. "We were getting close."

The memory of Daniel's terrified expression just before they snapped his neck.

I had to push that thought from my mind.

He laughed. "You're a hell of a lot closer now."

A wave of anger washed over me. "Well, it's not like I planned this."

"None of us planned this, dumb ass," Haley said.

"What do you mean you've been looking for them anyway?" the man's voice grew more serious.

I swallowed the lump forming in my throat. Most of me was so glad he asked though. It was something to think about that wasn't my idiotic ass getting into that van and Daniel dying for it. And something that wasn't my throbbing brain.

"It's kind of a long story. But to make it short, someone asked for my help finding their family who went missing a few years back. They were declared dead, but he was convinced that they weren't. We ran some tests and confirmed that they were alive. My fiancé's brother was declared dead without a body too, so we did the same tests for him and confirmed the same. We just kept digging and I guess they realized we were getting close. I don't know."

"How close? Like, figuring out the location close?" he asked. A ray of hope coated the edge of his voice.

"No, not that close. But we found two kids that escaped," I said. "I guess one of them escaped. I think they let the other one go to lure my family into a trap. I should have realized that then."

That aching silence rained back in for a second. Then the man spoke again. "As soon as I saw those headlights, I should have left. I could have just disappeared. But too little too late, I guess." He let out an ironic laugh. "Can't dwell on it now."

My head tilted. "Are you a teleporter?"

"Yeah," he said. "Or I was anyway. It's been a while."

"What's your name?" I asked with furrowed brows.

"Chris."

My heart thudded excitedly in my chest. "Christopher Skoulda?" I asked. He fell silent. "Is that your name?" He stayed quiet. I smacked the wall a few times, smile coming to my lips as I tapped it again. "Is that your name? Are you a Skoulda?"

"How'd you know that?"

I laughed. "Well, this was definitely intentional. But why? They know who we are. Is it supposed to be some type of poetic irony?"

"I can't hear you, speak up," he called.

I turned to the wall to feel the cold steel beneath my fingertips. "My fiancé is Jeremy Skoulda."

CHAPTER THIRTY

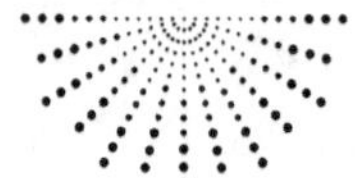

MARCH 11, 2019 - JEREMY

"We tracked the license plate," Ramirez said. We stood around the kitchen island where he sat hunched in front of a laptop. "It belongs to fifty-three-year-old Katherine Warren from Uniontown. She reported it stolen two days ago."

My ray of hope shattered. Tracked the license plate just for it to have been stolen. Therefore sent us fucking nowhere. "So a dead end."

"Sort of," Ray muttered. "We picked up the plate on a traffic cam heading into Ohio."

"So you found her?" Wyatt asked.

"No, they must have switched the plates again. But we know which direction they were heading, or at least a general idea. Her face is plastered all over everything. After news about Daniel came out, all the major news stations are reporting on it. Every station across this country is covering this on the morning news. She's a young and attractive pregnant businesswoman and a respected person in the community. Hell, she was a foster parent. The fact that Daniel was an immigrant, or at least suspected immigrant, made it blow up on the internet. The case has gone viral, check your social media. Someone's going to recognize her. We're going to find her."

Wyatt shook his head. "They're smart. It isn't going to be that easy.

They wouldn't have let her out of the car. Not to mention the fact that they could have changed vehicles."

My stomach sunk. I traced my tongue along my teeth, shaking my head slightly. Wyatt was right, cops weren't gonna be how we found her. Whether humans were responsible or not, this wasn't a human problem.

I stared vacantly at the wet bar behind the island. Slow breaths left my nose as I focused on the bottles of liquor.

She was gone. Just gone.

My world was crashing down around me. It felt like something heavier than a planet sat on my back. I pushed up against it so hard, fighting with everything inside of me not to let it smash me like a bug. I didn't want to crack under its pressure. But that bottle of Crown looked like a forklift big enough to lift it from my struggling shoulders.

"We're going to find her." Ray looked up from his computer to meet Wyatt's gaze.

"Maybe," Wyatt said. "But not with this. They probably already got wherever they were going."

"Laila is my only shot at getting my family back," Ray barked. "We're *going* to find her."

Wyatt said, "Alright. Sorry, I'm not trying to be a dick, man. I just don't want to waste any time."

"I bet that's why they gave us Daniel," Brody murmured from his seat on the stairwell. He chewed his thumb with a gaze as distant as mine. "That's how they were tracking her. I'd put money on it. They knew she'd take the kid in. They used him."

As those words left his lips, it felt like ligaments breaking as I struggled to keep that world floating above my head.

It was because I hit that kid. The child whose cold body lay on an autopsy table at the coroner's office. They found her because of something that I did.

My arms were breaking and cracking, sending stabbing pains of guilt through my entire body.

I needed that forklift.

I teleported to the wet bar, reached for a glass on the shelf, and set it on the counter.

"What are you doing?" Brody started to his feet.

"Don't." I spun off the plastic golden cap. Crown Royal. Laila's favorite liquor. The only time I'd tasted it since I was a teenager was on her lips.

"Jeremy—" Brody began.

"My pregnant fiancé was just kidnapped by the people who beat an eight-year-old boy so many times that it looked like he jumped straight out of the Civil War," I snapped with a tight jaw and darting gaze. "Don't. Just don't, Brody."

He frowned. He watched me turn back to the counter and pour the glass to its brim. I lifted it to my lips, tilted my head back and chugged. The room fell silent as Brody, Ray, Wyatt, and Celena witnessed my first relapse in six years.

When the liquor touched my tongue, I didn't even feel the urge to gag. It tasted good. Familiar. The burn stinging down my throat was warm, not so different from the way it felt when Laila and I kissed long and hard enough for her temperature to rise. The heat slid into the pit of my stomach, filling it with heat and relief.

When the first glass was gone, I poured another.

Rinse. Repeat.

"Jeremy," Leah murmured. She brushed past Brody down the steps and walked beside me.

"Please don't." I gave a slow shake of my head, eyes filling with tears. "Please. Just don't."

She frowned. "Let's go sit down in the living room, okay?"

CHAPTER THIRTY-ONE

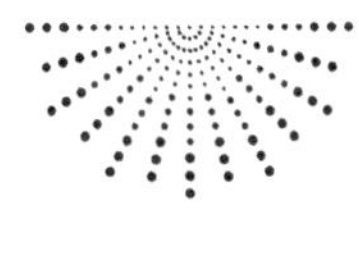

JEREMY

I leaned against the window twirling her engagement ring in circles between my fingertips. It looked like two rings through my drunken gaze. I stared down at it, stopping from time to time to examine the diamond.

"Hey," Celena said. She walked behind the love seat and leaned against the back of it to face me.

I glanced up at her and then back down at the ring. "Hey."

"You might want to put that back in the box and keep it somewhere safe." She gestured toward the ring.

I stopped spinning it. I pinched the loop between my thumb and forefinger, watching it sparkle against the lights above. "You know why she liked this one?"

She frowned. "No, I don't."

"She liked that it was small." I smiled, looking up to meet her gaze. "How humble is that? She could have gotten almost any ring in that store. But she just wanted one small, simple diamond. And she wouldn't get a real diamond. She wanted one of these scientifically created ones. What are they called?"

"Cultured diamonds, I think," she said.

"Yeah, that's it. Cultured diamonds. She wanted a cultured

diamond because she didn't want to buy a 'blood diamond.'" With a chuckle, I rubbed my watering eyes. "That's what she called it. Because of the children who die mining them in Africa or something?"

"Sounds like Laila." She gave a sad smile.

I looked back down at the ring. "She's so pure, you know? She's just so gentle and sweet. I know she's got a mouth on her and everything, but underneath it all, that's what she is. So sweet." Tears began to stream from my eyes. "What if they do to her what they did to Daniel?" I turned my eyes back up to hers. "What if they kill her?"

Celena's head shook. "We're not going to let that happen."

I nodded. I didn't believe it, but I nodded anyway because I had to hope. I had to hang onto hope that she'd be back in my arms soon.

But I didn't believe it for a second. If this was going to be easy, she'd be home already. She wouldn't be… Wherever the hell she was. I had a bad feeling from the moment we picked up Daniel, and I should have listened to that instinct, damn it. Some part of me knew something like this could happen.

"They won't even let me help." I made a drunken gesture to the kitchen.

"You're just too close to it."

I bit my trembling lip. "I can't feel her anymore. I've never not been able to feel her. Ever since our bond was completed, I always knew how to find her. I always knew that she was safe. And I know she's alive, but I can't find her mind." Celena pressed her teeth together, eyes softening. "I can't find her."

Tears burned across my eyes. I turned my disoriented gaze to the ground. "What if I never see her again? What if something happens to my son?" I gritted my teeth together to keep my lip from curling. "I won't be able to live with myself. I won't have anything to live for if something happens to her."

"Don't talk like that," she said. "You're drunk, Jeremy. It's only been a few hours. You just need to get some sleep."

"You don't get it yet, Celena. You've only known Wyatt a few months. Once you've been together as long as we have, once the bond gets tighter, living without him…" I wiped the tears that ran down my cheeks. "It's not living without being *with* them. Laila broke up with me before and it hurt but it wasn't like this. You can still live as long as you know that they're okay. But if something happens to her and our baby, I don't see the point in living."

She was on the verge of tears. But she took a step forward. She placed her hand on my upper arm. "It's gonna be okay."

Tears fell from my eyes and my stomach ached. I wasn't sure if it was the fear or the alcohol, but I didn't give it much thought regardless. I didn't give anything much thought. Aside from fear and pain, my mind was blank.

"I know she's only been gone for a couple hours but I already miss her so much." My quiet tears strived to turn into an all-out sob.

"We're going to bring her back, Jeremy." I took a step back and ran my hand over my mouth. "I'm not going to lose another sister."

"I was trying so hard to keep her safe." I wiped my red eyes. "She was so mad at me for telling her what to do but this was why. I knew something could happen to her and I—I was scared."

How ironic was that. I was the one who kept rambling on and on about how she needed to be careful. She was kidnapped because *I* sent her out to get her nails done. Daniel was dead because *I* told her to leave.

My chest grew so tight that breathing hurt. The room was spinning again, and my throat was thick. The water in my eyes turned to a quiet weep.

"We are going to bring her back, Jeremy." Her voice got firmer that time. I pressed my trembling lips together. "But you're going to have to be strong. You have to be ready when we find her. You can't be like this."

My lip quivered. Yeah, I wanted her back so bad, and my solution was to chug two glasses of whiskey. That was *definitely* gonna help. She'd be so fucking proud.

I looked away. "I know, I fucked up."

"But you're going to make it right. You're going to keep it together for her. Regardless of when we get her back, she's going to need you. You *have* to stay strong for her."

I was quiet for a moment. "I know."

"Let's sit down. I'll get you some water and bread. You need something to soak up that liquor."

I started around the love seat, gripping it for stability. "Yeah, you're right."

She gave a sad smile as I sat. "I'll be right back."

My eyes wouldn't stop watering. The corners stung where the skin dried and began to crust into raw flakes. Snot stuck to my long hair in giant clumps. Maintaining my composure was getting harder by the second.

Laila was gone with my unborn child and Daniel was dead.

Daniel is dead.

My watering eyes overflowed. He was just a kid. Practically a baby who lived through more hell than almost anyone could imagine. And he was dead.

They killed him to tie up a loose end. Like Laila said. Whatever Daniel had locked up in that head of his were threads they couldn't have pulled.

My shaking hand closed around the circle of white gold. I closed my eyes, and my head shook.

Suddenly, an intense, stabbing pain sliced up my wrists. I cried out. I grasped my palm around it. Simultaneously, I heard her scream echo between my ears.

The pain got more intense. I dropped the ring and gripped my aching forearms. I felt pressured, aching pains all over her body. Her ankles, around her ribs, each wrist.

She was struggling.

Her arms and legs were flailing against some type of restraint that held her in place.

My stomach churned as shocked, pained tears spewed from my eyes. I stumbled off the couch. My cries rapidly turned to sobs. They were cutting into her. I could hear her screaming. And there was nothing I could do.

The pain in my wrist got even worse, like the flesh was being ripped off. Or maybe like it was being ripped open.

"What's wrong?" Celena urged in the doorway.

"Are you okay?" Wyatt lowered himself to the ground beside me.

"They're hurting her." Tears rolled down my cheeks. I grimaced and drunkenly fell to the side. "I feel it. I hear her screaming." My hands went to my head, squeezing my hair in fists as her pleas echoed inside of my mind. "I can't get in her head, but I hear her screaming. They're hurting her."

I turned over and pushed my back against the couch. Gradually, I pulled myself up with trembling hands. The pain persisted. My head shook, hearing her screams turn to sobs in my head. I looked desperately up at Wyatt. Tears streamed down my cheeks, and I held my shaking hands in front of my face. "What should I do? What am I supposed to do? *What do I do?*"

CHAPTER THIRTY-TWO

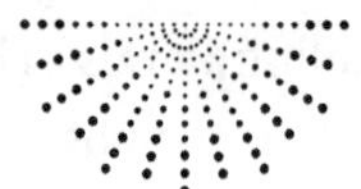

MARCH 11, 2019 - LAILA

"Jeremy," Chris murmured quieter than before. "You're marrying my brother?"

I laughed. Nodding fast, I said, "Yeah. Jesus, this is crazy. They had to have put me here on purpose."

"Jeremy's getting married?" His tone grew solemn. "How old is he?"

He didn't know how long he'd been here. "He's twenty-four now."

"Twenty-four," he repeated. "That means it's... What? 2020?"

"No, it's 2019. His birthday was two weeks ago."

Quiet for a moment. "So it's been seven years."

My gaze locked on the moon through the foggy glass-block window. "Yeah. Almost, anyway."

"Jesus."

"How do you know she's even telling the truth?" Haley snapped. "She could be one of them. They could be trying to get in your head or something."

"What? No. No, I'm not." I put my hand on the cool steel wall that separated us. He was the only sense of familiarity I had in there, he had to believe me. I needed him to trust me. We needed each other.

"Ask me anything. I can tell you just about anything about any of your siblings."

"You wouldn't know anything that they wouldn't," he said. "Not after this long."

"Well, I know that you were closest to Leah and Jeremy growing up. And I know that you and Leah tried to make cannabutter once and spilled it on the back burner of the gas range and that's why it doesn't work anymore. I know that you and Adam were playing catch once and he fell onto your aunt's two-thousand-dollar antique table and you took the blame for it and had to clean the bathrooms for six months." I paused. "God, I've heard other stories. Just give me a minute."

"Leah told you that?" he asked. He stopped for a second. He laughed quietly. "We swore to take that to our graves."

I smiled. "In all fairness, she thought you were in the grave."

"How is she?"

"She's..." I trailed off and chuckled. "She's Leah."

"But she's good? She's happy?" he asked.

"In her own way," I said.

"What about Jeremy? And Adam? And Brody? Oh God, how's Hannah? She's what, eighteen now?"

"Next month." I pulled my knees up to my face for warmth. "She's amazing. She's applying to colleges, taking the SATs. She wants to go to law school."

"She always was good at arguing," he muttered. "What about Adam? And Brody?"

I chuckled. "Adam is his usual, bubbly self. He just kind of bumbles through life, you know?"

"Yeah." He laughed quietly. "That's Adam."

My lips lifted in a smile. "And Brody is pretty good, I guess. As good as he'll ever be. Grumpy, but good." I licked my lips as I thought for a moment. Chris would have been the first to go to college, I was sure he'd want to hear that Brody was in school too. "He takes classes at the community college. He'll be graduating in a year and a half."

"What's he getting a degree in?"

"Well, he's considering going to a university still, but he's getting an associates in business management and an associate in accounting at the moment."

He laughed. "That's so lame. He always was a dork though. Definitely sounds like my baby brother."

I smiled. He was a dork. But the sophisticated kind, not the nerdy glasses kind. "He said he wanted to get a degree in something that there would always be a need for."

"What about Jeremy?" he asked. "Does he still play guitar?"

"He does. All the time actually." I thought about how he must have been feeling at that moment. Guilt washed over me. His shoes must have been some shitty ones to be standing in right about then. "Jeremy's great. Well, probably not right now, given the situation. But otherwise, he's really happy."

"That doesn't sound like my brother." Chris laughed. "He was always such a dark little dude."

I pulled a smile to my lips. "Well, he's not these days. And he's not so little anymore either. We got engaged about a month and a half ago." My fingers coasted over my belly. I paused, debating about how to go on. "And our baby is due in July."

"Your baby?" Haley butted in fast. "You're pregnant?"

"And you're in here?" Chris's soft tone picked up pace.

"Not really where I pictured myself either. But they were going to kill Hannah if I didn't go with them," I said quickly. I thought back to last night before lowering my voice. "They killed Daniel."

"So you'd prefer they kill your baby?" Haley scoffed. "You should have let the bitch die and saved yourself."

"I couldn't just let them kill her," I snapped. "She's practically my sister, I love her."

"Well, clearly you don't love that baby."

Those words would echo through my mind in the coming months. Then the coming years. She was wrong. I loved my baby more than anything, even more than I loved Jeremy. More than I loved my mom or my siblings or my friends. I loved him with everything I had.

I was just stupid. There was no way I could have saved Hannah that day with the lack of control I held over my abilities. But I was dumb enough to believe I'd be okay in that place until my knight in shining armor came to the rescue.

I was pathetic. I'll never say otherwise.

But I loved my son.

"Is she okay?" The wall shook a bit as Chris tapped his hand on it. "Is my sister okay?"

I placed my hand to the cold, smooth surface. My palm heated to a warm, orange glow. I hoped he'd feel its heat on the other side. "I saw her get into my car and pull out from the rear window. She's fine."

"Thank God." Hope touched the edge of his voice. "Thank you, Laila. Thank you."

The lights turned on suddenly and I got my first good look around what I would soon call my room. "Shhh," Chris urged. "Don't say anything."

The ceiling and walls seemed like a single, solid sheet of stainless steel. The floor was painted—or maybe epoxy-coated—gray over cement. Across from me sat a small jail toilet equipped with a tiny sink on the top, also sparkling steel. To the left, a spigot came out of the wall. A drain sat on the floor beneath it. The door with the four by four-inch window was stainless steel too, matching every other surface in the room.

So much steel. The bed I sat on, the toilet, the walls.

Not an ounce of color.

My door swung open. In walked two men in thick, white rubbery suits. Fire touched my fingertips as they started toward me. My arms lit aflame, and I said, "Don't touch me."

They laughed. Then they grabbed my shoulders and effortlessly hoisted my flailing, flaming body into the air. One of them plunged a syringe into my neck.

And I drifted away.

CHAPTER THIRTY-THREE

JEREMY

"Twenty-one-year-old business owner Laila Callidy out of Somerset County is still missing nearly twenty-four hours after her abduction," the lady on the TV said. I gazed up at it, licking my dry lips and chewing on the chapped pieces around the edges. "The young woman recently inherited a small business in her hometown after the death of her family friend late last October. Sources tell us that she has made charitable donations to the community center as well as multiple homeless shelters from here to Pittsburgh since she inherited Moe's Diner."

The woman sounded serious, but her lips curved upward at the end. As if she was happy to cover such a "big" story. My nostrils flared and my jaw tightened.

"Laila Callidy is pregnant and planning a wedding with her high school sweetheart. He could not be reached for a comment, but sources tell us he is entirely distraught. She and her fiancé were foster parents to a young boy who was killed here at the site of the abduction. The coroner has not yet released a cause of death."

"Fuck you, nobody asked for my comment," I mumbled at the screen.

It blinked over to a picture Laila had hung on the mantel in our living room. I wondered who'd given it to them. Probably Leah.

She just got it back from the photographer two weeks before. She was so proud of it. I remember the grin on her face as she opened the manila envelope. Her favorite, the one on the TV, was the one with me behind her. My fingers laced against her belly. I gazed down at her with a smile. Her bright red lips smiled at the camera, big green eyes nearly glowing with excitement. She held two blue shoes against the little bump on her white dress. Her dark hair laid in big bouncy curls against her chest, nearly reaching her bloated belly.

She looked so happy. So did I.

"The sister of the victim's fiancé witnessed the abduction and says that she wouldn't be alive if it weren't for Laila's actions last night, according to police reports. She is currently recovering from injuries related to the attack and has not been available for interview.

"The police are searching for a white or silver 2017 Luxury Mercedes Benz Sprinter, also known as a mobile office, as pictured here." The screen flashed to a photo of the van and a license plate number. "There is evidence suggesting the car was headed towards Ohio avoiding almost all roads with traffic cameras. If you see a vehicle with this description, or any suspicious activity near a vehicle like this, you're asked to contact 911 immediately.

"We are told that the people responsible are armed and dangerous. You are instructed to use extreme caution if any suspicious activity is suspected. Again, call 911 immediately. The police currently have no leads on the suspects but are using all available resources to search for the young woman. The Federal Bureau of Investigation was contacted after evidence surfaced of the suspects crossing into the state of Ohio. We were able to interview a few people close to the victims earlier this afternoon and this is what they had to say."

The screen flashed to an image of Max. His brown eyes were glossy, dirty brown hair falling in his face. A blue bar appeared under his face saying '*Maxwell Campbell*,' beneath it in a smaller font said, '*Head Cook at Moe's Diner.*'

He knew Laila longer than I did. Longer than anyone besides her mom and sister. They'd been friends since grade school. He looked almost as torn up as I was.

"Laila is probably the kindest person you'll ever meet," Max said. "She took in some little kid she literally found on the street. She doesn't pay any person who works at this little place less than ten dollars an hour, she gave us all a huge bonus for Christmas out of her own pocket, she donates to charities, she spends holidays at soup kitchens, she takes in every stray she finds. She loves everyone and everything with her whole heart and always has. This girl is the definition of an angel. I can't think of a single reason someone would ever want to hurt her." He bit his curling lip. He wiped the corner of his eye. "She just got engaged, she's going to have a baby, she's at the best part of her life and now she's just gone without a trace. It's just so unfair."

"If her kidnappers are watching this right now, what message would you want to send to them?" the reporter asked.

He turned to the camera with tears in his eyes. "Please bring her home. We'll pay you ransom; you can contact us anonymously and no one will know who you are. Please just bring her home. No one deserves to go through this, but especially not Laila. Her fiancé's heart broken, her friends are a wreck, her mom's terrified. Please just bring her home."

She pulled the microphone to her lips. "So you've been in contact with the victim's family?"

"I have, and they want everyone to give them some privacy. They're crushed and need some space right now."

"You shouldn't watch this." Adam grabbed the remote from the table and turned the TV off.

"Why?" I met his gaze. "Because I shouldn't think about it? I felt them cutting into her skin and ripping—"

"Because it isn't going to help." He sat beside me with a frown. "We have a guy on the inside. The news won't have information before we do."

I gritted my teeth together. He was right. I knew he was right. But I didn't know what to do. There was nothing *to* do. "This is so fucked up."

Adam bit his lip and gave a nod. "It's hard, man."

"I don't know." Rubbing thick knots at the back of my neck, my gaze turned to the ground. "Leah did the locator spell and it's doing the same thing it did for Chris and Ray's family. We even paid Helena to run a stronger one and it came up with nothing too." My heart hurt as I said the last line. "She's just gone."

"It's only been a day," Adam murmured. "We're going to get her back."

"You know how missing persons go." I looked up to meet his gaze. "The first twenty-four hours are the most crucial. If you don't find anything in that time, the case goes cold."

Adam turned his eyes to the ground.

"They're hurting her." My lips began to tremble. "They're hurting her and there's nothing I can do."

His eyes softened. "I'm so sorry you have to go through this, man."

"I just want to make it stop but I can't," I whispered. "I don't know how to help her."

"Jeremy," Ray said quietly from the cased opening to the foyer.

I stood, wiping my face. "Did you find something?"

He frowned. "Not yet. But I need to talk to you for a minute."

CHAPTER THIRTY-FOUR

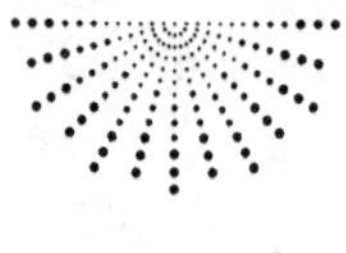

JEREMY

"What the fuck are you trying to say, dude?" My eyes shifted rapidly between Ray's. "You really think that's possible? You think that I'd hurt her?"

"He didn't say that," Adam said. "He's just telling you the facts."

"The facts don't fucking apply here," I shouted. "This isn't a human situation. Why did you involve the cops in the first place?"

"What would happen if we didn't?" Hannah rubbed her aching wrist at the breakfast nook. "What? You think no one would notice if Laila and Daniel just disappeared? You guys had to go to court in less than two months for his custody, Jeremy. We had to do this."

I turned around. My hand ran over my clenched jaw. I knew she was right. But cops just made it so much more complicated. What if I got in there and felt them torturing her again? Was I supposed to sit there calmly with the police officers as I felt them torture the love of my life?

"What's going on?" Celena set an array of coffees and a box of cookies on the counter.

"He thinks I have something to do with all of this," I snapped with an angry wave at Ray.

"That's not even close to what I said," he said. "I know how much you love her. I know you would never hurt her. But the FBI doesn't know you, Jeremy. Statistically speaking, most people who disappear have some personal connection to the victims—"

"I know the statistics." I rolled my eyes.

"Then you understand why they want to question you."

"None of you understand how hard this is. Half of me is fucking gone." Tears burned down my cheeks, and I angrily wiped them away. "She's just gone, and I don't know how to pretend like I'm okay. I know what they're doing to her. I fucking feel it." I bit my trembling lip. "I feel them torturing her. And there isn't a damn thing I can do. All I want to do is make it stop and bring her home and I fucking can't."

"No one expects ye to be all right," Kai said quietly from the breakfast nook. He continued peering out the window, eyes red with dried tears. He turned and met my gaze. "I ken what she means to ye, Jeremy. I know it's not the same as she means to me. But I'm not all right either. None of us are all right. Every one of us is worried. Everyone is scared. She's our family, too."

I rubbed my eyes between my thumb and forefinger. Obviously this was affecting all of us. But it was a little different because I literally *felt* what they were doing to her. "I didn't mean it like that. I'm sorry. I just..."

"I get it, Jeremy," Ray said quietly. "I've been in your shoes. My wife was taken by the same people who took Laila. I was interviewed, I was accused. I know how hard this is."

I stared down at the floor, fingers grazing the stubble on my chin. "Can you be there when they interview me?"

"I'll do what I can. But all they're going to do is ask you questions. Nothing is going to spark them as suspicious about the two of you. You're madly in love, anyone who's seen you together knows that. Neither of you have any history of violence, and the only record you have is some humanitarian bullshit. The two of you rarely fight and when you do it's never aggressive. You live above the diner; your staff would know if the two of you were having problems. And besides, you have an alibi. I'm sure we could talk to the jeweler about confirming where you were at the time."

Rubbing my mouth, I gave a nod. Although I could be at two places nearly simultaneously, they didn't know that. I wasn't going to jail for this. "Yeah. Yeah, you're right."

"And you aren't married yet. You don't have anything to gain from her death," Leah said.

The way she said that made my heart race. "She isn't dead. I would know if she was dead."

"No, I know," Leah said. "I just meant that it makes you less of a suspect."

"Not to mention the fact that you've been an incredibly perfect partner throughout the pregnancy," Celena chimed in.

"Yeah, I'm sure Laila's mom would testify to that," Hannah said.

"And Laila's doctor, and all the staff at Moe's who see the two of you every day," Brody said. "They have no case against you even if they wanted to pursue one."

"But you have to get that look of guilt off your face." Adam gestured to me. "I know you feel like it was your job to protect her." I opened my mouth to interject but Adam raised his voice to speak over me. "But this isn't your fault. You go in there with that look on your face and they're immediately going to think you did something to her."

I did feel guilty, I'm sure I looked it. I was the one who told her to go out with Hannah and get her nails done. I was the one who told her to enjoy her girl's night. But he was right, I'd done nothing wrong. I had to straighten up.

CHAPTER THIRTY-FIVE

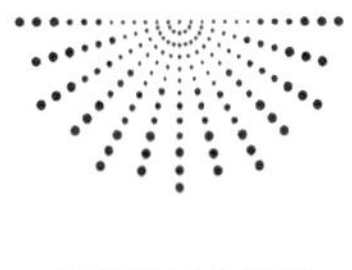

JEREMY

The smell of shitty coffee and lingering old spice drifted up my nostrils. A cool shiver moved up my arms, cold air wafting from the heater vent. My chucks anxiously tapped against the dirty white linoleum turned gray from years of dirty sneakers rubbing against them. The soft brown on the walls should have been remotely inviting but the lack of photos did the opposite. The "See Something, Say Something" poster of a man standing beside a car door in a big black hoodie wasn't exactly welcoming either.

I hated police stations. When I was on the other end, it wasn't so bad. I'd worked with cops at least a few dozen times when I was still working cases. But we typically met in diners, parking lots, and bars to discuss technicalities. Doing so in a police department would've looked too sketchy. With my long hair, baggy jackets, and unwashed jeans, I looked more like the person they were trying to find than a colleague helping with an investigation.

Guess I didn't look so out of place sitting at that steel table. At least my hands weren't in cuffs. But that door locked from the outside and that made my stomach hurt. It also made me think about Lai. She was probably staring at a door that locked from the outside too.

Ramirez set a cup of coffee in front of me. He lowered himself to the old rusting metal chair. "Do you need cream or sugar?"

"No, I'm good," I muttered. "Thanks though."

"She was just going to the bathroom. She'll be in in a second."

I lifted the coffee to my lips. Granules touched my tongue and slid down my throat. I made a sour face and set it down. "Do you really drink this shit every day?"

"If I don't have time to get coffee on the way in." Ray shrugged. "You get used to the grounds after a while."

"Get used to it tasting like piss too?" I wiped the corner of my lip with the back of my hand. "Is your coffee maker dirty? You should really clean it every few weeks. Every other month, at least. All you have to do is run some vinegar water through it."

He laughed. "I don't think any amount of cleaning can fix that coffee pot."

"Keurig's are only a hundred bucks or so. You should invest in one."

"Yeah, I have one at home. They're nice."

The metal door behind him opened and I sat up a bit. An older woman—probably around her late forties or early fifties—with salt and pepper hair came through carrying a file and a cup of coffee. A gray headband pushed back her tight black curls. She wore a yellow dress shirt over her pear-shaped silhouette that complimented her dark skin. She wasn't thin, but she wasn't very large either. She was an attractive woman with a friendly face and a gentle smile.

"Sorry to keep you waiting." She set her things down on the table and reached out to shake my hand. "My name's Tina Davis. I'm an investigator with the Federal Bureau of Investigation."

I reached across the table and took her hand. "Nice to meet you. Jeremy Skoulda."

She smiled as she sat. "Well, I've just got a few questions for you and you'll be on your way. Shouldn't take more than an hour."

"No one's waiting up for me," I muttered. "No rush."

Tina frowned at that, eyes sympathetic. After a moment, she cleared her throat and started with the basics. How did we meet? How long were we together? Was there anything about Laila that they weren't yet aware of, but I might find obvious? Easy enough questions to answer. The next question wasn't too bad either.

"So how would you describe your relationship? Are you guys happy?"

I gave a sad smile, glancing down at the grains floating in my cup. "Yeah. We're definitely happy."

"No crazy affairs? Not a lot of arguing or anything like that?"

"Oh, no. Nothing like that," I said. I remembered last fall. I knew she'd told Max, her mom, and her sister when we'd broken up. I didn't want to get caught in a lie, even if that break up was total bullshit. "Well, we did have a little rocky patch last October. But we worked it all out. It was the only time we ever really fought. Aside from the usual bickering over leaving my socks on the floor, I mean."

"Do you care to elaborate?"

"Not particularly, but if you need to know, I can go into the details."

"If you don't mind." She leaned back a bit in her chair.

"It was right around when Moe died," I said. "And she just found out she was pregnant, and she didn't tell me at first. She was just really stressed. We were arguing more than I would have liked, I guess. But once things started to even out at the diner, we started getting back into our usual groove."

It wasn't the whole truth, but it wasn't a lie either. It's not like I could have told her the whole truth. She wouldn't believe it if I begged her to.

Her head cocked to the side. "She kept the pregnancy from you?"

"Just at first. She wanted to get an ultrasound first so she could show me him. I thought it was sweet."

She gave a smile as she looked down at her papers. "So does Laila have any known enemies? Anyone who might want to hurt her? An old friend or maybe a drug dealer?"

I laughed. "No, she's not really into that sort of thing. She just smokes weed. Or at least, she did. Before she found out she was pregnant and everything."

She looked up from her papers. "The pregnancy wasn't planned, I take it?"

"A pleasant surprise, we call it."

"And you were happy about the baby?"

A smile pulled at my lips. I gave a nod. It shrunk away as I remembered that anything could happen to him. Laila, I could feel. The baby was another story.

"Yeah. I started working on his nursery the day after she told me. She wanted it to be Winnie the Pooh themed. Gender neutral and all that. I made these little shelves in the shape of a tree with a door at the bottom in this tiny little nook by the closet. He won't be able to use it for a few years, but I saw it online and..." I chuckled. "Sorry, I know how stupid this sounds. But that's something I could do, you know? She's growing a life inside of her. Refinishing some floors and painting some walls is nowhere close to growing another person but it made me feel like I was doing something for him too."

Her smile lifted. I was glad she was a woman. Being the sappy fuck that I was, it probably would've looked odd to a man. But it was endearing to a woman. "That's sweet. I wish my husband would have been that happy when I was pregnant."

I gave a smile and turned my gaze back down to my coffee. "I just want to be a good dad."

Tina sent me a sympathetic gaze, growing quiet. Apparently my grief was showing, because she smiled and asked, "So how did you propose?"

"We had a nice dinner, I got down on one knee and I just asked her. She said no." I laughed quietly.

She arched a brow but held her smile. "She said no?"

"She said something about how marriage was created to trade women like cattle. She asked if she should come up with a dowry too." I laughed.

"One of those new age hippies, huh?"

"I guess you could say that."

"But she said yes?"

I chuckled and gave a nod. "We were lying in bed and she asked if it was really important to me. I told her it meant a lot to me, but ya know, it is what it is. And she said, 'Fine, but I have conditions.'"

Tina laughed. "Oh yeah? What were they?"

"She doesn't want to be pregnant when we get married, she wants a small wedding, she's keeping her last name, and she wouldn't take my mom's ring. She wants my little sister to have it."

It felt good to talk about her. I hated the thought of going in there, but Tina didn't look at me accusatively. And it brought me some sense of calm and normalcy. Talking about shit always helps. I wished it were Laila I was talking to. But talking about her wasn't so bad either.

"The one who was with her the night of the abduction?" she asked.

My smile fell. "Yeah, Hannah. She went with her to get their nails done and dinner while I picked up our rings from the jeweler in Pittsburgh. We're all really close. She's been a part of the family for years."

"Pittsburgh, how far is that from here?" She glanced at Ray. "Two hours?"

"About an hour and a half traffic depending," Ray said.

"So you weren't even here the night that it happened?"

"No, I didn't know until I got home." I wiped a tear from the corner of my sore, irritated eye.

"Could you give us the contact information for the jeweler?"

"Yeah, of course. Anything I can do to help."

"Good. Thank you." She smiled again. It was almost like she was relieved as I was that she wouldn't have to build a case against me. "So now, I'm just gonna go over the basic questions we ask everyone involved in missing persons cases. We got some information from her mom but it's pretty clear that you spend more time with Laila than she does with her family these days." I gave a nod, and she went on, "I normally ask if the person smokes or drinks, but I'm assuming no since she's pregnant?"

"Yeah, she's never been a smoker. She'd occasionally hit a cigarette here and there when she drank before she got pregnant, but it was never habitual. At least, not since I've known her."

"Did she drink a lot before she got pregnant?" she asked.

She did love her liquor. But she wasn't exactly a party girl, at least not since I'd known her. "Sometimes. Usually, she just had a few glasses of wine here and there. But she likes whiskey too."

"What kind of hobbies does Laila have?"

"She writes. Or used to, anyway. She's been stuck in writer's block for a while now."

"What does she write? Does she keep a journal?"

Time to lie my ass off. She'd journaled every case we'd worked for the last three and a half years. She'd journaled our entire life up to that point. She didn't write it all but once a month or so, she'd sit down and recap important things that'd happened. Things she didn't want to forget. Things that she did. She said putting it onto the paper got it out of her head.

But there was no way in hell I was handing those over to the cops. Aside from pictures, that might be all I had left of her soon.

"If she does, I've never seen it. She's a perfectionist, she keeps her stuff pretty private until it's exactly how she wants it. I know she writes a lot of poetry. She helps me write songs sometimes."

Tina nodded, jotting down some notes. "I have her physical description here, but we're missing a few details. Does she have any identifiable marks that make her easier to stand out? Tattoos, piercings, scars? Or birthmarks most people wouldn't see?"

"She has a scar on her chest near her ribs. And a little birthmark by her back dimple."

"Which side?" She scribbled in her notebook.

"Um..." I envisioned her for a moment. "It's on her left. And she got her nose pierced when she was fifteen or something but it's pretty much closed now. On her right nostril. And she has a mole right above her belly button."

She wrote on her papers for a moment. She continued, "Now onto her personality. How would you describe her? Is she outgoing, introverted?"

I gave a chuckle. "Well, she's definitely not an introvert. I don't know if I'd say she's outgoing though. She's friendly but she's not the kind of person who has a lot of friends. Just a lot of friendly acquaintances. But she's a really bubbly, happy person. She's almost always smiling. She's fiery though. She can be pretty spirited."

"In an aggressive way?"

"On some things. She's passionate about a lot of stuff and she has no problem telling you about it."

"Oh, yeah? Like what?"

Another shrug. "Well, she cares a lot about women's rights. And public welfare and the planet. LGBTQ rights, immigration, gun reform, racism. Pretty much anything Bernie Sanders talks about."

She made another note and said, "Is Laila religious?"

Well, she's an Angel but she doesn't really believe in God.

"I guess you could say she's spiritual. She always says that what you put out into the universe will come back to you. Namaste and all that."

Tina scribbled silently for a few ticks. "So what kind of values does she have?"

"I don't know, I guess I'd say loyalty is important to her. Love and compassion are more important than anything else though."

She wrote in her notes a moment longer. "Does she have any health problems, physical or mental? Or medications she's taking?"

"No, she's pretty healthy. Just the prenatals. Oh, but her blood pressure was a little low the last time we went to the doctor. They told her to eat more salt and be careful when she stands up. And she has anxiety, but she doesn't take anything for it."

"Got it," she said. "Do you know what dentist she goes to?"

My heart hurt, realizing why they'd need her dentist's information. Dental records confirm identities on otherwise unidentifiable bodies. I shuddered at the thought.

"I don't know her name, but I can get it when I get home."

"If you could bring us in her toothbrush or hairbrush when you drop that stuff off, it'd be great."

"Sure thing."

Ray's phone buzzed at his hip and Tina's a second later on the table. Ray pulled it from his pants and gazed down at it, glancing at Tina as she looked at hers.

"I'm going to have to take this." Tina stood from the table. "But thank you for your time, Jeremy. We'll let you know as soon as we get some more information. Could you get those details before he leaves, Detective?"

"Sure," Ray said.

"Thanks." She rushed from the room and hastily shut the door behind her.

My heart skipped. I wasn't sure with excitement or fear, but any news would be better than no news. "Is that about Laila?"

"I think so."

CHAPTER THIRTY-SIX

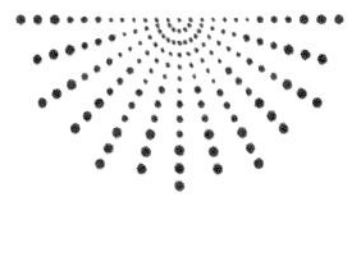

JEREMY

"They found the van," Ramirez murmured with a glance into the busy police station hallway.

"Where? Did they find her?" I asked.

"There's no sign of anyone. The car was abandoned and caught on fire, probably to get rid of any evidence. I think you guys might be able to help with some of your powers."

It felt like my heart was falling. Not with fear, but joy. A lead. "Wyatt and Celena might still be able to pick up her scent."

"That's what I was thinking. I don't know when the area will be clear though, they're not going to let civilians anywhere near it."

"If there's too many people there, it might throw off her scent. I'll get Celena and Wyatt there, you get the area cleared. Text me the address, we'll be there in twenty minutes."

"Twenty minutes isn't enough time—"

"You'll figure it out." I turned away and headed toward the door.

"Jeremy—"

"Thanks, Ray." I shot him a hopeful smile. I practically ran from his office. I lifted my phone from the pocket of my jeans. The tone rang as I paraded my way to the front door.

She'd only been gone for a day and a few hours and I was far from proud of the way I handled it. She'd be so ashamed that I relapsed. Or at least, how *fast* I relapsed.

I could have been doing something productive. But no, I decided to drown it out. I didn't even like drinking that much. But it was better than pills. It was definitely better than a needle, or so I rationalized it.

But I wouldn't fuck up again. I was going to fix this. I was going to bring her home.

And now, I had something to do. I had a lead. I had a way to help.

"Shit, I must have fallen asleep," Leah mumbled on the other end of the phone. "What's going on?"

"They found the car." I opened the door and hopped in. "I'm only a minute or two from the diner so I'll drop off the car and teleport to the house."

"Did they find her? Was she—"

"No, but it's something. Maybe Celena and Wyatt will be able to pick up a trail. Are they at the main house? Or the cabin?"

"Uh, I don't know. Let me call them. Just come here and you can go to the cabin if they're not downstairs."

"Alright, Ramirez needed time to get the area cleared for us anyway. But I'll be there soon."

"Alright. Love you, be careful." She yawned.

"Will do. Love you too." I clicked the shutter button and started the engine.

I quickly reversed from my parking spot and started out of the lot. Cutting the wheel a bit too tight, I peeled some tire as I pulled onto the main road. Not all that heroic or Hollywood—drifting out of a small Pennsylvania police station in a blue 2018 Subaru Forester. But you don't see the truth in movies and TV.

Nothing looks perfect when your life's falling apart.

The actors never have dried snot caked around the edges of their nostrils. They never have red sore spots beside the corner of their eyes from wiping their tears. Only their eyebrows change when they cry. Their lips don't curl upward as they swell, their faces don't turn the color of a tomato. They still look glamorous and stunning.

They don't look the way I looked as I touched sixty-five in that thirty mile per hour zone.

My hair was a greasy mess sticking to the edges of my cheeks like I had just worked a double shift at the diner. The stubble along my cheeks and jaw gradually turned the bottom half of my face a shade of gray from my black hair on my blanched skin. My eyes were red, partially from the sleep deprivation, and partly from the weeping I'd barely stopped since she was gone, and maybe in part from the hang over.

The image of Daniel's back flashed behind my eyelids like a skipping record.

That could be Laila. That could be our son.

My son experiencing anything less than a joyous, happy life was more devastating than the worst thing I could imagine. But the thought of him enduring what Daniel suffered made me sick to my stomach. Any person, especially a child, let alone *my* child, withstanding that kind of terror was the most monstrous thing I could envision.

What the fuck was she thinking? Why didn't she just kill them?

She could have, easily, if she would have listened to me. I told her she needed to perfect her powers, but she was convinced fire was enough. Laila never fucking listened.

I tried to show her, I tried to tell her how much potential she had. But she didn't think she needed it.

She could have used air to push the guns from their hands. She could have teleported them into her own. She could have used telekinesis. She could have used earth to grow a tree fast enough to smack them to the ground, if she wanted to add a flare of drama. Fuck, she could have controlled their minds.

She was stronger than anyone I'd ever met. Laila had a never-ending supply of massive energy and she only used a fraction of it. Not even a fraction. A tiny decimal of what she was capable of.

I tried not to think that way. She was ambushed, she didn't know she'd have to prepare for something like that.

But this wasn't her fault. Not really. Ultimately, I guess it all started with Ray. Then with Leah when we realized they had Chris.

Then mine for not doing more when we realized they knew we were onto them. We set a supply of boundless energy in front of a bunch of strength eating monsters. Laila was like a pot of gold to anyone looking for power. She was pregnant with the most powerful child the world had ever seen, in addition to everything she was capable of.

I should've never let this happen.

CHAPTER THIRTY-SEVEN

JEREMY

Everything looked the same as it did in the spot where Laila was taken yesterday. They were smart. The area was densely covered in vegetation, even for the early spring. The road was desolate, it'd be the perfect place to do anything they wouldn't want a passerby to see.

The smell of burned plastic filled the air and swayed into my nostrils. I studied the still smoldering vehicle. The sun had already set so the only light was Ray's flashlight, the ball of energy I held in my hand, and the orange embers that remained on the side of the van. Smoke still floated through the air above it, adding to the large black cloud that had alerted others to its location.

"It looks like the fire was set from the inside." Ray shined his light along the black, smog coated exterior doors. "Do you think Laila set it?"

"There'd be bodies," I said. "She didn't use her powers. Either she was unconscious, or she couldn't."

"The smell of the gas makes it pretty obvious it wasn't Laila," Wyatt muttered.

"Can I see her sweater?" Celena reached toward me for the bag that hung over my shoulder. "I think it's gonna rain soon. I don't want anything to get washed away."

I closed the ball of energy inside my hand. I pulled my backpack off my shoulder. I reached inside and passed her the cotton jacket.

"She was wearing this yesterday, right?" Wyatt asked as Celena sniffed.

"Yeah, right before she left with Hannah."

"Do you smell that?" Celena looked up at Wyatt.

He handed the jacket back to me and gave a nod. "Barely. But yeah."

"She was here," Celena said. "Something of hers' still is, I think."

A hopeful swirl spun in my stomach. She was there. We had something. Barely a shred, but something.

"You're sure?" I asked.

"Pretty sure," she said. "We should shift."

"In a minute." Wyatt took a step around the vehicle and kept walking until he was at the front.

"Do you have something?"

"Maybe," Wyatt said. He pulled a ball of swirling blue energy to his hand and lowered it as a light, bringing himself to his knees.

Celena took a few steps forward sniffing the air. "What is it?"

He extinguished the electricity. Celena crouched beside him. "Bring that flashlight over here, Ray." Ramirez walked around the car and aimed the light toward the ground. "You smell that, right?"

"There's something but it's faint. Maybe a piece of hair or something."

"But definitely something."

Ray handed him the flashlight. She lowered her head to the ground, squinting as she felt around.

"Do you have gloves?" Wyatt asked.

"You need to keep everything exactly where it is." Ramirez reached into his back pocket and passed Wyatt a pair of blue, nitrile gloves.

"Your guys won't find it here. My nose is better than their dogs, trust me. I'm just gonna move it somewhere slightly more visible."

"What is it?" I asked.

Wyatt pulled the glove over his hand and reached underneath. He shimmied a bit, army crawling until half of his body was beneath it. A second later, he squirmed out from under and sat up holding a small orange cap between his forefinger and thumb. He looked inside it and then back up to Ray. "It may not be much, but her DNA is in this."

I knew all too well what that orange piece of plastic was. A needle cap. Me and those little pieces of plastic went way back.

"Can you smell what it was? That they injected her with, I mean."

Wyatt shook his head. "Mom was always covered in different drugs from the hospital. I can't differentiate between most of them."

"Let me see," Celena said. She took a glove from Ray's hand and pulled it over her fingertips. "I wasn't a wolf yet when Kay was sick, but it might trigger something."

He handed it to her. She raised it to her nose and carefully took a deep breath in with closed eyes.

She paused for a moment, squinting in thought. After raising it back to her nose, she continued, "It's a benzo. A really strong one. It starts with a C, I think?"

"Clonazepam? Or maybe Klonopin?" Being an addict basically made me a walking drug encyclopedia. Usually didn't do much good but sometimes it was convenient.

"Yeah, that's it," she said.

"They were trying to calm her down?" Ray asked.

"They were trying to knock her out. This is a high milligram. God only knows how much they gave her."

"Why not use trazodone? Or ketamine even?" Ray asked. "They'd act faster and be more effective."

"They could cause birth defects," I murmured. My eyes widened. "They don't want to hurt the baby."

She nodded. "That'd be my best guess."

Wyatt brought himself to his feet. He took the cap from her fingers and set it against the rear tire. "When you guys are checking out the site, make sure to point that out if they don't find it."

"Will do," Ray said.

Celena wandered in front of the van to look for tire tracks.

"Do you smell something?" I asked close behind her.

"Just looking," she murmured with a gaze at the ground. "The kidnappers had already pulled off the road. If they were switching cars, the other driver wouldn't have pulled off. They would have stayed on the road to easily take off once the transport took place."

"Yeah, that'd make the most sense," I said.

She squinted, making the same face Laila did when she focused. Her nose wiggled and she sniffed again.

"What is it?" I asked.

"It isn't Laila." She sniffed. "But I smell something. It could be the car burning but..."

"What do you smell, darlin'?" Wyatt asked.

Celena's brows creased in focus, looking around. "When I was a kid, we had this one piece of shit car that kept breaking down on us. We usually kept it in the garage, but Dad moved a bunch of shit in there, so we had to park in the driveway. The car was leaking oil and Mom kept bitching about it ruining the fresh cement. He let me help him work on it one day. And when he revved up the engine, blue smoke shot out of the exhaust. That smoke, it had a very particular smell to it."

"My charger did that a few years back," I said. "And you smell that now?"

Celena walked across the street. Her eyes stayed shut while she inhaled. She continued sniffing the air for a few seconds. Slowly, she meandered along the yellow lines.

After a few long cricket chirps in the distance, she leaned down. "I think I found something."

We followed behind her and lowered ourselves to the ground. There was an oil spot on the cracked cement about the four inches in diameter.

"What is it?" Ray asked.

"A car that was leaking oil stopped here for a minute or two," Celena said. "I can't be sure it was them, but there's no stop sign nearby and no road to turn onto."

"Could they have stopped for an animal?" Ray asked.

"Must have been a slow animal." She stood. "I'd say they were stopped for at least two minutes to accumulate that much oil. How often does it take more than thirty seconds to get an animal off the road when you're driving?"

"That's genius." A breath I didn't realize stopped in my chest left my smiling lips. My heart skipped with excitement. "Can you guys follow it?"

"I think so." She glanced at Wyatt.

"Good eye, darling."

CHAPTER THIRTY-EIGHT

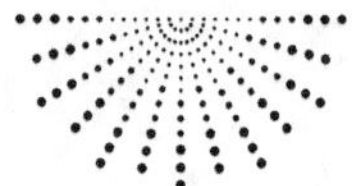

EARLY MORNING MARCH 11 - LAILA

LAILA

The bright, bluish fluorescent lights shined into my eyes. It was like accidentally opening them in a tanning bed after forgetting goggles. I blinked and tried to raise my arms to cover my face, but my wrist caught on something cold.

I pulled forward again. But the same cold touch pressed against my chest, and my hips, and my ankles. Brisk, clean-smelling air caressed my bare skin. A cold chill rose over every pore of my body.

I blinked fast in attempt to look away from the blinding light. My heart thudded against my naked chest. I shivered. I felt my teeth start to chatter in a combination of fear and a struggle to retain warmth.

"Well, good morning, Miss Callidy," a man's voice said above me. My vision was starting to adjust but I still couldn't make out much. Just the outline of a man and the slightest hint of my reflection in a pair of glasses. "Sleep well?"

I fought against the restraints again. "Where am I? Who are you?"

He chuckled. I looked for him through the bright light, trying to make out his face. "My name's Doctor Robert Peterson. It's a pleasure to meet you, really. Well, we've met before. But you wouldn't remember that." His steady hands tried to place a needle into the crease between my forearm and bicep, but I wiggled against the table. "Truly, a pleasure though. You look different than I expected. Sweeter."

"If you knew who I was, then you'd think a little harder before you treated me like this," I snapped. My shackled hand shimmied against his that strived to jab my veins.

He gripped my arm so tight that I instantly knew it would bruise. Anger flooded over me and I tried to pull a flame to my hand.

But I couldn't.

I tried to see his face but the light hanging above me was too bright to see anything. Although, I was almost thankful for it. Because my naked body was freezing, and it was my only source of heat.

"Out there, you're powerful. But here, you're just like everyone else. Kind of, anyway." He squeezed harder and jammed the needle into my skin. "It's not worth the battle, Laila. I have my ways of suppressing your abilities."

"What did you give me?" I said between chattering teeth. He pulled a tube from my arm and turned. My vision adjusted a bit, but he became a mere blur behind the sharp, dentist like light above me.

"Relax, I'm not gonna hurt the baby. Just some benzos. Something I know you're familiar with. They're safe during pregnancy. He may be born addicted, but the withdrawals are survivable if he's monitored. Which he will be."

Janis Wilson's voice echoed through my mind. *"You're carrying one very powerful child."* Maybe it had nothing to do with me. Maybe it was all about my son.

"Why do you care about him?"

He turned back to me. I got my first good look at him. Oddly enough, he wasn't unattractive. Quite the opposite, I hate to admit. At least, in a boring, dorky kind of way. He couldn't be past forty judging by his frosty black hair and beard. His lips weren't big but thick enough that they were still attractive. His tiny nose appeared almost dainty on his strong jaw and nasal root. I couldn't make out the color of his eyes, but they seemed dark behind his thick black glasses. Beneath his white coat, I noted his small, bony frame.

"I know who you are, Laila." He smiled, pushing his glasses up the bridge of his nose. "Everyone knows who you are where I'm from. You're one of the most influential people to ever walk this planet. Or any planet, for that matter."

I swallowed hard and creased my brows at a painful twinge at the back of my head.

"So is Jeremy. But he would've been too hard to get now. He's an experienced fighter and he's ruthless when it comes to protecting you. Plus, the two of you together, you would feed off of one another. It would make concealing our location far more difficult." He raised his arms in a gesture around. He shrugged. "I don't need him anyway."

Damn it, he knew what we were.

"Besides, I already have his brother who has the same powers as him. And that extra flare he gets from you isn't something I could use." He reached forward to put a piece of gauze and tape against the bleeding spot on my arm. "And this baby, a product of you, with his power too..." He smiled and his head shook. "Let's just say that I consider myself blessed to play a part in all of this."

"You're not going to touch my son," I growled.

He chuckled and pushed hair from my face with his other hand. His skin on my cheek made my stomach hurt. "Our intentions are good, Laila."

Our. He said *our*. He wasn't working alone, but he certainly was the figurehead.

"You killed Daniel," I said behind my gritted teeth. "You tortured him for years. Your men were going to kill Hannah. You don't have a good bone in your body."

"No, we just knew you wouldn't let her die. But that child wasn't your son. He barely had any power and never would. That won't happen to this baby. He's important." He pulled his hand away and reached to the table nearby. He slid another glove on.

"You torture, you kill." My teeth clicked together, quivering in the cold air. "You're evil. You'll never lay a hand on my child."

He frowned and met my gaze again. "That isn't justified. I haven't hurt you."

"You killed Daniel," I yelled, angrily ripping against the restraints.

"I didn't realize he'd mean so much to you," he murmured. "It was simply damage control, Laila."

"He was a person." Tears stung my eyes. I blinked at them quickly, writhing forward only to bruise myself against the metal holding me down. "A beautiful, sweet, kind little boy. And you fucking murdered him."

"Well, not me personally," he muttered. "But I do apologize if his death has affected you in a negative way. That wasn't my intent."

Affected me in a negative way. The child I'd been taking care of for more than a month was just murdered and he expected it to not *"affect me in a negative way."*

"Fuck you," I spat.

"I think we've gotten off on the wrong foot. I don't want you to resent the situation you're in. This is an opportunity for you."

"An opportunity for what?" My eyes darted around. "To be your little lab rat? Why the fuck would I want this?"

"Because of what the future has in store for us." He smiled. "You're far from an experiment. You will bring light to this world, Laila. I want to be a part of your story."

"You're psychotic," I said.

"The others here, they're a part of the story too. But you, you're the center of it." He chuckled, seemingly unfazed by my rage. Justifiably, I suppose. I was the one tied to a table after all. "You're going to do amazing things one day, Miss Callidy."

"I'm going to destroy you," I said with pride—as if I wasn't the one lying out before him to do whatever he pleased with.

He frowned for a moment. It turned to a soft laugh. "You can try. And one day you will. But not any time soon."

I narrowed my gaze. "What are you doing? What's your purpose in this?"

He gave a soft smile. "That's a complex question. One day, I'll answer it for you. But what I will say for now, you have more potential than you can even begin to imagine. And I'm going to help you. The other little monsters, they don't need my help the way that you do. But you, Laila Callidy…" His smile widened. "You have so much to learn. I sat around for a while waiting for you to improve but you haven't. Now is the time. You have to be ready. The shift isn't too far in the distance now, and if you aren't ready… Well, let's just say that I'd hate to see what that world looks like."

One day. That was practically Peterson's catchphrase. One day, one day, *one* day.

"If I'm not ready for what?" I snapped.

He held his smile. "The rest of them, the abominations, they'll be yours one day. You'll bring them purity."

"Are you hearing yourself?" My eyes heated up and shined a bright green toward him. "You capture us, you torture us, you murder us. And yet, *we* are abominations?"

"Not you." He smiled, eyes sliding along my naked body. "The Fae are a beautiful race. Truly magnificent. I've only ever met a handful. Your kind has always captivated me." He looked back up to meet my gaze. "But you especially. You'll understand what makes you so important one day soon, I'm sure."

My eyes glowed with fury. "Watch yourself, Doctor. You have no idea what I'm capable of."

"That's just it, Laila. I don't think *you* know what you're capable of." He licked his smiling lips. "I know you better than you know yourself."

"Fuck you," I said.

And *that* was my catchphrase.

His smile widened. "You are infinitely powerful. In another life, they'd call you a goddess. If you had any idea what you were doing with your powers, you could escape this effortlessly in a million different ways. But I've been studying you. I know you only know how to use your fire. You're amazing with it, but you'll be just as powerful with every other element once I'm done with you. And your mother, she's an old, extremely powerful Angel. Her powers alone are almost limitless. But her power, plus your father's, and your grandmother's…" He leaned closer and cupped my cheek in his hand. His dark hazel eyes met mine. "I want to watch you grow. I want to help you learn to be the most powerful creature this world has ever seen."

I pulled my face away to look the opposite direction. Out of the corner of my eye, I saw him shake his head and reach to the table.

Metal clanged as he said, "I wish I could say this isn't going to hurt, but you're tough. I think you can handle it."

I turned back to see what he was doing. He grasped my arm. He pulled two Velcro straps that laid beneath my arm around my bicep and wrist so the lighter, blue vein covered side faced him.

"What are you doing?" I vigorously shook my head.

He raised a scalpel to my arm. "It's just a couple cuts. It'll be over in no time."

I'll never forget the feel of that cool metal just before it sliced into my skin. The cold hurt worse than the cut itself.

I'd been stabbed or impaled with objects a number of times. But in those situations, I was actively fighting. My blood boiled, my arms licked with flames, and I usually had a knife in my hand. I could fight back.

But not from that table.

That scalpel was so cold.

For the first time since I discovered my abilities, I remembered how it felt to be completely powerless.

I can still hear the sound of my scream as I watched that metal slowly nudge deeper into my skin. I can still see the look of sadistic joy on his face as his tongue ran along his lips.

I fought against the tight straps that held me down to no success. "You can scream, if it makes you feel better." He pulled away and set the scalpel on the small rolling table beside him. "But no one's going to help you. And I don't mind."

"Just let me go," I begged. "Please, just let me go."

He chuckled. His fingers gently tapped my bleeding arm with a piece of gauze on a set of metal tongs. "Oh, Laila. We haven't even gotten to the worst part yet."

He laid the gauze down and raised a small black object smaller than a dime to his fore finger and thumb. His blue, gloved fingers reached forward, pointer and middle finger on either side of the inch and a half slit on my wrist.

He met my gaze. He ripped the skin apart. The pain sliced up my arm.

I screamed so loud, watching him smile as he stuck his fingers with the little black dot into my flesh.

CHAPTER THIRTY-NINE

JEREMY

JEREMY

I trailed behind Celena and Wyatt as they trotted through the woods following a scent my nose wasn't able to detect. Once they got out of my vision, I teleported to them. Then did the same thing again once they were out of my sight.

They ran faster than anything I'd ever seen, even faster than other werewolves. I supposed the bond affected all of their abilities. Celena dashed just a few yards in front of Wyatt, no matter how hard he tried to get ahead. It made sense. She weighed far less, and her legs were longer.

But it clearly irritated him. In human form, he may not have even realized he felt that way. But as a wolf, he almost looked insulted. The dominant wolf leads the pack. I'm sure Celena didn't realize that, but even if she did, I doubted she'd slow down for him. If she was anything like Laila, she already knew she was the one in control.

I held their clothes, keeping moving. I was getting dizzy, standing still for a moment and swirling a few feet down the way as they sped past me.

Normally, I'd be fine doing it. It was pretty easy with all things considered.

Nevertheless, I was exhausted. My vision began to distort around the edges. My legs started to feel like jello. My fingers tingled. My heavy eyelids rubbed against my irises like sandpaper.

Although, I knew if I lay down, I'd stare up at the ceiling for hours.

Emotionally, I was even more drained. I felt throbbing at various places all over, stinging in others, and aches on nearly every surface of my skin. But they weren't my wounds.

I could hear her crying sometimes.

I couldn't reach her mind though. It was like a one-way link. My end was working but her line just wasn't picking up my half of the signal.

All I wanted to do was hold her. I wanted to take her to Leah or Kai to be healed and make the pain go away. I wanted her to be safe. I wanted to take the pain away.

I just wanted things back to where they were.

We were happy. We were in love. We were comfortable. We were perfect.

I was finally going to have the big, happy family I always wanted. But now, I had a feeling that wasn't going to happen. At least, not any time soon.

After about forty-five minutes of teleporting, Wyatt and Celena slowed to a halt. Then they both turned toward me. Wyatt jumped at my legs, pawing at his clothes in my hands.

"Oh, shit. Sorry. Here." I set them on the ground and turned away. "I'll just stand over there for a minute."

There were some groans and grumbles accompanied by cracks and snaps as they shifted. A moment or so later, I heard them rustling with their clothes. Then Wyatt called, "Alright, we're good."

I started toward them. Wyatt buttoned his pants and met my gaze. "You traced it to here?" I asked.

"A few hundred yards from here." Celena gestured behind her, zipping up her jacket.

"Do you smell Laila?" I asked.

"Yeah, I got a whiff of something, but she's not here anymore," Wyatt said

Guessed it was what I'd expected. It'd been just over twenty-four hours since she disappeared. We were in Ohio, only about two and a half hours from home. If someone was going to kidnap Laila Callidy, they weren't gonna keep her that close. And certainly not thirty minutes by car from the place they switched vehicles.

But maybe they switched cars again. Maybe they realized they were leaking oil and stopped to get a new ride. Maybe we weren't too far behind their trail.

The two of them exchanged an odd look before turning back to me. "Do you hear that, Jeremy?"

I listened a bit closer. There was something of a hum, or a whir, followed by a loud, low pitched screech. It came from above. I looked up. I watched a passenger airplane rise over the tree line.

Time stood still in that moment. We weren't at an abandoned house or industrial building. It wasn't a cabin in the woods. Whoever had taken her thought big. Large, open skies big.

"No," I said. "No, she can't be... Planes can go so far so fast. It's been a day; she could be in Tokyo by now—"

Wyatt grabbed my shoulders and met my gaze. His firm eyes moved between mine. His hands clasped on my shoulders were practically the only things keeping me vertical. "If they did take her somewhere, they probably left a paper trail. If we figure out who, we can figure out where, right?"

"Let's call Ray. He's gonna need to know where to go," Celena said.

"Why don't we check it out now?" I asked. "If she's still here—"

"She isn't here, Jeremy." Celena looked behind her and sniffed a few times. "But she was. Most airports have security cameras, right? They'll have some proof of Laila being moved. They might even know where the plane was going. But if we are on those same cameras, we'll have to break in and delete it. Then they'll have nothing."

I paused in thought for a moment. "But a wolf could walk in there. That wouldn't give us away, right? We could—"

"We could get shot, man," Wyatt said with a shake of his head.

"What would an armed person do if they came across a wolf? Let alone a wolf indoors?"

It's not like I could expect them to risk their lives for Laila. I didn't even give Laila the opportunity to risk her life for theirs.

"Yeah. Yeah, you're right. I'm sorry, I'm not thinking straight."

He gave my shoulder one last squeeze. "You need to sleep. And eat. Let's go home. We'll tell Ramirez what we found, they'll investigate, and by the morning, we'll have more to go on. But we all need to breathe for a minute. It's been a long night. We'll have clearer heads in the morning. Alright?"

I wanted to storm that place. I wanted to teleport inside and search every square inch. But they were right. The law was involved, and we knew she wasn't there. They didn't smell her, and I couldn't feel her. On top of that, I was no good to her nodded out from exhaustion or vomiting from hunger and dehydration.

"Yeah. Yeah, okay."

I lay on the old couch, leather sticking to the small of my back where my shirt rode up. My hand floated to my mouth holding a blunt between my middle and forefinger. I took in a long, deep drag. It burned but I didn't have the willpower to sit up and cough.

My gaze shifted to the clock to check the time. 12:24.

In five hours, I would have been awake for two days straight. I was drained but every time I closed my eyes, I felt wider awake.

I reached for my phone and clicked the home button. I swiped to my photo gallery. It was practically a shrine to Laila. Every single photo of her had a memory I associated with it, even the less flattering ones I couldn't bring myself to delete.

I scrolled to a picture I'd taken last week of her with Daniel. She looked beautiful. She hated it because she was looking down at him, and she had "like, a million chins," but I didn't even see a second.

All that I saw was her great big smile as Daniel reached up and clutched her cheek with a grin. Her long black hair was lifted into a messy bun. She wasn't wearing any make up, but she looked adorable. And happy.

In just one week, or one day really, all that changed.

Footsteps creaked down the stairs a few feet away. I exhaled the smoke and took another drag before the rest had even left my lungs.

"Can't sleep?" Brody headed toward the couch behind me. He leaned over the back. He looked down at me, reaching for the blunt.

"Pretty much." I passed it to him.

"Me neither," he muttered. "I wish I could, but my brain won't shut off."

"You're telling me." I rubbed my eyes and sat up. He walked around the couch to sit beside me.

"Did you guys find anything?" he asked.

"Maybe. We found a needle cap with her blood and clonazepam on it. At least, that's what Celena thought it was."

"Something, I guess."

It wasn't much. All it proved was that we knew that van was the one that took her. It didn't give us anything else. "And a trail. We think it's from the car they moved Laila into. It led to an airport. Ray's trying to lead them there now."

"You guys didn't check it out?" Brody asked.

"Would've been too hard to cover up if we got caught. We're too close to the investigation to go unnoticed."

"Yeah, probably so."

He took in a long hit and gazed ahead for a moment. I studied his expression. I'm sure it was a lot like I looked. His wavy black hair was a mess of knots laying against his ears. Dark purple, nearly black circles drooped beneath his eyelids. His lips were chapped around the edges and his dry cheeks were beginning to flake away.

That was a rarity for my little brother. He always looked like he was prepared for a job interview. He, Hannah, and Chris always had that in common. More like our dad in that way. I suppose Adam and I were messier like our mom.

"You miss her," I murmured.

"Everyone misses her."

"But it's different for you." I took the blunt from his fingers. "You miss her like I miss her. Everyone else just loves her. We're *in* love with her."

His sad, shame filled eyes moved between mine. "I don't want to be."

That expression ached my heart. His brows pinched, his lips pressed together, his head tilted slightly downward. As if I was upset with him. It's ironic now to think back on considering where he'd be in a few more years. But it made my chest hurt. I didn't *like* that he had a thing for my fiancé. That didn't mean I held it against him though.

"You can relax." I chuckled. "I'm not gonna punch you again."

He was quiet for a moment. "I never planned on it, Jeremy. She actually annoyed me a lot in the beginning." I laughed and he smiled. "But I got to know her. Even now, there's a lot of things I hate about her. But there's so much more to her once you see past the bubbly, happy go lucky demeanor."

"What do you hate about her?" I grabbed my water off the table and took a sip. He looked at me puzzled for a minute. "You said, 'even now, there's things you hate about her.' What are they?"

"Oh. I don't know. How much she relies on you. The way she drives. How she never listens to anyone but her damn self. The fact that she rolls better joints than me." He met my gaze with a soft smile that I returned. Wasn't wrong about that, Laila rolled a damn good joint. "How she loves you and not me." I couldn't help the face I made at that one. "How stupid she is sometimes."

My expression grew defensive. "She's not stupid."

"Not *actually* stupid. She knows a lot of things; she knows how the world works. She's really smart. She just doesn't think before she acts and it's annoying. She makes rash decisions based on a moment's consideration. Like last year, that thing with the Siren?"

"Probably shouldn't go there, Brody."

He licked his lips and gave a nod.

Not that I wanted to argue but that was far more on him than it was her. I knew she'd have been hurt regardless of how she found out, but if I'd have been the one to tell her, if she didn't think I was hiding it;

things would have gone a lot different. And given the situation, I felt obligated to defend her. Even if part of me was upset over the rash decision she made that led us to where we were.

"Every decision she makes that seems stupid, she made for a reason. When she broke up with me, she thought she was protecting herself from more pain. She didn't have any reason to explain what she saw in *your* head."

"Yeah. You're right."

"And she let them take her because she didn't want them to kill Hannah and Daniel. Our sister is alive because of her." I said it in defense of her. But it almost felt like I was trying to convince myself more than him.

"Daniel's not," he muttered.

My hand instinctively tightened. "That wasn't her fault—"

"No, of course not. That's not what I'm saying, Jeremy. Not at all," Brody said

I hit the blunt, watching his concerned expression. "What are you saying then?"

"If you were in her shoes, would you have believed they weren't going to hurt them? Or would you have just killed them?" His gaze searched mine for a moment.

I squinted a bit. "You would have let them kill Daniel and Hannah?"

"I wouldn't have given them the time to touch either of them. Neither would you. And neither of us are even half as powerful as her."

He wasn't wrong. The second I saw that van, my head would have gone to Leah's description from Cage's thoughts, and I would have teleported out. Or in her case, called me. Or slammed the car in reverse and hightailed it to the shopping center she just left. Or locked the doors. Or a million other things *besides* getting in that van.

But hell. If I were the one carrying our child? Maybe I would've handed over my soon-to-be sister-in-law and foster kid. Awful as it may have been, I may have done it. Because I'd watch the world burn if it meant saving my son.

I looked down. "She's always been too compassionate."

Brody's voice was soft. "I guess it's not that I hate how stupid she is. I hate how naïve she is."

"That's fair."

He gazed at the ground for a moment. He looked up to me. "Isn't it weird for you?"

"Hmm?" I asked.

"The way I feel about Laila," he said. "Doesn't it bother you?"

I gave a smile and shook my head. "Not really. She's perfect. Part of me wonders why everyone isn't in love with her." A faint smile pulled at his lips. "If she would have had a history with you, or feelings for you, I'd feel differently. But she doesn't, not in a romantic way." I felt a twinge of guilt as he tried not to frown. "You're my little brother, Brody. I'm never going to hate you because of who you love. But I do wish it were someone else. Not because I blame you or because I'm angry with you for loving her."

He took a hit. "What is it then?"

"Because she's never going to feel the way about you that you feel about her. Maybe if she and I weren't what we are, she'd give you a chance. Because I do know that she loves you. I'm sure some part of her could have loved you instead of me. If you met her first. But with her moral compass, knowing what it would do to me..." I said. "She wouldn't cross that line. She wouldn't hurt me like that. Not after all the time we've been together, not after everything we've been through."

"You don't think I know that?" He turned his sad gaze to meet mine. "I know her, Jeremy. I know how she feels about me. I know how she feels about you. Nothing and no one could ever compare to you, even if you weren't together. Believe me, I know that." He chuckled. "What do you think? That I just chose to fall in love with her? That I wanted to love my brother's soulmate that I knew I'd never have a chance with? I wish I didn't, Jeremy. I wouldn't have chosen this just for the hell of it. But it just happened."

I took a hit, watching the smoke drift in the wind before me. "I don't blame you. She's easy to love."

"She really is."

Silence crept in for a moment as we passed the blunt back and forth. I cleared my throat. "I wish I wouldn't have sent her out with Hannah," I muttered. "If she would've been with me, there's no way I would've let them take her. I would have died first."

"You can't think like that," Brody said.

A thought dawned on me then.

I sat forward, head cocked to the side. "Laila and I are always together, right? Like, we're almost never apart. And when we are, we're never more than ten minutes by car."

His brows lowered in focus. "Yeah, the two of you are together more than you're apart."

I blinked hard a few times, glancing around the room. "So how would they have known I wasn't with her?" I paused for a moment. "They had to have been watching us."

"They have a Witch working with them, right?"

"They have to. I don't know how they'd be able to block their location without one."

"What if they bound themselves to Daniel?" he asked. "They could see through his eyes. They must have planned it out for the one-time Laila was with Hannah and no one else knowing that Hannah doesn't have active powers and couldn't defend herself."

"That could mean that there's still traces left of the Witch's power in Daniel's body." I sat forward. "If Ramirez can get us to Daniel's body, and I can get another Witch to cast a spell, we might be able to get a remnant of their power."

He smiled wide. "And do a location spell on them."

"I should call Olivia." I reached for my phone.

"Laila would love that," he muttered.

I narrowed my gaze. "Laila knows I don't have feelings for her."

"Maybe, but it's clear that she has feelings for you. She bashes Laila at every opportunity she gets. You think she's going to devote herself to finding the girl who has everything she wants?"

"If it's to help me."

He made a face. "I don't think you should talk to Olivia right now, man."

"It's not like I'm going to hook up with her, Brody. I can't even think about sex right now—"

"That's not what I meant."

I turned my head to the side a bit. "What did you mean then?"

"She's a physician's assistant. She has access to a lot of drugs."

"I'm not going to relapse, Brody."

His eyes flooded with disappointment. "You already did, dude."

"That was alcohol."

"Just because it wasn't your drug of choice doesn't mean it wasn't a relapse."

"If you're going about it the NA way," I said. "But if we go by that logic, I've never been clean." I gestured to the blunt.

"Weed and alcohol aren't the same thing."

I bit my tongue. "Fine. You're right, I fucked up. But I'm not going to do it again. It was a momentary lapse in judgment."

It wasn't just a momentary lapse.

When life was good, when I was happy, I didn't want to get high. A small part of me did from time to time, but mostly, it was just that small fraction.

When I met Laila, I'd been clean for almost three years. The only reason I chose to stop using then was because Aunt Annie begged me to days before she died. She was the closest thing to a parent I could remember, and I had to honor her somehow. I wanted to use every day from the day I got clean until I met Laila. The urges still wandered in my mind but nothing like they had before.

She gave me a reason to stay clean. She only knew sober Jeremy and she loved him. I didn't, but she did.

She was like my new drug. I didn't know how to function without her. It was pathetic, I knew that. I knew it was dangerously codependent. I knew it was toxic to put my happiness in another person the way that I had.

Granted, even when she broke up with me, I stayed sober. Because she was still there. She wasn't my girlfriend, but she was there. She was safe.

She was gone this time. The only tie to her I had now were the throbs and stings of her healing cuts.

When I hated my life, I loved drugs. My love for life was dissipating and my joy for getting fucked up was like a seed sprouting from the soil once more.

CHAPTER FORTY

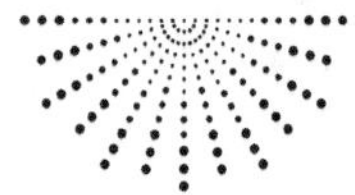

I gazed down at my arms. Hope of Jeremy finding me was beginning to fade. If he could have, he would have already. And it was my fault. As that humbling realization rained down, I realized for the first time since I discovered my abilities, that I was going to have a scar. Leah always healed any major wound I got in a fight. But she wasn't around to heal these.

I imagined what they'd look like once they mended. On either wrist, just below my hand, rested a slit somewhere between an inch and a half to two inches long. The skin around it was swollen and thick. Thin black pieces of thread held it together like the button on my jeans after Thanksgiving dinner.

The same slits appeared further up, one on each bicep. One at the base of my throat just above where my neck met my chest. Then one in the center of my ribs. Two more on the top of either thigh. Then two more on my calves. And one on each foot.

Twelve total.

Twelve massive scars I'd have to live with every day for the rest of my life. If I did manage to find a way to escape, my wardrobe would have to vastly shift. And I'd have to buy a whole hell of a lot of chokers.

"What did they do to me?" I asked, raising my voice for Chris to hear. "What did they put inside me?"

"They're implants," he said. "They put them in all of us."

"What kind of implant?"

"Morion and hematite, I think," he said. "I don't know for sure, but they dull our powers."

I pulled a flame to my fingertips. "They don't dull mine."

I didn't even have a hold on my Guardian abilities. Peterson knew very well that I was Fae. They had to have had a bigger purpose than just dulling our Guardian abilities.

"What are you? Guardian powers are nothing with them."

I huffed. "A mutt."

"What do you mean?"

"I'm part Fae, part Guardian, and part Angel."

"Holy shit," he said. "What blood line?"

I prepared for the backlash. As powerful as I should have been only to end up tied to a table and butchered like an animal.

"I'm Elite."

"Jesus Christ. How did they even capture you? You could've killed them all in seconds."

I could practically hear Jeremy's voice in my head. Telling me to go practice with Kai. Telling me to learn air so I could fly. Telling me to master water and air together so I could take us scuba diving without the equipment.

Then me telling him, "What's the rush?"

"I haven't perfected most of my abilities."

"Why the hell not?"

"I don't know, because I'm a fucking idiot. Most of the time, my ability to control fire has been enough. I've been able to get a good handle on air and I'm in touch with spirit pretty well, but that's about it."

"Well, that's stupid," he said. "My family didn't force you to learn?"

"It's pretty hard to force me into anything." I chuckled at the irony as my fingers traced the stitches on my right arm. "No one in your family has my powers, they didn't know how to teach me. My brother does. But he's not exactly pushy."

"What about Mary? She could have helped you with the angel side of things."

She had tried to teach me a thing or two in the past. But I was a little bitch who got annoyed and stomped her feet when it didn't work as I expected it to. "Mary's been out of the picture for a while."

"Oh God, is she okay?" he asked quickly. "She isn't dead, is she?"

"No, she's fine," I muttered. "Just a snake."

"What do you mean?"

"It's kind of a long story," I said.

"If you haven't noticed, we've got nothing but time here."

I chuckled. "Well, last October, my life—all of our lives—I guess, kind of flipped upside down. Mary told us we needed to investigate this breach. Apparently, someone had entered the earth plane and..." I paused and thought for a moment. "This is really hard to explain."

"Take your time, I've got all day."

I delved deep into the story. I explained what happened from the moment that Jeremy got home to the moment Mary insisted not to look for Chris. I told him what she'd told me at Moe's funeral. He asked questions, he put in his two cents.

We talked because talking was better than staring at the sewn flesh. It took my mind off of where we were and what I'd done to end up there. But as I finished, he grew quiet for a moment. After a long pause, he finally broke the silence.

"Maybe she knew this would happen to you. Maybe she was trying to protect you from what's about to happen."

"What's about to happen?" A long moment of anticipation passed, heart racing faster with each millisecond before I said, "Chris?"

"The stress tests."

CHAPTER FORTY-ONE

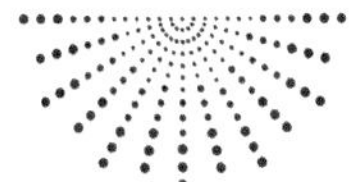

MARCH 12, 2019 - JEREMY

Ray and I leaned against the brick wall of the local hospital. Rain drizzled down and tapped my hands. I wished I'd have worn a longer jacket. The sun was shining a touch, but it was still so gloomy. Hospitals always were, I guessed, but it looked even sadder that day.

The smell of Ray's cigarette whooshed my way. He offered me one. I wasn't a smoker anymore; I'd only smoked for a couple of years in high school. But it was a hell of a day.

As I took one from the pack, I muttered, "I didn't know you smoked."

"I usually don't." He flicked his lighter, holding it in front of the cigarette. He handed it to me and sat. "But I can't drink on the job, so here we are."

I lowered myself to the short retaining wall beside him. My thumb struck it to a flame, and I lit the end. "I can relate." I took in a drag and tossed him his lighter. "Did you find anything?"

"Kind of."

"What is it?"

"Well, it's not good or bad really. Just something." I waited. "We followed that trail, the burnt oil Celena and Wyatt tracked. We had to wait for a warrant to search the airport. We got a judge to sign off and raided it. We found the car they used."

Sounded like good news but his bleak face said otherwise. "That's good, right?"

He rubbed against the back of his neck. "The plates were fake, and every VIN number had been scratched off. Even the one on the engine block, under the spare tire, the rear wheel well, the door. These fuckers are great at covering their tracks."

"And you're sure it was the car?" I asked.

"We found her clothes inside. The dog picked up her scent right away."

So, they changed her clothes. They, because I knew Laila wouldn't have done anything willingly. Not without something hanging over her head. She knew Hannah was safe, she'd seen Daniel die. I doubted she was being a peaceful prisoner.

I cringed. She was drugged. In the back of a car. Then they stripped her and changed her clothes.

Trying to get that thought from my mind, I said, "Were there cameras? Did you see anything on them?"

He huffed. "Every camera conveniently shut off from nine p.m. to nine a.m. the night she disappeared."

"What about flight logs?"

"It's a private airport. They aren't required to take meticulous record of what goes in and out."

"They have to have leasing records or something."

"They do. But they don't record everything that touches down and leaves. Our forensics are looking into them now. But in all honesty, I doubt they used a real identity to set up arrangements to fly in and out. If they went so far as to scratch the VIN of an engine block, why the hell would they use a traceable alias?"

I squeezed my quivering hand in my hoodie pocket to a fist. It was starting to feel like we'd never find her. She'd only been gone for a day and a half, but we were coming back to the same place we'd been for months. A trail that clearly shows what happened. But one that ended at a thick door that we couldn't get through. They were right there on the other end, but we didn't have the key to pass through it.

"What about witnesses? Employees at the airport?" I asked.

"Well, there was one person we attempted to question. He was wearing a uniform like Hannah described. Almost military, but not military. But when he saw us, he shot himself in the head."

I guess he was committed to his cause.

"But that's not the weird part. You know what is?" Ray met my gaze with creased brows.

"No, what?"

"His fingerprints were burnt off. None of his teeth were original, they're all veneers. And so far he hasn't been reported missing anywhere."

Odd, sure. But gave us nothing to go on. There was no way that'd help us. There was no way it *could*.

"So another dead end."

Ray blew out a puff of smoke. "It may not be an obvious clue, Jeremy. But every single thing they cover up is a clue. It shows us something about them. We may not know who they are, but if they have an airplane, we know they have money. If they can afford to burn a thirty-five-thousand-dollar vehicle, that's a clue. Their cleverness, covering their tracks, burning off employee fingertips and implanting new teeth so they're unidentifiable even in death? Those are all hints."

A clue that would lead us nowhere. A catch-22. The problem was the solution. Sure, it taught us something. But not something that would help in any way, shape, or form. "We already knew they were smart."

Silence settled in for a moment.

I looked to the parking lot, trying to people watch to get my mind off of everything. But I saw a man slam into park in front of the ER entrance and leap from his car. He darted to the passenger side and swung the door open so fast. He reached inside. And out stepped a woman.

Her round stomach was so large, I wasn't sure how she stood upright. Messy dark hair swung into her sweaty face. I couldn't make out what she was saying but her mouth was parted in an O shape. But the man was smiling. She smacked his chest. But his smile didn't fade.

A lump stiffened in the back of my throat. I wanted to be happy for that random couple. But I couldn't help the jealousy. Or the tears that strived to puddle in my eyes. They dribbled down my throat instead.

Fuck. Was I gonna get that opportunity? Or was my son gonna be born.... wherever the hell Laila was? Would he even make it to birth?

"Maybe your friend will have more information after she's done with that Witch shit she's doing in there." He nodded toward the building. "What's her name again?"

I cleared my throat. "Olivia."

"Right. Olivia."

We sat there in silence. I'm not sure how long, maybe ten minutes, maybe twenty. But after a while, Olivia rounded the corner with a notebook in her hand.

"Hey, did you find anything?" I stood.

"Yeah, I did. I'm not sure what help it will be though."

"What is it?" Ray asked.

"A Witch was definitely bound to him." Her gaze met mine. It was serious but her tone was gentle. "I have a trace of her magic, but I doubt it'll be enough to do a locator spell. And even if it is, this is one powerful Witch. I don't think we'll be able to track her if she knows what she's doing."

"She?" Ray turned his head to the side. "How do you know it's a she?"

Olivia shrugged. "I don't know for sure. But from how strong her power is, I'd be surprised if they were a man."

"That's a thing?" Ray asked.

"It's a thing," I said.

"But I found something else too when I was reading over the autopsy report." She pulled her phone from her pocket and handed it to me.

It was a photo. A series of little black spheres on a white towel. Small signs sat beside them numbering one to twelve. "What is that?" Ramirez asked.

"What do you see, Jeremy?" she asked.

I squinted. I'd never seem them on such a small scale. But if it was what I thought it was, it'd explain why I never saw Daniel use his powers. "Is that hematite?"

She gave a nod. "It looks to me like morion compounded with hematite. But more bizarre than that, they're electrical."

I turned my head to the side. "What do you mean?"

"I can't be sure but from my examination in there, it looked to me like they were blinking. I'd love to take one underground for us to study if you can find a way to misplace one, Ray."

"I'll see what I can do," he said. "What do you think they're for?"

"Hematite and morion are a Guardian's kryptonite," I said. "Kind of, anyway. They don't hurt us, but they definitely weaken us. But this is such a small amount."

"They were implanted all over his body." Olivia pushed up her glasses. "My guess is that they weren't used for just keeping powers at bay though. I think it has a GPS in it."

"That's how they knew where they were," I murmured.

That's what I'd felt the morning before. They were implanting those rocks inside of Laila. That's why it felt like her flesh was being torn open, because it was. And not just for the purpose of torturing her, but to stunt her abilities.

But it didn't make sense. Laila couldn't use her Guardian abilities. We didn't even know what they were. Maybe they had something to do with the bond being blocked. Then again, that wouldn't make sense either. I couldn't find her mind well before I felt that pain.

"You guys work on that," Ray said. "I'm gonna get back to the station and see what forensics knows about those pebbles."

"Alright. Thanks, man."

He gave a soft smile. As he headed toward his car, I turned to Olivia. "Thank you for everything. You want me to take you home?"

She gave me a once over. "I'm actually kinda hungry. Do you want to get lunch somewhere?"

"I'm alright."

She squinted, her blue eyes washing over me once more. "When was the last time you ate?"

"I don't know. I'm fine—"

"You're not fine," she said. "You couldn't be fine after the past few days you've had. Please, let me take you out for lunch. You need to eat."

I didn't particularly want to say yes. But my stomach was growling. And maybe she had more information she didn't want to mention in front of Ray or outside a busy hospital.

"There's a Panera down the road. But I can pay for myself."

"Alright. Separate checks then."

CHAPTER FORTY-TWO

JEREMY

I spun my chicken noodle soup in the cup in front of me. I was hungry but I had no desire to eat. It smelled good. Warm, relaxing, homey. It looked even better. But I just couldn't bring myself to raise the spoon to my mouth. Everything felt so heavy.

That plastic spoon. The air. The weight of my fiancé and unborn child's lives on my shoulders.

"It works better if you actually eat it." Olivia leaned across the table and put her hand over mine.

I pulled it away and set it on my lap. "I'll just wait for my sandwich."

Olivia lifted her coffee to her lips. Taking a sip, she gazed at me over the rim of her paper cup. Her look made me uncomfortable. Like this meant something to her.

I shouldn't have agreed to go. I guess I only did because it seemed like the polite thing to do. But Brody was right, it was clear that she still had feelings for me.

Any feelings I had for Olivia disappeared a few years shy of a decade ago. She was my first love. A part of me would always have a soft spot for her. But honestly? She was a horrible person.

When we were in high school, she was one of those girls that would take pictures of other people and post them on social media just to mock them. It was a rarity if she was decent to a server at a restaurant. She also had a thing for fucking strangers at parties, even when she was dating me. And even if I was one room over.

Back in the day, she used to brag about her perfect figure and pretty eyes. And in all fairness, she wasn't wrong. I didn't date her just for the fact that my grandparents were friends with her mom and dad. And she was still cute, but karma had come for her full throttle.

Her little ski sloped nose now looked misplaced on her round face. The pores of her skin were much larger than they used to be as wrinkles pulled at the corners of her cat-like blue eyes. It was barely noticeable, but I remembered her as a seventeen-year-old cheerleader.

Not to say that she was ugly. I still found her attractive. If it weren't for the fact that I loved my fiancé, there was a chance I'd still be interested. But I did appreciate the irony.

"It's really nice to see you." Olivia broke the silence. "I wish it were under better circumstances."

"Yeah. Yeah, you too."

She held my gaze for a moment. "It's crazy how life works, isn't it? One day, you're just kids falling in love for the first time. Then the next, you're grown, having kids and getting married." She smiled. "Did you guys set a date?"

"No, we're going to do that next week." I paused, considering correcting myself. We *were* going to do that next week. I cleared my throat. "She wants a long engagement anyway."

Olivia gave a sad smile. "Well, make sure I get an invite."

"Sure."

She definitely would not.

Licking her lips, she looked down for a second. She cleared her throat and looked up to meet my gaze. "We were kind of good once, weren't we?"

I raised my brows, unable to hold back the laugh that left my lips. "You're kidding, right?"

She smiled, shaking her head. "I wasn't actually."

"We were horrible together." I laughed quietly. "We didn't see eye to eye on anything. You didn't like music. I thought the whole football, cheerleading thing was stupid. There was nothing good about us as a couple."

"There were *some* good things." She flashed a flirty smile. "Kinda learned how everything works together."

I sucked my teeth. "Is that why you wanted to go to lunch? To talk about our adolescent sex lives? While I'm in the middle of the worst thing I've ever been through?"

"No." Her brows pulled together, and she frowned. "I just wanted to catch up. I'm sorry, I shouldn't have said that."

"Yeah, you really shouldn't have." Head shaking, I lifted my coffee to take a sip. She silently gazed down at the table and fidgeted with the wrapper from her straw.

As I looked over her, an annoyed, nearing angry feeling crept up inside of me. I wasn't sure if it was at her for bringing up a part of my life I'd rather forget or if it was at myself for agreeing to go out to lunch together because I knew how much it'd piss Laila off. I thought about that a little harder. The look on Laila's face when Olivia made a comment about remembering where my bedroom was. Everything she was going through. And the fact that I was on a lunch date with Olivia. And I just snapped.

Which wasn't fair. I knew that. But I was in a really fragile state right about then. Yeah, she was helping me, but she chose then to try and make a move? Not even two days since my pregnant fiancé was kidnapped? That was low.

"Why were you such a bitch to her the last time you saw each other?" I blurted.

She squinted, setting her coffee down. "What?"

"Laila." I studied her flinch as I said her name. "You didn't say a single decent thing to her."

"I'm sorry, I don't follow."

"You haven't changed at all, have you?"

"What are you talking about?"

"It's been six years since we really knew each other. Six years, and you still get some weird pleasure out of putting other people down."

"I seriously don't know what you mean, Jeremy."

"Last month when you came to examine Daniel. You made some shitty comment about her weight. Said something about how our baby wasn't planned. You even made a remark about remembering where my bedroom was in some pathetic attempt to make her jealous of you." I gave a weird, confused shrug. "Do you honestly think there's still a chance for us somewhere?"

She turned her glance to the coffee on the table. "No, of course not, Jeremy. I know it's stupid, but I'd be lying if I said I didn't have unresolved feelings for you. But I know you won't leave her. I know how important that baby is to you."

'How important that *baby* is.' Laila was my baby too. In the metaphoric sense of the word, obviously, but the fact remained. I didn't love her because she was pregnant. That may have been why I jumped the gun on proposing but it wasn't the reason I was with her.

An employee set my sandwich in front of me. "Thank you," I muttered.

Once she was out of hearing distance, I turned back to Olivia. "It's not just the baby that's important to me, Liv. Laila's my world. She's sweet, and happy, and strong. She's everything I've ever wanted and everything I didn't know I needed," I said. "She's the love of my life. It would've been nice if you could have been at least remotely decent to her."

"I'm sorry, I shouldn't have said anything."

I watched her carefully. "It seems like in some way, you're glad this happened. You don't care about her, you don't care about my son, you just wanted a way in with me. What better opportunity than when my fiancé's been kidnapped, right?"

"Of course not," she said. "Yes, I still feel something for you. But that doesn't mean I would have ever wished this. After seeing that little boy, I can't even imagine what you're going through. I would never want you to feel this way. I would never want you to experience anything like this, let alone your baby."

I gave one of those ironic, huff kind of laughs. "Right. But Laila, you couldn't care less about. Why? Because I love her, and I don't love you?" I stood. "I'll be in the car when you're done."

I started outside, disgusted with myself for ever being with her. Although, I wasn't actually that mad. Not at her, not really. Any other day, I wouldn't have lashed out at her the way that I had. But come on, bringing shit up like that with all things considered? I had the right to snap a little.

As I grabbed the door handle, a painful split slammed across my back. I gasped and braced myself against the window to keep from falling. It happened again, this time stinging the whole way down my spine. It was similar to the sting of getting hit with a rubber band but on a much larger scale and a hell of a lot deeper.

I jumped into the car, hoping no one saw my odd bout.

In that first moment, I wasn't even sure what it was. I wondered if it was some new anxiety symptom I'd never heard of.

I heard her. The ear-piercing scream. It was so high pitched that I reflexively covered my ears. But it didn't matter because the sound came from inside of my head.

"Please stop," I heard her say between cries. "Just please stop!"

Then the image of Daniel's back flashed behind my eyelids. Those thick scars that ascended every inch of his skin.

They were whipping her. I reached out for her mind. I reached out for her location. I'd done it a handful of times before and it was always so easy. Like dialing a number in my thoughts and being instantly connected. She didn't even need to click answer.

But this time? All that I got was feedback. A loud a buzz, like a microphone held too close to another.

My stomach tightened in a way it never had. This horrible sense of defense washed over me, but I couldn't do anything. I couldn't grab the fucker that hurt her like that by their throat. I couldn't bash their head off the ground into mush the way I wanted to. I couldn't shove a blade into their chest.

There was nothing I could do but sit there and cry.

"Baby," I said aloud. I grasped either side of my head, tears burning down my face. "Just show me where you are. Just show me, I'll be there. I'll leave right now."

Another whip cracked against my back. I arched forward in agony. She screamed again, louder that time. Then the screams turned to cries. Both hers and mine.

"Where the hell are you?!"

It cracked again, uncontrollably sending my body forward. My quiet cries turned to helpless sobs. I dropped my head to my hands. I punched the steering wheel over and over again. I didn't stop, I just kept punching and crying. I didn't know what else to do. There wasn't anything else *to* do.

But the moment I did, guilt flooded over me. What if she felt that? As if she wasn't in enough pain already, I had to add to it by losing my temper. I hoped she didn't. Maybe she was in too much overwhelming pain to feel mine.

The passenger door opened, and I tried to recollect myself. Olivia hopped in as I wiped my face. "I'm so sorry," she said quietly. She climbed into the seat. "I shouldn't have said all that."

Another snap tore against her back and I grimaced, closing my eyes and trying not to think about it. Trying not to hear her screams.

"Oh, shit. You're bleeding." She reached for my hand. I yanked it away. She pulled her hands back. "I have some gauze. Can I bandage that up for you?"

My throat was tight as I swallowed, looking down for the first time. All four of my knuckles were busted, steady streams of red drizzling to my elbows.

Olivia reached into her purse. She pulled out a few pieces of gauze and self-adhering wrap. "I'm really sorry, Jeremy. I didn't realize it'd make you this upset."

I fought the urge to snap at her the way I had inside the restaurant. It wasn't her fault, but it did tick me off that she flattered herself into thinking that spat meant so much to me. "This isn't because of you."

"What do you mean?"

Another tear cracked against my back. I closed my eyes, trying not to let any more sobs escape. My shaking hands tightened to fists. Slow breaths moved in and out of my nostrils. Another slam against my spine. It took everything in me to stay still.

Then again. And again.

Her screams filled my mind. It was like she was right beside me. I could hear them clear as day. Yet, I couldn't stop it.

It went on for another minute or so. Maybe a little less. Maybe a little more. I didn't know, I wasn't timing it. But eventually, it stopped. The pain didn't, not really. But the cracking of the whip did. Her cries did too.

When the pain subsided, I opened my eyes and met her gaze. "They're torturing her. Right now. I can feel it."

Her gaze softened. I think a tear even formed at the corner of her eye. I wondered if it was in sympathy or out of jealousy. "So the rumors are true." She laid the gauze across my knuckles. She took the wrap and began twisting it around my hand.

"About us being par animos?" I asked. She nodded, and I nodded back. "Yeah. She's my soulmate." I paused, throat thickening. "And I feel everything they do to her. Every needle prick, every grab. Every cut. Every whip."

"You can't find her location?" she asked.

Another smack slammed against my back and I awkwardly curved upward. I stifled back a grunt. I recovered for a moment. "No. The Witch must be really good."

"God, I can't even imagine." She moved to my other hand. "That must be awful."

"To put it mildly."

"I think you might have broken this one," she muttered. "I can give you something for the pain. Or at least something to help you get some rest."

"No, thanks. I'll just have Leah heal it when I get home."

She finished tightening the bandage around my hand. She reached in her bag and grabbed a bottle of orange pills.

"I don't want—"

"It's not an opioid," she said. "It's not even a controlled substance."

"What is it?" I asked.

"Neurontin. It's not a euphoric kind of drug. It's for nerve pain and seizures. We even give it to women in menopause for hot flashes."

One of the few drugs I was unfamiliar with. Because it wasn't much fun.

"It's not a controlled substance?"

"Not at all. It'll just help you calm down and get some sleep."

"It's not a benzo?"

She frowned. "I wouldn't give you something like that."

All things considered, I needed something. Anything to take the edge off. And hell, if it wasn't a benzo or an opioid, why the hell not?

I grabbed the bottle and twisted it open. I grabbed a few and tossed them into my mouth.

My addiction didn't pick back up because I took those pills. Still though, it wasn't worth it. It didn't even help me sleep.

CHAPTER FORTY-THREE

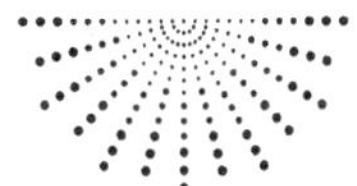

MARCH 12 2019 - LAILA

I didn't remember falling asleep. But I realized I had when I felt a quick, painful snap against my spine pull me from it. My body writhed backward as I struggled to sit up. But I couldn't.

I lay face down on some type of table. It was more like a massage bed than anything, like the ones they have at chiropractor offices, aside from the lack of cushion. The stomach section even dropped so the baby wasn't pushed against anything. How considerate.

Metal brackets held me down at the wrists, waist, thighs and ankles. There was no point in fighting. Fighting only bruised the skin where the metal held me down. I did though. Wouldn't be Laila Callidy if I didn't. I yanked my arms and legs against the restraints. But the moving just made the sting down my spine worse.

I didn't even have time to take it in. I didn't even grasp what was happening.

The snap cracked again, and a scream left my lips. "Son of a bitch!"

It whooshed through the air, slashing through my flesh like butter. My hand caught fire. The flames spread up my arms. Fire covered every surface of my skin from my hands to my shoulders.

That sound. *Whoosh!* Then *crack* when it met my skin.

It smacked my left shoulder this time. I screamed. It was reflex. I never screamed when someone hit me, but it hurt so much more than any stab ever had. Because I couldn't fight back.

Wires taped to my body began to melt down my bare skin, dripping like candle wax in some BDSM porn. Some on my head, others on my chest, even on my arms and legs. There were as many on my belly as there were on my entire body combined. But the longer I stayed aflame, the faster they dissolved.

My gaze stayed steady on the cement beneath me. Blood started to pool below my elevated feet. Red. The first color I'd seen since I arrived. Agony slashed over my spine again.

"Stop! Please stop!" I begged. But it was already flying to my bare back again. It caught my butt. My body curved upward.

The man behind me, the man beating me, chuckled. "Ya know, she doesn't even look pregnant from behind."

"She doesn't," another voice said. "She's got a cute little ass too."

"I don't know, too tiny for me," the first voice said.

"Go ahead and try, you piece of shit," I said. "I'd love to say I killed some fucker by setting him on fire with my ass."

The other guy laughed.

"What? That was funny."

He raised the whip, cracking it over and over against my flaming skin. He just kept going. And I kept begging.

As he did, the flames spread, growing brighter with each whack. I don't even know how many times he hit me. All that I know is that my mind and body were at war. I thought that I didn't want to kill anyone. But my body wanted to defend itself.

"Please stop!" I pleaded. I was no longer screaming. At that point, I was sobbing. "I'll do whatever you want, just please stop!"

For a second, only a millisecond really, I could feel Jeremy. His presence, or his soul. Something familiar. It wasn't a physical sensation but more of a mental one. It wasn't clear, like a fuzzy image on a TV when the HDMI cord starts to break. No words, no images, no real connection to him. But I could feel it. I could feel his fear.

The men laughed and the whip cracked again. It smacked against my back and ass before grazing my thighs.

And I couldn't hold back.

Air swirled around me as my body went up in flames.

The whip cracked one last time.

I couldn't see it. Not the flames themselves, but I saw the color. The vibrant orange that lit the room like the sun. I felt the heat swirling off of me like a tornado of fire. I saw the glow of the flames turn from red to orange in the air around me. Then orange to yellow. Then the yellow changed to a bluish color, Into a brilliant shade of violet.

I heard their screams.

As shamed as I am to admit it, I smiled when I smelled their flesh burn.

The flames disappeared and I was at peace for a moment.

"Wow," I heard the doctor say over an intercom. "Beautiful. Absolutely beautiful."

I wanted to scream profanities, but my throat was hoarse from crying. I began to open my mouth to utter something, but as I did. I heard his voice once more.

"You're amazing."

Suddenly, I felt a needle pierce my back. It all went black.

My knees ached against the hard cement. I used my hands as a pillow to hold my head on the metal table. I wanted to lie down but I couldn't lie on my back. It was torn to shreds.

I couldn't lie on my stomach because the makeshift bed was too hard on the bump of my belly. I couldn't sit on my ass because the cuts and slashes stretched down to the top half of my butt. All that I could do was kneel as if in prayer. But God didn't give a flying fuck.

Focusing on the pain on my back seemed like what I should have been doing. How to keep it from happening again. How to keep from killing again. But I couldn't. I couldn't focus on the anger I wanted to have.

Jeremy though. I couldn't stop thinking about Jeremy. How he must have been feeling. How scared he was. How I failed him when I got in that van. My chest tightened and my eyes filled with tears. I should have listened to him. I shouldn't have taken for granted how much he cared for my safety. Why did it agitate me? He knew something like this could happen. All he wanted was to keep me safe. Why didn't I listen?

Tears drained from my eyes as I clutched my belly. My son. I was sorry for what he must have felt inside my womb that day. I read once that that fetuses feel every emotion their mother does. He didn't have thoughts yet, nothing I could read, but it hurt so bad to think he felt what I just had.

The door slammed shut. I listened to the men who helped them do it to me laughed their way down the hall. I heard another bang, then a beep, followed by a click. The secondary door locked.

A gentle tap knocked on the wall next to my bed. "Laila?" I heard Chris say.

My throat was too hoarse from screaming to reply. I stared at my blurred reflection on the steel wall. I couldn't make anything out, not really. Just my long black hair resting against my paper white skin.

"Laila?" He tapped harder. "Are you okay?"

"No," I murmured.

"It'll feel better in a couple days," he said.

"He's lying," Haley called. "It just gets worse. In a couple days, they'll do it again before it's even close to healed."

Fingers quivering, chest tightening, I attempted to hold in my sob. But it was practically out of my control. "I just want to go home."

"We all do," Haley said. "But the wallowing in self-pity isn't going to help—"

"Shut up, Haley," Chris said.

"What? It's the truth. That's what you told me my first time—"

"You weren't pregnant with my nephew," he snapped. My teeth chattered as I wiped my face. "It's going to be okay, Laila. It is, you just gotta hang in there."

"No, it's not," I said quietly but still loud enough for him to hear. "Jeremy isn't coming for me."

"You don't know that," he said. "Like you said, he knows you aren't dead. If I know my brother, he isn't going to stop until he finds you."

"They can't make it in here anyway." I wiped my eyes, scratchy voice lowering. "What if I lose this baby?"

"Don't talk like that." He tapped the wall again. "He's a Skoulda. That means he's a fighter, he's gonna be fine."

Maybe he was right. Maybe we would come out on the other end. But that didn't take the pain away as I felt it soar over me.

"I don't know how I can go through that again," I said between tears.

"You just will," he said. "Some way, somehow, you just will. You'll hold onto whatever gives you hope. You'll remember something that you want to feel, or taste, or smell again and it'll give you the strength to carry on. Maybe it's the sun, or the wind. Maybe it's ice cream, or a margarita." I chuckled. His voice lightened. "There ya go. We'll make it through this, Laila. You have to hold onto the happiness for the short moments that you have it. Make that one second stretch out for days. Hold onto that little bit of joy. That's how you'll survive."

"I haven't even gotten to have a legal margarita," I muttered. "Just shitty ones with that cheap mix from Walmart."

"Really? How old are you?" he asked.

I knew he was trying to distract me. In most situations, I would have snapped and said to shut up. But I needed that distraction. I needed to think about anything that wasn't my pain.

"I just turned twenty-one last month," I said. "But I'm pregnant, so, you know."

"Damn, twenty-one," he said. "So when did you and Jeremy meet?"

"Three and a half years ago."

"Geez, you were just a baby. So was I when I fell in love for the first time though. How did you guys meet?"

"I was friends with Adam." I smiled at the memory. "He was dating my friend Adrian."

"Oh yeah?" he asked.

"Yeah, the three of us were at a concert."

"Who were you seeing?"

"Mumford and Sons," I said.

"No shit, I love them. Are they still together?"

"They are," I said. "Their older stuff is still better though. But maybe not. Maybe I just like their oldest stuff more because it reminds me of being that girl again, ya know?"

"Yeah. Yeah, maybe." He paused for a moment. "So did Jeremy tag along?"

"Not really his taste." I laughed. "No, we got a flat tire on our way home. Well, actually, we ran over a deer and blew out a tire."

"And Jeremy came to the rescue?" he asked.

I laughed as I wiped my cheek. "I guess he did. We didn't have a tire iron. He brought one but we couldn't break the bolts, so we loaded up into the Charger and he drove us home. Adam was staying at Adrian's, and it was on the way, so he dropped me off last. We stopped on the way and got Sheetz 'cause my fat ass is always hungry. And we ate and just talked in the car for hours. Before I knew it, it was five o'clock in the morning."

His smile was almost audible. "Did he ask for your number?"

I laughed. "No, of course not. He was a little bitch. So I gave it to him. He called me the next day." I smiled, remembering the look on his face when he met me at the diner for our first date. His grin was a mile wide, wavy black hair falling in his bright blue eyes. He was younger then, but that boyish grin never faded. "We started talking a lot after that, but we didn't actually start dating until a few months later. I made him ask me out."

Chris chuckled. "You *made* him ask you out?"

I laughed too, smiling at the memory. "He was supposed to come over for Christmas dinner with my mom, as a friend, of course."

"Oh, of course."

"But he bailed, and I was mad. I didn't answer his calls for a week. Then he showed at my work, and he brought my Christmas presents, and he finally kissed me." I closed my eyes, trying to remember that look on his face as he held my forehead to his, so close his breath teased my cheeks. "And I said to make it up to me, he had to take me out for my birthday."

"Did he? Make it up to you?"

My cheeks flushed, remembering that look on his face when we stepped outside the little Italian restaurant. I remembered his eyes grazing over my lips and his pupils dilating. I remembered wondering why he didn't make the move. And I reached onto the tips of my toes and touched my lips to his.

Still, I remember that kiss like it was yesterday. The world practically spun around me. His lips parted against mine and his hand moved to my hip while the other found my neck.

I could almost feel his thumb grazing my cheek as my eyes closed. I raised my hand to touch it, wondering what was going through his mind that day. Wondering if it gave him butterflies the way that it did for me.

Then I remembered that night in the cabin, and...

"He most certainly did."

Chris laughed. "And how did Adam feel about that?"

"He did not approve."

"Really?"

"Yeah, not at all. I didn't get why then. We had a lot in common and we got along really well. But both me and Jeremy were kind of wild in those days." I thought back to how simple my life once was. When all I had to worry about was getting my diploma, helping Mom with the bills, and waiting tables at Moe's.

I wondered if I should tell Chris the whole truth. About the problem Jeremy manifested when Chris disappeared. I decided I wouldn't. I didn't know if either of us would make it out of there. And if we didn't, I'd prefer his memories of his little brother be of his happily ever after with me than the addiction he struggled with.

Clearing my throat, I said, "He probably figured we'd have a fling and it'd make our friendship weird."

"It didn't though?"

"No." I smiled. "No, we both gave up our single days pretty quick."

"Well, I'm glad Jeremy found you. He was a good kid. He deserves to be happy."

"He would love to hear you say that," I said. "He's so worried you'll hate him for not finding you. They all are."

Chris let out a quiet sound. Something between a grunt and a huff. "If you get out of here, make sure they know that I don't. I'd rather all of them be leading happy lives than worry about finding me."

It was noble. Stupid, but noble. His brothers and sisters wouldn't stop searching until they either found him or a body.

"You don't want to go home?" I asked.

"Of course I want to go home," he said. "But I'd rather be here than them end up here trying to get me out."

Not just noble. Inspirational. I found myself feeling the same way in that moment. I'd rather it be me than them. Because that's love. You'd do anything to prevent someone you loved from aching the way you have.

"Yeah, that makes sense."

"So what's Leah up to? Is she still with Amber?"

I frowned. "No, Amber died a few months after you disappeared."

He got quiet for a moment. He murmured, "Do you know what happened?"

"Not really. She doesn't talk about it."

"Well, is there anyone else in the picture?"

"Leah doesn't date. She always says one heart break was enough to last a lifetime."

"I can relate," he muttered.

"So you know what happened to Mia?" I asked in the same sad, low tone.

"Yeah. I saw it." He paused. His voice grew somber. "I've seen a lot of shitty things. But that was definitely the shittiest."

I couldn't help but remember hearing Adam utter nearly the same words about Adrian. So far, all of the Skoulda kids had horrible luck with love. It was almost as if they were cursed.

I fell silent for a moment. "I'm so sorry for your loss."

"Thanks," he muttered. After a second, his tone picked back up. Not quite happy, but not so sad. "So what's Hannah like now? She's all grown up, huh?"

"She's amazing." I smiled. "A lot like Adam. She's really light-hearted and happy."

"Still no powers?"

I wanted to tell him, but I couldn't. Even if I could, I wouldn't. "Still no powers."

"Any boyfriends?" he asked.

"Yeah, actually. Remember the twin brother of mine I told you about before?"

"No way." He laughed. "What a weird world. Is he a good guy?"

"Yeah. Yeah, he is. He's a sweetheart. He's got that whole carefree, love is all you need, Fae attitude."

"I've never met one from the realm," he muttered. "Always wanted to though."

"Maybe one day you will," I said.

We went on talking for hours. It was nice because we both got to keep them alive through my memories. That was the start of a friendship I'd never lose. As much as I loathe Peterson, that's one part of the awful experience I can be grateful for.

CHAPTER FORTY-FOUR

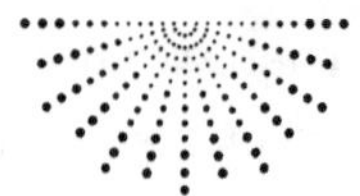

APRIL 10, 2019 - JEREMY

Salty air danced into my nose. Roars of the ocean vibrated to my ears. The light shining around was almost orange from the bright sunset overhead. A feeling of peace settled around me, basking in the beauty of the moment.

The warm air. The tranquil sound of the waves. The beautiful brunette before me.

"So, in other words, you think Pink Floyd sucks." Laila shook her head with a playful grin. "Wow, okay. We should probably just end this now. I can't see this working out long term."

"I did not say Pink Floyd sucks." I grasped her hips and lifted her onto the trunk of the Charger. "I just said that Zeppelin is better."

She stuck her finger in her open mouth and lurched forward to signify puking. "So basically, you're saying Pink Floyd sucks."

"Are you trying to say that Zeppelin sucks?" I pulled her hips closer to me, so they were flush against mine. Her long legs draped against the back of the car, feet resting on the bumper with my body between them.

"That is exactly what I'm saying." She smiled.

My jaw dropped. "You cannot call yourself a fan of rock and roll and think that Led Zeppelin sucks."

"I like his voice; I like his rifts. For the first minute. It's like, 'Oh, shit.

Did I restart the song? No, it's just Zeppelin with the same thirty seconds strumming on repeat for six minutes.'"

My smiling lips fell open as I looked between her gorgeous green eyes. "Ya know, I really like you and all. We just see things so differently. Maybe we should take some time to consider our options here."

"What a shame." She tossed her arms around my shoulders. "I will forever remember the days we spent together. They will always hold a special place in my heart."

I laughed and pressed my lips to hers, sliding my arms around her waist. I felt her bare skin beneath my palms just as I had a thousand times before. My fingers played with the string of her bikini.

She pulled away and bashfully looked around. "You can't just take my top off, Jeremy."

"Why not?" I huffed and moved my hand from her neck into the back of her long, dark brown hair. I grasped the locks at the nape of her neck. The silky texture was so real between my fingers, squeezing and tugging her head to the side. Her eyes closed and a sigh escaped her perfect lips. I lowered my mouth to her neck.

"Jeremy." A hand tapped my shoulder. "Jeremy, wake up, bro.'"

My eyes flung open, and I looked around. No warm sun. No salty, ocean air. No beautiful green eyes.

The smell of old coffee and fryer oil. The dreary fluorescent lights on the ceiling. The quiet hum of the refrigerator in the back. The cool air and even colder bar counter.

Moe's.

Max met my gaze. "Sorry, man. I just figured you might want to go up to bed."

"Shit." I looked at the clock ticking on the wall above the serving hatch. "Damn it. It's six thirty already?"

Max nodded. "Unfortunately."

"Shit. Shit." I looked down at my pile of paperwork spread out on the bar. "Oh, fuck. I have to have pay roll done today. Shit, shit, shit. Okay, I'm sorry. Give me five minutes to get all this shit out of your way."

He frowned, brown eyes shifting over me. "It's alright. Go get some rest, man. You're burning yourself out around here. I can help with pay roll."

"Oh, no. No, that's okay. I couldn't ask you to do that—"

"You aren't asking, I'm offering. Seriously, go get some rest."

I covered my mouth to stifle a yawn. "It's okay, I won't be able to fall back to sleep now anyway. I got a few hours in, I'll be alright."

His lips tried to stay in a frown, but he willed them into a gentle smile. "Did you at least sleep good?"

I tried to blink away the dream and come back to reality. "Yeah, you could say that."

He gave a sad smile. "About Laila?"

"They're always about Laila."

His sad eyes shifted over me. I rummaged the paperwork to a pile. "Are you sure I can't help with anything? I don't mind, man. The place is pretty clean, and I got most of my prep work done last night."

"No, it's alright. You work too much already. Don't worry about doing my work too."

"At least let me cook something for you."

"I'm good, man. Really." I stood and stretched my arms above my head. "Thanks though."

He glanced at the bottle of Jack Daniels on the counter. "Don't take this the wrong way, man. But I don't think you are."

He wasn't wrong. I was a shit storm. I could barely eat, I couldn't sleep. Not until I passed out over the desk in the office or here at the bar. I wasn't sure when the last time I showered was and I'd been wearing the same clothes for at least a week. Almost all day every day, I drowned myself in liquor. That whole staying clean thing just didn't seem to matter without her.

"I'm kind of a mess, I know. But I'm holding it together."

Silence crept up for a moment. "Any news recently?"

"No. No news at all."

He frowned. "The cops haven't said anything?"

"They ran out of leads."

"And the FBI? They just gave up?"

"She's been gone for more than thirty days and no new evidence has surfaced. The case went cold so they stopped investigating."

I knew it didn't matter that the cops stopped looking. The only reason to involve the police at all was to cover our asses on Daniel's murder and not raise any eyebrows while Laila was missing. They weren't going to find her; I knew that the moment Leah told me Ramirez put an APB out on her. They couldn't find Chris, they couldn't find Lydia and Amy, they couldn't find Cage's father. Hell, they didn't even know they were alive.

They were human. They had no idea what was really happening. Ramirez knew about our kinds for years, but he didn't have the slightest clue either, let alone a lead. Shit, neither did I.

"That's ridiculous."

"Yeah, well. They think she's dead," I said.

His eyes shifted between mine. "You don't believe that, do you?"

"No," I said. "I know she's still out there somewhere. I just don't know where."

"Well, for what it's worth, I think she's still alive too."

"Yeah, thanks. I'm not giving up on her," I muttered.

It was a lie. I knew she was alive, but we'd been chasing these people for months and had *nothing* until they handed Daniel to us like a brilliant, heart wrenching virus to destroy us from the inside. I wouldn't admit it aloud. Maybe I wouldn't even admit it to myself in my mind. But I was out of hope. I knew it even if I wouldn't face it.

Laila was gone and I had no way to get her back.

The empty liquor bottles in the recycling bin and the flask in the pocket of my dirty jeans were more proof than anyone needed to see that I'd given up.

Max returned the same forced smile. "She's gonna come home."

"Yeah. Yeah, I hope."

The bell rang above the door behind me. "Sorry, we're not open yet —" I began.

"Well, shit. I thought I was welcome any time." Rachel smiled.

Laila's mom. She wasn't in as bad of shape as I was physically. Her clothes were clean, her blond hair was done, it looked like she had a little makeup on. But I saw the smudges beneath those aching mint eyes.

I forced a smile. "Oh, sorry, Mrs. Callidy. I didn't realize that was you."

She smiled. "That's okay, hon."

"Hey, Rachel," Max said. "Can I get you anything?"

"No. No, that's okay. Thank you," she said.

"What's going on?" I asked.

She shook her head. "Nothing really. I just wanted to know if you were busy."

"Well, actually—" I began.

"He's not busy," Max said.

"Max, I have to get the—"

"The schedule can wait until tomorrow. I can take care of payroll. I'll add an extra fifty bucks to my check if that makes you feel better." He smiled at me before turning to Laila's mom. "He needs to get out of here. Take him."

She met my gaze with a gentle smile. "Get your jacket, Jeremy."

"I still need a shower, and—"

"No, just get your jacket. Come on," she insisted.

Saying no to a Callidy was close to impossible any day. I really didn't want to go. I didn't want to look Laila's mom in the eye and tell her I still had no clue how to find her daughter. But I respected that woman. And Laila would want me to listen to her.

I took in a deep breath. "Alright, let me take a piss."

Rachel and I sat at a quiet little coffee shop in town. I picked. Laila loved their coffee. It'd been a while since I'd eaten there. But it was warm, and it smelled like her two favorite things. Coffee and cookies. It brought back enough memories that I almost forgot she was gone.

"So how are you?" I wrapped my palms areound my coffee cup and looked up to meet Rachel's cool green eyes.

She sighed. "Really shitty."

I wanted to laugh. But it came out as more of a huff. "Yeah, I can relate."

"This is the worst thing I've ever felt." Rachel looked past me out the window at the cars driving by. "I don't know where she is. I don't know what's happening to her."

My stomach ached.

"But you do." I looked up to meet her desperate eyes as her lip struggled to stay steady. "What are they doing to my daughter, Jeremy?"

"You really don't want to know."

Pain reflected in her eyes. "Yes, I do."

"Mrs. Callidy—"

"Don't call me that," she asserted. "You call me Mom."

"We aren't married yet."

"It doesn't matter," she said. "You will be. You're the most important person in my daughter's life. You two are going to get married, you're having a baby together, you're my son."

I summoned a bare smile. "Alright."

She smiled back. After a moment, it collapsed. "If someone could tell you what was happening to your baby, you'd want to know what it was, right? Even if it was hard to hear. Even if it was painful. You'd want to know."

I look down at my coffee. Would I? I guess. Knowing what was happening to Laila was terrible. But it also gave me a shred of hope because I knew she was alive.

Rachel stared at me for a moment, waiting for me to go on. "It's hard to think about, Mrs. Callidy—"

"Mom," she corrected.

"Right. Mom," I muttered. "It's hard to think about. But it's harder to say out loud."

"Can you show me then?"

"No. I won't do that," I said faster than the speed of light. I leaned back in my chair and clenched my jaw. "I'm sorry, but I won't."

There was no way in hell. If I let her see those memories, if I let her feel what Laila was going through, she wouldn't want to live. I knew because that's how I felt.

Rachel nibbled her bottom lip. After a quiet moment, she said, "It's that bad, huh?"

"It's pretty bad."

Her eyes softened. She looked back to her coffee. She spun the spoon through it as some form of distraction. I knew she wanted to know more, and I understood.

I did *want* to tell her. Part of me did want to show her what they were doing. I wanted to get it out of my fucking head. I wanted her to understand how horrible it was. I wanted to talk about how it was tearing me apart. I wanted someone to hurt as much as I was hurting so I had someone to relate to.

Someone to understand how every few days, they ripped the flesh off of her back. How they cut into her skin on a daily basis. How they poked and prodded her every single day that ticked by.

But if it was happening to my son, I wouldn't want to feel those details. I might think that I did, but once you know something like that, you can't unknow it.

I wished I didn't know. At least part of me did. But part of me found comfort in the pain. At least I knew that she wasn't dead.

The pain kept me linked to her. I couldn't do anything to take the pain away, but it was a link. It was our only point of contact.

The pain made me remember that she was still living. She was in agony. But she was alive.

I'm not sure what would be worse. The fact that I knew everything they did to her and couldn't stop it or not knowing at all.

"You really want to know?" I asked quietly.

She looked up from her coffee. "I can handle it, Jeremy."

My voice lowered as I glanced around to make sure there was no one close enough to overhear.

"I don't see anything that's happening. I can't get into her head. I've tried spells to magnify my link to her so I can get a message through but" —I shook my head— "Nothing works. All I do know is the pain. I can feel it like it's happening to me, but I don't know why they're doing it or the context that it's happening in."

She nodded and I went on, "I feel needle pricks a lot. Several times a day. Some are in veins like they're taking blood. Others are just pokes, like something's being injected. Sometimes, it feels like she's fighting against something. Handcuffs or some type of bracket on a solid surface?" She listened carefully, watching my expression. "The first day, I felt these pains all over. On my arms, and in the middle of my ribs, one right below my Adam's apple, and some more on my legs. Like a cut and then the cut being torn open. I think that was when they put those things in her that we found in Daniel's autopsy."

"What are they?"

"We're not sure exactly. But we know they have GPS in them. We think that's how they tracked Laila in the first place," I said. "But they're made from hematite and morion. They're used by other races to deactivate our powers. But it doesn't work on Fae, it only works on Guardians. So I think they have to have a bigger purpose than that. Maybe just to track them in case they escape, I don't know." She waited for me to go on. "I feel these little cuts sometimes, different places at different times. I don't have any idea what they're from or what their purpose is."

"Are they like..." She paused to look for the words. "Are they scratches or are they deeper?"

"They're pretty deep."

She bit her lip. "Is that all?"

"Every few days, every Monday and Thursday, I feel her back getting hit. Whipped, I guess, would be a better word for it." Rachel maintained her composure, but I saw her breaths get short. "It never lasts long. Usually no more than a minute or two. The first time was a little longer, maybe five minutes. But since then, it's gotten shorter each time. I can hear her when they're hurting her back. She screams at first, and she gets mad, and..." I paused. "I feel nothing."

"Is that everything?" She tried to bite back tears.

"Yeah, that's about all."

She looked down at her coffee again. I looked at mine with the same solemn expression. I didn't know what to say.

We were both in horrible situations. But hers was worse. I'd been in both sets of shoes at one point or another. And I loved my fiancé with every fiber of my being. She was everything in the world to me.

But Laila was Rachel's baby. She was this beautiful creature that came into her life and completed her family. She was the only thing that she had left of her husband. She was her youngest child, the last she would ever have, and she was pregnant with her first grandchild.

I was beginning to understand what it was like to lose a child. But it wasn't the same for me, not really. All I had ever seen of my son was his little black and white face on an ultrasound. I never got to see him smile or watch him laugh. I never got to comfort him when he cried. I never got to hold him. I never even got to touch him, and I was still broken to pieces over losing him.

I couldn't imagine if I had watched him grow into a wonderful man just to be ripped away without any clue as to where he was or what was happening to him.

A moment or so later, Rachel broke the silence.

"I love my daughter," she said quietly.

"I know you do."

"And I know *you* love my daughter. I know your brothers and sister love my daughter. I know you guys are doing everything within your power to find her." She pressed her lips to a hard line. "But I don't think it's within our power."

"Yeah, it's starting to look that way."

"But there's someone else who loves my daughter. And it might not be out of her power."

I genuinely had no idea who she was referencing. "What do you mean?"

"I hate to even say this." She rubbed her tired eyes. "Have you been in contact with Mary?"

I scoffed, shaking my head. "She doesn't give a damn."

"I know it might seem like she doesn't care given everything that happened last year. But she didn't hurt Laila. She never would," Rachel said. "All of my baby's life, Mary checked in. I'd see her at dance recitals and spelling bees and chorus concerts. She was even at her high school graduation. She always brought her a gift for her birthday... We'd exchange a glance, and I wouldn't see her again, but she was *always* there. She was always watching out for her. In the shadows, not interfering, just checking in. Just making sure she was okay. But she always made sure she was safe. She loves her."

I traced my tongue along my teeth. "You want me to contact her."

"I would do it myself," she said. "I've tried actually. I pray to her, but she doesn't answer me. But you, she knows you. She's loved you as long as she's loved Laila. She'll come to you."

I didn't love the idea. Mary and I hadn't seen one another since that day in the Elder's Hall. But I'd walk across broken glass to bring her back. Talking to Mary was the easiest stone I hadn't thought to turn over.

"I can try, Rachel."

"Mom," she corrected again.

I gave a sad smile. "I can try, Mom."

She smiled back, knowing it gave me a sense of comfort to have someone I could call a parent. It'd been a long time since I had that. Despite everything else, it did give me a fraction of peace. I'd always love Rachel. Out of all the people I'd considered a parent over the years, she may have been my favorite. Next to Annie, anyway.

CHAPTER FORTY-FIVE

JEREMY

I sat at the edge of our bed holding a framed photo of me and Laila. We'd just started talking when it was taken. She didn't even have her powers yet. She looked so young and innocent. I guess we both looked young, but it'd been years since I was innocent. Wouldn't be long and I'd never use the word *innocent* and *Laila* in the same sentence again either.

Her hair was shorter then. That year was probably the last time she cut it. It rested against the top of her back, just barely below her neck. Her head tilted up to look at me in wonder with a sweet smile against her lips. It stretched up her cheeks to make her large, round eyes as small as an anime character.

She looked so bewildered by me, like she was trying to figure me out. She always knew I wasn't like other guys she'd been with, or other people in general for that matter. But she wasn't nervous about discovering what made me different. She was just full of amazement and curiosity.

I gazed down at the two of us looking so peaceful and happy. Every picture I was in for as long as I could remember, I didn't smile, or I forced it. I looked constipated in every one, trying to look happy—or at least content—when I never was. But in each picture with her, I smiled. A real, genuine smile.

From the moment I met her, I knew that I didn't want to live without her.

Yet there I was. Still living. Without her.

"I don't know if you're listening," I began quietly. "After everything that happened, I wouldn't blame you for ignoring me even if you can hear me. But damn it, Mary." Tears welled in my eyes and my lip curled. "I need you right now. They're hurting her. Every day, they are hurting her. And I want to make it stop. I want to end them, damn it. But I don't even know who they are. The other Angels couldn't help, they said it was a human matter and they couldn't interfere. But it's not just a human matter, Mary, you know that. I know that. We all know that."

"She's your daughter. And I don't understand why you did everything you did last year. But she told me you said it was to protect her. I'm not going to pretend to understand but I know you care about her. I know you want her to be okay. But I can't do this alone. I need you, Mary. Your *daughter*, needs you."

I looked around for a moment.

"I don't know what good I can do." Her quiet voice said at the doorway. I looked up to meet her hazel gaze. I couldn't help the smile that came to my lips. She gave one back, a scarce occasion for Mary. "It's nice to see you, Jeremy."

"Thank you for coming."

She sat beside me on the bed. The familiar smell of her jasmine and vanilla perfume wafted my way. I hated that it brought me comfort.

"How are you?" she asked.

"I could say I'm okay, but I'm not."

She was quiet for a moment. "Me neither."

I looked at her dismal expression. She wasn't lying. She really was heartbroken.

I'd known Mary for as long as I could remember. She was the closest thing I had to a parent after Annie died. And never in all of those years had I seen her like this. Her brows pulled together, lips curved low, eyes speckled red from tears.

"I know what you must think of me, Jeremy. From your perspective, the things I did were unforgivable. But if you knew what I knew, you'd understand."

"I don't care about that right now, Mary." I muttered. She held my gaze for a moment. "You know what's happened, right?"

A soft nod. "I wasn't sure if I should confront you guys. I know Leah wouldn't want to see me. Not that I blame her, really."

"Yeah, probably a good idea."

She took in a deep breath and slowly blew it out. "I love my children, Jeremy. I'm not their Mom, I know that. But I love every one of them. Everything I've done, I've done out of love. Even what happened last year. Even though you guys hate me for it, I was trying to protect you too."

I looked down at the picture in my hands. I didn't even care. What happened, happened. Hanging on it wouldn't change anything.

But I didn't know what to ask her. Although, it was nice sitting beside someone and knowing they were hurting as much as I was.

"She was so young there." Mary gave a quiet chuckle. "It's funny, isn't it? That wasn't even four years ago, and she looked like a different person."

"She *was* a different person then," I murmured.

"Before she fell in love with you."

A harsh reality I hadn't wanted to face. "If I knew this would happen to her, I wouldn't have let her."

"Don't say that." She gingerly placed her hand on my back. "The two of you give each other's life meaning. That's not a bad thing."

She wasn't wrong. Not really. But that didn't change the fact.

I would do anything to take her pain away. Anything. Even if that meant she wasn't mine, even if that meant I wouldn't have the family I'd been dreaming of, even if it meant that I had to die. I would do absolutely *anything* to make her stop hurting.

It wasn't about being a couple. It wasn't about my pain ending. It was about making it easier for her. No matter what, in every life, that's all I ever wanted. For her to be happy.

I looked up to meet her gaze. "Am I going to get her back?"

She pressed her lips to a line. "I like to think that you will."

My eyes filled with tears. "Do you know where she is?"

"If I did, she wouldn't be there. She'd be here."

"Is there anything I can do?" My tears beaded over. "Is there some way I can use my powers to bring her home?"

In a motherly fashion, she thumbed the salty water from my cheek. "The bond isn't working? You can't go into her mind?"

I wiped my eyes with the back of my hand. "No, not really. The only time I feel her is when they're torturing her."

Her tone was gentle. "You feel it?"

"I hear her screaming too. But It just stops."

"Your bond is that powerful." She smiled. "That's a good thing, Jeremy."

"What do you mean?"

"A Witch might be able to disguise her location, but if you can still feel each other's pain, that means the Witch isn't blocking the bond. Someone else is."

"Why is that a good thing?" I asked. "Regardless of who's blocking it, it's blocked."

"No, you don't understand. Whoever it is, they're inside Laila's head. She probably doesn't realize it yet or she would have pushed them out by now."

"But how does that help?" I said. "If I can't get in contact with her, there's nothing I can do."

"Once Laila realizes what's happening, which she will, this will end. But she has to do her part. You can't save her this time. She'll need your help. But until she blocks them out of her mind and contacts *you*, there's nothing that you can do, Jeremy. It's Laila's turn to save herself."

My brows furrowed further, and my chest got heavy.

I didn't realize it then, but Mary was right. It made me angry that I couldn't swoop in and take her pain away. But Laila had to be her own hero that time. In hindsight, I still wish I could have done more. Yet, if I had, I doubt Laila would have evolved into the newer, stronger species she was becoming.

To grow, to be strong, we have to survive the storms. We hate the rain as it falls, but without it, everything that grows will wilt.

CHAPTER FORTY-SIX

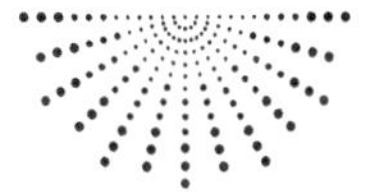

APRIL 10, 2019 - LAILA

Thirty-one days.

I'd been there for thirty-one days.

Thirty. Fucking. One.

In the past few weeks, I'd started to lose hope. I didn't want to face the fact at first. But my bubbly persona was fading. I hated my life. There wasn't much life to lead at that point.

I was nothing but a science project.

Still, I didn't know why Peterson was doing it. It seemed like he wanted to learn about us. What made us tick, what limitations we had, where our power came from. But he hadn't revealed his purpose. I wasn't sure he ever would.

For the first time in my life, I began to understand what depression really meant. I had been sad before, anxious from time to time, but I had never been truly depressed. Not until then. It all just felt so pointless.

My baby was growing and that gave me my only sense of joy. His kicks were the only thing that made me smile. But when I thought about where I was and what might happen to him when he was born, I began to wish I would have listened to Mary.

I wished I had an abortion. I wished I ran away. I wished that I never let it happen.

My baby was going to be born into that cold, awful nightmare.

He'd be born addicted to drugs I was unwillingly becoming dependent on. He'd be taken from my belly into the arms of a heartless, soulless human who could never understand what it was to have a child like mine. He'd be used as an experiment like I was. He'd be tortured in what that monster referred to as "stress tests" to challenge his abilities.

And if he was born without gifts like so many other babies born to supernatural parents, he'd be slain just as Daniel was.

I got to a point where I didn't care what happened to me. I wanted to go home, but if I didn't, I didn't mind. As long as my son was okay. But I knew he wouldn't be. I tried to hold onto hope that he was going to make it out of there, but my intuition told me he wouldn't.

Without him, I had no purpose in living. A life like that was pointless.

Come to think of it, that's probably why we didn't get bed sheets.

Stress tests took place twice a week.

At first, Peterson wanted to see how skilled I was with the powers I already knew how to use. But after the first two stress tests, he suppressed my ability to manipulate fire and air. I didn't know how he was doing it. But it forced me to wake up the other powers within me.

I didn't know how to use spirit offensively. In fact, I didn't know it was possible. Until I wanted my victimizer dead so badly that I imagined him taking the gun from his holster—the one that all of them carried—putting it in his mouth, and blowing his brains out. Suddenly, the whip stopped cracking through the air. I heard the boom of a gunshot. Without even realizing I'd gone into that man's head, I made him kill himself. Just like that. Pure instinct.

And the pain stopped. And I was relieved that he was dead. Proud, even, of my conquest.

The first time I used water, I didn't realize I was doing it. Not until I heard the woman who was beating me gag and gurgle. She choked on her own saliva just as I'd visualized. I drowned her in her own spit just by thinking it.

But the pain stopped. And I was pleased to know she was dead.

The next time stress test day came around, my abuser couldn't have imagined what I'd do to him. I couldn't use fire, air, water, or spirit that time around. There weren't any plants in the cold, sterile room. I couldn't kill him with earth. Or so I thought.

When I tried to summon fire, it didn't work. Air failed just as miserably. So did spirit and water. When nothing worked, I begged the earth for help.

I felt the room quake. The lights flickered like those of a police car. Then massive thuds shook the room. Tiles and light fixtures fell from the ceiling, sending debris and dust all over my bare, bleeding back. Then screams.

Then nothing.

And I was delighted. Because he was dead. I didn't even know how I did it. But I didn't give a shit. The fucker was dead.

I wasn't the girl I'd been a month ago.

Each terrifying day that went by, I was becoming the girl I *thought* I was a month ago.

But as time went on, as I continued to kill those men and women, I realized that I had no power in it. I was getting my revenge for their momentary infliction of my pain. But ultimately, they weren't the ones doing this.

It was Peterson. He was the one I really wanted to kill.

He sent them in to torture me knowing they wouldn't walk out.

I was becoming the monster Peterson claimed we were. And I was praised for my murders.

He'd come onto the speaker and say how *beautiful* what I had done was. How gorgeous. How awestruck I'd made him. Like I was some sort of artist on a stage he'd paid to come see.

It made me fucking sick.

He'd shoot me with a tranquilizing dart, and I'd wake up in my cell a few hours later.

I was at twelve people then. Twelve lives I'd taken.

I hated myself for it.

I hated that I had to do it.

I hated what I was becoming.

It was a matter of rinse and repeat after a while. I was getting a better handle on my powers every stress test day that rolled around. I was getting stronger, just like he said that I would. But I would have rather been a powerless human than continue to use my powers like that.

The irony in it all was that he was just as naïve as me. He could see how powerful I was but yet, he thought he could keep me within his restraint. He was trying to make me stronger. He wanted me to reach my full potential. The paradox in it was that he was creating a force he, and no one else, could ever control. At times, a force that even I couldn't control.

I pulled a flame to my fingers as I gazed out the frosted block window. The sun shined in to cast warmth across my cool skin.

I missed the sun. All the times I bitched about it shining in my eyes or my pale skin peeling after being out in it for too long seemed so arbitrary then. At that point, I'd literally kill for a sunburn.

I missed food. I'd been eating some type of gray, unidentifiable mush for the past month with my hands as spoons. I didn't even know what it was. It smelled like tuna, but it *wasn't* tuna. Or maybe it was, just mashed up with something else. Chris called it oatmeal. What I'd have done for a real bowl of oatmeal... Fuck, what I would've done for a fucking salad.

I missed coffee. I fucking *missed* coffee. Coffee used to be the one thing I never went a day without. Now, I was forgetting what it tasted like. All I drank in thirty-one fucking days was lukewarm water.

I missed shampoo. And body wash. I'd only been able to rinse my body since I arrived there. We weren't given toiletry items. Shit, we weren't even given a pillow.

I missed physical contact. The only time I felt another person's touch now was when Peterson belted me down to that freezing table and drew my blood. But his touch made me want to vomit.

I missed my mom. The way she smiled when I walked in her front door unannounced. The smell of her famous chili on the stove. The way her hug made me feel safe.

I missed so many things.

But most of all, I missed Jeremy.

I started to forget what he looked like. I knew his eyes were blue and his hair was black, but all the details started to blur. I couldn't remember his smile. It was like a mannequin's face on his body when I tried to recall it in my mind.

I couldn't remember what he smelled like anymore. I knew I liked the smell. But I couldn't remember it.

I couldn't remember the sound of his voice either. I remembered thinking that it sounded peaceful and melodic, yet strong and deep, but I couldn't hear it in my mind. I could still hear his guitar as he played a song. But not his voice. Not him.

The only thing I vividly remembered was the way he made me feel. That his arms were the safest place in the galaxy. The way his hands gently held my face like a priceless sculpture when he kissed me. The way my stomach flipped when I saw his smile. The way his lips felt against mine.

CHAPTER FORTY-SEVEN

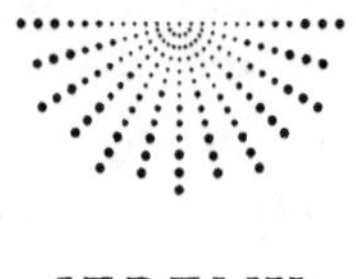

JEREMY

"N o."

"But it's for a good cause, Jeremy," Max insisted.

"If nothing else, it's good publicity for the place," Hannah said.

"But more importantly, it could help us find her," Max said.

I slammed the binder in front of me shut. "It won't make a difference."

"Why are you being so pessimistic?" Max said.

I huffed. "Why are you being so *optimistic*?"

"What's going on back here?" Celena asked in the office doorway. She pulled her blonde hair into a ponytail. "Customers were complaining."

"Tell them their food's on the house and apologize for the inconvenience." I stood and turned to the filing cabinet.

"Max and I thought it would be a good idea to host a fundraising event for a missing person organization in honor of Laila since the police have declared it a cold case, and Jeremy's against it," Hannah said.

I glared at her over my shoulder. "I'm not against the fundraiser. I just don't want anything to do with it and I definitely don't want to perform in it."

Hannah's gaze softened, dewy blue eyes moving between mine. "But you're a great musician."

"And you're her fiancé," Max continued. "It doesn't look good if you don't—"

"I don't give a shit how it makes me look, Max," I snapped. "Hosting some stupid event isn't going to magically bring her home. But if you guys want to do it, go ahead. Just don't expect me to stand there and talk about Laila to a room full of strangers who don't even know her."

"Jeremy—" Max began.

"I'm not fucking doing it. And don't ask me again." I slammed the filing cabinet shut. The bang was like a gong, casting silence through the room. His eyes met mine, jaw tightened.

"Jesus," he said. "Whatever, dude."

As he turned away, I took in a slow breath. I closed my eyes. Then rubbed them with my thumb and forefinger.

Yeah, that'd make Laila happy. Yelling at her best friend. Pulling the 'I'm the boss now that she's gone, and you're gonna do what I say,' card.

I could practically hear her. *"What makes you think you can talk to him like that? He's been working at this place way longer than you. And who the hell do you think you are talking to anyone like that anyway? You aren't a god. Even if you were, is that the kind you'd wanna be? The asshole that barks at people when they say something you don't like?"*

I could see myself conceding when I met her glowing green eyes. Listening to her like my second conscience. Fuck, she'd hate the man I was being.

Celena walked into the office and shut the door behind her. I turned to the old wooden chest behind me, grabbing a short glass and a bottle of whiskey. I opened it up and poured until it was about half full. I turned back to Celena and Hannah, raised the glass to my lips, tipped it back, and chugged.

Hannah gazed at me as I burped. "Sorry, do you guys want one?"

Frowning, she shook her head.

"I'm okay. Thanks, though," Celena said.

I poured another glass. Hannah reached across the desk and grabbed it from my hand. "You could have just said you wanted some."

"Jeremy." She set the bottle down. "What the fuck are you doing?"

I gave a shrug as my stomach filled with warmth. I teleported the bottle back to my hand and filled my glass again. "Getting drunk. What the fuck are *you* doing?"

"Wondering why my brother who has almost six years clean and serene is pouring himself glass after glass of whiskey."

I laughed, shaking my head. "C'mon, we both know I'm not 'clean and serene,'" I said, making air quotes. "I fucked up the day she disappeared, remember?"

I hadn't been close to clean. I hadn't bragged about it; I hadn't drunk with my siblings. But I definitely hadn't been clean.

"What's going on, Jeremy?" Celena lowered herself to the chair next to Hannah.

I lifted the glass and took another gulp. "I had breakfast with Rachel this morning. She thought it'd be a good idea to see if Mary could help find Laila. So I talked with her."

"Mary?" Celena asked.

"You know, mommy dearest?"

I was a dick when I used. Some of the time, anyway. Context depending, of course.

"You and Laila's birth mom." Hannah turned back to me. "What did she say?"

"Basically, she said that there isn't a damn thing I can do. Laila has to save herself," I said. "But she doesn't know how. It could be months before she figures out how to contact me. Years, even. Or maybe never at all." An ironic laugh left me. "So. I'm getting shit faced."

Celena reached for the bottle. "Do you have another glass?"

I reached behind me and grabbed one from the wooden chest. "Have at it."

"Celena," Hannah said.

"I'll see you at home, alright?" She spun the lid off and poured her glass.

Hannah shook her head in disapproval. She turned to me and stood. "Just think about it, okay?"

I had no intention of thinking about it. Performing was never my thing. Let alone for something I knew would embarrass the shit out Laila. She hated being the victim. If she ever made it home and saw the shrines erected all over town in her honor, she'd tear them down.

"Mhmm." I took a sip from my glass.

As the door shut behind her, I turned to Celena. "You know everyone's going to chew your ass out for drinking with me."

She leaned back in her chair and took a sip. "I'm sure they will."

"Then why are you?" I asked.

A shrug. "Because no one should drink alone when they're in your state of mind."

She reminded me so much of Laila. Not in a 'I want to fuck her because she looks like my fiancé sort of way.' Just in the sense that she felt familiar. Although, she was a little less responsible than Laila.

"I'll drink to that." I took another swig from the glass.

"Plus, you're going to be my brother-in-law." She smiled. "Everybody should get whiskey drunk with their in-laws at least once."

"Is that a thing?" I asked.

Celena shrugged. "I don't think so. But it should be."

A chuckle left my lips. I swirled the brown liquid in my cup. I sighed, watching small bubbles rise to the surface.

"How are you holding up?" she asked. Not in the gentle, babying tone my siblings used. She almost said it as a statement. She knew what I was gonna say but just wanted to get the conversation started.

"I hate my life."

"I'll drink to that." She took a sip from her cup.

"You've had a shitty couple months too, huh?"

"Yeah, you could say that."

"Life sucks."

Her brow raised, almost in a shrug. "Mostly."

"Blows you didn't really get to know her before all this too," I muttered. "She's the best person I've ever met."

"Well, why don't you tell me about her? I can get to know her through you."

I laughed. "I could talk about her for hours; you don't want to hear all that."

"Well, I'm supposed to be at work right now. But my boss is really cool. Lets me drink on the job and bullshit in the back." She grinned. "So I've got nothing but time."

I chuckled. "What do you want to know?"

"I don't know. Just tell me about her. It helped a lot to talk about my sister when I lost her. It's not the same, I know Laila's still out there. But it helps." She forced a smile. "How'd you guys meet?"

"You really want to hear all this?"

"I really do."

"Well," I muttered. "She was friends with Adam. It's funny actually. Before we met in person, I saw a picture of them together and was like, 'Hey, that girl's cute as fuck, what's her name? I'm gonna add her on Facebook.' And he said no 'cause I'd ruin their friendship." She laughed. I smiled for a second, It fell. "And because we thought she was human. So I let it go or whatever. But this one night, they hit a deer coming back from the city and blew out a tire. Adam calls me and asks if I'll come pick them up, and I was like 'Nah, I'm already in bed,' and he was like, 'Remember that cute girl whose number you wanted? She's here, we're her ride home.' And I was like, 'Okay, on my way.'"

"That's adorable."

My shoulders lifted in a shrug. "I get there, and Adam and Adrian are sitting in the car trying to keep warm. But not Laila."

"No?"

My chest got warm at the memory. "Not Laila. She was sitting in the brush on the side of the road with the dying deer." I smiled, envisioning her muddy boots and shivering hands as she stroked its fur. "When I asked her why, she said because no one deserves to die alone."

"Sounds like Laila." She smiled.

My smile gradually lowered. "And when she said that, I just... I don't know, I couldn't even bring myself to flirt with her. It's not like I was looking for my soulmate or anything. I was twenty, I just wanted to fuck around. But she was... She was better than me. She had her shit together, and she was so sweet. She was like a princess or some shit and I didn't even think I stood a chance." Biting my lip, I looked down at the whiskey in my glass. "I didn't think I wanted to fall in love then. But I just... I did. Like, instantly. It's like I already knew her. I guess we probably did in a past life or something."

She smiled, waiting for me to go on.

"We started driving home, and Adam and Adrian were making out in the back seat, so we just talked. It was almost a three-hour drive, so we really made a dent in that awkward first meeting phase, you know?" She nodded and I went on, "We dropped Adam and Adrian off at her house and she asked if we could stop and get food before I took her home."

"Because Laila always has to stop and get food." Celena smiled.

I laughed. "Yeah, so we stopped and we sat in the parking lot for, God, I don't know. Three or four hours? Just talking and talking." I smiled. It slowly faded. "I remember looking at her and thinking about how beautiful she was. I thought Adam was right, you know? Like, there's no way that this girl would ever have any interest in this pathetic asshole. She had all this ambition. And I was a loser, ya know? I didn't have a job, and uh..." I paused. "I wasn't gonna try anything. I got in my car that night with the intention of bringing that girl home with me. And I met her, and I couldn't even try to get in her pants. I wasn't enough for her, you know?" Celena gave a gentle smile, nodding slightly. "But when we finally pulled up to her house, she asked me out." I laughed. "Well, she said we should hang out and gave me her number."

"So she asked you out." Celena's smile widened.

I smiled back. "Basically."

CHAPTER FORTY-EIGHT

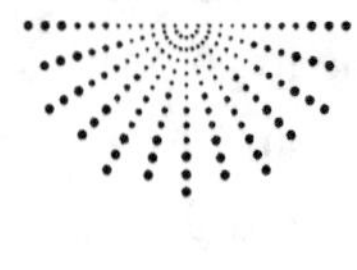

JEREMY

Celena and I talked for hours. I poured drink after drink. Mostly, I just rambled about Laila.

She let me talk about her without a twinge of awkward annoyance. I think that in her own way, her heart was breaking too. Celena lost a sister already and although she didn't really know Laila yet, she wanted to. Especially since she didn't have to hide who she was with Laila.

Celena didn't say much. She lightly conversed, but more than anything, she just asked questions about Lai. She asked about me a bit too, but her main focus was her sister whose photos hung all over the mostly refinished apartment. I'd been busy with the diner but since I wasn't getting much sleep, I had a lot of time to work on painting and finishing touches. I wished she could see how nice it was coming together.

"Hannah said you were a musician, right?" Celena sipped her Coke.

"I play guitar. Wouldn't really call myself a musician."

"Nah, you're a musician. I can see it." She studied me for a moment. "You've got the whole long hair and tortured gaze thing going on."

"Eh." I took a sip from my glass.

Celena gave a half grin. "Did you tell Laila you played guitar the night you met? 'Cause I can definitely see that being something she would be into."

"Maybe, I don't remember. We talked about a lot of stuff that night," I muttered. "Her dad just died so we talked a lot about loss. I have a lot of experience in that department."

"Yeah, me too. It almost makes you wish you didn't love them at all when you lose someone, ya know? Those memories, they're beautiful, but they hurt so bad because you know you're never going to make any more."

"Almost. It hurts when you think about how you won't get to make any more with them. But if I didn't have those losses, I wouldn't be who I am. I wouldn't know what happiness was without them."

"Yeah. Yeah, that's true."

I took another sip from my glass.

"Are you any good?" She gestured to my guitar that hung on the wall.

I glanced up at it and laughed. "Not really."

"Do you love it?"

"What—Playing guitar?" I asked. She nodded, and I shrugged. "Yeah, I guess."

"Have you been playing since this all started?" Celena said.

"Not really."

"Then you should play something," she insisted. "Artists need their release. Even if you do suck. If you love it, then you should do it when you're sad."

I huffed. "You just want to know if I really do suck."

She smirked. "Kind of."

I laughed. Maybe she was right. Maybe it'd feel good to hold a guitar. I started toward the wall. "Fine, I'll play something but I'm pretty tipsy so it's probably going to sound even worse than it normally does."

"Fair enough." She gave a soft, friendly smile.

I sat on the chair by the window. I turned the keys for a minute, checking the tune. I began strumming.

The first song that came to mind was *Tiny Dancer*. It was one of my Dad's favorites when I was a kid. It was also the first song Chris taught me to play on guitar. I always knew the song with piano as the primary instrument and I remember thinking how cool and different the beginning sounded on the old, well-maintained acoustic. I could play just about any instrument I picked up now, and I'd always love the piano, but guitar would always be my favorite. Every song sounded better on strings.

Once I wrapped up the last chorus, I set my guitar down. "I'm pretty drunk so I think I fucked up a good bit."

Celena put her hands together in a slow clap, shaking her head. "No, man. That was amazing. I really was not expecting that."

"Shut up." My eyes fell on the pick between my fingers. Laila gave it to me two years before. She caught it at a Jack White concert and told me it'd bring me more luck than her. Literally every single thing I touched reminded me of her. "I'm slurring my words and shit, that was awful."

"That was so far from awful, dude," Celena said. "You're insanely talented."

I took a slurp from my glass.

"There's no way you actually think you're bad," Celena said. "Hannah's right, you should perform at that fundraiser."

"I'm gonna pass on that." I stood and walked to the entertainment center. I reached into the drawer and pulled out a pack of papers and a small bag of weed. "You smoke, right?" Before she could answer, I continued, "Yeah, you smoke. Duh."

"I think that would mean a lot to Laila," she said. I sat back down on the chair diagonal from the couch.

"How?" I laughed. "It's not like she's going to be there. She won't know. And even if she were, the whole thing would make her uncomfortable. Laila doesn't want to be seen as some victim. She's going through hell right now, but if we ever get her back, all of these posters and trending stories are going to embarrass the shit out of her. If I participated in that, she'd probably hit me."

"Maybe at the other stuff, but not you performing a song for her. You two are as sappy as they come. She'd get all teary eyed just thinking about it."

"You don't know Laila that well. Trust me, she wouldn't care if I didn't sing her some stupid song."

"She'd love it and you know it."

"She wouldn't even be there."

"We'll record it and show it to her when we find her," she said. "And like Max said. It'll look good to the public. There's a lot of attention around Laila's disappearance, people around here are curious. And people don't see you much. Everyone in this town knows each other but not you. They know your face, but they don't know *you*. This, your music? It's you. Part of you anyway. You can't show everyone the big picture, but you can show them that side of you."

I broke up some buds on the table. "She'd think it's stupid."

"What's your song?" she asked. I puzzled up at her. "You can't tell me you sappy fuckers don't have a song."

I looked back down and sprinkled weed onto the paper. "You know Panic! At the Disco, right?"

"Of course I know Panic! At the Disco."

I laughed. "I don't know, you're young. I guess they're bigger now than they've ever been though, huh?"

"You do realize you're only six years older than me, right?"

She waved me off. "So what's your song?"

"*Always*." I rolled the paper between my fingers and licked it shut. "It's kinda lame. I don't really consider it our song, but she does. I had my AUX cord plugged in and it came on while it was on shuffle and she got super stoked about it. She started, like, jumping up and down and was like, 'Oh my god, you like Panic!?'"

She gave a gentle smile and tossed me a lighter. "You should play it."

I sparked the joint. "It's been a minute since I sang that high. Don't make fun of me when I fuck up."

"Oh, I'll mock the shit out of you. But I'll tell you what you need to fix before the show."

I rolled my eyes and hit the joint a few times. I passed it to her and raised the guitar to my lap and began strumming. I started singing a moment later.

In the beginning, it was just words and notes. I didn't think too much into it.

But as I moved into the chorus, my voice started to shake when I made it to the softer, emotional lines. As I moved into the next verse, I recovered a bit. Until the last line that says something about being lonely and pretending to be okay. Tears started to stream down my cheeks, and I stopped playing. I moved my hand from the neck of the guitar to wipe my face.

"Shit, man. I'm sorry," Celena murmured as she set the joint into the ash tray.

I leaned the guitar on the floor against the couch. "No, don't be."

"That was dumb."

"No, it's okay. I'm okay. I just…" I coughed a bit from the tears and snot running down my throat. I wiped my wet hands against my jeans. "I just miss her. I miss her so much."

Celena awkwardly pressed her lips together. I supposed bullshitting was her thing, not emotions. She grabbed the joint from the ash tray and passed it to me. "I know you do."

I held my breath for a moment to keep my tears from turning to heaving cries. "Sorry, I'm kind of a mess right now. I thought the liquor would help and I guess it does for a second. But I don't know. At least it helps me sleep."

Silence set in for a moment. I lifted my glass and chugged. The burn settled in my stomach. And life didn't feel so bad. It didn't feel good. Really, it didn't feel like anything.

When I was drunk, looking at the pictures of her on the wall didn't hurt so much. The soft feel of the shag carpet beneath my toes didn't make me feel so guilty. She hadn't been here when it arrived, and she'd been so excited about it. Each morning when I walked on it, I thought about how cold she was. I downed some whiskey to take that feeling away.

"Why does everyone make such a big deal about you drinking?" Celena asked quietly.

"Nobody's told you?" I asked. She made a face, like asking me to elaborate. "I wasn't always the Jeremy you know. I, uh... I started doing pills when I was fifteen and was onto heroin around sixteen. I got clean but I... I can't just use drugs like you guys can. Especially downers."

"Oh," she muttered. "I didn't realize."

I shrugged as I took a hit off the joint. "Ya know how they say addiction's a disease?" She nodded and I continued. "It is. I mean, I see almost everyone else drink or do party drugs and call it a day. But I physically can't do that. If I get fucked up, I don't know how to make myself stop. It's a disease, it's definitely a disease. But it's like a secondary disease, at least for me. Like with some types of diabetes, how it starts out as an overeating disorder."

"What was your primary disease then?" she asked quietly.

"Depression." I laughed. "PTSD, maybe? I don't know."

"How did Laila feel about that?"

"Me being an addict?" I asked. "I don't know, she never made a big deal about it. She knows I am, but she's never treated me like it. Most people glare or make snide comments even if they say they support rehabilitation. But Laila never has. I mean, I'm not perfect and I know that. But I think to her, I kind of am. Like she is to me. I love everything about her, even the bad shit because it's a part of what makes her her. I think she sees my addiction the same way. It sucks but it really is a big part of what makes me the person I am."

"That's kind of beautiful," Celena murmured. "You should write a song about it."

"That's not really my thing. I can write the music, but I can't write songs for shit. Writing's Laila's thing."

"Fair enough." Celena sat forward and ran her hand along the bridge of her nose. "Is there anything that we haven't tried to find out where she is?"

"Magically speaking?" I asked. She nodded. "Yeah, everything I can think of. I even paid Helena to try some spells. No location spells worked, and we can't magnify our bond because she isn't here to do the spell. It's like I'm completely blocked out of her head."

Silence followed. She met my gaze, squinting a bit as she thought. "This is probably a dumb idea, but you guys can still feel each other's pain, right?"

"Yeah, why?"

"This is a really gruesome thought…" I squinted, waiting for her to continue. "But if you were to carve a message into your skin, she'd feel it right?"

It was as if a light bulb went off over my head. "I didn't even think about that. That's genius."

I teleported to the kitchen, grabbed a knife from the sink, and lowered it to my skin. I'd barely drunkenly touched the surface before Celena rushed up to the counter and pulled it from my grasp.

"I didn't mean right now, Jeremy. You're drunk as shit, your blood's thin."

I reached for the blade. "I don't care, somebody can heal me—"

The front door pushed inward. Wyatt walked in. His mouth fell agape, watching the two of us tussling over a carving knife.

"What the fuck are you doing?" He hurried over and effortlessly ripped it from my hand. "Jeremy, you can't kill yourself—"

I laughed. "I'm not trying to kill myself."

"It's my fault." Celena rubbed her temples.

"What do you mean?" Wyatt asked.

"Can I heal you, Jeremy?" Celena asked.

"I guess."

She held her hand over my arm. I grimaced as the white light penetrated my skin. It was barely there, maybe the depth and width of a cat's scratch. The small cut mended quickly but disoriented me a bit. I stumbled backward. Wyatt gripped my shoulder to steady me.

"Woo, got a little lightheaded there," I said with a chuckle.

"I think we should get you to bed, man." Wyatt held my swaying shoulder.

"I'm fine. I was having a good time." I gave a childish grin.

"You can have a good time tomorrow," Wyatt said the way a parent would. "Let's go to bed."

I turned to Celena. "Thanks for chilling with me. Sorry I cried a lot."

She gave a sad smile. "We all cry sometimes. It's alright."

CHAPTER FORTY-NINE

JEREMY

I stared up at the white ceiling. It was so cold. I could have pulled the blanket over me, but it felt wrong. She was shivering, I could feel it. Why should I be warm when she was so cold?

The bed still smelled like her. I wasn't sure how, but it did. Like honey and tea leaves. With a meandering hint of weed.

Raising the joint to my lips, I took a slow drag before resting my hand against my chest. I watched the smoke rise and fall to form miniature mushroom clouds before dissipating into the air around me.

I wasn't holding up very well.

Every few minutes, I felt stinging and stabbing pains all over my back as she turned and ripped open scabs struggling to heal. It was especially hard at night. She couldn't get comfortable.

I felt the skin pulling against cloth on her aching back. Every part of her was sore. During the day, I didn't feel as much pain. Her knees hurt though. It was a pressured, bruising kind of pain. She must have kneeled a lot. It was probably the most comfortable way to be positioned because of the never-ending wounds on her spine.

My gaze turned to a picture of us together on the side table. It was taken last year when we teleported to Hawaii for the day. We were whale watching and asked another tourist to take it. She looked so happy curled against my chest on the picnic blanket. We both did. I wished I could go back and relive those moments.

There wasn't a reason for us to scramble off to the beach that day. It wasn't our anniversary or anything, but she was working a lot and finally had a day off, so I just took her. It's not like it was a big feat. I could go anywhere in the world any time I wanted. But she loved it.

She always talked about how badly she wanted to travel before she learned what we were. She'd ramble about how she'd probably never make enough money to see the world. Once she knew what I could do, I had to show her everything I'd seen. I'd been everywhere. I'd seen every great city that existed.

I saw the Alps from their highest peak. I'd cheated my way to the top of Mount Everest and ended up feeling like shit for days because of the rapid elevation change. I'd seen the clearest water in the world at Jiuzhaigou Valley in Sichuan Province of southwest China. I'd seen anything beauty on our little blue planet worth seeing.

I couldn't give her much, but I could take her anywhere she wanted to go in the world.

There were so many more places I wanted to take her.

And I couldn't even find her.

Every time I felt that sting or stab against my skin, I was reminded of just how horribly I was failing her. It was hard to even look at myself in the mirror. I was trying so hard not to give up, but I was losing hope. Not only in finding her, but in life itself.

"I'm so sorry, baby," I whispered.

CHAPTER FIFTY

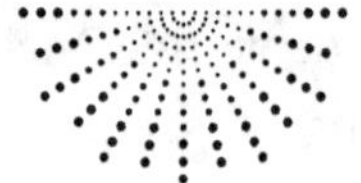

MAY 2, 2019 - LAILA

Day fifty-five.

I was up to nineteen murders. I killed nineteen people. Not Demons or Ghosts or Vampires. Not innately evil creatures. Not lives my conscious could justify as the days dragged on.

I killed *nineteen humans.*

Nineteen sets of blood on my hands.

Nineteen souls I had sworn to protect.

Who was I? What the fuck was I letting him turn me into?

I was glad there wasn't a mirror in my cell, because I couldn't look at myself if I wanted to.

I killed nineteen people.

But it was stress test day.

And I wasn't going to let my total turn to twenty. Not yet, anyway.

I awoke again to the cold leather tips of the whip slicing against my back. It scraped all the way down my shoulder to the middle of my ass. The skin tore a seamless line down my body like a paper cut but fifty times as deep and a hell of a lot wider.

I moaned, feeling the wind swirl around me and fire spark the tips of my fingers. But I held it in, focusing on keeping the pain at bay. I stayed steady. I'd made it through—What? Fifteen of these so far? I could do it. I didn't have to kill anyone else.

The whip kept cracking as I struggled to maintain my composure. I took slow even breaths. Just letting it slash my back to shreds. I silently chomped on my lip until the warm metallic taste of blood danced on my tongue.

Peterson thought that my abilities were centered around pain. While that was true to an extent, what he was doing forced me to lose control. When I maintained power over the abilities, that's when I truly became a force to be reckoned with.

It slammed against my back again, slicing like a piece of meat at a butcher. The sound as it whooshed through the air used to scare me. It meant that the pain was coming. But I'd stared at that floor as they tore my body to shreds so many times then. I'd watched my blood puddle in front of me week after week. It didn't scare me anymore. I knew I was too valuable to kill.

The pain became less agonizing. It still fucking hurt. But once you know that pain is temporary, once you know that you won't die, pain isn't so intimidating. When you remove the concept of death, pain is just an annoyance.

"Aren't you gonna do something?" the woman holding the whip said behind me.

I shook my head against the metal, toilet seat shaped head rest. "No." I grimaced as another slash split through my flesh. "I'm not going to kill anyone else."

She cackled. "I'd like to see you try."

I couldn't help my chuckle when she slammed my back again. It seemed to make her angry because the next slash cut even deeper. I cried out before I laughed again.

"C'mon, bitch." I bit my tongue when it whacked against my spine once more. "Show me what you can do. You can kill me, right? Do it then."

Gritting my teeth together as the leather cracked through the air, I let the wind swirl around me. In the shadow on the floor, I watched the strings of leather whirl like a tube man outside of a car dealership.

I wasn't gonna kill her. But I was gonna make a fucking point.

She gasped. I yanked the wind in the room toward me, pulling her into me like a vacuum. I heard a thump. A shriek followed. She screamed as I dragged her closer. In less than a second, she lay on the ground beside me fighting the cyclone of air with no success.

Her brown eyes widened in horror; mouth open like she was trying to catch raindrops within it. That short blond hair slid into my puddle of blood, turning its golden hues a dark shade of crimson. Her lip trembled in terror as tears flooded her eyes.

"He sent you in here for me to kill. You realize I have killed every single one of you that tortures me, right?"

Eyes still wide in fear, she swallowed hard.

"You don't actually think you matter, do you?" I smiled, laugh leaving my lips. "You would be dead if I didn't decide I wasn't going to kill you."

Her body trembled in panic while I stared deeply into her eyes.

I went into that room with the intention of staying peaceful throughout the torture. To remain calm. To prove that I was better than the person he was forcing me to become.

But there it was. A bland, human mind, easy to hop inside of. An able body on the ground with a gun at her hip and a set of keys to the locks that held me.

I saw my opportunity. And I fucking took it.

I enveloped myself into her mind until I stared up at myself through her while still looking at her through my own. I slowed the wind and stood her up. That's when I saw the stress test room for the first time. I noted the door in the corner and the large two-way mirror on the opposite wall, but I didn't have time to pay attention to all of the details.

I had one goal. Release the cuffs around my hands, shackles around my ankles, and the metal band around my neck and thighs.

I hurried to it and fiddled with the locks for a moment. Peterson yelled over the speaker, but I ignored him. The blood rushing through her veins pumped like a drum in our ears.

The locks needed keys, but I didn't have time to undo them. I reached to the holster and pulled the gun out. I cocked it and blew each hunk of metal out with a bullet, chunks flying across the room in a shower.

I heard the beep and click of the handle on the steel door to my left. My hand opened. I sent the wind to hold it shut with thousands of pounds of force like that of an airplane in flight.

They yelled on the other side, pounding against it like the police with a search warrant. I pulled the locks through the metal at each notch while keeping the wind against the door like my own interior barrier.

When the last piece of metal came through the final hook, I slammed out of my abuser's mind back into mine. Stammering to my feet as the wind swirled around us like we were in the eye of a tornado, I didn't waste a second of the short window of time I had. I leaned down and lifted the gun to my hand to be sure she couldn't grab it.

I glanced around. My eyes caught on the large window with a mirror effect over it. My hand stayed outstretched to hold the air against the door as I walked toward the glass.

"I'm not killing for you," I screamed over the howl of the wind. "You want to see what I can do? Get out here and let me show you."

The mirror effect faded like a slideshow. After my eyes adjusted, I found myself staring at Peterson. He frowned, deeply disappointed, as if he expected this but hoped I'd be smarter.

But it wasn't Peterson's face that stopped me in my tracks.

Had it not been for her, I may have made it out on day fifty-five. I didn't realize it until a moment or two later, but she was at least part of the reason I didn't make it out on day one.

She didn't look identical to the pictures. But it was her. It was fucking her. She stood beside him like a queen to a king.

She didn't wear the scrub like gowns the rest of us wore. No. She had a pastel pink lace blouse draped over her torso. As if heading to her nine to five at the local bank. Her red hair rested against her chest in loose, beachy curls, like she'd spent hours perfecting each lock. Her bangs were pulled to the side with a yellow, cloth flower clip.

She was bright and full of life. Her blue eyes shined at me like an old friend visiting their drunkard uncle with pity.

Her skin looked soft and supple, gently dusted with a coat of foundation. Her high cheek bones and rounded chin were beginning to droop with cracks and crinkles but there was no denying it. Her long, flowing copper hair was impossible to confuse with anyone else, although it now had thin lines of silver throughout.

What shocked me so much, what terrified me to my core, what made me drop the wind against the door, wasn't the woman standing beside him.

It was the little girl. With warm brown skin, curly black hair, and pale blue eyes who sat in a chair beside her mother. She couldn't have been more than twelve. She was different now, as I'd known she would be. But that complexion was unforgettable.

They were just as beautiful as Ray described them.

Amy and Lydia.

My heart sunk to the floor with the gun.

I'm not sure what shocked me the most. It wasn't because they were there, I expected that. Part of me even hoped it.

I was astonished to see their obvious alliance. The most alarming thing in it could have been the fact that a child was watching me being tortured. Or maybe it was that her mother let it happen. Maybe it was that I was standing in that room swirling the wind around butt naked, dripping in my own blood and holding a pistol in front of a child. The daughter of my friend, no less.

The wind stopped spinning and my stomach churned. The adrenaline wore off and my back began to throb.

I gazed at her completely flabbergasted. She began speaking into my psyche but not so much words as a barrier. Had I not let my guard down for that split second, she would have been incapable of blocking anything in my mind.

I heard the door slam open. I tried to bring a fire to my hand, but it wouldn't ignite. The wind wouldn't move.

Then men and women in suits came in with guns drawn. I started to run. I didn't know where I would run *to,* but it was the only option I had.

But it was already too late. The gun shot echoed off the cement walls and sent shockwaves through my ears. As I fell to the ground, I watched the little girl scream. She cupped her hand over her mouth.

It replayed in my mind like a slow motion clip a thousand times. That terrified little girl watching some naked pregnant lady covered in blood get shot and fall to the floor.

Amy wasn't the victim Ray thought she was. She worked for him.

She was helping him.

CHAPTER FIFTY-ONE

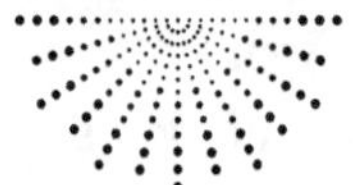

MAY 4, 2019 - LAILA

Beep. Beep. Beep.

The smell of Axe cologne mixed with rubbing alcohol. Cold air wisped around me from an air vent. My leg throbbed. I tried to lift my hand to soothe it away but caught cold metal. I groaned at the ache shooting up my arm.

"Rise and shine, Sleeping Beauty." His disgusting voice pulled me from my sleep.

My eyes fluttered open, blinking through the bright light that shined against my face. He pushed it to the side. My vision became clearer. Peterson sat beside me in a rotating chair, face slightly leaning over mine. He pushed his glasses up and brought a smile to his lips. "Glad to see you again. Had me worried there for a while."

"You wanted to see how powerful I was." My voice cracked between my dry, tearing lips.

He grabbed a light pink cup off the wheeled table beside us and held the straw between his pointer and fore finger. "Here, drink."

I turned my head to the other side, coughing a bit and avoiding his gaze.

"It's just water, Laila." He softly grabbed my chin and turned my face to him. It was oddly gentle. Sweet, almost. "Look." He raised the glass to his lips and took a sip, careful to avoid the straw. "Your body has been through enough; it doesn't need to be dehydrated too. I've been pumping you with fluids but I'm sure you're thirsty."

I tried to swallow, but my throat was too dry. My tongue felt as parched and scratchy as cotton against the roof of my mouth. I don't think my mouth had ever been so dry in my life. I wanted so badly to turn it down. But I wanted that drink so much more than the pride of refusing it.

I raised my head a bit. He delicately put the straw into my mouth. My lips closed around it before I aggressively slurped it down. "There you go," he murmured softly.

The ice clanged in the plastic cup. That freezing water felt so good sliding down my esophagus. And it spiked guilt through me. Chris and Haley, as well as the countless other people they were holding there, drank lukewarm, mediocre tap while I slurped down ice cold water.

"Alright, alright. Give yourself a minute." He pulled the cup away.

I coughed and gagged a bit when the water went down the wrong pipe. He jolted forward, the way you do when a baby chokes on their bottle. He grabbed my shoulder with alarmed eyes. I recovered a moment later.

Water spilled from the edge of my lips. He tenderly wiped the corner of my mouth. Chills erupted down my spine.

"You didn't care what my body had been through when they were beating me," I murmured.

His eyebrows fell sadly over his eyes. "The stress tests are to help you. To teach you."

"It's horrible," I said as loud as I could.

He was quiet for a moment. "No more stress tests. Not until the baby comes and you're back to normal."

"Are you going to quit doing them to everyone else?"

He huffed, then chuckled. "Everyone else isn't pregnant."

"Then keep doing them to me."

He laughed again. "I couldn't if I wanted to. Amy needs to work on her technique because we can't have a repeat of the other day, can we?"

My teeth chattered from the familiar chill in the room. He reached down and pushed hair from my face. I moved my head to the side, but I couldn't go far. His hand gently caught my other cheek and pulled my face back to his.

His warm palm against my skin was almost comforting, and that thought made me sick. I hated him. I hated that he'd taken so much from me that something so small, something *he'd* given me, was a comfort.

"Are you cold?" His thumb caressed my cheek.

"I'm always cold." My teeth trembled together. "You keep it freezing in here."

His brows pulled together and his lips curved down. "Hang on." He hurried to his feet and disappeared behind me.

My thigh ached as if being ripped from my body. I looked down to see it, but my belly wrapped in a large monitor made it impossible.

An off-white hospital gown covered my torso like a sheet to a corpse. It wasn't much but it was more than what I had the last time I was belted down to that table. My legs were shackled to it, but it felt different than the last time I lay there. There was some type of foam beneath me, and my legs were tied down further apart against a set of stirrups. I assumed it was for easier access to the birth canal if I were to go into premature labor from the trauma of surgery.

"Here," Peterson said. He draped a pastel green blanket over my body. It was soft and fuzzy, similar to the small throw blankets I laid on my couch at home. But a cheaper, thinner material that almost resembled felt. It wasn't as warm as the ones Jeremy and I curled beneath while we watched movies and argued about who had more and who didn't deserve to pull it any further to their side.

He tucked it under my sides. As it laid against my skin, I immediately felt warmer. The smell of his cologne, or maybe his laundry detergent, filled my nostrils and made me nauseous. But I was warm.

"I keep this here for the long nights." He smiled as he sat in the chair beside me. "I'm glad I left it in my office."

I said nothing, just watched his sweet, gentle eyes as he pushed his glasses up. I couldn't figure him out. His expression, it looked like he cared. But how could you care for someone and do to them what he did?

He stared back for a moment. He cleared his throat and reached to the table beside me. Bags rustled as he rummaged for something. "I wasn't sure what you'd want, but I figured that everyone loves chicken strips."

He lifted a cardboard box with a logo to his lap. The word *Harvey's* was sandwiched between two pieces of a blue and orange hamburger bun. I'd never been to Canada. But I knew enough from Television to know that's where most of the Harvey's franchises were located.

I caught a whiff of it. My throat bobbed with a swallow. Water puddled in my mouth as he opened the lid. My stomach growled like a bear preparing for hibernation.

I wanted those fucking chicken strips so bad. But I couldn't. Not when everyone else was eating fish mush.

"I got barbecue and honey mustard," he said.

"I can't eat that."

"Of course you can."

I shook my head.

He looked at my face and then back to the chicken strips. "Is this because you don't want special treatment?" I said nothing, just turned my gaze away. "What if I got pizza for dinner Sunday? For everyone. I'll get everyone pizza if you eat this."

I turned back to meet his gaze. "You wouldn't do that."

"I will." He nodded fast. "I will, but you have to eat. The OB is worried about your weight, you need to eat more."

I rubbed my tongue against my teeth. "You'll really get everyone pizza?"

He smiled, nodding fast again. "I will. I promise." He reached out and squeezed my hand. I tried to jerk it away but only moved about a quarter of an inch. His smile fell as he brought it back to the box. "Just eat, Laila."

I looked down at the chicken strips more intently than I'd ever looked at food in my life. My stomach gurgled. I wasn't sure if in hunger or guilt. But holy fuck, I wanted that chicken strip. He lifted a piece to my face and waited for me to open my mouth.

I did, and he fed me a bite. My mouth tingled and watered like a flash flood. It was cold and kind of dry, but it was somehow pure heaven. My taste buds exploded. Grease stung the tips like fireworks against my tongue. Garlic danced along my taste buds like it never had before. I could taste the hint of onion powder and the glimmer of stinging pepper as I swallowed. The salt jumped along my tongue and filled me with a rush of endorphins.

He laughed when I closed my eyes, enjoying the bliss of every chunk. I devoured each bite like a rabid animal. It had been almost two months since I'd eaten real food and I'd forgotten how much I loved eating. It was the best moment I'd had in so long.

Once I finished the chicken, he lifted a cup from the table and held it in front of me. An orange straw protruded from the whitish mush. "What's that?"

"An Oreo milkshake," he said. "I didn't know if you'd want chocolate or vanilla."

I moved my head forward and sucked through the straw until the cool, slushy ice cream made its way into my throat. My head pounded with brain freeze as I guzzled it down. But I didn't care. It was delicious. Oreos were my first craving when I became pregnant. I couldn't even attempt to act like I didn't want it.

As I drank the last sip, I met Peterson's smiling gaze. "Are you one of those freaks who gets off watching girls eat or something?" I said as he set the empty cup down on the rolling table.

He chuckled and wiped the corner of my mouth with a napkin. "No, you just really seemed to enjoy that."

"No shit. I've been eating garbage since you took me. When I can keep it down."

He frowned. "You should have told me. I could have gotten you something else. Our baby needs you to eat."

My brows fell as his words repeated in my mind.

"This isn't your baby."

He smiled, chuckling. "I wish you would just see the reality that you're living in, Laila."

I felt my face begin to tremble, teeth chattering in fury. "My baby's father is Jeremy. You'll never be my son's parent."

"Your mother is Rachel Callidy, and you don't share any blood." He pushed up his glasses and held my gaze. "As much as you'd hate to admit it, one day this child will love me. Maybe even as much as he loves you."

"My mom didn't want me," I said with gritted teeth. "I want this baby more than anything. Jeremy wants this baby more than anything."

He smiled and reached forward to cup my face in his hand. "You saw Amy and Lydia, Laila. You can be his mother," he said quietly. "I won't take him from you. I wouldn't do that to you."

"Aren't you considerate."

His smile began to pull down at the sides. "I'm not doing this because I *want* to hurt you. That's just a sad part of the way this has to be."

"What—you think it's helping me?" I shook my arms against their restraints. "You think locking me in a room and only taking me out to torture me and run tests on me is a positive experience, Peterson? You honestly think that you're doing a good thing?"

"I'm doing what needs to be done." He frowned. "You need to be prepared."

"For what?" I snapped. "Because nothing can be worse than this."

He scoffed. "You have no idea what the future has in store for you."

"You have no idea what I'm gonna do to you when I get out of here." I shrugged my shoulders against the cold metal behind me. "You evil piece of shit. I can't wait until I get to fucking kill you. Because I will, Peterson, I'm going to kill you."

For the first time, I saw a spike of anger instead of smug confidence over his sad little face. But it didn't scare me. It gratified me to realize I'd made it under the surface of his skin.

He grasped my neck, pressing slightly into my throat while the palm of his hand squeezed. Where it was positioned, I was able to siphon just a touch of air into my lungs. It was barely enough to refrain from fainting.

"You aren't getting out of here." He squeezed tighter as his face screwed up in anger and a bit of fear. "You aren't going home." I gasped for air as things began to blur around the edges. "You are *mine*. That baby is *mine*. I know what I have to do here, and it is going to be done. Until I say otherwise, your existence is in the palm of my hands, do you understand me?" He squeezed so tight that I felt my face begin to swell.

He yanked my head back and forth like a rag doll. His teeth gritted hard. He stared at me with eyes that could cut diamonds. He pushed his hand harder into my neck until I heaved out a deep wheeze. I moved my head up and down slightly in what I could make of a nod. He released my neck, still glaring.

It was the first time I saw him genuinely angry. Prior to that moment, I was a pet. He wanted to teach me new tricks. But when you teach a dog to attack, you unleash a different kind of beast within them. For the first time, you realize how dangerous your domesticated creature really is. It leaves you with two options.

Put it down, which was out of the question to Peterson.

You end its life, or you brutalize it into compliancy.

Peterson took the latter.

"I try to show you how much you matter." He leaned back in his chair. His hand ran along his jaw. "I could have hurt you for that stunt you pulled, I could have killed you. And if you were anyone else, I would have. I would have killed you so quick." He gritted his teeth together. "But instead I reward you. I sew you up, I feed you, I assure you that you won't have to endure any more pain until this baby comes."

"You won't." I choked out between heaving coughs. "Not while I'm pregnant."

He narrowed his gaze further. "I still wouldn't kill you."

"Why?" I swallowed to ease the tightness in my throat since I couldn't with my hand. "Why, because it's fun to watch me squirm?"

"Because he that overcometh will inherit all things." His gaze softened a touch but still appeared angry. "You're important. I care about you, Laila. You're a part of it all, don't you see? You're the missing piece. You're the center of it. The earth protected the woman. Don't you see?"

I had no clue what he was fucking talking about.

Jeremy would have known exactly where those verses were from though.

I gritted my trembling teeth together, seeing for the first time how insane he was. "You don't do this to people you care about. You don't beat them and torture them. You don't care about me. And I certainly don't care about you." My eyes locked with his. "I will *never* care about you. This baby will *never* care about you. No one could ever love you. You're the most disgusting thing that's ever walked this earth."

His hand went back to my neck and his eyes filled with rage. His grasp was so tight around my throat, I was sure that was it. It was my last breath.

I smiled, trying to say, "Do it," through his grasp. He released his hand and blinked to see straight. He took in and blew out slow, uneven pants. His teeth gritted to a hard line.

I was practically swimming beneath his skin. And I fucking *loved* it. For the first time since I was there, I had the power. He was struggling to maintain his composure. In that moment, he wanted to hurt me more than any time before. I wouldn't submit, and it infuriated him.

"Fucking do it. Just kill me," I yelled in outrage, followed by a laugh. Admittedly, I was losing it a bit too. "This life isn't worth fucking living. If I have to see your disgusting face, I don't want to be alive. Fucking kill me. Do it. Just kill me!" My limbs contorted against the restraints. I slammed against them like a lunatic. I felt my eyes begin to glow. "I'm never going to fucking be yours. I'll die before my son is. Just kill me—"

Before I could go on, he grabbed my neck and lowered his face to me. His lips were musty as they touched mine, stinking of mouthwash and a smell that almost reminded me of sulfur. My stomach churned and vomit crept its way up my throat. I gagged it back down. The prickle of his freshly shaved face scratched my cheeks and chin. He shoved his tongue into my mouth.

I squirmed against his hands, flailing my arms and legs as much as I could against the tight restraints. I fought so fucking hard. But I was already tied down. And he had his hand around my throat.

There was no escaping his grasp.

His slimy tongue invaded mine and I attempted to yell. I tried shaking my head, but he held it still, disabling my ability to breathe, squeezing tighter.

Still holding my neck, he moved his lips to my ear. "You are mine."

His mouth at my neck started something of a kiss before his teeth dug inside. Stinging, aching, burning. I gasped. Blood trickled down my neck. "Until I say that you aren't."

"Stop," I begged between gasps. "Stop. Please stop." Tears began to spouted from my eyes. He released my neck and walked to my legs. He unbuckled his belt and threw it to the ground.

"No." I shook my head furiously. My back ached, attempting to scoot upward on the maternity table. "No, please. I'm sorry. I'm sorry, just don't."

There's no way that bitch didn't hear me. She had to be nearby to hold my powers down the way that she did. She was the only reason he was able to get close enough to hurt me. She was probably on the other side of that wall hearing my pleas and cries of agony and ignoring them. She didn't do a goddamned thing.

He pulled the keys from his belt loop and undid the metal bar at my hips. He flung it to the side. I continued to beg and plead as he undid each shackle. I screamed and kicked as he freed my legs. But my right leg hurt so bad that no amount of kicks would be enough to stop a mouse.

My hands were still latched down with large metal bracelets that attached to the table. I screamed. He pulled a latch below the bed that made the lower half collapse. He grabbed my hips and slid me down the table, jarring my wrists to the sides against the metal bars.

I kicked against him again. But he grabbed my legs and gripped them against his waist. I pulled as hard as I could, but he pushed his thumb into the wound on my thigh. I heaved out in agony. He gazed down at my legs like they were some object he'd been dreaming of touching his entire life. His other hand found my neck.

"I don't care what bond you have to him." He squeezed my throat and pulled me upward as far as he could through the restraints. "He doesn't deserve you anyway."

CHAPTER FIFTY-TWO

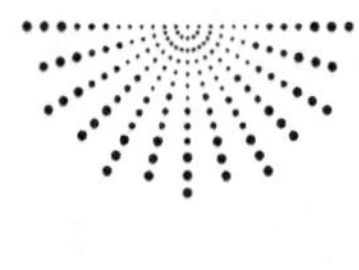

JEREMY

I gazed out the window at the cars quickly filling our little parking lot outside. The smell of burned weed touched my nose. Running my tongue across my teeth, I lifted the fifth of Jack Daniel's to my lips. It burned the ulcers along my tongue. I took a long swig as I watched them step from their vehicles with smiles. Happy. To go to a fundraiser for a missing woman.

My hand slid to my thigh where another shooting pain stabbed upward toward my waist. I stared down at it in frustration. My nostrils flared. I angrily clamped my teeth together. The pain was a constant reminder of my failure.

I raised the bottle back to my lips and took another gulp. I wiped away the brown liquid that trickled from the corner. I didn't care about being sober anymore. I didn't care about much of anything.

The only thing I did care about besides Laila and the baby was the diner. It didn't matter all that much to me, but it mattered to her. Moe's was her pride and joy. I couldn't let it fall apart.

There was a quiet knock at the door. I didn't have time to open it before Leah came in carrying a couple coffees from Dunkin Donuts. I wrapped my lips around the bottle and took another swig as she turned to face me.

Her purple hair rested against her dark skin, gracefully caressing her cheeks and sticking to her light pink lipstick. Her eye makeup was dark with thin black lines pulling upward at the ends on top of gray and black sparkly shadows.

"You look nice," I said.

"You look like shit." She grabbed the bottle from my hand and set it on the counter.

"Don't flatter me."

She handed me the paper cup. "Drink this. You've got to sober up."

"I'm not even drunk."

It wasn't a lie. I'd been drinking so much that the quarter of a bottle I'd drunk was just enough to disorient my vision a bit. My words weren't slurring, the room wasn't spinning. Had it not been for the liquor on my breath, there wasn't a way to tell I was even drinking.

"Either way." She sat at the bar stool. "Go get dressed. And pull your hair back, you look homeless."

"I'm not going on for an hour and a half." I sat beside her at the other stool. "This is stupid anyway. Hannah and Max keep saying this is 'in her honor' like she's fucking dead or something. Like it's going to help. I get it with Max, he doesn't know anything. But Hannah knows it won't make a difference."

She grabbed the bottle of Jack and raised it to her lips. "Have you felt anything new recently? Laila's getting closer to birth, have there been any contractions?"

"I feel him kick sometimes," I muttered. "But no contractions. Something happened to her leg the other day though."

"What do you mean?"

"It was right after they beat her. Maybe she was stabbed? Or shot?" I set the bottle back to the counter. "I don't know. I just kept getting these really bad aching, stabbing pains in it. But nothing since."

"You don't think she's..."

"No. No, I don't think she's dead. I haven't felt much but I did feel something right before you walked in. She's still alive."

"I'm going to do that spell when I get home. Just to be sure."

She wasn't dead. I was so annoyed with everyone assuming she was dead. We all just accepted that Chris was alive, but everyone still acted like Laila died. We had physical proof of her life that we didn't with Chris or Ray's family, yet everyone was so quick to suggest that she was gone forever. It hadn't even been two months yet.

She snatched the bottle. She tilted her head back, guzzling before she went silent. A few seconds later, she turned up to me with big, sorrowful green eyes. "I know I'm generally pretty cold. I don't like to talk about how I feel or what's going on in my head. But you're not like that. And I'm sorry I haven't given you the opportunity to be open about what must be going through your head."

I chuckled. "You already know what's in my head."

"We both know it's not the same thing." She reached forward to touch my upper arm. "Do you want to talk?"

Spinning the liquor through the glass until it formed a little tornado, sitting with the silence for a while, I eventually broke it with, "I want to die."

"Jeremy." Her lips fell to a frown.

I laughed. "I'm not going to kill myself. I just don't want to live this life anymore."

"You don't want to die," she said quietly. "You just want the pain to go away."

"It's not even that. I can deal with the pain. I hate the pain, but at the same time, it's what keeps me going. I know she's alive. She might be in misery, but she's alive." I chewed my dehydrated, peeling lip. "I could be okay without her, I think. It's not being apart from her that's killing me."

"It's the helplessness."

Yup. That's exactly what it was. "I was supposed to protect her. I was supposed to keep her safe. And now she's in that place. She's cold, and she's sore, and she's hurting." I angrily wiped a tear away.

"We both know that Laila can protect herself," Leah said.

"She could if she knew what the fuck she was doing," I said. "I know this is horrible. I know it is, and I wish I didn't feel this way." She looked up, patiently waiting for me to go on. Then for the first time, I said it aloud. "I'm so mad, Leah. If she would have just learned to use her powers, if she would have unlocked her potential, she wouldn't be there. Or if she would have just..."

"Let them kill Hannah?" Her voice stayed calm.

"I love my sister," I said.

"We all have thoughts like that in situations like this."

"I know it isn't Hannah's fault," I said. "I wouldn't want anything to happen to her."

"You're a person, Jeremy," Leah said. "You're allowed to have meandering thoughts like the rest of us. Trust me, you're not the only one who's thought it. Even if you don't blame her, Hannah does. That's why she did all of this, you know. She feels helpless too. She just wanted to do something."

"I figured." I ran my hand along my tense jaw. "It's not her fault. They were watching us; they were waiting for an opportunity for the two of us to be separated. They waited until it was just Laila and Hannah for a reason. And they knew Laila. They knew she'd take in the haunted little boy that wandered into our life. They knew we wouldn't question it because Laila's kindness is her best attribute. That's what I love about her, that's what makes her Laila. But it's also her biggest weakness." My head collapsed to my hand. I rubbed my temple. "Is it horrible that I wish we would have just kept driving after I hit him?"

She was quiet for a moment. "We've all thought it. It isn't right, and we all feel guilty for thinking it, but... He wasn't our family. We didn't really know him. We cared for him, but he wasn't one of us. Laila and your baby..." She sucked her teeth. "That's our family. Our sister, our nephew... It's horrible, but it's the reality we're living."

That it was, and it fucking sucked.

It sucked for everyone involved, and I hated feeling so damn powerless. I hated that there was no way for me to make it stop. I hated that there was no way to make this better.

"I don't know what I'm supposed to do. I know it isn't getting drunk and crying about my problems. But *what am I supposed to do*? We can't find her. Whoever they are, they're fucking brilliant. They've thought of everything. They're blocking her energy signature, they're blocking her mind, there's nothing we *can* do. Even the sample of energy we got from Daniel was too small to use a tracking spell. What do I do, Leah?"

She stared at me more pitifully than ever. All the times I'd been like that before, drowning my sorrows with booze or drugs, she looked at me like I was pathetic. But this, she felt too. She knew I wasn't being a dramatic little bitch. I was truly hanging on by a thread.

"We're not going to stop looking, Jeremy. We're not giving up. Somehow, we're going to find her. We're going to find them all. I know we will. I'm still working on the when and how, but I'm not going to stop looking until we do." She reached for my hand and pulled it off the bottle.

She wrapped her fingers around my knuckles and held them tight. Leah was far from an affectionate person. She was distant, smart, and mostly serious. Quirky, at times, but never sweet and rarely gentle. Especially in the past few months since learning about Chris. But the look she gave me then wasn't fearful for them. She was scared for me.

We lost Chris. And when we realized he was still alive, we lost him again. We lost Daniel and Laila and the baby. And now, she was losing me.

"But I can't do this alone, Jeremy. I need you to be here. You're free falling and it's just a matter of time until you hit rock bottom." I watched a tear form in her eye before she blinked it away. "You're not a teenager anymore. I can't tie you to the bed and cover your room in hematite and morion. When you hit the ground, I don't think I'm strong enough to pull you back up."

She was right. I was a plane with a broken wing gradually spinning through the sky, just waiting for the explosion when I plummeted through the atmosphere.

No matter that I knew she was right, and I should have stayed strong, the impact was about to happen. I was about to crash and burn. I could have kept it in the air a while longer but the thing about a spiraling plane? The impact is inevitable.

CHAPTER FIFTY-THREE

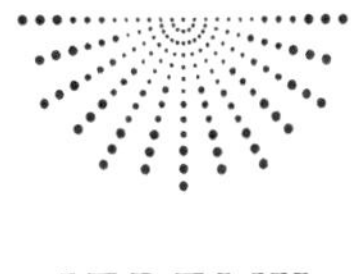

JEREMY

My eyes shifted around the crowded basement. I sat at a bar stool in the back. Hints of perfume, booze, cigarettes and sweaty bodies masked the wet basement odor. The speakers were loud but played a soft melody from the acoustic trio on the stage in the corner. Lights shined from there onto the dense crowd standing around the tables.

I was sure we were breaking at least a few fire codes with all of those people in there at once. But I doubted the cops would have the nerve to crash a fundraiser for the missing pregnant girl whose face was plastered on every telephone pole in the county.

Besides, Laila was friends with half the cops in our bunk little town. Moe's was a frequent stop for them. There weren't many options for cheap, decent food around here. Most of the stores were more of novelty shops than anything with short, bizarre hours when they were even open. We opened at seven a.m. every day except Sunday's when we opened at eight—besides on major holidays when we closed for a day or two and a week between Christmas and New Year's.

Laila was always working. She was friendly with every customer that came through her doors. Most of them, she knew by name. She was never rude to any of them but especially not to the cops. She may have been naïve, but she understood how important the risk of exposure was, especially after Ray saw her using her powers on film.

She may have been a little past friendly into the realm of flirty with them at times. Not that I really cared. It was like an elegant dance. She'd smile a little wider at certain comments, gently brush her fingers against a shoulder here and there, or 'forget' to charge them for their second doughnut. It was smart.

If questions arose about some unexplainable event close to us, no one pointed fingers in our direction. Not the pretty little harmless waitress with the bubbly smile and happy laugh. Not the happy, young high school sweethearts that lived above the quaint diner on the edge of town.

We were the last people anyone would suspect of anything *because* of Laila. A bunch of young adults living in a giant house on a few hundred acres of property a short while out of town was pretty weird. But when Laila entered the picture, she normalized us.

It was her town. I grew up there too, but I wasn't nearly as involved as her. She walked in the parades as a kid, she biked the streets with her friends as a teenager. Everyone knew her and everyone loved her. We all spent so much time with her at that place, people kind of just accepted us on her word. But Celena was right, they didn't know me.

"Hey." A finger tapped my shoulder.

I turned and pulled a smile to my lips. Laila's sister peered at me from behind her glasses. She smiled and extended her arms for an embrace. I leaned forward, doing one of those awkward half hugs to avoid brushing her boobs.

"Hey, Jenna, how are you?" I asked, pulling away.

She forced a smile and shrugged a shoulder. "I don't know, really. Numb, I think."

"Yeah. Yeah, I know what you mean."

She lowered herself to the stool beside me and set her bag on the counter behind us. "Mom told me the police stopped looking. I don't understand that, she's only been missing for seven weeks. It hasn't been that long."

"The local police are still working on it, but the FBI is out until new evidence surfaces."

"I just don't get it." Jenna angrily rolled her hands as she spoke. It reminded me of Laila, the way she talked with her mannerisms when she became passionate about something. It must have been a learned behavior because they didn't share any DNA. "How could they just give up? How could they just decide she must be dead with no evidence to suggest it?"

"I don't know. The trail went cold after they found the airport. They used an alias for the facility and never used the same one again. Not at other airports, on vehicles or property. Nothing. The last place it was used was for the lease."

"It just doesn't make any sense. Laila is just a girl from a small town. All of this is something that would happen to someone big, you know? Like a war criminal or foreign leader, not someone like Laila." She was quiet for a moment, eyes distant yet focused in thought. "Who would go to those lengths to kidnap someone so normal?"

Because Laila is anything but normal.

"I don't know."

"This is nice though. It's putting pressure on the cops. Reminding them that we didn't forget." I glanced around at the people watching the small band on stage. "It's nice to keep her alive here in everyone's mind."

"I think it's stupid." I lifted my glass of whiskey to my lips.

"Why?"

"It's like a vigil," I muttered with a gesture around. A picture of Laila sat on the counter of the bar and another on one of the metal columns supporting the structure of the building. "'In honor of Laila,' on every flyer, people talking about her like she's dead, singing sad songs about grief and shit. When she sees this stupid flyer, she's gonna be so fucking pissed at my sister for embarrassing her like this."

Jenna laughed. "Yeah, she always hated being the victim. Hurt her pride, I think."

"She'll be happy the money went to a good cause though."

She smiled. When she went on, her smile drooped. "You don't think she's dead, do you?"

"She's not dead."

She gave me a look, as if wondering why I was so sure. "I guess I'm just starting to run out of hope. When the FBI gives up, you kinda lose your faith in things getting better."

"I don't really know what to think any more. We're all just sitting around with our thumbs up our asses."

She chuckled. The band on stage stopped singing, applause following. Max stepped up to the microphone, saying the band's name and how cool their performance was.

I was next.

I loved music, but I hated performing. Musicians are generally egotistical bastards on stage. You have to be cocky, or at least confident, to perform in front of people like that. I was quiet and awkward, at least about my music. Confidence was never my area of expertise.

"After a lot of begging and pleading, we finally got Jeremy to agree to come up and perform a song for us. Now, for those of you who don't know Jeremy, he probably knows Laila better than anyone in this room." He gestured to me from the stage.

"You sing?" Jenna asked. "How did I not know that?"

I shrugged. "Because it's not that big of a deal."

Max continued, "He hasn't prepared a set, so he's just going to perform a song that would mean a lot to Laila."

I stood, finished off my drink and set it back to the counter.

"Wish me luck." I started toward the stage.

"Yeah, break a leg," Jenna muttered. Looking back on it, I think that was the moment that she realized she knew next to nothing about her sister. More importantly, how much Laila kept from her.

"Ladies and gentlemen, let's give him a warm welcome," Max said. He met my gaze as I climbed the three steps to the small stage. He patted my shoulder with a smile. The audience applauded quietly. I grabbed my guitar off of its stand and pulled the stool from the side of the stage to the microphone.

I sat down and raised the mahogany, acoustic guitar to my lap. The audience grew silent as I leaned to the microphone. Clearing my throat, I gazed out over the bobbing heads through the bright lights.

"It's been a while since I did something like this, so try to cut me some slack if I fuck up, alright?" There were a few chuckles followed by a clap here and there. "The first time this song came on my playlist when me and Laila were driving down some back road, she turned to me and said this was her favorite song when it first came out. She said that her little thirteen-year-old self fantasized about being serenaded to it. So today, I'm gonna sing it for her. Really wish I could sing it *to* her but." I adjusted the strap around my neck and went on, "Yeah, well. Here's *Always* by *Panic! At the Disco*."

Claps sounded quietly through the room. I started to strum. I dazed off as the words left my lips, trying not to think about them too hard. Trying to remember it was just a song and refrain from crying the way the people in the audience began to.

As I made it to the final verse, I felt a tightness around my throat. It was just pressure at first, there wasn't any pain. I pulled my face from the microphone at a lull to clear it away before I went back to singing. I thought it was anxiety at first. But it got so intense, it almost hurt.

I finished up the verse and moved into the last chorus. I rushed through the last few lines while the pressure got tighter around my neck.

That wasn't normal. No one had grabbed her neck before.

The crowd applauded as I finished the last riff. Some people even stood, wiping their eyes and raising their hands together. But my chest started to hurt. My vision was getting disoriented. The tightness grew into dull throbbing pain and breathing became more difficult.

Realizing it was Laila, I hurriedly pulled my guitar off of my lap. I set it down on its stand. I rushed off the stage without saying another word. I wasn't sure I could talk if I wanted to. Everything was growing fuzzy around the edges. I hurried across the room and past the crowd of people clapping for me.

Thankfully, they seemed to chalk up my reaction to being choked up.

It was different than the times before. It had always been calculated, business official type of torture. No one had grabbed her throat, not like that. And it was eight o'clock on a Saturday. She was never tortured on the weekend. It was usually Mondays and Fridays in the mid-afternoon.

I was nearly at the steps when Adam caught my arm. Leah and Brody stood behind him, worried eyes on me. "What's wrong?"

A tear left my eye. "I have to go."

My body wasn't actually being affected, but I was afraid my reaction to the pain would be unexplainable. Adam released my arm. He followed close at my flank. Max spoke into the microphone on the stage, suggesting I get another round of applause as I hurried upstairs.

The pain slowed to a dull throb as if the skin began to swell but the cause dissipated. I hurried past the counter in the front of the diner to the swinging steel door. I brushed past a few servers, nearly running to the apartment steps. I took two at a time to be sure the customers and employees didn't see the pain if it started again.

"What's going on?" Leah asked.

I rushed into the doorway and gripped the wall for support. "They were choking her."

"Are they still?" Brody asked, desperately searching my gaze.

"Not at the moment."

"Jesus," Adam muttered. "The girl can't have one day of peace."

I gasped at the tight grip around my throat again. Her heart thudded in her head like it would explode out of her skull. My hand flung to my throat, trying to fling it off of her, as though that were possible from however far apart we were.

Adam grabbed my shoulder, teleported me to the couch, and sat me down. "Is it happening again?"

I nodded. I felt a sharp pain against the side of her neck. I gasped. My brows creased in confusion. I knew that feeling, but never so deep. Teeth. Digging into her flesh until blood dripped down to her collar bone.

Then the same pain on her lip.

My eyes widened.

I knew that pain.

I'd done it to her a thousand times. But never so hard. Not until she bled.

"Oh my God." Leah covered her mouth, reading my mind.

My breathing became short as the hand around my neck got heavier.

"No." My heart raced so hard against my ribs that I thought it would break them. "No," I said again, hearing her voice echo the same within my mind. She repeated it, over and over, begging and pleading him to stop.

"What's happening?" Brody said.

My stomach turned as it sunk in. I had grown used to the beatings. They were excruciating and terrifying, but I wasn't prepared for this.

Leah grabbed the small garbage can near the TV and rushed it to me. She put her hand on my shoulder, but I shoved it away, taking the waste basket instead. Vomit burned up my esophagus and emptied into the plastic lined bin.

"Leave." I made out between dry heaves.

"Jeremy—" Adam began.

"Fucking go!" I screamed, looking up from the garbage bag with vomit leaking from my lip.

Leah nodded. "Let's give him some space."

"What's—" Brody began.

I heard Laila's scream in my mind, simultaneously yelling, "Get the fuck out!"

Leah was quiet for a moment. Then she put her hand on Brody's shoulder. Adam and Brody looked confused but disappeared.

The pain in her thigh got worse, shooting all the way up my body. Her wrists cracked and throbbed like she was pulling them against something. She was nearly breaking her arms against some type of handcuff or brace. She was fighting so fucking hard.

The tightness at my throat came back and her screams stopped.

But I felt it.

The sensation made me sick to my stomach. I leaned forward and puked again.

I knew that feeling too.

I loved that feeling.

The slight sting inside of her as her legs stretched around my hips.

But it wasn't just a bare, pleasurable sting. It felt like she was being torn apart.

CHAPTER FIFTY-FOUR

JEREMY

I lay against the couch cushions covered in puke, sweat and tears. I couldn't catch my breath. I couldn't process what I just felt. I knew what happened, but I couldn't even think the word.

When it happened to me, there wasn't any pain. I barely even remembered it. It fucked me up more often than I liked to admit but it wasn't brutal like that. It wasn't violent and full of agony. It was a blur in my mind, barely even there.

Her back stung like it was on fire with each push. Her wrists throbbed from fighting the restraints. Her neck started to bruise from his hand at her throat. Her leg throbbed and stung at the same time, as if she'd ripped out stitches.

I grabbed a throw pillow and hugged it against my chest, struggling to breathe as hot tears continued to stream down my face.

I needed it to go away. I needed to get out of my head. I needed to stop thinking.

I pulled my phone from my pocket and scrolled through my contacts until I found Olivia. My shaking finger tapped the green symbol and I held it to my ear.

"Hey, you," she answered. "What's up?"

I cleared my throat, wiping my cheeks. "Can I get your help with something?"

"Uh, yeah. Of course," she said, tone confused. "What do you need?"

"Regardless of what you say, I'm gonna do it anyway." I sniffed snot into my nose and wiped my eyes. "Can I talk to you in person? Is there anyone nearby?"

"No. No, I just got home. You can come by."

"Okay." I ended the call and stood. I used the inside of my shirt to wipe the stray vomit from my lips and teleported to her living room.

"Jesus," Olivia said from the white leather sectional. She walked toward me. "Are you alright?"

"No, not really."

She walked my way with furrowed brows, reaching out to comfort me, but I involuntarily cringed. Physical contact, especially from her, was the last thing i wanted right now. "What happened?"

"I... I—" I shook my head violently, tears overwhelming me each time I tried to speak. "I can't even say it."

She was quiet for a second. "What do you need then?"

"You said you could give me something for pain." My voice was hardly audible, trembling. "It isn't my pain, but it won't fucking stop."

I knew it was wrong, even at that moment. But I just needed out of my head. I needed to breathe. I needed it to go away.

"You're not hurt, Jeremy." She frowned. "I can't just give you pain pills."

"If you don't, I'll just find another way. I could have just stolen your pad, but I didn't. I can get any drug I want; you know I can. I can teleport into a hospital and get morphine or an evidence locker for heroin. I have a million options if you won't help me." My lips trembled. "I don't want to do something like that, I just need the pain to go away."

She gazed at me for a moment, just watching me cry. I think it was only the second time she saw me in tears. And the last time had been when she told me she cheated.

"Jeremy..."

"Please, Liv." My lip pathetically quivered. "I'm going to get high either way. At least you'll know how much I'm doing."

Her eyes closed, and she rubbed one. "I don't have much on hand."

"I don't need much."

She knew it was a bad decision, but she started toward the kitchen anyway. That was the moment I realized that all I needed to do was give her that look.

Olivia was my own personal pharmacy.

She was an enabler. She always had been. Although the last time I was hard on drugs, she didn't have a prescription pad with her name on it. But I knew how to manipulate her when we were kids, and I hadn't forgotten as an adult. It wasn't hard, especially with someone who loves you. Addicts make excellent puppeteers.

As she walked back into the room, she unscrewed the lid from an orange bottle and poured a few to her hand. "If the pain is that bad, it'll help. But please be careful."

"What are they?" I opened my palm for them. "Fifteens?"

She nodded, "You don't need any more than this. You've been clean for years, Jeremy. Your tolerance isn't what it was the last time you used."

My heart skipped with excitement. Aside from getting Laila back, that was the best thing that could have happened to me. "Yeah, I know."

"But I didn't give these to you."

"Your secret's safe with me if mine is with you." I closed my palm around them. "Thank you, Liv. I owe you one."

She opened her mouth to speak again, but I already teleported home. I sat down at the table and opened my hand.

Four. Just four.

Whatever.

Better than nothing. Still more than a recommended dose. Plenty to get me high.

I dropped them on the table, grabbed the dusty, decorative candle in the middle and began tapping them to pieces. Once they reached a thin, powdery consistency, I leaned forward and pulled my wallet from my back pocket. I flipped it open, pulled out my debit card, and a dollar bill. I set the bill down with my wallet and slid the card through the blue powder until it made two even lines.

I stared down at it for a moment, realizing that I was about to hit rock bottom.

But hey, at least it wasn't dope.

It was just a few roxies. I used to be able to take a fistful of them before breakfast.

I grabbed the dollar bill and rolled it into a tube. Leaning forward, I held it to my nose and closed the other nostril. I carefully sniffed down each line.

It hit almost instantly.

The weight lifted off of my shoulders. My body flooded with euphoria. A wave of calm washed over me and slowed my racing heart. The stabbing pains dulled until every muscle was soothed.

It was like a warm breeze. Or being snuggled up on the couch with a fuzzy blanket and a cup of hot chocolate after a day in the snow. The grayish tinge I'd seen over everything, the black looming cloud slowly floated away, shining vivid color over the world around me. The cool chill I hadn't been able to bundle up since this all started began to thaw. I felt warm and relieved, maybe even safe. My clenched joints finally relaxed.

Warm. I felt warm for the first time since she was taken.

I felt like a person instead of a tense set of bones. I could breathe again.

An hour or so later, the effects began to dampen. I was still high. Not as high as I would've liked to be, but high nevertheless. The euphoria was fading, and mood swings were kicking in. It hadn't even been an hour, but an hour of euphoria was better than no euphoria at all.

I missed her so much. My stomach hurt at the thought of what just happened. Tears pearled down my face and my hands began to tremble.

I just wanted to hold her. I wanted to tell her I loved her. I wanted to make it all go away.

I remembered Celena's idea.

CHAPTER FIFTY-FIVE

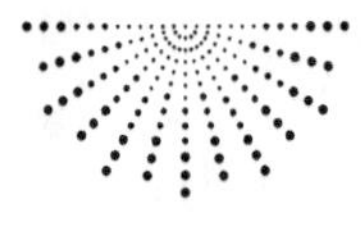

LAILA

My eyes fluttered open in the nearly dark, steel walled room. The hospital gown laid haphazardly over my body. It pulled against all the loose, fraying scabs and broken skin. Everything hurt. My back, my ace bandage wrapped wrists, my gauze tied leg. Even my fucking vagina.

I tried to pant through the pain as I brought myself forward.

My teeth chattered when it flashed through my mind. Tears welled in my eyes. A thick lump formed in my throat. I lifted my hand to my mouth covering it to keep Chris and Haley from hearing my cries.

But Haley had wolf ears and Chris practically had supersonic hearing.

"Laila?" I heard. "Laila, that's you, right?"

I cleared my throat, trying to hold in my tears. "Yeah."

"Thank God," Chris said, relief coating the ends of his voice. "We were so worried. Where were you?"

"How long was I gone?" I asked.

"A day and a half or so. What happened?"

My aching, ace bandage wrapped wrists rubbed my eyes. "They shot me."

"They shot you?"

"I thought I heard a gunshot," Haley said.

"Why?" Chris asked.

"Yeah, what'd you do? Try to escape?" she asked.

"No. I probably could have." I wiped my eyes again, taking in slow, calming breaths. "I went into one of their heads and set myself free. I... I'm so fucking stupid. I could have blown the roof off and flew out of here."

"That would've been too Hollywood for reality," Chris said.

I said nothing, just looked out the glass block window at the moon in the distance.

"What did they do to you?" Haley asked. "The gun shot was just to take you down, right?"

I traced my tongue along the swollen welt on my lip. I wanted to brush my teeth. I wanted to boil them, actually. I wanted that taste out of my mouth. But I couldn't make it to the sink.

"Laila?" Chris tapped on the wall beside my bed. "Are you okay?"

I put my hand to the steel and let heat radiate from my palm. "Not really."

"Do you want to talk about it?" he asked.

"No."

Silence crept in for a few long, painful moments. I didn't even have thoughts in my mind. Only the pain. And the last couple hours replaying in my head like a broken record.

Then a sudden pain sliced down my arm. I grimaced, pulling it in front of me and rubbing my other hand across it. A small line, maybe an inch long. "Fuck." I rubbed in an attempt to soothe the pain. But it didn't stop.

More importantly, it wasn't my pain. It was his. It was the first time I'd felt him hurt since I was there. There may have been times before and it was either too short to make a real connection or I was too intoxicated to notice, but suddenly, I felt him.

Jeremy.

My stomach flipped like a little girl waiting by the silent phone for her crush to call when it finally rang. A very gruesome phone, but a way to relay a message all the same.

Another cut began just above it but much smaller. A dot, almost. I followed each slice with my finger, trying to piece it together. Fear struck through me at first.

I realized they were letters.

Another line to the right. Then a slow circle beside it. Then a parallel line meeting another parallel line at a point at the bottom. Another parallel line with three horizontal lines coming from it. Then a small horseshoe shape.

Following each painful cut with the tip of my pointer finger, my eyes filled with tears, and my heart skipped a beat. It was like a puzzle at first, following each line and murmuring out the syllables.

I laughed.

I love u

The u touched my vein an inch or two from my palm.

I smiled, cupping my hand over my mouth. Tears of joy burned across my eyes. My finger slid against each letter as he formed them into another word.

AlwAys

A joyous cry left my lips, but I stifled it the best I could.

He was still there. He hadn't given up. I may have but he hadn't.

It occurred to me.

I hadn't thought of it. I assumed that since I couldn't reach his mind, he couldn't reach mine. I thought he'd felt none of my pain.

I grazed the bite on my neck. My tongue found the cut on my lip.

If I felt his cuts, he felt mine. He felt my aching wrists. He felt my burning back. He felt my pulsing femur. He felt the throbbing between my thighs.

He knew.

CHAPTER FIFTY-SIX

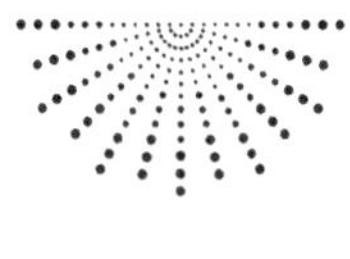

JEREMY

I stumbled into the living room gripping a white dish cloth around my forearm. "Where is everyone?"

Everything was black around the edges. My head throbbed worse than the cuts along my skin. I was so lightheaded that I could barely tell where I was. Honestly, I don't know how I even had the energy to teleport there.

"In here," Leah called from the kitchen.

"Do you smell that?" I heard Wyatt say.

I staggered down the hall. Holding myself vertical was harder than it'd ever been. No matter how doped up I'd been in the past, no steps were harder than the ones I took into that kitchen.

"I need a little help," I groggily muttered in the doorway.

Kai rushed toward me. Gasps sounded behind him. He clutched my arm with one hand and my face with the other. "The hell'd happen?"

I pulled the towel from my wrist. "I had to make sure she knew I loved her."

I love u always

It was carved in jagged lines from the crease where my elbow met my bicep to my wrist.

"Jesus, Jeremy." Leah rushed toward us.

"I just needed her to know that I love her," I repeated.

Leah clutched my chin, yanking my face to look at her. Her teeth gritted together. "Your pupils are fucking pin pricks."

I pulled away and looked from Kai to Celena. "I can't get it to stop bleeding."

"Here." Celena held her hand above mine.

I watched the white light penetrate my skin, not even flinching as the tissue melded back together.

"Doesn't this hurt?" she asked.

"He's high as a kite, Celena," Leah snapped. "I bet he wouldn't feel it if he had a bullet in his chest."

I narrowed my gaze. Celena continued to heal my arm. "I'm barely even high now."

Leah huffed. "Bullshit."

"It was pills, not heroin," I snapped.

"Did ya shoot them? Or snort them?" She put a hand on her hip. "Because lord knows you aren't going to swallow them."

"Does it matter?" I said as Celena got closer to my wrist.

"I guess not." She ran her tongue against her teeth. "I don't know why I'm surprised."

My face screwed up in discomfort as Celena finished my wrist. "Neither do I. You said it yourself. Just a matter of time, right?"

"Guess I should know better than to second guess my instincts."

"Guess so. But don't worry, I don't expect you to pull me up." I pulled my hand back, holding Leah's gaze. "And the reason I barely felt that was because I've gotten pretty used to excruciating pain recently. Not because I'm high."

"Jeremy," Adam began before I turned to Celena.

"Thank you," I said. I disappeared and dropped to the couch in my apartment.

CHAPTER FIFTY-SEVEN

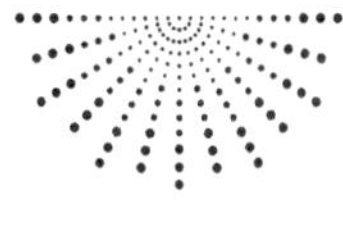

JEREMY

"Wake up, dude." Adam threw a wet rag at me. I jumped at cold water trickling from the cloth down the side of my neck. "Clean yourself up."

I blinked through the dawning sun that cast in through the open curtains. The scent of cleaning agents nearly gagged me. My hands curled around a bottle of Jack Daniels beneath my head, propping it up like some pathetic excuse for a pillow. I sat up on the hardwood floor rubbing my fists against my eyes. My back cracked like a glow stick. I stretched my arms above my head with a yawn.

"What time is it?" I asked.

"Ten thirty." He sprayed the kitchen counter with bleach. "Figured I'd let you sleep in."

I stifled a yawn once more, stumbling to my feet, gripping the dining room table for support. "Thanks."

"Yep." He glanced at the counter while he scrubbed my blood with paper towels.

"You don't have to clean that. I can handle it."

He looked up and took in a deep breath. "You can't handle all of this on your own, Jeremy. You need to stop pretending that you can."

I licked my lips.

"How many did you take?" He looked up as he waited for a response.

"It was nothing."

"It was something to someone with no tolerance." He set the rag down and his gaze locked with me. "If I was in your shoes, I would have just slit my wrists." I made a face, and his remained serious. "That's what I did when I killed Adrian, you know. Leah found me in my bedroom and healed me. I made her promise not to tell anyone and." He shrugged and scratched his head. "Well, yeah. No one else knows that except for the two of us. And now you. So. There's that."

My brows dropped. "Why would you tell me that?"

"Because I don't blame you, Jeremy." His eyes met mine with sincerity. "With what they've been doing to her, what you have *felt* them doing to her, if I were you, I'd get high too."

"I just wanted to breathe for a minute, you know? I was so..."

"There aren't words," Adam said. "It isn't close to the same thing, but I lost the girl I loved too. To some end, I can relate to what you're going through."

I huffed. Yeah, vastly different than what happened with Adrian. But both situations sucked ass. "I don't know who's had it worse."

He flashed an ironic grin. "The debates of Skoulda men, who has worst luck with love."

I walked beside him, grabbed some paper towels, and ripped them from the roll. I reached for the bleach, turned to the ground, sprayed the floor, and lowered myself to wipe it up.

"Where'd you get that idea?" He gestured to the blood on the counter and floor.

"Celena mentioned it a few weeks ago." I stood and dropped the blood coated napkin into the trash. "I forgot about it until last night.

"Props to her," he said. "That was smart."

"If it worked," I said. "I don't know if she'd even be able to read it, you know?"

He shrugged. "I don't know."

"It's pretty morbid, I guess. Even if she did read it, I don't know how she would have felt about it. I mean, she was hurting enough already. And here I am, cutting myself and shit." I laughed quietly. "Just bizarre."

"I bet it made her happy. She hadn't heard from you since she was taken, and after that... Hearing you say you loved her must have meant a lot."

I hadn't told him. I remembered the look on Leah's face as I looked up from the trash can. Damn it.

"That's another thing. Now everyone knows about this awful thing that happened to her, and she..." I rubbed my eye. "That wasn't right, Leah shouldn't have told you guys. That should have been something she told you when she was ready, or never at all if she didn't want to. I... I shouldn't have known unless she wanted me to. But I know, and... I just want to make it stop."

"Well, I think we have a way to do just that." Adam smiled. "Or at least, a way to find her."

My gurgling stomach danced with butterflies. My eyes widened. "What? How?"

"Okay, so try and stay with me." He set the bleach down and turned to face me. "We were brainstorming last night before you showed up and we started talking about why you would torture someone with abilities like ours. It's routine, every few days, right?" I nodded and he went on, "Okay, so the only reason we can think of is to see what they're capable of, right?"

"I guess." I crossed my arms against my chest.

"Okay, so that must be what the implants we found inside of Daniel were. Like little remotes that they can flick the abilities on and off with."

"But that wouldn't work on Laila's powers because she's a Fae," I said.

"Right. And what did Mary say about what was blocking your bond?"

I thought for a moment. "A psychic. Someone inside her head."

"Right, so there's someone blocking Laila's powers, but not all of the time, right? It'd be too strenuous on any psychic to block powers like Laila's long term, no matter how strong they were."

"But then why can't we pick up on her energy?"

"Because it isn't *just* a psychic. They have a Witch who uses barrier spells, not only to keep their energy masked—"

"But to keep their powers inside the perimeter, right." I held his gaze. "But how will that help us find her?"

"Well, the bond isn't broken. You still feel each other's pain, but Laila probably just realized that when you cut yourself last night. Any other injuries you've had may have been so mild that she didn't feel them through the pain she already has from the beatings."

"Still not following."

"Blocking the bond, at least the part that shields her location and thoughts wouldn't be nearly as hard as blocking out her powers. That *could* be done long term."

"But either way, if Laila can't push them out, that still means there's no way to find out where she is."

"But that's just it," he said quickly. "Is there anyone so strong that Laila can't push out?"

"Probably not. But then, why wouldn't she have done it already? If she realizes..." I thought for a moment. Then my eyes shot open. "She must not realize they're in her head."

"Exactly."

"But how? How wouldn't she know that? She knows our bond is blocked."

"That's just it, she knows the bond is blocked, but doesn't realize how."

I rubbed my temples. "I'm confused. Just explain it to me."

"So Laila knows that this person is in her head when her powers are suppressed, but then, she gets them back. Maybe when the torture is over, maybe during the torture. I don't know, but at some point, she has to be using her powers because no one could block her abilities for extended periods of time. I think that when she's using her powers, she thinks no one else is in her head. Because they're not *all* the way in. They're doing one thing in there."

"They're blocking her location and mind from you. But Laila thinks it's something *else* blocking your bond. She probably thinks it's the same person who's put up the perimeter spells. That, she wouldn't know how to break. Spells aren't something she's familiar with. But she doesn't realize your bond makes it through the perimeter spells. She doesn't realize she can contact you because she doesn't realize it's someone inside her head that's keeping her from talking to you. She thinks it's the Witch because—"

"Because she thinks the psychic left when her powers came back," I said. "Okay, I think I get it."

"But if we can get a message to her, if she realizes they're in her head—"

"She can block them out and I can find her." My eyes widened. He smiled and gave a nod. I smiled back, heart skipping joyously in my chest. "We can find her."

He smiled. "We can find her."

Finally, I had hope again.

I reached for a knife on the counter, but Adam caught my hand. "Get dressed first. We'll go back to the house and do it where someone can heal you. Hopefully, she can send us a message back, but we'll need to heal you between each one so there's enough room to respond."

A trill left my lips. "So I'm going to have to see Leah."

"Looks like it."

"Hey." I leaned against the door frame of the kitchen. Leah sat at the bar looking down at her laptop.

She didn't even look up from the screen. "Hey."

Chewing my lip, I said, "You gonna hate me forever because I fucked up?"

She turned up from her computer and closed it shut. She pushed her glasses up and frowned. "I don't hate you, Jeremy. I'm frustrated. I thought you knew better."

"Yeah, well." I shrugged. "I was pretty fucked up. I just wanted to feel better for a minute."

"Well, did you?" She crossed her arms against her chest. "Feel better?"

Another shrug. "For a minute."

She ran her tongue against her teeth in annoyance. "Well, at least there's that."

"Look, I'm not proud of it, alright? But try feeling what I felt. Try knowing that was happening to someone you love. Try feeling every awful second and not being able to stop it. Wouldn't you want to get high too?"

"I'm not saying I don't understand, Jeremy. I just know that when we do bring her home, if you're strung out on dope—"

"I wasn't on dope—"

"Or booze, or pills, or whatever it is that you decide to take that day, she isn't going to want you. She has her shit together and she isn't going to want to be with some little fuck boy who's snorting pain pills in the bathroom of her restaurant. You're a different person when you're high. You aren't the person she fell in love with."

Obviously, I knew she was right. But it happened. I fucked up. And I couldn't change it. But if I could get her home, it'd never happen again.

"Let's just do this so we can bring her home."

Leah stood from her stool. "If we're able to communicate back and forth, you're gonna lose a lot of blood so you need to sit down."

I pulled a chair from the edge of the breakfast nook. "Sounds like a plan to me. Do you have a knife?"

"Yeah, I got a scalpel from the hospital. It'll be a cleaner cut. We should grab Kai and someone else. If I faint, they can go on healing you and someone else can write down the conversations."

I pulled my phone from my pocket and texted Kai to come downstairs and to bring Hannah. Lowering myself to the chair, I sighed. Leah came over with a tablet and a pen.

She sat beside me and met my gaze. "I watched you destroy yourself for your addiction, Jeremy. And you were finally doing good. You were the best I've ever seen you."

I pressed my lips together. "I want to be that good again too, Leah. But she's gone. I don't have anything to be happy about now."

She laid the scalpel on the table. "Let's bring her home then."

CHAPTER FIFTY-EIGHT

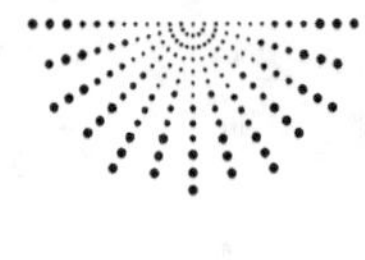

LAILA

The cool surface caressed my spine. My cell didn't smell like rubbing alcohol and bleach anymore. It wreaked of iron and sweat. Or maybe it was just me that stunk.

I bounced a ball of fire from my left to my right hand. The warmth was comforting as I watched the sun peak through the window behind me in the reflection on the wall. It brought me to a place of tranquil, yet firm thought.

Never again.

I would never participate in stress test day again. The moment that door opened for them to shoot me with another dart of benzos, I'd burn them alive. I could use my powers in my cell. That bitch couldn't control me in here.

A few days before, the thought of killing another person made me ill. But after what had happened, I didn't care. No one was going to hurt me again.

It wasn't even about the rape. That played a part. But just a fraction.

He called my baby his. And he was full of fucking shit. I may have done what he wanted up until then, but I was fucking done. If I was gonna kill again, it'd be because *I* wanted to. If I was gonna kill again, it'd be to get my baby out of there. Or to keep someone else safe. Not for him. Never for him.

It was about Lydia too. That sweet little girl who watched someone so powerful get taken down by a gun shot. I had to show her that no man could control us if we fought hard enough. If we had to kill, we had to kill. But no man, especially not one so punitive as Peterson, could use us like tools and toss us away when he was done with us.

None of them would ever lay a hand on me that I didn't want after last night. None of them would ever touch my baby. I'd stay in that room until I starved if that's what it came to. No one was taking my son. No one would hurt us again.

No one was as strong as me.

Last night and my failed escape a few days prior were the impetus I needed to remind me of that. I was the strongest creature my world had ever seen. I was damn near unstoppable.

No way in hell was I going to let him raise my son the way Lydia was being raised.

A sting rang down my arm the same way it had the night before. I absorbed the fire and moved my finger to my forearm. I followed the lines as they began to form letters, then words.

t-H-E-r i-N u-r H-E-A-d

I looked around, searching for something I could use to cut a message into my skin. Of course, there was nothing. If there was something in that room sharp enough to cut myself, I would have slit my wrists by then.

I sat up shaking my head in frustration. She wasn't in my head, at least not then. If she was, I wouldn't be able to use my powers.

I glanced down at my stinging arm. It writhed in stabbing pain and dissipated. Someone healed him.

I ran my fingers across it, eyes catching on my long, jagged fingernails.

The day I was captured almost two months prior, my acrylics were brand new. They were melted on the edges where my flames had licked them, but I hadn't had a way to cut them. I'd scraped them across the floor from time to time in some desperate attempt to file them down. But they were there.

I began scratching with my forefinger until the skin bled. It was barely anything, but it was something.

N-o-t N-o-W

It wasn't as deep as his were, so I hoped he'd feel it.

A moment later, the pain came back. This time on my right arm.

b-l-k-i-N

Black?

b-o-N-d

Blocking bond.

She wasn't in my head; she couldn't be blocking our bond. The barrier spells blocked every spell we'd attempted when we were searching. It locked the energy of our bond inside the barrier. That's what I'd assumed when I got there and couldn't reach his mind.

But if it were the barrier spells, I wouldn't feel that. *He* wouldn't be feeling that.

I felt the familiar, burning heat as the aching stopped in his arm.

G-E-t E-M o-u-T

If she was in my head, she'd know if I pushed her out. If I pushed her out right now and Jeremy stormed in to rescue me, I *might* make it out. That is, if Jeremy somehow managed to make it in without getting himself killed. But all of our people would stay there in suffering.

And even if he found me, he wouldn't be able to teleport in. The barrier spells didn't only keep magic inside of it, but they kept outside magic from coming into it as well. Clearly, or the countless tracking spells we used would have pinged off of Chris, Lydia, or Amy.

It wouldn't be easy to get me out of there. Especially not in my condition. I couldn't even stand.

My leg needed to heal.

And if they were coming for me, they needed to come for all of us. I wasn't going to let my people perish in there. No, we needed a plan.

Now that I had a means of communicating with him below the radar, I had a way to conspire with them. If we were going to do this, if we were going to get me out, we were going to do it right and get all of us out.

I would be the Trojan horse I planned to be when I was taken. But I needed to be able to fight. I needed to be able to get Chris and Haley and Lydia out. I needed to get *everyone* out.

That was why it all started. To save them.

I couldn't just save myself. I needed to save them too.

S-H-E-l N-o

I scratched each letter with careful, but not too harsh, precision.

A moment later, the cutting began again.

J-S-t 1 S-E-C

Just one second. One second. Did he really think one second was all he needed? Surely, he knew better.

I began scratching again, pulling the skin until it coated up the abrasive part of my nail.

2 r-I-S-k-y

Then, it went quiet. He was thinking of what to say.

But I began scratching again.

N-E-E-d A P-l-A-N

I was running out of space on my arms. The scratches would soon group together, and Jeremy wouldn't be able to make out the different letters. I needed a larger canvas.

l-E-G, I scratched, sitting forward and pulling up the hospital gown.

I felt a cut on it a moment later. It stung with the warmth of healing, as if to tell me he was ready, and I resumed scratching.

H-A-V 2 S-A-V-E u-S A-l-l

H-o-W-? I felt on my wrist.

I-d-k Y-E-t 2 W-E-k 2 F-I-G-H-t

The pain stopped for a moment as the heat of being healed ran against my wrist.

R u o-k

I smiled. Not really. But I was talking to my fiancé for the first time in almost two months. That was something. Enough to make me smile.

b-t-r N-o-W

My wrist stung again.

l-E-t M-E H-E-l-P

I could practically hear his heart breaking. He hated being helpless. He loved being my hero. But that time, he couldn't swoop in and carry me off into the sunset.

u-l-l G-E-t k-I-l-d

I W-O-N-t

u W-I-l-l

I-d-C

I d-o

P-l-S

He would never understand how badly I wanted him to come rescue me. Tears spouted down my face. I wanted out of there so badly. But I wanted *all* of us out even more. And I didn't want him to die trying either.

It was like Chris had said on day one. I didn't want any of them to end up where I was. Or even worse, for *all* of us to end up inside. Then to have no one capable of finding us at all.

G-T R-d-Y

W-Y-M

What the fuck do you think it means? Get prepared.

T-E-l-l u W-E-N r-d-Y

S-o-o-N-?

I-d-k

There was a lull as he thought of what to say.

W-A-T W-I-l-l I N-E-E-d

E-V-r-y 1 u c-A-n G-E-t

H-W M-A-N-Y o-F u

I wasn't sure. But there had to be a fair bit. When I looked out the window, I couldn't make out much detail through the frosted glass blocks, but I could see the building stretch on either side into a horse-shoe like shape. It was huge, like a school or a hospital. There could be hundreds of us. Maybe even thousands.

A L-oT

T-H-E-M-?

There was a long pause this time. I didn't have a clue. It seemed that a new guard peeked into my room each hour check.

A L-oT

W-H-E-r-E-?

c-N-d-A-?

Another long pause as they healed him.

C-H-r-I-S-?

I smiled, giving a nod I knew he couldn't see.

Y

H-E o-K-?

Y

b-A-b-Y o-K?

Y

U o-K?

I bit my lip as it began to tremble.

I wasn't okay.

I was so far from okay.

Y

L-I-A-r

I laughed. Smiling, I shook my head.

I W-I-l-l b

I wiped blood onto my nightgown as I began scratching again.

R U o-k

N-o

Tears burned my eyes. All of the things he'd felt in the past fifty-eight days. The aches, the swelling, the bleeding, the tears, the throbs, the whips, the pricks, the cuts.

The rape.

U W-I-l-l b

N-t t-I-l u-r w M-E

Not until you're with me. I smiled and ran my hand against my arm. He always had a way with words.

I l-o-V-E u

l-o-V-E u M-o-r

I smiled, chest growing tight. I wiped my watering eyes. The corners felt tender and sore from all of the wiping.

Fuck, I missed him.

The pain returned.

d-N-t C-r-Y

I M-I-S-S u

I M-I-S-S u M-o-r

My eyes traced over the blood running down my skin onto the metal table. The cuts were superficial, but they spanned my entire thigh. I didn't want to stop but I wouldn't have a choice when I ran out of room.

A-l-M-S-T o-u-T S-P-A-c-E

S-r-Y A-M-o-u-r

I smiled, remembering the sound of his voice when he spoke in his first language. It brought the sound of his voice back into my ear. I could almost hear it.

It carried me back to the first time I heard him speak in French. We were lying in bed at the cabin, bodies curving together like two halves of a whole. He played with the hair resting against my chest, twirling it between his fingers like it was the softest thing he'd ever felt. I'd only just realized he was bilingual, and I asked him to say something. He came back with, "Tes yeux, j'en rêve jour et nuit."

It meant, "I dream about your eyes day and night." Apparently, a common romantic phrase he heard his dad say to his mom.

For the first time in months, I remembered his beautiful smile again. I remembered the sound of his voice. I remembered his face. I remembered how much I loved him.

N-o I carved, *H-o-P-E A-G-A-I-N*

A-l-W-A-Y-S H-E-r-E

I smiled as I gazed down at my arm, tears falling from my eyes to the running blood.

A-l-W-A-Y-S. I scratched back.

CHAPTER FIFTY-NINE

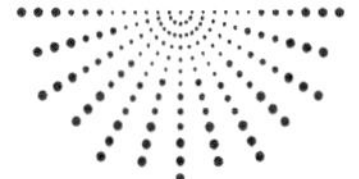

MAY 12, 2019 - LAILA

Six days passed when I hit twenty.

As usual, the two guards opened my door. In my defense, I told them to leave first. But as they aimed the dart gun at me, I melted it in their hands. Obviously, that didn't go over well. They started into the room to grab me—decked out in their fireman like suits. But fire wasn't the only thing I could use any more. Aside from that, those suits were made for human temperatures of fire. Not violet, hottest fire in the universe fire.

I flung the man holding the gun against Haley's door. His head slammed to the metal, followed by the floor, so hard that blood immediately poured from a crack in his skull. The other ran away in terror and slammed the door shut behind him.

A few hours later, a doctor came to the door. She looked like a sweet, middle-aged woman. Her graying hair was pulled back in a neat bun. She wore a light gray sweater beneath a white lab coat. Her eyes reflected a cold, dull blue on her pale white skin. Her cheeks were chubby but sagged slightly near her jaws. Her eyes crinkled with large crow's feet and deep laugh lines cracked against the corners of her mouth. But the frown lines between her eyes were even more prominent.

"Laila?" She tapped at the window.

"Fuck off." I tossed a ball of water from one hand to the other.

"Laila, I'm a doctor. I'm not here to hurt you." She raised her hands in surrender.

"Doctors don't hold much merit to me these days." I raised one hand above the other, swirling my fingertips to make the water spiral into a miniature cyclone.

"I understand that," she said. "But I swear I won't hurt you. I just want to examine your leg and the injuries on your back. I have the ultrasound machine with me too. I just want to go over some things."

"I said fuck off!" I looked to the door with glowing green eyes.

She got quiet for a few heartbeats. "Laila, your body has been through a lot. That means your baby has been through a lot. We need to make sure everything is okay."

"Why?" I absorbed the water back into my hand and met her gaze. "So he can take him from me? So he can grow up in this shit hole?" I said. "No one needs to worry about my baby but me."

"And aren't you worried?"

I gritted my teeth together, contemplating for a moment.

I was. Besides getting out of there, I thought of nothing but my son. I'd felt him move, so I knew he was alive. But I was definitely scared. I hadn't been taking prenatals, I didn't have a diet close to what I needed, and I'd been tortured for the past eight weeks of my pregnancy.

"You aren't giving me any drugs."

She shrugged off her coat. "I know you can't see it, but I don't have any pockets. I don't have anywhere to keep a needle if I wanted to." I watched as she gazed through the window. "I'm going to open the door now, okay?"

"If you try to hurt me, I'll kill you quicker than you can say stop,"

"I believe you."

She opened the door, pushing a small white machine in front of her. She moved it to the corner of the room and came toward me. She held her arms upward, spinning in a circle to show me she didn't have anything on her.

"May I sit?" She asked with a gesture beside me. I scooted to the left, spinning my legs so they touched the ground. "Can I look at your leg?"

I pulled up the dirty hospital gown. She moved her hands to the gauze. She carefully pulled off the tape and examined my wound. The pain had given me a good idea of how severe it was.

"Hmm," she murmured. "I don't like the way this looks. I'm gonna get you some antibiotics, an infection like this could be very bad."

"How bad are we talking here?" I asked.

"If it goes on untreated, we may have to amputate."

That's just what I like to hear.

"Or you could just let me go home where one of my siblings can heal it."

She chuckled, shaking her head again. She walked to the cart. There she grabbed a bottle of sterile water, gauze, and tape. "That's not my call."

I huffed. She returned and sat beside me. She opened the water and gently poured it over the wound. I winced when it stung the torn flesh. "Why do you work for him?"

"Because we're discovering solutions to every human problem there is, Laila. We're going to build a better future. With your abilities, we can heal the sick. We can move things around the globe with zero carbon emissions. We can end deforestation. We can generate endless energy without a single shred of pollution. We can solve everything. You and this baby are going to purify this planet."

Although stretching the truth, that wasn't a lie.

"You think he cares about saving the planet from its impending doom?" I laughed. "If you really believe that, then you're more naïve than me."

"What do you think he cares about then?" She placed the gauze over the wound and ripped strips of tape.

"Power," I answered. "Men like him only care about one thing and that's power."

"I may not agree with his methods but—"

"If it were *really* about solving the world's problems, don't you think he would have done it by now? He's been at this for at least a decade, right? My kind can grow at least ten trees a day, and yet, deforestation is still happening. My kind can teleport, and yet, everyone out there is still traveling by car and plane. He's had countless people here who can generate energy, and yet, we're still using fossil fuels. I can heal the sick, but they're still dying," I said. "You're a doctor, you can't be that dumb."

"It isn't all that black and white. Power is not his priority, Laila. There are forces at work much bigger than Doctor Peterson. The future is all that matters." I laughed again. "Can you turn around for me? I need to examine your back."

I shifted a bit. "That's as far as I can get."

"That's perfect. Thank you." She pulled the gown down on either side. I could almost hear how hard it was to look at from the sound of her breath. Maybe it was easier to see on someone who wasn't a couple months from giving birth.

"Pretty nasty, huh?" I muttered.

I could practically hear her holding her breath.

"Gotta admit, used to have a thing for whips. The whole handcuffs, blindfolds, *Fifty Shades of Gray* sort of thing. But I can't imagine enjoying it now. Kinda creeped Jeremy out anyway. Not really his thing. Maybe it's a good thing that I don't like it anymore."

"Is that your boyfriend?" she asked as she poured sterile water over my back.

"Fiancé." I winced. "He was on his way to pick up our wedding rings from the jeweler when they took me."

She fell silent, finger gently grazing a few places on my back.

"These are healing up nicely. I brought you a fresh hospital gown and a set of scrubs, but I think you should wear the gown with some pants for now. These need to breathe. I don't want you having to fight two infections at once."

"Probably couldn't get a shirt on if I tried."

"Could you lie down for the sonogram?" she asked.

I lifted myself with my brittle wrists, scooted down the metal table, and lay against the cool metal. She sat beside me near my legs once she rolled the machine toward us. She clicked some buttons as I pulled up my gown.

When she turned and saw my genitals, her jaw dropped. I didn't know what they looked like below my third trimester belly, but her face told me everything I needed to know.

"How did that happen?" Her eyes were wide in horror as she stared between my legs.

"Peterson."

"He... He..."

"Raped me?" Her face screwed up when I said that. "Yeah."

The woman swallowed hard and grabbed some gloves off of the machine. "Can I examine you?"

"Yeah. I'm pretty sure there's something going on down there."

She moved her hand to my pelvis and carefully maneuvered around the sore areas. "Have you had any bleeding?"

"A little the day after." I shrugged. "Just when I wiped. Not anything that would affect the baby."

"Trouble urinating?"

"Yeah, it burns a little. Feels like a UTI."

"It's probably all the swelling," she muttered. "I'm gonna get you some acetaminophen. I can get you a low dose painkiller too, if you'll take it."

"That's okay. Tylenol's fine."

"Have you had any blood in your urine?"

"No, it's just really sore."

"I bet. There's a lot of bruising."

"So that's what it is?" I asked. "I can't really see over my belly these days."

"Let one of the guards know if there's any other symptoms. Discharge, vomiting, inability to urinate, anything like that."

I nodded as she pulled one glove into the other. She turned back to the monitor, grabbed a bottle of gel and squirted it onto my stomach. "When you're done looking at the baby, can I get a picture?" I asked. She looked to me. "It's not like I can hurt myself with it or anything. I just want to be able to look at him." I moved my hand to my stomach. "I haven't seen him since I was taken."

She thought for a moment. "I don't see the harm."

I smiled. "Thank you."

Raising the probe to my stomach and gently pushing it over my skin, she gazed up at the screen. I waited, watching her move it around the blurs for a moment. Then, I saw him.

A smile came to my lips and tears welled in my eyes.

It was in high definition, he actually looked like a baby. No longer a rotisserie chicken.

He had a giant head, knee craned up to his face. His eyes were massive. Huge, just like his dad's, but they looked even bigger on his little face. His lips. Those were something I couldn't see as clear because he appeared to be sucking on the lower one. But they looked wider than mine, perhaps. The top appeared to have my shape though. And that nose was not mine, I could tell that in a second flat. Mine was small, Jeremy's was...not. We'll just say that.

I watched his hand move, almost like he was waving.

I'd remember that moment for the rest of my life. That sweet little hand, swaying inside of my stomach. Telling me hello.

"He's in a great position," she said.

"He actually looks like a baby now. I mean, still kind of alien-like, but definitely a baby. He looked like a chicken last time."

She laughed. "I've never heard that one before, but I can see it."

I smiled, just staring at him in amazement.

As I looked at him, I wondered what it would feel like to hold him in my arms. I wondered how his little cry would sound when it rang into my ears. I wondered how he'd smell. I wondered if he'd love Oreos like he made me crave the entire pregnancy.

I wondered if he'd even make it that far. Because even though I was damned and determined to get out of that place, I was still crippled and trapped in a steel room.

But it did give me hope to count those little fingers and toes.

As she printed out some pictures and handed them to me, I turned with a smile. "Is there any way you could slip one under the door to the room beside me? He's my fiancé's brother, this is his nephew."

She smiled. "I'll do that. As long as you promise to take the antibiotics and Tylenol."

"You've got yourself a deal."

She stood with a smile. On her way out, she left a few containers of gauze on the back of the toilet. "If you notice any bleeding from your leg, use these to slow it and call for help."

She headed toward the door. When she left, she turned over her shoulder with a smile. "Thank you for being so cooperative."

Those words made my stomach churn and my blood boil.

I couldn't even bring myself to nod. I wasn't cooperating to be compliant. I was cooperating to make sure my son was safe.

I gritted my teeth together as she closed the door. A moment or two later, I heard the beep and click of the secondary exit and knew she was gone.

I tapped on the wall. "Chris?"

"Yeah?"

"A doctor just did an ultrasound on the baby. Do you want to see it?"

He chuckled quietly before he paused. He said, "I'd love to."

"Okay, I had her put one of the pictures under your door. Go look at it—"

"Lai." He paused. "I would love to see my nephew, but I... I guess you wouldn't know this since you've never seen me."

"Know what?" I asked.

"When I first got here..." He trailed off, silence lurking in for a moment. "Peterson was pretty ill informed on the whole teleportation thing. He thought that if I couldn't see, I couldn't teleport."

My stomach sunk. "You're blind?"

"To put it lightly."

Well, now I felt like a piece of shit. "Oh, God. That was really insensitive of me. I'm so sorry."

"It's okay," he said. "You didn't know. But how 'bout you describe him to me?"

CHAPTER SIXTY

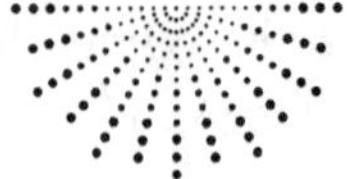

JUNE 10, 2019 - LAILA

ay ninety. Ninety fucking days. A third of my pregnancy wasted in that stupid, cold fucking room. They'd locked me in there after Peterson raped me and I'd refused to leave since. The OB came in every week and examined me, taking blood samples from time to time and doing more ultrasounds.

But I could feel it then; the wall in my mind that kept Jeremy from reaching me. It was hard to describe. Almost like when you do a horrible thing and lock it away far from your consciousness. You could tear down the wall, but you know it'll be like knocking down a dam.

The thing about knocking down a dam isn't that it can't or shouldn't be done. It's a matter of preparing for what will happen when it crumbles. You have to build a different kind of blockade for the water. You have to keep the flood routed in the direction where you need it. You have to manipulate the flow, so it doesn't destroy the important things along its reckless path.

That's what I was doing. I was figuring out which way to send the water after I blew up the dam.

It wouldn't be long now. It *couldn't* be long. I had to get out before my baby came. I was almost healthy enough to fight again.

Without the haze of whatever benzodiazepines they were drugging me with before, I was amazed at how well my abilities worked since I'd unlocked them.

The first week or two without them were difficult. My body ached most of the time and felt uncomfortably tingly at others. I couldn't sleep, the slop made me even more nauseated than usual, my emotions were a roller coaster, and my muscles spasmed periodically. But once they tapered off, I felt better than I had in months. At least, in some respects. Maybe the lack of beatings contributed to that.

Once those unpleasantries passed, I carefully collected information. I'd creeped into a few guards' minds as they headed past my room. The barrier spells made it difficult, but I had a good minute and a half in their mind before they crossed the door outside of the hallway my cell attached to. The images and thoughts were blurry, but it was enough.

Two weeks ago, I managed to stay in a guard's mind long enough to follow most of his rounds.

Four floors high. Four wings. Eight units on each wing. Three of us per unit.

Three-hundred and eighty-four—if my math was right and every room was occupied. Almost four hundred of us. Almost four hundred lives I had to save.

I'd recycled the plastic lined medical tape by folding it into a small triangle the size of a quarter. I melted it with my fire and squeezed it together with the tips of my finger to create a little shiv. It wasn't enough to hurt anyone else, but it was enough to send messages to Jeremy in thinner, more careful lines than my melted, acrylic fingernails.

Once I had a general idea of the buildings structure, I sent him a rough diagram and description from what I could make out. It wasn't as thorough as I would have liked, none of the messages were. But it gave them an idea of what they were walking into and what to expect.

He carved a message into his arm every day. It was bittersweet. I felt so guilty for letting it happen to me in the first place and his loving messages made me feel worse. He was right before, when he said I was too weak to fight Celena's war. Maybe I wasn't now but I was then.

Every day, I thought about selfishly tearing down that dam inside my mind. I suppose it would have been selfless, at least to Jeremy, but he wasn't thinking clearly. He wasn't thinking about the other people in there. He wasn't thinking about his brother, or himself, for that matter. He was too blinded by wanting me back. Not that I blamed him, I probably would have felt the same way if I were in his shoes.

Although, it brought me joy in the same instance. I smiled every time I felt that sting in my arm, but I was just so depressed. Hopeful, but depressed.

It was torture writing those secret little love letters back and forth. Cryptic, yet still so beautiful. Haunting, almost. Every cut left me craving, and still dreading, another.

I wished I said more than I did, but I had to make sure the scratches would heal before the doctor came. After we spoke, I'd scrape the skin until it was just one messy blur of irritated flesh I could crack up to a result of the irritating detergent on the ratty clothes.

It was a messy, yet calculated way of communication. Brutal, I'll admit.

Still, proof that we could withstand just about anything.

I bounced a ball of water between my hands. My eyes shifted over the sun outside the window. It was so bright. Almost summer, in fact. I'd missed my favorite season. But I'd be home for summer. I was sure of it.

"When we get out of here, what's the first thing you're going to do?" I called to Haley and Chris.

Haley laughed. "Pretty bold of you to assume we're going to get out of here."

"Fine, Haley. *If* we get out of here, what's the first thing you're going to do?" I retorted.

"God, there's so many things," Chris said.

"Like what?" I asked.

"Well, hugging all of my siblings, that'd be the first thing," he said.

"And then, I'd get a fucking big mac. Jesus, I miss big macs." I chuckled. He went on, "And a Sprite. An ice-cold cup of sprite. Oh, and French fries. So many French fries."

"I can't wait to eat a salad again. I miss green food," I said.

"And I'd go to a bar and order all of those drinks I always heard the adults talk about but never got to try. An old fashioned, whatever that is. A Manhattan. A martini."

I shrugged. "Well, you've probably had a martini. It's just vodka and a little fancy wine. Or gin, if you prefer."

"Okay, so not a martini then. But all of that. And I'd eat so much candy. Chocolate bars and Reese cups. God, I would fuck a buckeye up right now."

"I miss strawberries," Haley said from her cell. "And human fucking blood. I'm so sick of the synthesized bullshit they give me. One of these days, I'm gonna eat one of those fucking guards, man. If I die in the process, it'll be worth it."

I couldn't help the quiet laugh that left my lips as Chris nearly gagged. "Jesus, Haley."

"What? I'm half carnivore, I eat meat," she said. "That fat one with the heavy breathing looks fucking delicious. Probably be easy to take down too."

"You're disgusting," Chris said.

She laughed. "And fucking weed. I'd probably kill for just one hit off of a bowl."

I laughed. As much as I'd craved a smoke before I came here, all I wanted now was to feel the sun on my face and drink anything that wasn't lukewarm tap water.

"What would you do, Laila?" Haley asked. "If we ever get out, I mean."

"I'd find my favorite fuzzy blanket—"

"God, I almost forgot about blankets," she said. "Actually, I take my strawberry thing back. I'd get a blanket first."

"And a big ass cup of coffee. Like, huge. No—you know what? I'd just grab the whole pot. I'd sit on my couch all snuggled up and watch the sun rise in the window," I said. "That'd probably be second actually. I'd kiss Jeremy first. I'd hug my mom. I miss my mom."

"Me too. She probably thinks I finally did it. Jumped off a bridge or drowned myself in a river somewhere." She laughed. "She was always so worried I'd finally hang it up. These days, I wish I had."

They didn't know what I was planning. I couldn't tell them that this was it. That they'd be out soon. That they'd be home.

"You have to hold onto hope, Haley," I said. "I know you think I'm just naïve but we're going to get out of here."

She laughed. "I'll tell you what. We ever get out of here, and you can slap me in the face for calling you a liar. I won't even defend myself."

I chuckled. Just as I was about to rebut that I would never, we heard the click of the hall door and fell quiet, as we always did when it opened.

A moment later, his grimy face appeared in the window with a friendly smile. It made my stomach turn. I hadn't seen him since the night it happened. Suddenly, despite my current point of comfort as I spoke with my cellmates, my hands clenched in fury. Not to mention fear, loathing, and terror.

"Hello, Laila." He smiled in the window. He slid a tray through the encased metal box in the wall.

"Go fuck yourself," I snapped.

"Well, that's not very nice." He frowned. I glared at him with glowing green eyes. "You can put those away. I'm not here to hurt you."

"Oh, I'd love to see you try. Go ahead and open that door, I dare you."

He sighed. "How's our baby doing?"

"*My* baby?" I asked. "He's great. Kicking like a soccer champ."

He smiled. "I'm glad my boy's doing good."

I gritted my teeth to a hard line. "Fuck off."

He sighed again. "I'm sorry for the way things went the last time we saw each other. I didn't want it to happen like that, it was supposed to mean something. That wasn't how I envisioned it. I've been trying to give you space—"

"Good, give me more. Like a continent worth," I growled. "Because I swear to God, the next time you touch me will be the last time you breathe."

"I wish you would just give me a chance, Laila. We could make an amazing team—"

"After what you've done?" I brought myself to my feet, adrenaline drowning the pain in my leg. I wobbled toward the door. "Look at what you did to me, Peterson. You think even a fraction of me would *ever* want to be near you? Let alone work with you? Get the fuck out of here. You're a disgusting excuse for a man."

His lips lowered in a frown. "I'm not perfect. I'll admit that. But I'm not evil, Laila."

I gripped my flaming hands against the wall for support. "You're nothing. You will always be *nothing*." I spoke behind gritted teeth. "I will *always* be Jeremy's. Jeremy will always be *mine*. This baby will always be *ours*. No matter what life, no matter what reality. You will never even come close to comparing to what we have."

He swallowed hard, hazel eyes shifting sadly over me.

I brought a smile to my lips. "You know what the sad thing is? You genuinely believe you're better than him. That you matter. Why? Because you're a doctor? Because you're older?" I said. "Those are your only valuable attributes. You're a rapist. You're a sadist. You're a murderer—"

"I'm not a murderer."

I wagged my finger and laughed. "You are though. You may not be the one actually killing, but you're the cause of their deaths. You're the gun, Peterson. You're not the one who pulled the trigger, but without you, they'd all still be alive."

He chuckled, pushing up his glasses. A terrifying smile came to his lips. His eyes widened a bit, darting between my own. "You may not want to admit it, but you *are* mine. Look around you, Laila. I have you. Won't be long and I'll have your baby too."

I slammed my fist against the glass. He staggered backwards. I laughed.

"If I were yours, you wouldn't be talking to me through a piece of glass. You wouldn't be terrified of me." I smiled. "But I'm glad you're scared. Because one way or another, I'm going to be the one to end you. Remember this face, you worthless piece of shit. Because one day, maybe not today, maybe not tomorrow, but one day. These eyes are going to be the last thing you see."

"A beautiful last sight then." He managed a smile that gradually receded. "I know who I am to you, Laila. It's an inevitable yet necessary burden I will always carry. You'll one day understand why every single awful thing had to happen the way that it did. I'll be long gone by then, but that's okay." He smiled softly as he looked between my eyes. "I'll always be a creator in your evolution. You may not appreciate it now, but one day you'll be glad I've done what I've done. I'll be long gone then, I know that. But it's okay. As long as you learned what you needed to."

"You're pathetic."

He sighed. He walked to the side and clanged open my cell mate's food boxes. "I got you and your friends dinner. I hope you like KFC, 'cause that's where I went."

Like treat training a dog. "Fuck you."

He sighed again, looking back into my cell. "One day, you'll thank me for the knowledge I've given you. I just hope it's sooner rather than later."

"Fuck. You." I gritted my teeth to a hard line.

He shook his head and made his way to the door. I heard the familiar beep and click, then exhaled the breaths that shortened at his presence.

A moment later, the relief turned to pain. I cupped my hand over my mouth, trying to keep my cries silent while I turned my back to the door. I gently slid down it, trying to prevent the heaves that inevitably collapsed themselves from my lungs.

"He raped you?" Haley asked quietly, almost sympathetically.

I said nothing, just tried to level my breaths before I fell into a panic attack.

"The day after you were shot..." Chris said. "Jesus, I didn't realize. I knew it had to be bad, but I didn't think he did things like that."

"Because he usually doesn't," Haley said. "I've only met him once. Definitely didn't get that vibe."

"Three times for me," Chris said. "I usually just see the guards. Well, don't *see* but you know what I mean."

"He doesn't normally talk to us like that either," Haley said. "Let alone bring us real food." She paused. "Why are you so important to him?"

I wiped my snotty nose. "I'm kind of a big deal or something."

"What do you mean?" Chris asked.

"I'm a hybrid," I muttered. "Fae, Guardian, and Angel."

"Yeah, we knew that, dummy," Haley said.

I shook my head against the cold door behind me. "You probably won't believe it."

"Try me," Chris said.

I was quiet for a few heartbeats. "Jeremy is my par animo."

Haley laughed. "And I'm Santa Claus."

"Told you that you wouldn't believe me," I muttered.

"How do you know?" Chris asked.

"I got my powers after we had sex for the first time. It activated them," I said. "Jeremy's abilities damn near doubled. And my brother, my twin brother, actually, is half as powerful as me. He has all the same abilities, but he can't use them like I can. He's strong but his energy signature is half of mine," I said. "Jeremy and I have the bond. It's hard to explain."

"And you're sure?" Chris asked.

"It was the general consensus from upstairs. Mary confirmed it."

"Damn," Haley said. "So I guess you are kind of a big deal."

"More like living legend," Chris said. "Jesus, poor Jeremy. I knew you loved each other and everything, but that's... That's different."

"Yeah, he's probably a mess," I said, knowing well that he was.

"You have the bond, and you haven't tried to contact him?" Haley said. "What the fuck is wrong with you?"

"It's being blocked." I gazed down at the scratch on my wrist. I wanted to give them hope, but I didn't have any way to do that and be sure no one else would hear it. "But Jeremy's going to figure it out. I know he is."

"He will," Chris said. "To protect their partner, a paired soul will go to the ends of the earth. A love that can create and destroy worlds. That's what the stories said, anyway."

CHAPTER SIXTY-ONE

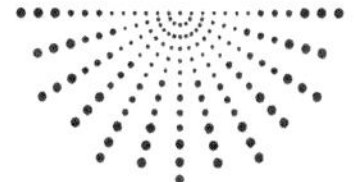

JUNE 22, 2019 - JEREMY

Forty days passed since Laila spoke to me for any length of a conversation. I still cut my skin every night to tell her I loved her. She'd replied with a heart each time. It wasn't deep, it was barely even there. But it was better than nothing.

It was redundant, I suppose. She knew I loved her; I knew she loved me. But I had to say something. I'd gone nearly two months without telling her I loved her, and I wouldn't let another day pass where I didn't. It was gooey, pathetic even, but that was us.

I'd show up at Kai's, Celena's, or Leah's door gripping my arm with a dish towel for them to heal me. I knew I was annoying them, but they didn't mention it.

They were probably just relieved that I wasn't drunk or on drugs.

I didn't want to get high anymore. I guess part of me did. Part of me always does. But I didn't want to drown it out because I had to be ready. As soon as she gave the word, I'd be ready. I couldn't be inebriated when she needed me.

On the twenty-second night, when I told her I loved her, she scratched into her arm, *don't give up on me.*

It stung that she even questioned that I could. I carved back, *never.*

She wasn't ready to fight. I could feel it. Her leg ached all of the time. She said she was getting better, but I knew that was only partly true. I felt her stand and plummet to the ground a few times. Part of me worried she'd never regain full function of her leg. It was easily the worst pain I'd ever felt. It was even worse than the slashes over her back which led me to believe there was muscle or tissue damage.

Her back still stung when she moved sometimes but it was nearly healed. She hadn't been beaten again. That made things a lot easier. It was still painful and terrifying that she was gone but I knew she was okay.

I didn't know if it was out of mercy or because of how bad of shape she was in and they didn't want her to die. Regardless of why, it was a relief. True relief wouldn't come until she was home, but it was better than it'd been.

She was thirty-five weeks pregnant then, almost far enough along to safely give birth.

The more I thought about that, the angrier I became. I missed almost half of the pregnancy. The exciting half, to make it even worse.

I missed watching her belly grow into a basketball on her torso. I missed the point where we could do a 3-D ultrasound. I missed getting to see him drop. I missed seeing her stretch marks appear. I missed getting to see her grow clumsy from the ball forming on her belly. I missed getting to count his little kicks. I missed getting to tour hospitals for his birth.

Eight months prior, I wouldn't have even known what half of that shit meant. But the moment after Laila told me she was pregnant, I studied like the valedictorian for the SATs.

It's ironic now. All that I wanted was to raise a child. He didn't have to make a difference in the world. I didn't expect him to be someone notable. I didn't care if he was flawed. I just wanted him to have a simple life.

But all of our destinies were written in the stars long before we were born. We were far from simple, definitely flawed, and more notable than almost anyone who walked that little blue rock.

"Hey." Celena knocked at the office door.

I smiled and shut the filing cabinet. "Hey, what's up?"

She shrugged slightly, smiling. "This is kind of stupid, and if nothing can be done about it, it's really no big deal. But I just checked the schedule for next week and I noticed me and Wyatt were both on it for the twenty-eighth, which is the date of our grad party. It's not really a big deal for me but—"

"Oh, shit. I'm glad you mentioned that; I remembered afterward and remade it. I need to go take that down and put the right one up. Thank you for reminding me."

"Awesome. It's not a big deal for me, but it's important to him."

"Well, it should be important to you too, you know. You've worked for thirteen years for that piece of paper, you ought to be proud."

"I guess." She stepped in and closed the door behind her. "So have you heard anything from Laila?"

"Not really. She responds sometimes but she's still healing. I haven't felt any new pain in a while. Which is good, I think. No bullets, no beatings, no cuts except for the little notes she sends me."

"Well, at least we have a way to talk to her now."

"Yeah, it's a hell of a lot better than nothing." I smiled and sat back down at the desk. "But how are you and Wyatt doing with your powers and all that?"

She raised her hand. A long, swaying strike of red fire protruded from her palm. She gazed at it for a moment before absorbing it. "Not too bad. It's not perfect yet but it's coming along."

"Are you guys going to go back to West Virginia any time soon?" I asked.

"Not yet. Wyatt still needs to figure out how to use his when he's in wolf form. I've figured out how to use air once I've shifted, but I'm still working on the others too. We're not ready to take on the pack. When we do, we have to find some way to do it so that the least amount of people get hurt. It's going to take time to come up with a plan. We can't just go in killing people. That's what we're trying to stop by taking Damon down, ya know?" she said. "And you guys are gonna need me when Laila gives the word."

I cocked my head to the side. "I don't know about that."

She chuckled. "Jeremy, you and the guys' powers won't even work there. You need all the Fae you can get. Laila said it herself."

"Kai, yeah. He can be there. But you're different. I'm sorry but you're kind of an amateur and people could die in there. Laila won't forgive me if something happens to you. She wants to keep you safe."

"I selfheal. I'm safer than any of you." She made a face. Her arms pulled across her chest. "Look, I'm going to need Laila for my war. She needs me to fight for hers, too."

"Celena—"

"You're not my keeper, Jeremy. This is my call. Not yours. I'm an adult, I can make my own decisions. And I've already decided. I'm going to do whatever I can to bring my sister and nephew home." No denying the family resemblance. "The thing is, what's happened to Laila affects all of us. This isn't just a battle against her, this is a war against our kinds. Everyone who isn't human is at risk. If we don't stop them, it could be any of us next. Me, or you, or Wyatt," she said. "The next generation. Who fucking knows? This is a lot bigger than just my sister. This is an attack on who and what we are. We have to end them."

I huffed. "You know, you've got a lot of pride in our kind for only being a part of this world for a few months."

She shrugged. "It's not pride, it's survival."

"I guess so. I've talked to a few other clans; they've agreed to help when Laila gives us the go. We have three Fae, nine vamps, four Wolves, twelve Guardians, and three Angels. Ray's built something of an arsenal for those of us whose powers won't work when we get there, but everyone's getting a gun. It's not much of an army, but it's better than nothing."

"What is that? Thirty?" she asked.

"Thirty-one, not including us."

"So with all of us, that makes—what?" She counted on her fingers. "Almost forty?"

"Thirty-eight including you and Wyatt," I said. "So far, anyway. I'm still trying to recruit some others. Especially Fae. The Angels are going to make a huge difference too, nothing can control them. The Vampires are good because unless they have silver bullets, nothing's taking them down. Wolves are strong and fast. The Guardians will probably be the least valuable and who we have the most of. We're pretty good with guns and physical fighting too though, so who knows. Border spells are going to cause issues for all of us. Either way, she said there were a lot of people we're helping escape. They can help organize the survivors at the very least."

"Will Mary be there?"

"Yeah, she's probably our most valuable asset next to Kai. I know that might be awkward for you—"

"A little weird." She shrugged. "I don't really care to meet her but if that's what it takes."

"I don't really care to see her either but." I scratched the back of my neck. "Do you know how to use a gun?"

She laughed. "You point and pull the trigger, right?"

I laughed, brows raising. "I'll tell Wyatt to show you. We have some pistols in the basement."

"How am I gonna keep a gun on me if I'm in wolf form?"

"We have some holsters that go around your waists. They'll fit between the shifts." She nodded nervously. "Do you have an issue with guns?"

"I'm a leftist. All those shootings and shit, you know?"

I laughed and sipped my coffee. "Yeah, well. You can still back out."

"No, I'll be okay. Sometimes you've got to sacrifice your ethics for the greater good."

I'd tried not to think about the fact that we were going to kill an unknown number of humans in the near future. My entire adult life had been dedicated to protecting them. And now, I was about to murder a shit load of them.

I rationalized it. I excused it, telling myself that they weren't good people. They weren't the type of people I wanted to protect.

They beat the love of my life until she could barely move. They cut into her flesh like butchers. They jabbed her with needles. They raped her. While she was carrying my son inside of her, no less.

If people had to die for me to get them back, then people had to die. I'd kill anyone, and I do mean *anyone*, who stood between me and my family. They were all I cared about. They still are.

And I wouldn't feel an ounce of remorse for it.

CHAPTER SIXTY-TWO

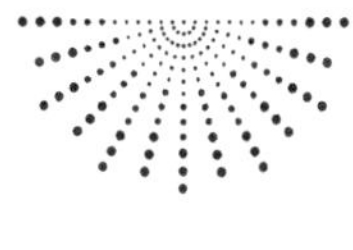

JEREMY

I hummed along to *Paint It Black* playing over the speakers in the corners. My gaze narrowed on a splotch of ketchup, refusing to come loose from the Formica tabletop. I dipped my rag in the bucket of warm, soapy water, flowery scent from the cleaner wafting to my nose. The bell rang above the front door. I was just about to say 'we're closed,' but I turned. Olivia smiled back at me.

"Hey," she said.

I gave a friendly smile back. "Oh, hey. What are you doing here?"

"I had an errand to run out this way so…" She lifted her hands on either side. "Here I am. I figured I'd grab a cup of coffee, maybe enjoy some decent conversation."

"Might take me a minute. I just dumped the last pot." I walked around the bar. "Decaf or regular?"

She sat at the counter in front of me and plopped her purse down. When her mouth opened, I almost gagged at the harsh aroma of liquor.

"Definitely regular." I grabbed a coffee cup from below the sink, set it on the counter, and passed her the sugar shaker.

She chuckled, bashful smile tugging up her cheeks. "I'm not even that drunk."

I raised my brows and gave a nod. "Sure."

"What? I'm not."

"I didn't say you were." I turned to the coffee maker and poured some fresh coffee grounds on top of the new filter. I glanced at the clock reading 10:52. "What errands did you have all the way out here?"

"Okay, I didn't really have errands. I just wanted to talk to you."

"I do have a phone." I turned back with a soft smile. "You could have called."

"I wanted to see you."

I made sure to pull down my grin. I didn't want to give her the wrong impression. "Well, it's nice to see you too. Are you hungry? Let me get you something to eat."

"No. No, that's okay."

"At least have some scones. We always make too many because we didn't have enough once and you'd have thought hell froze over. I'd rather not waste them."

Olivia nodded with a smile. "Okay, I'll have a scone."

"And some water."

I knew what she was getting at, but she seemed so helpless. She'd driven more than an hour away just to see me. Given the way I used her the last time we talked, I owed her an ounce of friendship.

I headed back into the kitchen and grabbed the lid off of the serving dish on the counter. "It's good you came when you did, I was just about to throw these out."

"Yay me," she said as I came back through the door. When I set them on the counter, she said, "Don't you pay people to do this shit?"

I creased my brows. "What do you mean?"

"All this. Cleaning and everything. You have employees, don't you?" she asked.

I fought the urge to say something about how her privilege was showing. There was a reason our elders were okay with us dating back in the day. My grandparents were loaded, so were hers, they were all on the Chamber together. Back before they disowned me for my addiction, I think they had some fantasy about us growing up and taking over their businesses together.

Nonetheless, the girl had everything handed to her. Most of my life then wasn't much different either, I guess. But Laila humbled the shit out of me. She taught me what hard work was in that diner.

I cleared my throat. "Yeah, we have employees. But I work here too. It's a small business. More than just paper pushing goes into running it."

"Ah," she said.

I grabbed the pot of coffee from the burner, poured our cups, and turned back to the counter with them. "So are you alright?"

"Yeah, I'm good. Just a rough day."

I managed a smile. "Wanna talk about it? We can find comfort in each other's misery."

She chuckled, dashing some sugar into her coffee. That's okay."

Then she lifted a flask from her pocket and splashed some clear liquid into her mug.

I glanced at her crooked car in the parking lot.

Look, I was the last person to judge anyone for substance abuse. And I wasn't judging. But if you're gonna drink or get high, do it responsibly. Don't put other people's lives at risk.

"Aren't you driving?" I asked.

"I'm fine." She raised the glass and took a sip.

I leaned against the counter behind me, searching for a way to ask her for her keys. No, I didn't want any part of the conversation we were having, and yes, I wanted her to leave. But I didn't want her to die in the process. I didn't want her to wreck and kill someone else.

She looked up from her coffee. "Oh, shit. I'm sorry. You want some?"

I did. But my craving for my fiancé and our little family was far stronger than my craving for that liquor. "Nah, I'm good."

"You sure? It's Ciroc."

Shaking my head, I laughed quietly. "You're mixing vodka with coffee?"

"It's vanilla." She smiled.

"That's still really gross."

"It's delicious."

"You always did suck at making drinks. What was that one you used to rave about? The one you made for that party in our junior year?"

She laughed. "The hurricane. Blue wave, cotton candy vodka, and a bottle of white wine. And I don't care what you say, it was amazing."

I wrinkled my nose. "It tasted like rubbing alcohol."

"It got you drunk as hell though."

"Yeah, it did the trick."

Quiet came in for a moment or two. She looked up at me over her glasses. "Do you remember that night?"

I shrugged. "Bits and pieces. Like I said, that shit did the trick."

"I do," she muttered. "We went out onto the roof top, remember?"

Should I have responded? Maybe not. I saw where the conversation was headed. But I was just trying to be nice.

"Yeah, I remember."

"I was so scared I'd fall off, and you told me you'd catch me if I did." She smiled, looking between my eyes. "It was stupid, I guess. I mean you probably didn't mean it the way I took it, but it was one of the sweetest things anyone has ever said to me."

That's sad. No one she'd been with since me said anything sweeter than that? I couldn't really believe that.

I pressed my lips to a line. "Why did you come here, Liv?"

She gave an embarrassed laugh. She paused and looked down at her coffee. "I don't know. I just missed you."

And that was it. The conversation had to stop there.

"I think I should take you home. I'll pick you up in the morning so you can get your car."

She laughed. "I'm sorry, was that a boundary I shouldn't have crossed?"

It was. But I wasn't in the mood to argue, and I damn sure wasn't going to stroke her ego . "You're just really drunk."

She pulled out the flask, tilted her head back, and poured what remained into her mouth. "If I wouldn't have treated you the way I did, neither of us would be feeling the way we do right now. I wouldn't be missing you; you wouldn't be missing her. She wouldn't be pregnant with your fucking baby wherever the hell she is."

I wanted to say something awful. But she was drunk. So drunk she could barely keep herself upright on the bar stool. God knows I'd been in a similar state and said far worse.

"What we had is literally history. I've been with Laila for almost four years now. You're just too late—"

"But, Jeremy—"

"Can I be blunt with you, Liv?" I asked. She nodded. I rubbed my mouth. "If I would have been with you when I met her, there just would have been more heart break. The moment I met her; I wouldn't have been with you anymore. I'm not exaggerating when I say that I fell for her the moment I saw her. The world stopped spinning for a second. She's my world. I'm sorry if that hurts you but it's the truth."

"But she's gone now."

My jaw clenched. *Nope. Nope, nope, nope. Time to leave.* I shook my head and started around the counter. "I think it's time for you to get to bed."

"Jeremy, I'm sorry. I didn't mean it like—"

"It's alright," I said as I got closer. "You're drunk, you won't even remember this tomorrow. Let's just get you home."

As I reached out to touch her shoulder, the least invasive and most platonic way possible to teleport someone, she grabbed my shirt. She pulled me toward her and touched her lips to mine.

I quickly took a few steps back. She smiled up at me. "That was really not cool."

Her smile fell a bit as she stood. "You can't tell me there wasn't a part of you that didn't enjoy that."

In some way, she wasn't wrong. Part of me, the part desperate for human contact, wanted to lean into it. I missed kissing. I missed hugging. I missed fucking. But she wasn't the one I missed kissing, hugging, and fucking.

"No," I said. "You're drunk. You need to go home."

"But you know that I want to," Olivia said. "You know that this isn't just a drunken mistake."

I shook my head again. I'd shaken my head so much those days, I was starting to think I'd be a bobble head in the next life. "I'm sorry. I know you still have feelings for me and I'm sorry you're having a hard time dealing with them. But I love her. I couldn't hurt her like that."

She frowned, looked down, and wiped a tear from her cheek. "I don't know what I was thinking."

"Let's just get you home."

I placed my hand on her shoulder, and we teleported.

We landed in her bedroom, and I flicked on the light, helping her into bed, but doing my best to touch her anywhere that she could interpret as coming onto her. Once she lay down in the mound of blankets, I pulled her glasses from her face and laid them on her nightstand.

She opened her eyes and gazed up at me. "Why don't you love me?"

I fought the sigh that echoed within me. Because we were kids when we developed feelings for each other. Because we'd gone two very different paths with our lives. Because she cheated on me. Because I was engaged to my soulmate and expecting the birth of my first child.

"I'm always gonna care about you, Liv. But what we had has been gone for a really long time."

She wiped her cheek. "Maybe for you."

"Sleep tight, okay?"

"Wait." She caught my hand. "Can I ask you something?"

"Sure."

"Does she make you happy?" she nearly whispered. Tears welled in her eyes. "When things are going right, I mean. Not right now, but just, in general."

"She does."

"Happier than I did?"

I knew she didn't really want to know. But I answered anyway. "Happier than anything ever has."

She smiled as tears escaped down her cheeks. "I want you to be happy. Even if it's not with me."

"I feel the same way."

"But how do I stop loving you?" She squeezed my hand.

One of life's greatest questions. "I don't know, Liv."

"Guess I just have to figure it out, huh?"

"I guess so."

"You're gonna come get me tomorrow so I can get my car, right?"

"I will." I gave a smile before pulling my hand away. "Sleep tight."

She smiled. And I teleported back home.

I dropped to the couch like a dummy in a car safety test. I held my hand to my head and rubbed my eyes.

That's not how I pictured my Saturday night going.

At some point or another, I was going to have to explain to Laila that she kissed me. I rolled my eyes as I envisioned the look on her face. The 'I told you so' look.

Suddenly, out of nowhere, I felt an ache in my stomach. Almost like diarrhea cramps but so much worse. It sent me doubling over and clutching my abdomen.

It went on for a few seconds before it stopped. At first, I chalked it up to something nasty I'd eaten. But then a few minutes later, it came back. It stopped again a moment after. Then came back a few moments later.

No.

No, no, no.

No, not yet. She was only thirty-five weeks.

He couldn't be born there. He needed to be at home with us. He needed to be born around family.

Laila needed to be around family. She needed all of my siblings in the waiting room. She needed her sisters. She needed her mom.

She needed me.

CHAPTER SIXTY-THREE

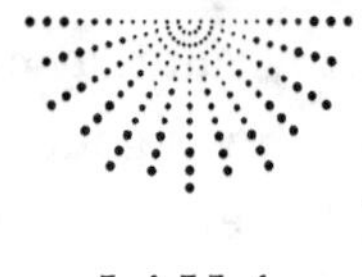

LAILA

Eleven days had ticked by since Peterson showed up at my door. Every second that passed, I grew more and more angry with my body. I wanted my leg back. It was better but it was still painful when I moved. I could hardly bare any weight on it, and it was infuriating. I just wanted to be better so I could get us out.

I lay on the cool table, gazing at the setting sun in the distance. I couldn't really see the sun; the frosted block was close to opaque. But I could see the colors of the early summer's sunset. The beautiful pinks fading into purple, goldish clouds licking the edges against the pale blue sky.

I still stunk. Worse than before, actually. But I'd be ready soon. And when I was, when I was out, I'd take the longest shower of my life. With bubbles, and lavender essential oils, and shampoo. So much shampoo. Oh, and a razor. I was starting to look like a woolly mammoth.

I just wanted out. I wanted to feel that sun. I wanted to taste the humid air in my throat and feel it coast into my lungs.

I wanted to knock that wall down in my head so bad. But I knew if I wasn't ready, if I couldn't fight, things wouldn't end well.

Jeremy loved me more than anything, I knew that. And I knew the moment I knocked that wall down, he would be there. He'd do whatever it took to get me out of that place.

But if he stormed it before I was ready to help, he might not make it out. There was a good chance none of us would.

All of them. My family, my friends, our allies. They might not live if we weren't prepared. I couldn't have their blood on my hands too. I'd killed enough people recently. I couldn't add those I loved to the list. Daniel would be on it for the rest of eternity, and I wouldn't let someone else I loved pass onto it too.

In my peripheral vision, I saw a guard meander by. He glanced in my room before the door clicked down the hall. I turned my gaze back to the window.

That's what I needed to focus on. I needed to think positive. I needed to think about how the air would smell and how the sun would feel. Bubbles on my skin. The smell of lavender.

Just one more week and I'd be ready.

Feeling the urge to piss before I let myself drift to sleep, I sat forward on the bed. I gripped the wall and began pulling myself vertical.

It was simultaneous. The moment I stood, a giant splat fell to the ground and exploded at my feet.

I gazed down in confusion, questioning if I'd peed myself at first. I'd leaked some piss from time to time, but it wasn't just a leak. It was a puddle.

As soon as the light hit the liquid on the floor, I knew something wasn't right.

It was green with hints of brown throughout.

"No," I said aloud. "No, no, no. Not yet. I have five more weeks. Not yet."

There was a tap on the wall where I braced myself. "What's wrong?" Chris asked. "Are you alright?"

I shook my head, unable to look up from the liquid on the floor. Words couldn't even form behind my lips. It wasn't time yet. I needed more time.

"Laila." Chris tapped on the wall again. "Laila, are you okay?"

"I..." I said. "I think my water broke."

"What?" he said. "I thought you had another month."

"I do." I ran my hand along my dry face. "I do. My due date isn't until July."

"Shit," he said. "Shit. Okay. Okay, should we call a guard?"

"Are you fucking stupid?" Haley barked from her cell. "You call the guard, and they're taking that baby."

"Well, what the fuck, Haley. I'm not a gynecologist," he snapped.

Hardly able to bring in air, the inevitable occurred to me. I was going to have my baby in that place. My teeth started to chatter, and my stomach began to turn.

"Something's wrong, it isn't supposed to look like this." I looked down with trembling hands.

"It doesn't matter," Haley said. "When he's out, you can heal him."

I heard what she said but it didn't register. I just stood there, staring down at the mystery fluid on the ground.

She hit the wall and made me jump. "Listen to me, Laila. Listen."

"I'm here."

"You're gonna make it through this, alright? Women have been having babies for eons. In fields and stables and rivers. Without running water, without electricity, without anything." Her voice sounded strict yet affectionate. "You can do this, Laila. Your body is made to do this."

My stomach tightened so taut that I stumbled, suddenly glad I was still bracing the wall. It was like the worst period cramps I'd ever felt. I lowered myself back to the table, taking slow breaths as I grimaced.

"Laila, are you listening to me?" Haley said.

I took in and blew out slow, deep breaths. "I'm scared."

"I know." Her voice was as level as a scale. "I know you're scared, Laila. But you can do this. Just think about how much you've lived through. Think about all the horrible things you've seen, all the shitty fuckery you've survived. You can do this. This is nothing compared to all that."

My lip began to quiver. "I can't have this baby. Not here. Not right now. I can't do it, Haley. I can't."

"Yes you can," she said fiercely. "You can do anything, Laila. You got this, okay?"

I struggled to slow my fast-moving breaths.

"We're going to be here the whole time." Chris tapped on the wall. "We're here, you aren't alone."

The pain continued, forcing me to close my eyes. I tried to remember to breathe, whole body trembling.

The walls seemed to be closing in on me. It felt like an elephant sat on my chest. My vision grew blurry around the edges. My palms got hot and sweaty. My extremities even started to go numb.

"Laila," Haley said, angrily hitting the wall. "You have to stay with me, okay? Don't you panic. You're the strong one here. You have to keep it together. To keep that baby safe, you have to keep it together. He needs you."

I blew out a slow pant. "He needs me."

I felt the now familiar—almost enticing—cuts cascading against my arm. My finger ran along each one.

B-A-B-Y-? he wrote.

I clenched my trembling teeth together. I reached below me to the small lip of the table where I kept my shiv. With trembling hands, I carved the words into my upper thigh.

H-E-s C-o-M-I-N-G

There was a long lull as Haley said, "Laila. Talk to me, girl."

"I hear you, Haley."

N-o-T y-E-T

My chest had never ached so badly in my life when I stared down at those words.

This wasn't fair. He deserved to be here. He wanted this baby so badly, and he wasn't going to see him born.

I-M S-c-A-r-E-D

The response was instant. *I-M r-D-Y l-E-t M-E H-E-l-P*

If he came then, he wouldn't have made it out. I know that with certainty. I was in labor, I couldn't help. As vain as it may sound, he couldn't have pulled it off without me.

Even if he managed to get inside of that hell hole, which was incredibly unlikely, how would he make it out? And that's a big if because he didn't have a clue what this place looked like. I was on the fourth floor. He'd have to get through countless guards, Amy, Peterson, and the Witch working with them.

He needed my inside access first. I had to get out of that room before he could come.

We had to do this as a team or no one behind those walls would make it out, myself and our baby included. Not me, not Chris, not Haley, not Lydia, and not whoever was coming to our rescue. We would all die if I couldn't do what needed to be done.

U-l-l D-I-E

IDC I H-A-V 2 b T-H-E-r

I bit my trembling lip so hard that I tasted blood. There was nothing that I wanted more than him to be there with me. But I couldn't do it. I couldn't be the reason he, or any more of our people, died.

He wouldn't be able to get to me. The moment they stormed the doors, the guards would immediately move me to a secure area, and I couldn't fight in labor. There was a reason they kept me so high up. This baby and I were important, they'd do anything to keep Jeremy from getting to us.

And if we went into lockdown while I was in labor? Then they'd know for sure that the baby was coming. And they'd take him. I was sure of it.

I l-o-V-E Y-o-U, I carved.

P-l-S, he begged.

I-M S-r-Y

N-o

There was a pause. I started to cry. He was going to miss our son's birth because of me. And I'd feel remorse over that every day for the rest of my life.

W-T c-N I D-o b-b-Y

What could he do? That was a great question. I wished I knew the answer.

D-N-T l-E-A-V-E M-E
I-M r-I-T-E h-E-r-E

CHAPTER SIXTY-FOUR

JEREMY

Blood poured down my wrist to my elbow. I pounded on Leah's mahogany colored door. The warmth had drained from my face, struggling to keep my eyes open. I'd already lost so much blood. I heard her maneuvering in her room and banged on it harder.

"Jesus, hold the fuck up," she yelled. I gripped the door frame, trying to stay on my feet. I was too weak to teleport again, I could barely hold myself up.

The door swung open and her mouth followed. "Shit, are you okay?" She grasped my shoulder with one hand and squeezed the towel tighter around my forearm.

"She's in labor." I tried to meet her gaze through the black haze and tears clouding my vision. "She's having the baby. I'm not there, Leah. I'm not with her."

"Adam, Brody!" She gripped my shoulders to keep me upright.

"I want to be there," I said. I pressed my fingers into the door frame as her tiny arms struggled to keep me on my feet. "I need to be with her. I need to meet my son."

"It's okay, Jeremy," she said. "*Adam! Brody! Kai!* Fucking Christ, I need some God damn help out here!"

"What's happening?" Adam opened his bedroom door. "Oh, shit."

He rushed to me. He grabbed my shoulder to take the weight off of Leah and held my bleeding wrist with his other hand.

"Get him downstairs so I can heal him," Leah said.

Adam nodded. We suddenly stood in the living room.

"Sit down." He wrapped his palms around my arms and lowered me to the couch.

"She needs me," I said. "She needs me, but she won't let me help. She says I'll die, but I won't. I won't. She just—she needs to believe in me. She needs to trust me. She can't do this on her own."

"Jeremy." Adam's face was before mine, but I couldn't focus on it. "It's going to be okay."

"It's not. It's not okay. It's not. I've missed it all and now I'm going to miss this too. I'm going to miss my son's birth."

"She's in labor?" He steadied my swaying shoulders while Leah came down the steps.

"He's coming."

I felt stinging against my thigh and my fading heart rate picked up. "Shit, it hurts too much. She's writing on her leg. I need to see what she's saying."

"Here." Leah sat on the coffee table, not wasting a second. She grabbed my arm, the white-hot heat radiated from her palm against my skin, and the wounds closed.

I pulled my hand to my leg to trace each letter.

I c-N-T D-o T-H-I-S

"I need a knife." I looked from Leah to Adam as my vision cleared. Adam nodded and disappeared.

"What did she say?" Leah asked.

"That she can't do this," I whispered. "She needs me, Leah. I need to be there for her, but she won't push them out."

"She has a reason, Jeremy." She took my hands in hers. "If she needed you bad enough, she'd let you come. But she's got this. You have to believe in her. She can handle it."

I shook my head, tears flowing down my face. "I just want her back. I want to meet my son."

Adam appeared in front of me with a knife. "Here."

I took it and put the blade to my wrist. But I had no idea how to respond. I couldn't beg her to let me save her again. She was dealing with enough; she didn't need my hero complex.

"What do I say?"

Her eyes filled with pity. "Tell her she can make it through this."

I pushed the knife into my arm.

U C-A-N

"What's going on?" Brody asked from the steps.

"Shh." Leah hushed. I extended my arm for her to heal.

I-t H-u-r-T-S

I N-o b-b-y

Leah took my arm and started healing it again before I yanked it away. "You need to give her enough time to read it."

"I'm sorry, you tell me when."

I-M s-O s-C-A-r-E-D, I felt in small, shaking print against my thigh.

U G-o-T T-H-I-S, I wrote. *I l-O-v-E Y-O-U*

As I felt the scratches on her leg, I extended my arm to Leah. She healed it while I used my other hand to trace her words.

I-M s-O s-r-Y

D-n-t W-r-Y b-O-u-t M-E

U s-H-d b H-E-r-E

I-T-s O-K

I-m s-r-Y

s-H-H

Leah grabbed my arm that poured blood once again. "Wait," I said.

She grasped it tight before letting the warmth shine into my skin. "You won't be able to help if you bleed out, Jeremy."

I let her heal my arm. I felt the rough, uneven shaking scrapes on my thigh again.

D-n-T H-A-T-E M-E P-l-S

Tears burned my eyes. The cramping continued. I bit my quivering lip.

"What is she saying?" Adam asked.

"Don't hate me," I whispered.

Brody sat across from me, hand grazing his cheek and rubbing his lips. His eyes were full of water too. Adam swatted away at his tears. Leah gazed at me with sad, mopey eyes.

I took the knife back to my forearm.

I l-o-v-E U M-o-r-E t-H-N A-n-Y-T-H-i-n-G T-h-A-T-L N-V-r C-h-A-N-G-E

Tears began to spew from my eyes like waterfalls. I dropped the knife to the ground with a clatter and raised my bloody hand to my face.

CHAPTER SIXTY-FIVE

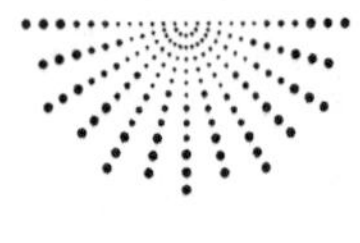

LAILA

I'd been in labor for a few hours while tearing my skin apart to talk to Jeremy. He wasn't there with me, but he was there for me. I felt his chest tightening as he quaked with tears. I felt the corners of his eyes getting raw from all the wiping.

He felt awful and I felt awful for being the cause of his pain. But he just couldn't come yet. He couldn't.

As the contractions got more intense, the harder it became to focus. My vision blurred as I watched my stomach get tight and loosen. I dripped sweat, panting through each pulse.

I tried to sit on the toilet as much as I could for it to catch as much blood as possible. The guards walked by every other hour or so shining a flashlight through the window of the door. When we heard the click, we all fell silent and pretended to sleep.

My lip swelled from biting it in place when they walked by, trying to stay as silent as possible while my stomach contracted. It was hard to refrain from screaming, but some how, I managed. I just kept holding my breath, then panting heavily when the door clicked shut.

Haley was coaching me through it. She spoke more kindly than she had since I met her. Her voice was soft when she counted the seconds of each contraction. "You're doing great, sweetie," she said. "Just a little bit longer and you'll see his sweet little face."

I panted heavily and wiped sweat off of my brow. I laid my head against the cold metal table. Another contraction began and I took in a deep breath.

In and out. In and out.

Just keep breathing.

"I don't want him to come here," I said between pants. "What are they going to do when they find us in here in the morning?"

"Don't think about that," Chris said. "Just think about how cute his little cheeks will be."

"It hurts so much." I ran my hand along my stomach. My brows scrunched down and tears escaped from the corners of my eyes.

"Let's think about something else," Haley said. "What are you going to name him? Have you thought about that?"

I took in another deep breath, waiting for the contraction to subside. When it did, I said, "Jeremy wanted to go with Christopher."

"After me?" Chris asked.

"After you."

"That's so cool," he said quietly. "What did you want to go with?"

"Micah," I said. "I love the name Micah."

"Then that's his name," Haley said. "Micah'll be here soon, alright? You're going to hold that little boy in your arms and it's going to make all of this pain worth it."

I nodded, running my hand against my belly.

"Okay, hon, you have to do something now," she said. "Kind of a weird question, but how familiar are you with your uterus?"

"What kind of question is that?" Chris said.

"Shut up, Chris. Laila, you aren't prudish with your pussy, are you?"

"I'm pretty familiar with my vagina but my uterus is another thing." I panted out another deep breath. My heart was beating so fast that I could hardly see.

"Okay, good. Good. So now, I want you to put two fingers inside of yourself, okay?"

"What am I feeling for?"

"Your cervix, it should have descended by now. It's far to the back, almost near your ass. You need to see how far along you are."

"How do you know all this?" I asked.

"I've got some medical training."

"That makes me feel a lot better actually." I pulled my knees apart, trying hard to think about what I had to do and not to focus on how much it hurt.

My finger slid up into my body. It didn't feel as it always had before. I guess it wouldn't, being in labor and all. I could barely make out anything through all of the thick, slimy blood. It almost made me gag.

"Are you doing it?" she asked.

"I'm trying," I muttered, feeling around. When my hand touched something hard, my breath caught. "I feel something."

"Soft and squishy? Almost like lips?" she asked.

"No, not at all. It's... It's hard."

She paused for a moment. I stroked my finger along it, feeling the smooth, velvety texture beneath my fingertips. Suddenly, I got a rush of some strange, hopeful feeling. It was oxytocin, I know that now that I think back on it. Because I was immediately in love as I ran the tips of my fingers across it again.

"That's really fast," she murmured. "But I think that's the head."

"Oh my God," Chris muttered.

I kept my hand there for a moment, basking in some emotion I never experienced before. An overwhelming wave of love deeper than I'd felt for anyone or anything in my life. Then the urge to hold him inside of me, to keep him safe inside my womb, came over me almost as quick as the love.

"I think it's time to push, Laila," Haley said.

I shook my head. "No. No, I'm not ready."

"It isn't up to you, girl. If he's coming, he's coming. There isn't a thing you can do to keep him in there."

I pulled my bloody hand out of me.

"Are you in a good position?" she asked.

"I'm kneeling," I said.

"Whenever that next contraction comes, you're gonna have to push, alright? Just hold your hands underneath to catch him as he comes. He might slip right out so be ready. He'll be slippery, hold him tight."

I couldn't help the tears that came from my eyes. I wanted to meet my baby, but I was terrified. Not of pushing him out, that was easy. This whole labor thing wasn't even that bad, not compared to the torture I'd been undergoing for months. The emotional turmoil was what made it so agonizing.

"You can do this, Laila." Chris tapped on the wall.

"I wish Jeremy was here," I whispered.

"Me too."

"I need him." My teeth chattered. The lump in my throat got thicker. "This isn't fair."

"You're gonna get to hold your baby's hand any minute now," Haley said. "Just think about that, okay?"

I bit my shaking lip. My stomach cramped again. I hushed the moan that strived to leave my lips, rocking my hips back and forth, closing my eyes.

"Is that another contraction?" Chris asked.

"Yeah."

"Alright, sweetie, you've got to push. Push until it stops and then breathe. I'm gonna count, and you push until I get to ten, okay?"

"Okay," I said.

"Okay, here we go. One, two, three, four..." She trailed on, and I pushed. My body shook. My trembling hand rested between my legs. A stinging sensation began when the skin stretched. "Alright, sweetie, breathe."

I cried, "It hurts."

"Take a breath for a minute, but you're doing great, Mama. You got this."

I felt stinging up my arm and outlined each letter.

U-r A-M-A-z-I-N-G b-b-y

My lips trembled and I broke out in heavy cries. I wanted him there so badly. I needed him.

I grabbed my makeshift knife and began scratching.

A-l-M-o-S-T

"You're doing great," Haley said softly, almost like a nurse off an old sitcom. "You're about to meet your little boy."

Another contraction began and I had to bite my tongue to keep from screaming. "Alright, one, two..." I pushed again. There was a gush against my hand as I continued to thrust my muscles downward. Then, I felt the hard velvet against my fingertips.

"I feel his head! I feel his head, he's crowning."

"You're almost there," Haley said. "You're almost there, Mama. One more big push and he'll be here. Just one more big one."

I nodded, breathing heavily. Sweat soaked hair stuck to my cheeks. I kept my hands just were they were but wished I could put it from my face. "Just one more."

"Just one more," she repeated. "You've got it in you, just one more big push."

I took in one more deep breath. Then the contraction began again. As soon as it did, I pushed like hell. My eyes stayed closed from the moment that I pushed until the moment that he entered the world.

It's surreal to think about how that one strong, agonizing push changed my entire life. I went from one person to two in that single second. All of a sudden, that little baby was all that ran through my mind for that moment and all the years that followed.

His head was born. I felt his soft hair beneath my fingertips. I can still remember the texture. I can still recall the way each soft little strand felt against my finger.

I pushed again. It was excruciating but relieving at the same time. Joyous, even. Beautiful. It showed me how amazing the female body truly is. A living, breathing miracle of creation that creates within itself to bring new life into a dying world.

I felt his little shoulders begin to bare weight onto my pinkies. I held his head between my palms, and I pushed one last time.

My eyes struggled to lift open and there he was. But I couldn't see him.

His sweet little body glowed white. The same blinding white light that my hands produced when I healed. I lifted him out in front of me and gazed in awe for a second. I couldn't see his face or any of his features, but I saw that beautiful light. I felt his magnificent spirit radiating from his skin in every direction.

It was this overwhelming energy filled with love, and innocence, and purity. *He* was that energy.

Micah was literally my light in the darkness. I collapsed from my knees to my butt and stared at him in awe a second longer.

I couldn't see him. Not really. I saw a glowing ball of light in my hands. He shined so bright, I'm sure he lit up Haley and Chris's rooms.

"Laila." I heard Chris say behind the blood pumping in my ears.

"What is that?" Haley said.

It occurred to me.

He wasn't crying.

My heart raced faster. I lay him onto my wounded thigh.

I remembered that home birth video Jeremy made me watch. Their baby didn't cry either.

I began furiously rubbing him the way they had in the clip. That made their baby cry.

Fuck, I never wanted to hear a baby cry so badly in my life.

Chris and Haley called for me, hitting their walls to try and get my attention.

"C'mon, Micah," I mumbled. My hand rubbed him furiously and I grew queasy. I pulled his little body against me, trying to warm him up. I anxiously massaged his hot skin. I even slapped his bum the way doctors did in old movies, just praying I would hear something.

His glowing little body rested against me as the bright room grew blurry. My heart thudded so loud, I'm not sure I would have heard it if he did cry. My warm, sweaty skin grew clammy and cold, as if I just came down with a terrible flu.

I lifted him against my chest, feeling that bright warmth for the first time and praying it wouldn't be the last.

I rocked back and forth.

I saw the flood of crimson between my thighs pouring onto the floor like an oil spill into the ocean.

And then, I saw nothing. I heard Chris and Haley screaming for me. I felt Micah's warm skin on mine. But everything else faded to black.

CHAPTER SIXTY-SIX

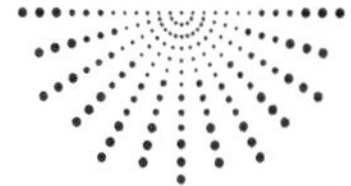

JUNE 25, 2019 - JEREMY

I f I thought I'd lost hope before, I wasn't just naïve but stupid.

Three days passed since my son was born.

Three days since I last heard from her.

Almost.

That was the last thing she said. I hadn't stopped crying since those words appeared across my arm.

I didn't feel a thing from her since then. Not a stinging tear in her eye, not a needle prick, not a cut, not a slash. Nothing. Total, absolute radio silence.

It was worse than the beatings. At least then, I knew she was alive. Now, I didn't know if her or my baby were even breathing.

I kept staring at my phone, pondering picking it up to call Olivia. Besides bringing them home, there was nothing I wanted more than getting high.

I'd locked myself away in my apartment the morning the baby came and hadn't left since. I'd spent every waking moment staring at pictures of her, and then of the ultrasounds, clutching them pathetically to my chest as I drowned myself in my own tears.

My mom died giving birth. Maybe Laila did too. It'd be poetic. Fitting for my catastrophe of a life.

"Jeremy." A knock sounded at the door. Leah yelled, "Jeremy, open the God damned door."

"Just leave me alone." I gazed down at a picture of us on my phone.

"Damn it, Jeremy. This is important." I rolled my eyes. I turned over on the couch. "Jeremy, I know your heart is broken. I know, man, I fucking know. I can feel how much you're hurting. And I am so sorry that you're going through this." She paused before she tapped on the door again. "I miss her too, you know. Laila's my best friend and I'm just as worried as you are. But I think I found something that will help. Please just open the door."

I hurried to my feet, bolted that direction, and flung it open with wide eyes. "What did you find?"

"I have to show you." She brushed past me and set her computer bag down on the table.

I huffed and shut the door. "What, another article?"

Leah turned back with a glare. She yanked her laptop from her bag. "You remember those implants inside of Daniel, right?"

I walked to the table and sat beside her. "What about them?"

"Okay, so we know that they're little remotes, right?" She powered her computer on.

"Right."

"So I started thinking about it. If they're remotes, they aren't just magical little crystals anymore. They're genius little super computers. Something has to work to turn them on and off, right?"

"Obviously."

"But how would you turn something with magical properties into a super powered computer that can deactivate and reactivate the qualities of the stone?" She angrily clicked buttons.

"I don't know, you're the programmer."

"Lucky for you, I'm an *amazing* programmer," she muttered.

"Can you just get to the important part? I don't need all the tech mumbo jumbo."

"Okay, look." She reached into her bag and pulled three little rocks of hematite from inside. "Basically, the only thing I could think of was some type of radiating energy." I made a face. "Like Wi-Fi. You know, energy that travels outward."

"And what does that mean?" I asked.

She grabbed my hand and set the crystal in my palm. She pulled my fingers shut around it. "Try to use energy."

I brought a small, plum sized ball of electricity to my opposite hand.

"Okay, put it out. Now keep holding those." She tapped away on her keyboard. I did as she told.

"Now, use energy again." I did so and brought a ball nearly the size of a basketball to my hand. She smiled. "I hacked into their network. I can disable them, Jeremy."

I nodded slowly. "So if we find them..."

"You guys won't be powerless in there," she said. "It might still dull the prisoner's powers, but they'll have them. Not as strong as they will be once we get these things out of them but should be enough to not affect you guys. That is, as long as they're all on the same network as these. I'm hoping, anyway. Might take me a few minutes to get into the system so we don't alert them we're there before we're ready. But I can do this, I know I can."

I gazed down at the small rocks in my palm.

"This is a good thing, Jeremy. Smile," she said.

I forced one to my lips. "Yeah, that's great."

"We're going to find her," Leah said. "I know we will."

"I hope."

CHAPTER SIXTY-SEVEN

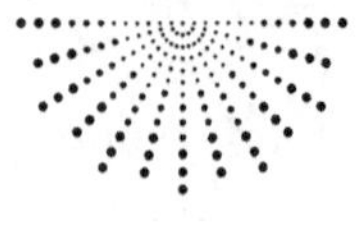

LAILA

"Well, good morning, Sleeping Beauty," a disgustingly memorable voice said.

My eyes fluttered open. That time, no burningly bright lights shined in my eyes. Instead, the sun cascaded in from a large open window just ahead of me. I blinked a few times, trying to focus on what was behind it.

The sun reflected against the crashing waves slamming the shore. It was so close that I could smell the salt in the water. I could even hear the roar as they rose and dropped against the sand.

His palm grazed my bracketed hand. I flopped it away, looking up with daggers to meet his gaze. "Where's Micah?"

He frowned. "Was that what you named him?"

"What do you mean was?"

He sat in a spinning chair beside me, pushing up his glasses, frowning. "He's gone, Laila."

My teeth began to tremble, chest so tight it was hard to breathe. I shook my head. "You're lying. You're a liar, he was here. He was alive."

"He was when he was inside of you," Peterson said. "He aspirated because he didn't have proper medical care at his birth like he was supposed to."

My head shook. "No, he was here. He was here."

He frowned and reached out to touch my cheek.

I flopped around against the restraints. "Don't fucking touch me."

He sighed, grabbed a cup of water off the table beside us, and held the straw between his fingertips for me to reach. I spat at him.

Peterson ran his tongue against his teeth. He wiped my saliva from his cheek. "I'm very sorry for your loss, Laila. I've been pretty distraught myself."

My eyes heated in their sockets. "Fuck off."

"This isn't my fault." He puckered his brows. "If it hadn't taken you so long to wake up, I would have let you hold him. But he's already rotting."

That image made me nauseous and my body ache. My head shook, tears gushing from my eyes. I'd lost him. Just like Jeremy had feared throughout the entirety of my pregnancy. I fucked up worse than anyone ever could.

"I hate you," I said behind gritted teeth. Tears raced down my angry cheeks. I shook against the restraints. My glowing eyes looked between his. "This is all your fault, I fucking hate you."

His nostrils flared. "The moment your water broke, you should have called for help. He would still be with you if you had."

"Fuck you," I growled. "None of this would have happened if you would have never fucking kidnapped me. This is all because of you, you worthless piece of shit."

He gritted his teeth together. "I get that you're hurt, Laila. But you don't have to take it out on me."

"You're the *only* person to blame for this." I struggled desperately to ignite my fingertips and failed.

I felt her there in my mind now, just like I felt the dam. I could have pushed it down. I could have bulldozed the whole thing.

But it wasn't time. If I did, I *might* kill Peterson, but even if I did, I wouldn't be able to get everyone out. By the time Amy realized what I was doing, she'd heal the volatile little excuse for a man, and I would be back to square one.

He gritted his teeth together. "I loved that baby. This is because you decided to selfishly exclude me from his birth."

"You're delusional." I let out a bare laugh. "The fact that you genuinely believe that you loved him. You did *not* love him. You realize that a baby feels what their mother feels, right? Every moment that I bled and feared for my life, he did too. He wouldn't have been so early if I hadn't been so stressed. What you did, *everything* that you did, is a part of why *my* son didn't survive."

"You'll never understand how much I loved him, but I hope one day you'll understand how much I love you."

I gritted my angry, trembling teeth to a line. "You don't love me. You're obsessed with me."

A smile pulled at his lips. "Isn't that what love is? That's how you and Jeremy are." He leaned closer so that his face hovered a few mere inches above mine. His hand moved to my neck. "True love is about being captivated by someone. To have your breath taken away when you lay eyes on them. To be mesmerized by the good and bad within them." He rolled my long hair between his fingertips, leaned down, and put his lips onto mine.

As our mouths met, I opened them against his and dug my teeth into the bottom one. I bit so hard that the taste of his blood filled my mouth. He tried to pull away, but I held it tight, ripping a piece of flesh off. He held my neck down and yanked his face away. He stumbled backward cupping his hand over his bleeding lip. And I laughed.

"Aww." A deranged cackle left my lips. I was still disoriented from whatever drugs he'd put in me while I slept, but I was also infuriated. "Poor little psychopath got a boo-boo."

He raised his hand and slammed it against my cheek. He wagged his finger in my face. "Don't ever do that again."

"Aww, poor little guy." I laughed again. "All butt hurt over a little cut. Fuck you. Fuck your stupid face and your fucking experiments. Fuck your goddamn existence. Fuck. You."

He reached forward to grip my throat and squeezed. I smiled up at him.

"Go ahead," I choked. "No balls. But I guess you know that as much as I do. Huh, little guy?"

He released my neck as his gaze narrowed. His nostrils flared. He moved back with gritted teeth. "I thought you'd appreciate my kindness in bringing you here. I didn't have to let you see the ocean. I didn't have to let you breathe fresh air. I should have known better than to expect gratitude from you."

"Fuck you," I said again, practically singing. "Fuck you, fuck you. Fuck you."

Peterson reached to the table and pulled out a vial and syringe. "You wanna know one great thing about you not being pregnant anymore?" He gripped the IV at my arm and plummeted the syringe into it. "Trazodone. Beautiful drug."

I laughed. "I could use a nap after this. Thanks, asshole."

He gritted his teeth to a line. I felt my eyes slowly seal shut.

I awoke in my cell as the sun was setting. It created a similar work of art in the sky as it had the night Jeremy proposed. I sat up on the table and gazed down at the red stain that still laid beneath me.

I was haunted by the memory, I always would be, but I wouldn't let myself cry. I had to keep it together just a little while longer. I could cry for weeks.

I raised my hand to cover my mouth, trying not to think about it. But then, my eyes caught my thigh.

The scabbing bullet hole was gone.

All that remained in its place was a perfect white circle with scarred dots around it from the stitches. There was no pain or throb. It was almost as if it never happened. But I didn't understand how. How could that be possible? I hadn't been asleep long enough to have a scar.

The more I thought about it, the more I realized that nothing hurt. There was a slight ache around my wrists where I fought Peterson's restraints earlier. Aside from that though, I felt nothing. I felt better than I had in months.

I lay his glowing little body on my thigh. Then against my chest.

He healed me.

Micah healed me.

He must have healed whatever was happening inside of me when I fainted too because there were no bruises or injuries on my still swollen belly to suggest the doctors resolved the bleeding.

As I realized that I was back to normal, I knew that that was it. I needed to act now before stress test day came back around.

A familiar, almost comforting, sting radiated up my forearm.

l-A-I-l-A

I bit the edge of my fingernail to make it sharp and began scratching. I dug my nail so far into my skin that I knew he'd feel it.

J-E-r-E-M-Y

Instantly, he began cutting back. *U-r A-l-I-V-E*

T-O-N-I-G-H-T

He carved back a question mark.

R U R-E-A-D-Y

I CAN B

I-l-l T-E-l-l Y-O-U W-E-N

1 H-R 2 P-r-E-P-A-r-E

<3

That was it. I wasn't spending another night in that cell. I was getting out. And I was taking as many of my people as I could get.

CHAPTER SIXTY-EIGHT

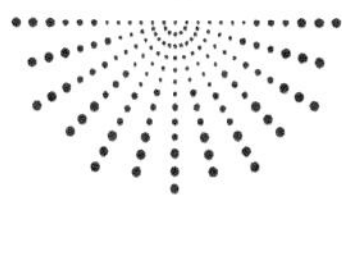

JEREMY

"Guys!" I landed in the living room. Brody sat on the couch watching an old episode of Friends with a joint in his mouth. I grabbed it from his lips and threw it to the ash tray.

"What the fuck, dude?" He sat forward.

"She's alive," I said with a large, excited smile. "She's alive, and she's ready. Tonight's the night."

He sat forward. "Are you sure?"

I nodded. "Start calling everybody. I'm going to get Leah, Adam, and Kai."

He smiled wide. He pulled his phone from his pocket. "I'll call Ramirez too and tell him to get the guns together."

"Good move. Make as many calls as you can. I'll finish up after I let everyone know."

I teleported to the kitchen where Leah sat hunched over her computer. I rushed to her, wrapped my arms around her from behind and swept her into the air. I set her on the ground.

She laughed, spinning around. "You're in a good mood."

"We're getting her back. Tonight." I excitedly gripped her little shoulders. "Tonight's the night."

She gazed down at my arm. Her shirt where my blood had rubbed against it. "I just got this."

"You're worried about your shirt?"

She took my arm and healed it quickly. "She said tonight?"

"Tonight. Can you get Adam and Kai? I'm going to grab Wyatt and Celena."

"Yeah, of course. When is this going down?"

"Soon," I said. "Brody's contacting everyone as we speak. You have your computer and everything?"

"Let me put it on charge, but yeah. I'll be ready."

My arms wrapped around her in another hug. She awkwardly patted my back. "Thank you for not giving up."

She smiled. I teleported. This time, I landed on the cabin's doorstep. I pounded on the door. "Wyatt! Celena! Open up!"

A moment later, Wyatt pulled it open a few inches, peering at me through the crack. "What's up, dude?"

I glanced at his messy hair and boxers. "Oh, sorry to interrupt. Hate to be a cock block, but you guys need to get dressed."

"What do you mean?"

"Laila. She told me to get everyone ready."

Celena pulled the door the rest of the way open and tightened her robe. "What's going on?"

"Laila, she's alive," I said. "We're bringing her home. Are you guys still in?"

She nodded and Wyatt joined in. "Absolutely. We'll get dressed and meet you at the house."

I smiled. "See you there."

Within two hours, almost forty of us gathered around the living room and kitchen of the main house. Ray brought an arsenal of guns to equip each of us with at least a pistol and fifty bullets in case Leah was wrong. Everyone seemed unsure at first, tiredly wiping their eyes as we waited while sipping coffee and telling old stories.

They were hesitant, but I was sure. I knew this was it. She'd be in my arms before the night was over. I was getting my best friend back. I was getting my brother back. Maybe I'd meet my son too.

I tapped my foot and twiddled my thumbs for two and a half long hours after she first wrote on her arm. But just after the clock struck midnight, there she was.

Hey, baby, I heard her voice in my mind, bringing with it a smile wider than the sky. *Did you miss me?*

CHAPTER SIXTY-NINE

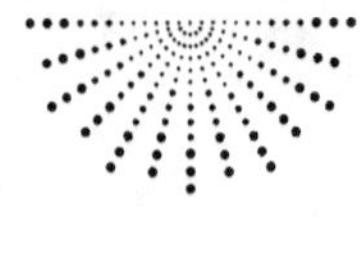

LAILA

I'd been planning how I would get out of that cell in grave detail for the last two months since my leg incapacitated me. I had a good idea of how I'd do it. But there were a few kinks I hadn't been able to work out until that night.

At first, I thought I'd try to escape when the guard came to take me for my next stress test or when the doctor came in to run tests on the baby I no longer carried. But I realized it would draw too much attention. They carried little phone like walkie-talkies with panic buttons. The moment they pressed it; we'd be on instant lock down.

I had to be sneaky. Aside from that, it wouldn't have left Jeremy and everyone enough time to get in. If I did it that way, I would have had to fight off two guards at once, not to mention Amy who would try to mute my abilities. I really hated the bitch, but she was my friend's wife, and I was hoping I wouldn't have to kill her. But I didn't have time for error. If I had to, I'd kill the bitch without a second thought.

The barrier spell around my room that kept my powers in wasn't a force field. It just kept the energy from escaping. It didn't keep my body from exiting.

The box they used to pass us our food and clothes was my way out. Obviously, I couldn't fit my body through it. But all I needed was my hand. If my hand surpassed the force field, I could use air to spin the lock on my door from the other side.

But I had to time it just right. I had to do it just before the guards made their rounds because I needed one of their handprints to open the door between the sectors.

My best shot to unlock the door was just as they switched the light off. The camera in the hall would have to adjust to the difference in lighting. They always went out just after the sun set when the guard made their final round before shift change.

I watched the guard walk by my room and glance in quickly before heading toward the end of the hall. I heard the familiar beep, followed by a click, and knew I had to act fast.

I hurried from my bed across the room to the small stainless-steel box. My fingers flipped open the door of the metal box. My heart slammed in my ears. I carefully grasped the outer door. I pushed it slightly ajar. Just enough so that it was open, but still appeared closed.

The lights switched off and I snuck my hand into the hallway. I spun the air from my hand like a miniature tornado, spiraling toward my doorknob until I heard a click.

I ripped my arm back inside, seeing my door move inward ever so slightly out of my peripheral vision.

My heart thudded with angst in my chest. This was it.

I was about to have nearly four-hundred lives in my hands. Four hundred men, women, and children. I had to make sure they lived. I had to save them from that hell.

No pressure or anything.

I gazed at the door from my table and anxiously tapped my foot.

A quiet knock sounded on the wall behind me. "Laila?" Chris said.

"Chris," I said.

"Are you okay?"

I chewed my lip. "I will be."

"We were worried," Haley said softly. "We didn't know if you were going to make it."

"What was that energy?" Chris asked. "Haley said she saw a big flash of light and I felt something huge."

"Micah," I muttered.

They fell quiet for a moment. A few seconds later, Haley broke the silence.

"I'm really sorry, Laila."

"I don't want to talk about it."

It wasn't that I simply didn't want to talk about it. I *couldn't* talk about it. I had to keep my head level. I couldn't break down, not then. I had too many people counting on me, even if they didn't realize it.

"Yeah, I gotcha," Haley said.

The silence crept back in for a moment. I gazed out that little square window and waited for the guard's next round. My fingertip outlined the small circle on my thigh.

"Do you guys trust me?" I asked.

"What do you mean?" Chris asked.

"If I told you we were going home tonight, would you believe me?" I said quietly. So quiet that no microphone could have heard it, but Haley's wolf ears and Chris' advanced hearing could.

Haley laughed. "Keep dreaming, baby girl."

I chuckled. "I'll remember you said that when we're smoking those blunts."

She laughed. "Hold onto hope if it helps you sleep at night."

I smiled. She had no idea.

"How do you plan on accomplishing that?" Chris asked.

"Haven't worked out all the details yet. But it's going to happen."

He paused for a moment. He said, "If you do, can you get a message to my brothers and sisters?"

"You can tell them yourself."

"But if I can't. Will you?"

"Sure."

"Tell Leah to try and be happy. Make sure she knows that I want her to be happy whether I'm around or not. Don't let her throw her life away being so angry at it. It's too short to be unhappy."

Good advice, but he was going to tell them all that himself. I was damned and determined to make it so. "Okay."

"And Adam. Tell him that I miss his happy-go-lucky dumbass. Tell him to never lose that." He paused. "And tell Brody to quit being a little bitch." I laughed as he went on, "Tell him to smile once in a while. Tell him to find something he loves and not to give up on it." He paused again and chuckled.

"Make sure Hannah knows I'm proud of her. She'll be the first one of us to go to a university and make sure she knows how proud that makes me." He paused once more. "Tell Jeremy how happy I am that he found you. And tell him to have faith in the world. And in himself once in a while." He got quiet again.

"Just make sure they all know how much I love them. And make sure this doesn't happen to them too, okay? Keep them safe for me, Laila."

"You can tell them all that yourself, Chris," I said.

"But if I can't and you can. Just tell them, okay?"

"I will."

CHAPTER SEVENTY

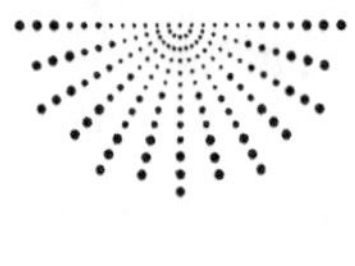

LAILA

It was about an hour later when I heard that now familiar beep and click. The moment I heard it, my heart sunk before it began slamming against my chest. I prayed to hell and back that it wasn't as loud to everyone else as it was to me.

I wasn't scared so much as I was worried. I didn't really care if I died at that point. I just wanted everyone else to live. I wanted to end that hell hole. I wanted to blow it off the map.

The thump of each footstep had the hair on my arms standing on end. The inevitable realization that I was about to kill yet another person sunk onto my shoulders. You'd think I was used to it by then but that was hardly the case. The kill got easier and more creative with each murder, but the weight of the guilt got heavier.

It wasn't so bad before because it wasn't premeditated. But I sat there knowing I was going to kill the man. It wouldn't be self-defense. I was just gonna kill a guy.

Thump, thump, thump.

I darted across the room and crouched to the ground beside the door. The flashlight illuminated the hallway. It cast a bare light over my cell, bouncing with each step. It turned to my window and I stood.

I heard him mutter something. He shined the light around my room in confusion.

I grabbed the wind, sent the door wide open and turned to face him. His face was a mere shadow. I stepped through the threshold and siphoned the air so that he couldn't scream. The darkness made it easier. I didn't have to see his expression as he took his last breath.

He dropped the flashlight and clutched his throat. He reached for his gun. But I spun the wind around him and sent it flying from his holster. It was the first good look of him I'd gotten.

I pushed away my humanity when both of his hands flailed at his neck. His face turned an ugly shade of purple. Veins pulsed in his forehead. His mouth was open, desperately trying to get a breath. But I continued sucking the air from his body. I gripped his shoulders to take him down slowly.

My arms helped his corpse to the floor. I stepped over his lifeless body into the hallway, grabbed his flashlight, and rushed over to Haley's door.

I released the lock. Then, I pushed her door open.

"I told you we were getting out of here."

I saw her for the first time. Her long, curly black hair poofed up in a messy afro around her small head. Her dark brown eyes blinked through the blinding flashlight, casting a grayish glow on her ebony skin.

"Laila?" she asked.

"Let's go, we don't have time for chit chat. They're going to see us on the cameras soon." I made a rolling motion with my hand. I turned and rushed to Chris's door. I spun the lock, grabbed the handle, and flew it open.

He heard the sound and sat forward. I jolted back when I saw him. He, like Haley and myself, was skinny and frail, clearly malnourished. His dark blue scrubs hung loosely on his bones, almost like a child in adult clothing. But what took my breath away wasn't his tiny, starved body or hollowed cheeks. It was his eyes.

Or rather, the lack there of.

Two empty pink sockets stared at me. I walked toward him.

Still, he was the boy in the photographs that hung around the house back home. All that was missing were those glowing, electric blue, signature Skoulda eyes.

"Hey, Chris." I pulled a smile to my lips. "You ready to go home?"

He turned his head slightly. I took his hands in mine. "What's going on?"

"I told you I was getting us out of here." I tugged him into the hallway.

"But how?" he asked. "There's too many of them, you can't take them on by yourself and we aren't much help."

"I'm not." I released his hand. "Haley, you're strong, right?"

"How strong are we talking here?"

I gestured to the guard on the floor. "Think you can rip his hand off?"

"Be easier in wolf form, but probably. Hold up."

Haley dropped to the ground and straddled his bicep. She pushed her knee into his forearm. She grabbed the wrist and began to pull but made little progress.

"Damn it," she muttered. "I'm not as strong as I used to be, but I got this."

She tilted her head back, eyes glowing a bright shade of brown. Thick canines pultruded from her gums. She raised his arm to her face and dug her teeth into his flesh. As she chewed, she rolled the limb from side to side as if eating corn on the cob. She made a circle of ripped flesh around his wrist, grabbed the hand, and pulled—still chewing—until it popped off.

"Alright, let's go." I grabbed the dead hand. "You can eat later."

She pulled away still chewing. She lifted herself to her feet. "Sorry. Told you I'd take a bite of this fat fuck eventually."

"Grab the extra clip from his belt." I reached to the ground and lifted the gun.

Haley fumbled with his belt before raising the clip. "Got it."

I started toward the hallway door. My toes bared my weight as I peeped out the small window. There sat a small empty foyer with eight doors, nine including the one I looked out of. Just as I expected.

A light shined in from one a few doors to my left, so I knew that was our way out once we made it through the one in front of us.

"Okay, listen." I turned to Haley and Chris. "There's eight other units outside this door. I'm going to let them all out, I'm going to the next wing. I'm going to work toward the wing beside us first and get the units on each out. We're moving to the adjoining hallway. But until I give you the signal, you stay put in the room we're about to go into. You're going to need to guard the door, Haley. Anyone that isn't like us, you kill on site. You can smell the difference between us and humans, right?"

"Works for me. But how are we going to get out? And what's the signal?"

"You'll know. But I have to contact my back up first. The moment I do, they're going to know they're under attack. And we're gonna be swarmed with guards. I'm hoping there's another Fae or two on this wing that can help you until my people get here, but until then, you're the one with the gun." I handed it to her.

She flicked the safety and cocked it. "Gotcha. Shoot first ask questions later is kind of my motto."

"Your back up," Chris said. "That's Jeremy, right?"

I nodded but then remembered he couldn't see me. "Yeah, Jeremy and everyone else. I wasn't completely honest when I said I had no way of contacting him, I just didn't want anyone to overhear. But I'll explain it all later."

"Do what you have to do," he said.

"I might be out of it for a second, so be ready to shoot, Haley," I said.

I closed my eyes.

Pushing Amy from my mind was almost as easy as thinking it. It only took a moment. She wasn't that strong; she wasn't even close to as strong as I was. It was harder to use air to swing the lock open on my door than it was to push her from my mind.

The moment I did it, I traveled to Jeremy's mind.

Hey, baby. Did you miss me?

Laila.

His voice was music.

There was no better way to describe it. I'd been surrounded by deafening silence for months, and Jeremy's voice was pure music. The moment I heard it, I was elevated. I felt lighter, happier, stronger. I couldn't say it was euphoric, but it somehow brought me peace while simultaneously filled me with energy.

Can you find me now?

Hang on.

Take your time, I said into his head. *Not like I'm trying to save four hundred people or anything.*

Got it. Should we come now?

Yeah, but don't try to get in yet. Stay as far back as you can get without being seen while still having a view. I'm going to make you an opening.

Which direction are we coming in from?

You'll know when you see it.

What do you mean?

Just trust me. I won't be here when you get here but get out everyone that you can. Chris is here.

I wanted to see him so badly, but to get as many people out as possible, I didn't have time for our sappy reunion. I was going to be too busy moving people. Although, more than that, I didn't want him to see that I wasn't pregnant anymore. I didn't want to explain why I wasn't getting our son out of here. I didn't want to explain why we'd never even get to see his face.

I just couldn't think about that.

Where will you be?

I'm setting them all free. As many as I can get. You'll be in my head; we can meet up once you guys get in.

Okay. We're ready. Shouldn't take us more than a minute to bring everyone. We're starting now.

Good. See you soon, baby. Be careful, I thought.

I always am. Don't get yourself killed, alright?

Believe me, that's not in the plans. Stay far back when you get here until I give you the signal.

And it wasn't. I may not have wanted to live all that much after losing my baby, but fuck, I wanted to tear this place to dust and live just to spite the bastard who'd done this to us all.

Will do. We're far back.

You're here already?

Kai and I are. Brody, Adam, Mary and Camael are bringing the rest in groups of three.

We'll argue about you bringing Mary later.

He laughed. *I can't wait.*

I smiled as I opened my eyes. I glanced out the window to see that nothing had changed. I turned to Haley. "You ready?"

"Fuck yeah."

I raised the hand to the small glass panel in front of me. Hearing that beep and click was the most liberating sound I'd ever heard.

I grabbed the metal handle and pulled the door open.

That moment was one of liberty. You don't realize how much it means to open a door until every handle you pull for months is locked. Being trapped in one place for so long makes you see the poetry in every part of reality. The doors that let us move from one place to another, the walls that segregate us, the windows that give us a glimpse of the outside world. Every single thing in the world means something different to you once you've been a prisoner.

I started toward the door on my right, clutching the severed hand between my fingertips and raising it to the glass screen. The door beeped and clicked. I darted inside, rushing to each door handle and opening it wide. The prisoners gazed at me confused, mumbling, "Who are you?" and "What are you doing?"

To which I said, "We're going home," each time.

Three more prisoners set free. I hurried to the next screen, held the dead hand to the pad and ignored its blood dripping down my arm.

There were more confused "Huh?"s and "What's going on?"s. But I didn't have time to explain. I just had to set them free.

I kept repeating the process, rushing to each room, and opening each door. My heart thudded like a drum against my ribs, and my palms were sweaty, but I didn't care. I just had to set them free.

"We've got company, Laila," Haley called as I opened the second door of the fifth unit.

I rushed to the last one before running to the foyer. In the window of the door that led to the next wing, I saw three guards barreling toward us.

I passed her the hand. "Open doors. Take Chris with you. I'll handle them. We should save the bullets."

She pulled Chris's hand toward the room. I made my way to the door, bringing large flames to my outstretched arms. They opened it with guns drawn.

"Stay back," I said to the herd of supernatural creatures behind me.

They made it through the threshold with guns aimed at my head. I stood tall in front of the small crowd. I heard the bang and shot bright, purple fire toward them before the bullets could get remotely close to any of us.

My fire wasn't like it used to be. I wasn't surprised when it melted the bullets flying toward me. What shocked me was the fact that as it met the guard's skin, their bodies abruptly turned to ash. They didn't even have time to scream before they were piles of dust. It was unfortunate though because we could have used their guns.

I turned around to meet Haley's gaze, but instead found fifteen or so awestruck faces. Haley was still opening one of the units. They stared at me for a moment with dropped jaws and wide eyes.

I cleared my throat. "Sorry you had to see that."

"Don't apologize," a guy in the back said. "That was the most beautiful thing I've ever seen."

I brought a smile to my lips. "Well, I hope you see something better when we're out of here."

"Who are you?" asked a young girl toward the front who couldn't have been more than fourteen.

"Laila." I smiled. "Laila Callidy. But I don't have the time to go into detail. There's at least another three hundred people I need to get out before we're done here." Haley rushed from the hallway carrying the gun in her waist band, the severed hand in hers, and Chris's in the other. "Who wants to help unlock the rest of the doors while I move to the next wing?"

There were a number of "I will,"s and "Me,"s as I turned to Haley. "Guard this door."

She dropped Chris's hand. She passed the severed limb to another prisoner. She moved him toward the crowd and lifted the gun from her pants. "Go. I got this."

I brought flames to my hands and started out of the room in a slow jog. I didn't have the severed hand anymore, but I didn't need it. Once I saw what my fire abilities were now capable of, it wasn't necessary.

I went out the door into a narrow hallway. The fluorescent lights shined above me as I jogged toward the first door I saw. It was identical to the last one with a small piece of glass to peek through.

Raising myself to my tiptoes, I peeped into the next unit. Another guard stood there in the dark, glancing into a cell with a flashlight. As she started to turn, I turned my back against the cool, cement wall beside the door.

My head rocked against the wall. I closed my eyes. I waited a while for her to come toward me. That few seconds, or maybe minutes, felt like decades.

I sat there pre-meditating her murder. Maybe it was because that guard was a woman, or maybe it was because I knew I could get out at that very moment if I wanted to. Regardless of why, a wave of remorse flooded over me. I always hated the kill, but I recognized that it was a necessary evil. Especially in that situation.

I struggled not to think about who she was, but it was easier said than done. There was an engagement ring on her fourth finger, but no wedding band. Someone was going to wake up in the morning without a fiancé. Maybe someone else would wake up without a mother.

But someone else was in their bed fighting the urge to think about their dead or missing sister. Maybe a Mom was sitting on the floor of her shower to keep everyone from hearing her sob. Maybe someone was sitting in their car with their weeping head in their hands listening to music so loud that they couldn't hear themselves scream while they mourned their brother.

I blinked away a tear in my eye. I heard the beep. Then click. I took a breath as I felt the wind of the door rush open.

Before I could look at her and lose my motivation, I focused on the saliva behind her lips. I pushed it down her throat, hearing her choke and gag. The illumination of her flashlight bobbed up and down. I closed my eyes. I brought stomach bile up her throat and pushed it downward into her lungs.

I heard her gurgle for air before her body dropped to the ground. Once the gagging stopped, I opened my eyes. My stomach churned. I stepped over her dead body on the floor.

But it didn't matter now. All that mattered was saving those people. I was going to save lives.

My legs felt like jello as I made it to the first door. I reached to the keypad with fire in my hands. I realized that melting the scanner may make the door malfunction or set off an alarm. I needed to clear the floor before that happened if I could.

Then a memory from my childhood flashed behind my eyes.

"You know what the most important part of a door is?" Dad asked.

His voice echoed in my mind. I said the handle before he told me that was one of the least important parts. "The most important part is what holds the door in the wall." I remember him pointing to the hinges. "A door without hinges is either a wall, or a hole in the wall."

A smile came to my lips. I raised a hot, dancing ray of purple from my palm toward the metal. I watched it drip down the seam of the door like water in the crack of a dam. My hand moved from each piece of metal like a gentle dance. I grabbed ahold of the handle and yanked it downward.

I stepped onto it, feeling it rock beneath my feet. I hurried to each door. As I opened each one, I yelled "Let's go!" before scurrying to the next. Then the next, and the next. Before I knew it, all eight units were cleared. Twenty-four people.

Twenty-four more people going home.

I urged them all into the hallway that connected the two wings. We headed toward the group Haley stood in front of. She held the gun toward me. She saw my face and lowered it.

"This way everybody." I rolled my hand toward the hallway I just instructed everyone from the second wing into.

As they flocked toward me, I met Haley's gaze. "I need you to guard the next door."

She nodded as they scurried into the hallway. Someone held Chris's hand, carefully ushering him beside them as he reached around aimlessly. Haley hurried out behind the last person with me close at her tail.

Haley stood in front of the next door, gun raised defensively toward the window that led to an unfamiliar part of the building—the long section that connected the north and south wings. I joined them in the hallway, clearing my throat before I spoke. "Okay, I need everyone to get as close to the floor as possible and cover their heads with their arms."

"Like you do for a tornado drill at school?" a teenage boy asked.

"Exactly like you do in a tornado drill at school. Get as close to this wall as you can." I smacked the wall Haley faced.

No one so much as questioned me after that. All of them, nearly fifty people, dropped to their knees and pushed themselves as close to the wall in the narrow hallways as they could. They had instant trust in me.

Haley glanced at me quizzically. I turned to the wall that led to each wing. I closed my eyes and stretched my arms out on either side.

I summoned every ounce of power I had inside of me. The wind swirled around my body like I was the eye of a tornado. Breathing a slow, deep exhale, the wind beneath my arms picked up speed.

I thought about every horrible thing that had happened since I showed up there. Each painful, now scarred welt on my back. The hand around my throat. Every blood draw done while I was comatose on benzodiazepines. Each now healed slice on every section of my body.

The hand I never asked to slide between my thighs.

That *beautiful*, dying bright light I'd watched come into the world and leave me as quick as he came.

The wind spun around me until I raised my arms above my head. Screaming, I pushed it toward the roof.

CHAPTER SEVENTY-ONE

JEREMY

A small island a couple dozen miles from Vancouver. Not even our country. I wished I'd known. But that didn't matter now. We were here.

The smoke from Celena's cigarette wafted toward me. It mixed with the smell of the ocean. The only thing I heard were those crashing waves. We stared at the H shaped building that sat on an island a few thousand feet away.

I raised my hand to her and said, "Can I hit that a couple times?"

"Do you just want one?" She reached to her back pocket for her pack. "I didn't know you smoked."

"Not usually." I shrugged. She dropped the cigarette to my palm and pulled a flame to her fingertip. I raised it to my lips and leaned toward her to light it.

"Unusual circumstance, I guess." She absorbed the flame back to her hand.

"Yeah, that's one way to put it." I took in a long drag.

"What do you think is happening in there?" Brody gestured to the other side of the crashing waves.

"I wish I knew. Laila was pretty vague."

"What's the signal again?"

"She said we'd know it when we saw it."

"Why does she have to be so cryptic?"

"Because she's Laila. Always has a flare for the dramatics."

Brody made a noise in his throat, as if to say he knew. He seemed almost as anxious as me. I felt bad in a way. Getting her back meant something far different to me than it did to him.

It was the wind thrusting my black cloud away. My light coming back. But Brody's cloud would only stop dumping rain on him. His was just returning to its usual dark gloom.

As for me though? I felt great. Scared and anxious, yes, but she was back. I felt her again. I could close my eyes and see through hers within that dark building. I could feel her heart beating in my chest. I could hear the sound of her breath as she ran. I could *feel* her.

I had my baby back.

Her mind against mine was that whoosh of warm air the drugs had given me. Our souls joined back together was being wrapped safely in that fuzzy blanket with a cup of hot chocolate. She got me higher than anything else ever could.

"C'mon, Lai," Mary said quietly a few feet in front of me. Her palms pressed against each other, resting in front of her mouth. She anxiously rolled back and forth on the balls of her feet. She looked so different today than she had on any case or mission we'd worked before.

For so long, I'd thought Mary was a cold, heartless bitch. Especially after the shit she pulled last year. But the way she stood there, practically holding her breath, would always remind me that she was so far from heartless. She may not have cared about most things, but she loved Laila. We didn't have much in common. But that was one thing we would always share.

Suddenly, just behind Mary's head, I saw the section of the building directly in front of us begin to shake. I blinked a few times to be sure I saw what I thought I saw. I flicked the ash to the cool grass. I raised the cigarette to my lips and took another drag. I squinted a bit, watching carefully. I felt the ground start to shake beneath my feet. I watched the waves crash harder into the shoreline and cliff side.

"I'm not the only one seeing this, right?" Wyatt squinted at the building.

"No," Celena said. "Definitely not."

I took another hit off the cigarette. I lowered to the ground and rubbed the burning end into the grass. My eyes stayed locked with the building. I slid the cigarette butt into my back pocket.

I was glad I looked up when I did. At that moment, I watched the most beautiful calamity I'd ever seen.

Suddenly, the top of the building lifted into the air. I can still see it like a slow-motion replay. Each section of cement flying through the sky as if hit by a bomb.

Although, I suppose it had been. That bomb just so happened to be the love of my life.

The rocks plummeted through the air to the waves beneath it like falling stars. They flew down and outward through the dark night, drifting so carefully that it couldn't be an accident.

I smiled. I gripped Kai and Celena's shoulders. "Like I said. A flare for the dramatic."

All of us who could teleport grabbed the shoulder or the hand of the person on either side of us. We landed just outside the building. Kai moved between Celena and I. He gripped either of our hands.

"Hold on tight," he said. The air whirled around us. It twisted to create something of a vortex beneath our feet that lifted us upward into the air.

I gripped his shoulder for stability as we soared into the sky. My gaze noted the thick glass block windows on each room. Within a second, we came to eye level with the floor whose roof and walls crumbled to the cool dewy grass. We coasted through the rubble and dust, hovering just beside the ground of the fourth floor. Kai moved us through the air toward the interior of the building. He lowered us to the floor through the thick, gray cloud of dust. I couldn't make anything out visually, but I heard her voice.

"Go!" she yelled. "Everybody go!"

I stumbled when we landed, coughing as I inhaled the thick gray smog.

"Laila," I called, starting toward the sound of her voice with Celena close behind me. Bright red lights flashed. Loud alarms roared over the shuffling crowd.

Kai stayed where we landed, moving his hands to create a cushion at the ground. He yelled, telling people to jump.

I made my way through the herd. At least forty of them rushed past me in a stampede, hurrying to jump from the precipice Laila created.

It slowed me down, but I kept pushing through them and calling her name. I made it to a doorway with bright fluorescent lights. It was impeccable how that part of the structure wasn't remotely phased by the explosion through the doorway. She was careful and precise.

I glanced around the wide and long hallway. Had she gone straight, I would still see her. I turned to my right where another doorway stood. But the door had been blown down the stairs it led to.

Smiling, I ran toward them, gripping the metal rail for stability as I took two steps at a time. Halfway down the metal staircase, I looked below.

For a second, only a split second, I saw her. Just the top of her head, but it was her. I could feel it.

"Laila!" I yelled. I tried to teleport to her but only vibrated a bit.

Leah must not have turned off the implants yet. Or maybe she had, but they cleverly placed the crystals around the building. I tested my electricity and was able to pull a few glistening strands of blue swirling energy to my hand. It wasn't as big as it could have been, but it was enough to interfere with electric signals and at least have a tasing effect on someone.

I knew she was busy, but I needed to see her. Christ, I just needed to see her.

I made it down the second flight and ran through the open door.

And then, I did. I saw her.

She held bright, violet flames in her hand angled upward, melting the hinges of a door. She kept a steady wave of wind against it to keep it from falling on top of her. I stared at her in awe for a second, marveling at how different she looked today than I remembered her.

Her small body looked dainty. Maybe even frail. Her shoulders weren't much smaller, but far bonier than they had been. She used to fall into that perfect line between thin and chunky but in those scrubs, she looked so skinny. Her stomach came out a bit further than it did before she was pregnant, but she clearly wasn't a few weeks from giving birth anymore either.

She wasn't pregnant.

And our son was nowhere in sight.

I pushed that thought from my mind. I gazed at her determined expression in the strobing red lights. Her dark blue scrubs were covered in dust and pieces of rubble. The long dark hair that reached the middle of her back the last time I saw her now nearly touched her ass. Even from the distance, I saw the scars on her arms. As I got closer, I noted the singed ends of her sleeves resting against deep purple needle marks. I would've thought they were the result of long-term heroin use if I didn't know better.

After she melted the bottom hinge, she side-stepped and pulled the air downward with her arm.

"Laila," I said.

As she turned, I got my first look at her face.

She was nearly a different person than the one I remembered. Yet still the most beautiful thing I had ever seen. Her cheeks hollowed slightly into her mouth. Deep purple circles laid beneath her glowing green eyes. They looked bigger and brighter now that the roundness of her cheeks had receded. The once bright red lips I'd dreamed about for months were now chapped and bleeding at the edges, but a big, radiating smile lifted them.

"Baby." She darted toward me. I ran to her, threw my arms around her tiny body in a tight embrace, and nuzzled my head against hers. I felt her ribs beneath my hands around her fragile back, inhaling the musty smell of her hair.

Her thin arms made their way around my waist and squeezed me tighter than I'd ever been held before. I wanted to stay in that moment for the rest of my life.

A wave of relief. She was alive. She was on two feet. She was back.

But she pulled away. "We don't have time. We need to get them out." She turned and glanced at me over her shoulder. "Do your powers work?"

"Not entirely. I can't teleport but we have a few Angels that can. They're coming now, Kai is getting everyone in."

She darted through the doorway she opened. She made it to another door, only to do to it the same she had done to the last.

"Okay. We could use them right now. Even if they can't teleport through the perimeter spell. If they could at least get us in and out of these doors."

I pulled my phone from my pocket. "I'll tell Mary to come down to the third floor."

She melted the second hinge. "No, I can handle this floor. Tell her to go to the second. Get Celena in here though, I could use her fire right now. Tell Kai to come down once he gets everyone on that floor out. I'm going to blow the ceiling off of this floor next, and when I do, I'm going to need him to get everyone on this floor out too." I typed angrily and sent the message.

I walked toward the door beside her as the one she was working on fell. I held my hand to the small keypad, sending electricity into it to see if it would unlock the door. Instead, it caught fire.

Laila turned and thinned the air that allowed the fire to burn. I looked at her in awe as she shifted to the door I was working on and began melting each hinge. I reached into my waistband, pulled out a gun, and handed it to her. "This might be a little quicker."

"Ah, you're a lifesaver." She cocked the gun and quickly shot off each hinge. I gazed at her in a bit of wonder as she sidestepped into me and pulled the door down effortlessly. "Go into that hallway while I work on the next one and open all the doors. There should be three. Then tell whoever is getting people out that they need to move everyone as far away from the building as possible so they don't get hurt when I blow the roof off."

I stared at her in amazement a moment longer. She was always a little naïve about these things in the past. She went along for the ride, and she was a good fighter, but she'd never called the shots. Here though, it was clear she had thought of everything.

When I didn't move, she turned to me with furrowed brows. "We're about to be swarmed by guards, I can hear their thoughts. We need to move, Jeremy."

I started toward the doorway she'd just knocked open. "Right, sorry."

She went on shooting off hinges and knocking down more doors. I started into the hall, opening each to get the only glimpse I ever would of how Laila lived for the past three and a half months. Four steel walls, a jail-cell style steel toilet, and a metal bench like table a couple feet off the ground which I imagined was the bed. My heart sunk, flooding with guilt while I watched the people run from the rooms like a bomb went off behind them.

Some of them had hospital gowns that hung open at their shoulders. The stripes carved into their bleeding flesh would haunt me for years. It was more brutal than *The Passion of the Christ* and *Outlander* combined. Some of them even had yellow, puss filled cysts protruding from them.

But the look of hope on their faces as the alarm lights flashed against their pale skin overrode the guilt of not helping them sooner.

I followed Laila from each door to the next, releasing more and more people little by little. I was in absolute awe of her. *She* did this. She saved all of those people. Just a few long months seemed to have turned her to a new person. But I suppose that's what these things do to you.

It fills you with something. You become a different person because the instinctive will to live kicks in. Suddenly, life isn't about the dirty dishes in the sink or whatever that mystery liquid puddling beneath your new car may be. Nothing matters but survival.

Survival, and vengeance.

CHAPTER SEVENTY-TWO

JEREMY

Laila started to the next sector. It was connected to the last by a small, narrow hallway. As we made it to the next room, she turned to me and said, "Do you have another clip?" I nodded and reached to my hip to swap guns. "You do have more bullets though, right?"

The way she turned to meet me; I saw the scar at the base of her neck for the first time. It was about a quarter of an inch above her collar bone and stretched about two inches across her throat.

I remembered the way that felt when it happened. I remembered feeling her hands nearly break against the cuffs that held her down. I remembered the sound of her scream.

Her hand moved to it, brows falling a bit. I flooded with culpability. She felt the scar beneath her fingers as though she'd forgotten. After quickly blinking, she moved her hand from her neck. She took the gun from my fingers and passed me the other one.

"Yeah," I said. "I have two full magazines and a bunch of bullets in my back pocket."

"We're going to need them so put in your next magazine. There's about ten guards heading toward us." She paused. "Actually, you take down the doors. I'll handle the guards."

She looked away and started to brush past me, but I clutched her hand. She caught my gaze and said, "What is it?"

I knew we didn't have much time, but I didn't care.

I grabbed her waist, yanked her against my chest, and took her face in my hand. My lips found hers, and everything froze.

The sirens were still blazing overhead, but they dulled to the background. The flashes had been all but blinding a moment prior, but when I was holding her, when she was kissing me, she was all that existed.

Nothing about that kiss was sexy. Her lips were so dry and cracked that they caught against mine. Neither of us had mint on our breaths, we were both drenched in an anxious sweat, and we were coated in debris.

It wasn't sexy. But it may have been the most romantic kiss I'd ever had. Because it was one of victory, reunion, and freedom.

She was okay. We were together again.

And she was amazing.

She'd orchestrated all of that from a small cell with help from no one. She'd studied and prepared. She was going to save every life that she possibly could.

It was beautiful. *She* was beautiful. An amazing, beautiful calamity.

Her lips stayed on mine longer than she wanted. After a few seconds, I pulled back and met her gaze. "I love you."

She smiled as a tear formed in her eye. She grabbed my hand and lifted our knuckles to her lips. "I'll be right back."

I nodded with a smile, releasing her fingers. "Go."

She turned away and started to the door we'd just came from.

I began where she left off, blowing the hinges off of each door and pulling them to the ground. The whistling of wind sounded through the air followed by a roar and a rift of swirling fire. She couldn't get burned, so I looked back to the door. I thought it'd be quicker to pull all eight doors down and then move from room to room. Just after I blasted the hinges off of the sixth door, I heard a gunshot that I didn't fire.

"Laila?!" I called.

"I'm fine," she yelled through the whistling wind. "Just let them out."

I went on shooting off more hinges and pulling down more doors. I finished with the eighth and ran between each hallway, quickly turning each handle and yelling to follow me. The people flocked like sheep behind me.

The more people I let out, the quicker the doors opened. They all joined in setting their fellow captives free. Before I knew it, there were twenty-four people following me to the hallway that adjoined the two sections.

As we gathered beneath the blinking, flashing lights, I got a better look at the people, the survivors. So many innocent lives that all looked like they hadn't eaten in weeks and were covered head to toe in cuts, scars and bruises. There was no age range or MO that depicted the group. They all had different skin tones and nationalities. They ranged in ages from young adolescence to mid and late fifties.

They were *my* people. Nearly fifty of my people. Another nearly fifty free outside. Nearly a hundred people going back to their families. Nearly a hundred people my soulmate saved. Nearly a hundred of *my* people.

She amazed me.

I always knew she was capable of great things, but I was overwhelmed with pride for her in that moment. Maybe Mary was right. Maybe she had to be her own hero that time. She made a better hero than me. I was so proud to know that she found the courage in that awful place to attempt, let alone succeed, this kind of escape.

"Everybody, get down and cover your head with your arms." I gazed out the doorway that led to the long hallway Laila went down. I loaded the next magazine into my pistol.

I saw purple flames erupt from the stair well we'd come from and I beamed.

She was such a fucking bad ass.

I watched a moment longer as the light dulled. Then my heart sunk in fear. Only for a second before her pretty face bobbed up the steps in a fast jog. I smiled as she ran toward us.

She rushed through the doorway. Her hand grazed mine, meeting me in the threshold. Her green eyes turned to me. "Get down and cover your head."

I lowered myself to the ground. I raised my arms above me as she looked but when I saw her feet spin around, I looked up at her.

She lifted her arms at her sides and let out a slow, deep breath. Her face was calm at first but as the wind became to spin around us, her brows started to fall. She closed her eyes, and the structure began to quiver. The wind got faster, spinning around us like a tornado. It was amazing how we all stayed in place given the power of the air. The ceiling vibrated and an ear piercing, angry scream echoed from my mouth.

I watched the ceiling quake violently. It flew into the night sky like a missile, breaking to chunks and flinging to the earth in a million pieces. The rest of the first floor followed. She flung her arms forward, directing a massive amount of wind to the wall in front of us. They flung through the air and broke to chunks and dust before plummeting to the earth.

"My brother controls air," Laila yelled to the crowd. She reached down, took my hand from my head, and helped me to my feet. "He's going to create a bolster to get you to the ground. From there, you're going home. Just jump when I tell you to."

Whooshing my hand through the dust, struggling to find her gaze, I used her hip as a guide to pull myself vertical.

As I squeezed her right side, I felt a pain in mine. I felt a warm, wet substance against my palm. And I realized it wasn't my pain.

"Shit." She glanced down at her torso.

"You're hurt." I pulled my hand away.

She huffed, eyes on the blood. "I was sure it missed me. Guess I didn't feel it with all the adrenaline."

"You should go," I said. "We can handle—"

"Fuck off." She narrowed her gaze. "I'm not even halfway done, and you guys don't know anything about the building."

Figured that was coming.

"Okay," I said over the alarm. "Can I see how bad it is?"

She pulled up her shirt to the side, careful to avoid pulling it the whole way up. An inch or two above her hip sat a perfect circle gradually streaming blood. I lifted her shirt a bit toward the back, studying the exit wound on her hip beside thick white scars. It was a small flesh wound and wasn't losing too much blood, so I nodded.

Through the gray cloud in front of us, I saw three figures rise through the air. Mary and Celena rushed toward us. "Now!" Laila yelled. The crowd hurdled toward the edge of what remained of the large building.

Celena ran our way and grabbed Laila's arms. Laila smiled and clutched her shoulder. "I'm so happy to see you."

Laila gave a soft smile. "Follow me."

Celena and Mary nodded in return. Laila turned to me. "Help get people out of here. Once I clear the next level, I'm tearing this floor down too. Once we get to the main level, I need everyone able to fight. They can help me get to the other two wings. But send more people in, just keep them off of this floor. And tell them to kill anyone who isn't in scrubs or a hospital gown."

"Be careful," I said.

She smiled and squeezed my hand. "I'll see you soon."

CHAPTER SEVENTY-THREE

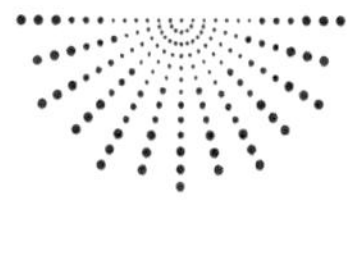

LAILA

Celena followed close behind me, Mary just at her flank. "There are a total of four wings on each side of the building. So far, I have cleared half of two of them. The other two wings are on the far side of the building, so we have to clear these two wings before we can move there."

"What connects them?" Celena asked.

If Jeremy knew what they did to me, so did they. Running down the steps, I said, "That's where the bad shit happens. But it's also where Lydia is."

"Lydia?" Mary asked.

"Ray's daughter," I said.

"Is his wife here too?" Celena asked. We started toward the door at the bottom of the staircase.

"She's here alright," I muttered. I began melting the hinges. Then Mary grasped mine and Celena's shoulders and teleported us to the other side of the door.

To our right, I heard, "Put your hands up!"

I turned to the group of patrols and raised flames to my arms. Before they could pull the triggers, I shot the fire toward them. They didn't even scream as their bodies engulfed in purple flames, flesh turning to ash and plummeting to piles on the ground.

"Jesus Christ," Mary muttered.

"Wait." Celena gripped mine and Mary's arms to keep us still. "Do you hear that?"

"What is it?"

"I think it's a plane," she said.

My heart sunk.

Damn it. He was going to load whoever I hadn't gotten out away, to some new, undisclosed location it'd take years to find.

"Fuck," I said. "Okay, you guys start letting people out. Just get everyone you can and bring them up to the floor we just came from. I'm going to create another opening but I'm getting Lydia first. I think I know where she is. I'll contact Jeremy and tell him to start bringing our team through. How many of us are there?"

"About forty," Mary said.

"That many?" I asked.

"A lot of them have loved ones that were never found. They have hope that they're here."

"Maybe they are. But hopefully not for much longer," I said. "Celena, I'm going to kill every guard I see along the way, but you have a better shot at killing any stragglers than Mary. Mary, you get the doors. Celena, you stand guard at the end of each wing. There's eight units per wing on each floor, three people per unit, so it'll take Mary a few minutes to break each one down. During that time, kill *anyone* that isn't ours that approaches." She swallowed. "You good?"

"I'll be fine. Just go," she said. "Save people and shit."

I smiled. "I love you. Be careful."

She gave a smile. I turned, not saying a word to Mary and darting down the long hallway. I took large strides, jogging, holding bright flames against either arm.

It was only a matter of seconds before I got swarmed by more guards. Twelve, I think. Twelve more people I turned to ash. Twelve more sets of blood on my hands.

I stepped over their ashes and kept running until I came to another door. That one didn't have a window in it like the rest. Just a solid, thick sheet of metal and a round hatch like that of a submarine. That was where they conducted the experiments, whatever the fuck they were, while we lay unconscious on metal tables like mice in a laboratory.

Suddenly, I had an even larger appreciation for Jeremy's criminal record. He'd saved thousands of animals being used for cosmetic testing as a minor and was still paying fines for it. However, the organization never got those animals back and ended up switching to humane testing.

My stomach flipped when I thought about him. He looked so different. Hopeful that day, but overall, a bit broken. His normally clean shaved jaw now had a several inch long, messy black beard. His dark hair hung even longer than it had before, reaching just past his shoulders. His eyes had deep, black circles below them. He'd even lost a bit of weight, or maybe just muscle tone.

I looked a hell of a lot worse, but it was clear he had been a wreck recently too.

In hindsight, I know that it was the right thing to do, at least for me and my family. Waiting until my body healed was smart. But part of me will always wish that I hadn't. Part of me will never forgive myself for not allowing him to swoop in and save me before I lost my son.

I would always blame myself for that. I could have saved myself. I could have saved my baby. But I chose to save those four-hundred people instead.

Although, as shamed as I am to admit it, I'd have let them perish for eternity if there'd have been a way for me and my baby to make it out of there with his uncle.

The hinges were on the opposite side of the next door which made my job a lot easier.

I thrust the wind beneath my arms outward in a giant gust. The door slammed open, instantly destroying the heavy metal lock. Four guards stood in front of—you guessed it—another goddamned door.

But that door was different than any other I'd seen. In fact, this entire section of the building was drastically different than the rest had been. It wasn't hospital or prison like at all; it was near homely.

We got metal doors with bulletproof windows. Amy got a set of beautiful glass French doors separated into twelve sections by pieces of thick, elegant mahogany wood. Instead of painted cement, an exquisite gray laminate flooring rested beneath my bare feet. White trim, thick white baseboards, and white metal window frames that looked out over the ocean framed the soft gray walls.

They raised their pistols and fired, but I urged the air toward them. Their bullets flew backward, some firing into them and others into the wall and door they stood in front of.

I slammed fire into them, letting their bodies turn to ash. I rushed air through the glass. It shattered inward to a million little pieces. I reached inside to unlock the knob.

I pushed them open, cutting my bare feet on broken glass. I walked through a dimly lit hall. A light shined into it from a modern, elegant bathroom. That room, or apartment, even, couldn't be described as anything less than a presidential suite.

Some expensive, genuine hardwoods creaked below my feet as I walked inside. All of the walls had recently been painted a gentle, modern shade of blue trimmed in impeccable white baseboards and expensive crown molding. Plants sat and hung on nearly every surface in sight. I hadn't been certain I was in the right place at first, but I was then.

I made my way into a large, open living room lit with intricate hanging chandeliers. They sparkled like diamonds against the light that came in from the floor to ceiling windows that captured gorgeous views of crashing waves on the beach. My gaze shifted to the round, kid friendly coffee table littered with children's books, small figurines, and stuffed animals.

That was what Peterson meant when he said we didn't have to be enemies. This was what he was offering.

My gaze shifted to the other window in the room. But it didn't lead to the outside world.

Instead, it overlooked the stress test room.

My stomach sunk and goosebumps erupted over my skin. A view of the crashing waves to your right, a live snuff film to your left.

On the other side of the open floor plan toward the kitchen, I heard a clatter. I brought a flame to my hand as I made my way toward it, carefully stepping so I could keep an eye on every direction. When I made it to the far side of the island, I gazed downward with a violet flame outstretched in front of me.

But as my eyes met the culprit of the racket, I immediately absorbed my flame to my hand and dropped to the ground.

That little girl. Alone, shaking on the hardwood floors. Trembling knees pulled into her chest. Pale eyes wide in fear as they met mine.

"Lydia." I reached out to grasp her narrow shoulders. She stared at me, lips trembling. Eyes wide in fear. Yeah, guess she didn't have an endearing picture of me in her head just yet. I offered a sweet smile. "It's alright, I won't hurt you."

"You're the pregnant lady," she whispered, tears streaming down her cheeks.

"Yeah." I struggled to make out the words. "Yeah. That was me."

"Why aren't you with your baby?"

"He... He—" A sharp breath cut me off. "That doesn't matter. We have to go."

"Who are you?" she asked.

I smiled and reached my hand out to shake hers. "My name's Laila. I'm friends with your dad."

Her forehead scrunched up. "My dad died."

My brows collapsed over my eyes. "No. No, sweetie. Your dad's been looking for you for years. He asked me to help find you, that's half the reason these people found me."

She shook her head fast. "No, Mom said so. You're lying."

"I'm not, Lydia. I promise you; your daddy is my friend. Come with me and I'll bring you to him."

Lydia was young, but not so young that she didn't understand what was happening. I had to be up front and blatant, because if not, she wasn't moving, and I really didn't want to knock the kid out to drag her out of here.

"I know you've seen me do horrible things, and I know it's hard to understand. But I was so scared, Lydia. I had to. I couldn't die, I was pregnant. You saw what they were doing to me. You know what they put us through. What they're putting *our* people through. I know it's hard to understand, sweetie. But your mom and Doctor Peterson are on the wrong side of history. I'm not the bad guy here."

"Why were they doing that?"

"I'm not sure. Maybe to see what I was capable of? Or maybe to get my powers to grow? I don't know. I was just trying to find my fiancé's missing brother and you and your mom and they just..." I trailed off. "I woke up here. And then a few days later, those horrible things started."

She said nothing for a moment, considering. "You'll take me to my Dad?"

"I promise. I swear on my life. I will take you to your dad."

She extended her hand to me. I accepted it, stood, and pulled her with me. "Lydia, if I tell you to close your eyes, you close your eyes, okay?"

She gave a nod as we started from the room. I carefully positioned her behind me, and we went out into the dark hallway.

I pulled her hand behind me as we ran down the hall to the next door. I gazed into its window and saw a flight of stairs. I was kind of wandering aimlessly because most of the guards weren't familiar with that part of the building, but I had to keep moving.

A familiar voice called behind me. "Laila!"

I turned and absorbed my flame. Brody ran toward me. A smile came to my lips as he wrapped his arms tight around my shoulders. I hugged him for a moment. I stepped back. "We have to get to the other side."

"Twenty-five people are already moving that direction. The first two wings are cleared." Tears of joy welled in my eyes. "Where does this take you?" He gestured to the stairwell.

"If I'm not mistaken, it goes to Peterson," I said.

"Who's he?"

I gritted my teeth together. "He's the bastard responsible for all of this."

Or so I thought.

"Let's go then." He gestured toward the steps. I hoisted Lydia to my arms, taking two steps at a time. "Who's your friend?"

"This is Lydia," I said, "Ray's daughter."

"No shit. You found them," he said.

"You know my dad?" she asked him.

"Yeah," Brody said, clearly unaware of how to talk to children. "He can be a real pain in the ass sometimes, but he's a cool guy."

"Shut up, Brody." I paused to listen closely. I heard yelling. Indistinguishable and impossible to focus on over the sound of the alarm. But still, the voice made my hands shake and my stomach hurt.

I hated that I was afraid of him.

"I hear him," I said quietly.

Brody teleported in front of us. He looked through the door and pulled a gun from his waistband. "I'm ready when you are."

"How did you—"

"Leah figured out how to hack into the microchips they put inside you guys. She just managed to shut 'em all off. We have our powers back."

I exhaled with relief. "That makes me feel so much better."

He smiled and gave a nod. "Let's end this."

I pulled Lydia to my side.

I melted the hinges off of the door and pulled it down the same way I had the rest. At least ten guards turned. I looked to Lydia. "Close your eyes."

She closed them tightly and looked down. I brought my arms to a flame and stepped onto the door. I heard the click of their guns, but the moment that fire left my body, any bullets they'd expelled fell to the ground with the ashes that remained of their bodies.

"Jesus," Brody muttered.

I grasped Lydia's hand and we started from the stairwell. "You can open them now."

Down the hall to my right a bit, I saw them. Amy had a gun in the hand that hung at her side. Peterson raised a phone to his ear. Someone else stood a few feet in front of them guarded by a few patrols.

Brody raised his gun and fired, shooting the phone from Peterson's hand and grazing the side of his head. So fucking close to a head shot that could have ended it all. Before he had the time to turn around, he teleported to him and held the gun to his head.

That's when Amy turned abruptly. As did the guards and their captor.

My heart sunk.

No.

He was in the first unit I released. He was half the reason I ended up there. How was he back in hand cuffs?

Amy pulled him from the guard and held the gun to his head.

No.

No, no, no.

Not all of this for nothing.

"Put the doctor down or this one dies," Amy said.

"Fuck you," Brody spat.

"Brody?" Chris said behind a quivering lip.

"Chris?" Brody asked.

Fuck. Fuck, fuck, fuck.

"Let him go, Amy," I said. Lydia stepped in front of me to look at her mom. "This can all end tonight. You can go home. You can see your husband again. You can have your family again."

She laughed and shook her head, holding Chris's body tight against hers. "I am home, Laila. As far as I'm concerned, Ray is dead. I have a family right here."

"I'm bringing Lydia home with or without you, Amy."

A half laugh left her nose. "You can't use her as leverage over me."

"I'm not," I said. "But I'll be damned if this fucker destroys another child before their life even starts. She doesn't deserve to grow up like this. She deserves a normal life."

She shook her head. She turned the gun toward us and pulled the trigger of her gun so suddenly, it almost didn't register what had happened until it was too late.

Lydia fell backward into me. I gazed down at her bleeding chest in utter disbelief. I realized where the bullet went.

Straight through Lydia's little chest, ricocheting upward.

Through my stomach.

Into my upper abdomen.

My mid stomach, to be more specific.

She shot her own daughter. Maybe she didn't mean to, maybe she was aiming for me. Nonetheless, she didn't stop to ask if she was okay.

Brody rushed toward me and released Peterson.

"Run!" she yelled to him. Brody caught my falling body.

I'd already lost a decent bit of blood after the flesh wound, but that one was quickly losing a lot more.

No.

God fucking damn it.

Amy and Peterson started down the hall, disappearing into another doorway. Brody yelled at me to stay with him, and blood poured from my lips. Everything was getting blurry. It didn't even hurt; I just couldn't believe it.

Fuck.

All of this fucking effort for Amy to be the villain, Chris to be taken again, and me and Lydia to bleed out on the fucking floor.

Brody pressed his hand into mine and Lydia's wounds simultaneously. It grew harder to breathe. He was screaming, trying to meet my empty gaze. But I couldn't hear him, I couldn't even really see him.

I had them. I fucking had them both.

And now, all four of us were gone again.

Micah healed me and I blew it.

Then Jeremy appeared. He dropped beside me and took my face in his hands with widened, terrified eyes.

He was talking too, but none of it sounded like words. It was just his voice. His sweet, melodic, beautiful voice. Like a song I couldn't get out of my head. Running in circles like a hamster on a wheel.

He turned upward, yelling at someone. I tried to tell him I was sorry. I just wanted him to know that I was sorry. I could have done so many things differently. I could have saved every single one of us if I would have listened when he told me I needed to harness the rest of my abilities.

But it was too late. Everything had already faded to black.

CHAPTER SEVENTY-FOUR

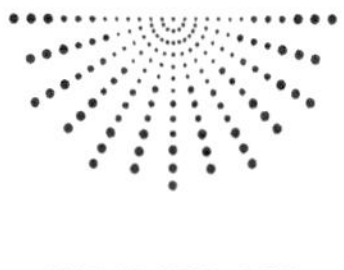

JEREMY

I pushed my hand into the wound of Laila's stomach, panting heavily as Kai ran through the threshold with Mary at his tail.

"Baby, you got to stay with me." I pulled her body close to my chest. Her eyes could have been open, but I couldn't make out much in the strobing red lights.

"The hell happened?" Kai yelled to Brody. He dropped between Laila and the little girl.

I felt guilty for it later, but I hadn't even thought about the child who lay bleeding beside my fiancé. Laila was all I could think about. I just got her back. I couldn't lose her again.

"Just heal them," Brody barked. He staggered to his feet and took off down the hall. I didn't know, let alone care, about what he was running off to.

"Move," Kai insisted. He held a healing light over the little girl's chest and pushed my hand from Laila's bleeding abdomen.

My heart raced as I watched the white light cast a warm glow on the bleeding hole in her stomach. I watched the skin mold back together. I watched the blood stop oozing.

The child beside her shot forward screaming in agony as her

consciousness reappeared with the regeneration. But Laila's eyes stayed closed.

Mary climbed on top of the little girl and held her down. Kai continued to simultaneously heal the two of them.

At first, I thought it was just healing slower than usual because he was using his energy on two people at once. But after a few minutes, her skin closed shut. There was no more blood leaving her body. Her pulse was racing a mile a minute beneath my fingertips that held the side of her neck.

She was alive but she wouldn't wake up.

The little girl screamed bloody murder as Mary climbed off of her. She grasped her shoulders and put her into some peace-filled Angel dream. Kai continued to work on Laila.

"Why isn't it working?" I said.

"Just give me a moment," Kai urged. His hands continued to glow over his sister's body. But nothing changed.

I blinked hard at the blood spot on her blue, dust-covered scrubs. She wasn't bleeding. There was no wound. She was healed.

"Something's wrong," I said. "It isn't working."

"It is," Kai insisted as he continued to hold the white light over her stomach.

"Where are we taking the survivors?" I asked Mary.

"Closest hospital we have for our kind," she said. "Vancouver Private Health Center."

"I know the place."

I teleported to my feet with her in my arms. Then to the threshold where the next power barrier was. I rushed through that doorway to the stairwell where I teleported to the third floor. Then through *that* doorway and to the cliff she created.

In that moment, I didn't even think. I knew something was wrong and I had to get her help.

I just jumped.

I prayed I would be out of that barrier spell's proximity before I hit the ground. Thankfully, I was. I landed about twenty feet from the flag line still being placed that showed where the barrier ended. The jog to that line of little orange flags felt like the longest race I'd ever run.

The moment I passed it, I flashed to Vancouver Private Health Center. As soon as I landed, a nurse I teleported in front of jumped nearly ten feet in the air. "Where's the emergency room?"

"End of the hall." She gripped her chest.

I teleported to the end and hurried to the front desk. "I—I need help. She won't wake up. Her brother healed her, but she won't wake up."

The nurse at the station rushed to her feet and yelled for a gurney. I turned down to Laila in my arms.

She looked so broken. I'd just witnessed her do the strongest thing imaginable and yet she looked weaker than ever.

Laila always looked soft and dainty. Even on her bad days, she looked gentle. But that wasn't soft or gentle. It was feeble.

It looked like she'd made a round trip to Hell. I'll never forget the way that hurt. I was staring down at the barely living personification of my failures.

I should have kept her from it all. I should have protected her. This had nothing to do with her, this was my family's shit. And it got her, and our baby killed.

That's all I kept thinking as they wheeled a bed over and instructed me to lay her on it. What I didn't realize then was that I couldn't protect Laila from much, but I especially couldn't protect her from this.

CHAPTER SEVENTY-FIVE

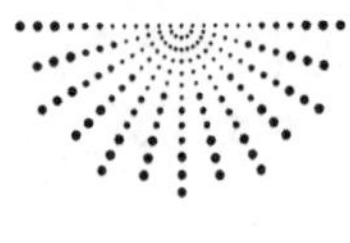

JEREMY

"You said that she was shot?" the doctor asked.

I pushed matted hair from Laila's dirty, sleeping face. I nodded, watching her chest slowly move up and down. "Twice. But her brother healed her."

"She should be awake." He raised his stethoscope to her chest. I tried not to look at the scar between her breasts when he pulled the nightgown down. "Physically, everything looks normal. But something is..." He frowned as he tugged back. "I'd like to run a brain scan."

"A brain scan?" Hannah asked from the chair beside the bed. "Why would she need a brain scan?"

"I just want to be sure of a few things," he murmured. He wrote on his clipboard. "Situations like this—"

"She didn't die," I said. I looked up to meet his gaze. "She wouldn't have lost brain function from blood loss."

"Have you checked her mind?" the doctor asked gently.

I had. And it was empty. No dreams, no thoughts. Nothing. But I felt her soul. She was there, she was alive.

"That doesn't mean anything. I can't always see something when she's asleep."

The doctor pressed his lips together. "We'll just run some tests. But do you have any contact information for her next of kin?"

"I talked to her mom," Leah murmured from the corner of the room. "She's figuring out travel arrangements. As are the FBI."

"Right," the doctor said. "Well, I should be back in an hour or so to run some tests."

"Thanks." I took her hand and held it tightly between mine. I held my gaze steady on her cold, lifeless face. Leah murmured something to the doctor before he turned to leave.

Nearly simultaneously, just as that door clicked shut, the heart monitor began to move slower. It started to beep. And then the green mountain of lines fell to a plateau.

I'm not even sure what I screamed out as I watched that line fall. All I remember was rushing across the bed to hold her, or maybe to shake her back to life. It's a messy blur now. But I'd never been more devastated.

I remember Leah and a nurse grabbing my shoulder as they wheeled in a crash cart. I tried to explain that the shock wouldn't hurt me and that I needed to hold her hand, but they had to usher me from the room. But just as they backed me into the hallway, I watched her body pulse upward into the metal plates against her chest.

Leah held me back. She grabbed my face, pulling it from the chaos behind that doorway. She said something, but all that I heard was that long, ear piercing beep and the blood pumping like a drum in my ears.

I couldn't bring words to leave my lips. All that left my body were sobs. Leah wrapped her arms around me as my legs wobbled.

Then the beep stopped.

Hannah smiled from the foot of the bed. I pushed past Leah and whatever nurses staggered in front of me. I dropped to the bed beside her and took her loose, practically dead hand in mine. Tears raced down my cheeks. I begged her to wake up. I don't remember what I said, just that I kept begging and begging.

After a few minutes, the nurses and doctors cleared out. I could barely make out words. I couldn't process anything that they told me.

I knew what they knew. Medically, she was fine. But her soul was fighting like hell to leave. It didn't want to live. It was broken. *She* was broken.

"Jeremy," Leah murmured. Her hand grazed my shoulder.

I knew what she was gonna say, and I didn't want to hear it. I coasted my hand along Laila's cheek. "Can—can someone get me a rag? I—I need to get this shit off her face."

"Sure." Hannah stood.

"Jeremy," Leah repeated quietly.

"I don't want to hear it." I blinked tears away.

"Sweetie." She sat beside me. "Did you hear what the doctor said?"

I fought the lump in my throat.

"Her body's fine, there isn't any trauma that would point to something like this," she said quietly.

"She's going to be okay." I gritted my teeth together to keep my lip from curling. "She almost died once before, remember? She woke up then too."

"I just want you to prepare yourself," Leah said. "It isn't looking—"

"Shut up." I shot my head to her. Hannah walked toward us with a bed pan and a couple washcloths. "Shut up right now, Leah. Don't even say it."

Leah stood. "We should give you some time with her. Do you want something to eat? Some candy or something?"

I shook my head and turned back to Laila.

"I think I'll stay," Hannah murmured. She sat the pink tub onto the rolling table. "Is that okay, Jeremy?"

I nodded and reached into the tub, wringing the rag over the warm water.

"Alright, I'll grab you something at the food court," Leah murmured.

As I ran the washcloth over Laila's cheek, Hannah started to her feet. She reached into the bin and squeezed out the other rag. She walked to the other side of the bed and sat beside Laila's opposite hip. She lifted the cloth, wiping away at the gray dirt along the edges of her fingernails.

"She's not going to die."

"Of course she isn't. She's Laila. A couple bullets aren't going to be what takes her down." Hannah gave a sweet grin, meeting my gaze.

A smile pulled at my lips, tears forming in my eyes.

"She's here." Hannah looked back down to Laila's hand. "She's back and I'm not ready to see her leave again."

I smiled wider, eyes filling with tears. I nodded again.

I may have lost her, but I'd get her back. I always got her back.

EPILOGUE

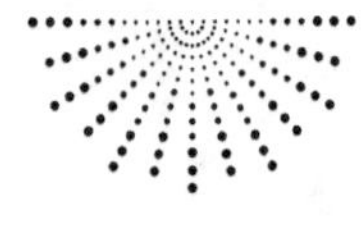

CHRIS

amn it. God fucking damn it.

That's all I kept thinking as the man half my height ripped me from the cold ground and carted my stumbling body down a long hall. It was hard to hear anything over the blaring siren above. But I did hear the clang of a set of keys against the gun at his hip, and I thought about grabbing it.

But we were surrounded.

I could hear their heavy pants as they dragged me through a doorway. I could hear the shuffling of their feet as I smelled…something. Something I hadn't smelled in years. It was masked by the odor of fuel and jet engine smog, but I still smelled it.

Saltwater.

I almost smiled, until the man grasped me harder, and I stumbled.

I remembered I'd never smell it again.

But I left the signal. It was there. Brody saw that they had me for certain, they'd find it. They'd find it and then they'd find me. I knew they would. I fucking *knew* they would.

It smelled so good for that single second that I stopped. I knew the man beside me could kill me but that smell. Fresh air. Fuck, I missed fresh air.

The man yanked my shoulder. "Hurry up, Stevie Wonder," he said. "Move your fucking feet or you're gonna be Hellen Keller next."

My hand tightened to a fist. It took everything in me not to turn and punch him. But that'd be my first blind fight. I knew what I was doing once upon a time, but I didn't exactly have Daredevil's training. I'd been drugged and tortured daily for seven years. I didn't stand a chance against that piece of shit.

But my family did. They'd find me. I knew they would. After all the people Laila had just saved, they wouldn't stop until they found me. And then the rest of us. They'd find my message and then they'd find me.

So I moved my feet.

"Twelve steps," he said over the roar of a jet engine. "Move your god damned feet."

I lifted my foot. The metal step felt hollow beneath it. So did I.

But they'd just lit a fire under my family's ass. They saw me, they knew for a fact that I was alive now. And they wouldn't stop until they found me. I knew it.

Each one hurt. I counted each of those stairs as I grasped the cold handrail. But they'd find us. I just kept telling myself that they would find me. Laila found us then, they'd find us again. And they'd set us all free. They would, they'd set us free.

"Sit him up there," Peterson's voice yelled as I stepped into a quieter space.

It was warm.

"Where at?" the man who held me by my arm called.

"Up there, idiot!" he yelled. "Beside Nastya. But strap his ass in. And make sure his chips are in still. Hopefully she was dumb enough not to cut them out."

"Oh, she was." Another voice laughed. It was familiar. But I couldn't tell where I knew it from. It was an old memory, almost like one from a childhood but somehow even older. "Don't worry. He's not getting out of here any time soon."

He shoved my back and I fell flat to my face. Aches soared through my knees and then my head. It hit so hard that it almost knocked me unconscious.

"Are you fucking kidding me?" the man carrying me said. He grabbed ahold of my shoulder and ripped me up. "You fucking idiot."

"You pushed me, asshole!" I screamed, stumbling upward. "I can't fucking see and you—"

His fist cracked against my cheek. I almost fell again, but he grasped my shoulder.

"Oh, bloody hell," a woman's voice said. "Just help the poor bloke to his seat."

My brows raised in shock. I may have been disoriented but he called her Nastya. And I knew a Nastya with a British accent. Or at least, I knew *of* a Nastya with a British accent. We'd met once, and her voice sounded different, but I knew her. Everyone did. She was infamous.

The man scoffed. He grasped my shoulders and nudged me forward. I took a few steps before he pushed my shoulders downward.

A soft cushion caressed my bony ass. A breath of relief left my lips. I hadn't sat on a soft surface in seven years, not once. Not a couch, not a bed. Not once.

Then a warm hand touched my leg. "Remember me, love?" Nastya's voice whispered, warm at my ear.

The hair on my neck stood and I inched away.

She laughed. The warmth of her breath drew closer once more. "Don't worry, I don't want you that way. We play for the same team. And your secret's safe with me if mine is safe with you."

No one, and I do mean *no one*, knew that. Then again, I was in the presence of one of the most powerful Witches alive. It made sense for her to know just about anything.

"Quit harassing him," the familiar man's voice muttered. "Give him the lamb."

The lamb? How the fuck am I supposed to hold a fucking sheep?

"Open your arms, Chris," another dainty woman's voice said.

"What?" I asked.

"Christ," the familiar man's voice said. Then two strong hands grasped my arm and ripped it from my side. He slammed my right hand to my left hip. He pulled my elbow out.

"What are you—"

"Just shut up," he snapped.

I swallowed hard. Knew better than to argue.

Then something soft caressed the skin of my forearm. Fuzzy, yet silky. A substance that I hadn't touched in years. A blanket.

A hand grazed my forearm before weight within the crease shifted downward.

A smell wafted into my nose. Clean cotton. Warm milk. An odor I hadn't taken in since my sister was born eighteen years prior.

Then a sound moved into my ears and my mouth fell open. A quiet little coo. Not quite a cry, but almost.

My stomach flipped and my head spun.

Laila was wrong.

"He looks a lot like him, doesn't he?" the soft female voice said.

"Aside from the eyes," Peterson muttered. "Or the lack thereof."

I heard them, but I didn't care. I didn't even think to make a quip. All I could think about was that warm little body against my chest.

"Micah," I whispered.

"Not as dumb as you look, love," Nastya said.

My left hand lifted, gently touching the fuzzy blanket and making my way toward his face. As my finger touched that cheek, an over-whelming sense of love washed over me. He may not have been my baby, but he was my family. And he was alive.

That chubby little cheek was the softest thing I'd ever felt. I couldn't see him, but he was beautiful. He *felt* beautiful. He was perfect in every meaning of the word.

"You're all he has now," Nastya said.

"Did you hear her?" Peterson grasped my face and ripped it toward his. I couldn't see him, but I smelled his filthy, sulfur breath against my face. My jaw tightened as I thought over the last seven years. But I couldn't lash out, I was holding my nephew. So, I just nodded.

"They're dead," he said. "His mother. His father. Your brother and your sister-in-law. They are dead."

My stomach sunk. "No. No, I just—I just heard Jeremy."

"And then Laila got shot in the head," he snapped. "Not on my orders. Don't worry. The Fae couldn't heal her. And your brother put the gun to his own."

Jeremy was the one who found our dad hanging from a ceiling fan. He wouldn't kill himself. He knew how much we'd resent him for it because that's how we felt about our father. No matter what. Even without Laila, he wouldn't put his brothers and sisters through that.

I shook my head. "No. No, he wouldn't."

"Laila and that baby were all that mattered to him, love," Nastya said in a soothing voice. "He didn't want to live without them. He's gone, Chris."

My eyes filled with tears. My head shook and my arm tightened around my nephew.

"You're all he has now," Peterson said. "I wanted it to be her that cared for him. He needs his blood. But you'll do."

I couldn't really process it. It'd settle in over the coming months. But he was right about one thing. We were all each other had.

And I was gonna do right by him. From the moment I held my blood in my arms again, I'd decided. I was gonna do right by him.

It was just me and Micah against the world.

But I didn't forget that message I'd left behind. Someone would find it. Maybe not Laila and Jeremy, but maybe Brody or Leah. Maybe Adam or Hannah. Maybe Laila's brother. I didn't know. But someone would.

And then they'd find us. They'd find us all.

The story continues in *Aftershocks*. Turn the page for a sneak peek, or click the link below to download now:
https://www.amazon.com/dp/B08WJXR8RX/

Sign up for Charlie's newsletter and receive a free copy of the Eluding Destiny prequel, *Blood Bar*:
https://liquidmind.media/eluding-destiny-prequel/

If you enjoyed this story, please consider leaving a rating or review on
Amazon:
https://www.amazon.com/dp/B08T17G7S2/

Join Charlie's private reader group on Facebook and discuss all things
Eluding Destiny and Charlie Nottingham:
https://www.facebook.com/groups/661440911724435/

AFTERSHOCKS CHAPTER 1

JUNE 26, 2019 - CHRIS

Slow breaths rose and fell from the little chest beneath my palm. He hadn't cried since that bitch put him in my arms, and that seemed odd. Babies cry. A lot, from what I remembered of Hannah as an infant. But I felt his chest moving. The warmth of his skin radiated into mine. The moisture of his hot breath slid against my hand. He was okay. He was alive.

It'd been so long since I touched another person, I didn't even mind how much my back ached throughout the ride. Of course, with each turbulent bounce, my heart skipped. I kept thinking, *Great. Lived through eight years of torture, finally have a piece of my family back, and we're gonna plummet to the ground.*

But we didn't.

"Who's that?" An elbow bumped mine.

I reflexively glanced that way and felt him jump back. A typical response, one that didn't bother me anymore. But I wasn't sure why my head still turned when people talked to me. I knew I couldn't see them. They obviously did. The whole empty eye sockets thing made that pretty clear.

"My nephew," I said.

"Really?" he asked.

I gave a nod. His little fingers wrapped around my thumb and I smiled. That might have been my first smile since this all started. But it really was something to be happy about.

"He's so little though," he muttered. "What is he? Like, a week?"

"Something like that," I said.

"How'd he end up in here?"

My jaw clenched. I didn't want to get into Laila's story. Not only was it not my place, but it didn't matter now. She was gone. He was here, but she wasn't.

She'd done a great thing on her way down though. Said from day one that she'd get us out of that place. And sure enough, she had. We were out. Still in captivity, but out of *that* prison.

I had to give her an A for effort.

Either way. Micah was alive and he was with me. And they'd have to kill me before they did to him what they'd done to us.

"His mom was taken when she was pregnant." I cleared my throat. "She's the one that blew the roof off."

He huffed. "No shit." I nodded. He paused. Then he said, "But they got her kid."

A knot stiffened in my throat.

That didn't matter. Only for now. Someone would find it. Leah, or Adam, or Brody. Hell, maybe even Hannah. They'd find it. Then they'd find us. I knew they would.

We'd get out. Micah and I wouldn't die in here. We'd make it home.

I had to believe that.

"What's his name?" the guy asked.

"Micah." I ran my thumb against the smooth skin of his knuckles. "Micah Christopher Skoulda."

He got quiet for a second. Then he laughed. "Like, *the* Skouldas? Raphael and Adele Skoulda, those Skouldas?"

Didn't surprise me that he knew my family name. We weren't exactly unimportant in the supernatural world.

"Heard of us?" I asked.

Another laugh. "Uh, yeah. Everyone has. Shit, which one are you?"

"Chris," I said. "Raphael and Adele are my grandparents. And you?"

"Noah. Noah Jackson."

Didn't ring any bells. But it wasn't like I took tabs of every name in our world. I was only eighteen when I was taken, I hadn't worked that many cases.

"But I'm no one. Just a Witch. I can barely cast a conjuring spell." His voice lowered. "Don't know why they want me when they have a La Fay sitting in the front row."

I was right then. The infamous Nastya La Fay. She was the Witch working with Peterson. It didn't come as a shock; the bitch was crazy from what I'd heard. But her dad was on the Chambers. What the fuck was she doing working with a human that kidnapped, held captive, and tortured our people? What could she possibly gain from this?

"Who knows what the fuck they're doing with any of us," I muttered.

"Yeah, true," he said. "You don't think—"

"Alright, shut the fuck up," the voice I'd heard earlier, the one that sounded familiar, said just above my shoulder. "Not a peep or I take him away. Got it?"

I clutched Micah closer to my chest. Not like that would do much good. Clearly the guy had the upper hand. Probably a gun at his hip. A voice that roared like thunder. And more than likely, vision.

A big, firm hand grasped my shoulder. His fingertips dug into the pressure point at my clavicle. My neck curled but I tried not to shift. I couldn't drop the baby. "Did you hear me?"

I nodded.

"Good."

***

The scent of mildew slithered into my nose. The air around me was cool, but not windy. Just cool. Dirty water sloshed between my toes, then damp, dusty concrete. I heard the sound of feet peddling and keys jingling but dripping too. Like water from the ceiling of a tunnel. Maybe that's where we were. In a tunnel. It was warm when we got off the plane, ridiculously warm. Humid, too. But it wasn't a place I'd been before. Which was saying a lot because, prior to the implants, I was a teleporter. I'd been just about everywhere.

"Drop that kid, and I'm breaking your neck." Cold metal pressed against the back of my shaved head. "I already took your eyes, don't think I won't."

I considered saying the last thing I planned to do was put this baby in anyone else's arms, let alone let him hit the chilled concrete beneath my bare feet. But I'd learned over the last eight years to keep my mouth shut if I didn't want to pay for it. Sometimes, I'd make a quip back, but not now. Now, I had a reason to stay alive.

Micah needed me.

And I knew we'd make it out. Not today, clearly, but we would. We'd get out of here. Wherever the fuck here was.

"Did you hear me?" Peterson repeated, pushing me forward with a fist wrapped around the back of my scrubs.

"Yes," I said. "I won't drop him."

"Good. Keep moving."

"Take the gun off him, dumbass," that familiar man's voice said. "What do you think he's gonna do—run? Just help him down the damn steps."

A tunnel. Now going down steps.

I was right. Thank god, I was right. I thought I heard the pilot say we were going underground. Good thing I was paying attention. I hoped I didn't miss one of the numbers though. That would've fucking sucked.

The gun lowered. Peterson grasped my elbow beneath Micah's head. "Eighteen, about a foot each."

I didn't respond, just carefully lifted my foot forward. It would have been easier if I had a hand to grasp the wall or a handrail. But no way was I handing Micah to the bastard that got him in here. I made do.

Carefully, I moved one foot in front of the other. Hate to admit it, but I braced myself against Peterson as I counted. One to eighteen down the cold metal stairs.

Then my feet touched something different. Something I hadn't felt in years.

Vinyl. Fake hardwoods, or something of the sort. Clean, textured. My brows fell in confusion.

"This way." Peterson pulled me forward. "Low door frame, duck."

I lowered my head and took another step forward.

Warm air. Circulated and crisp, but warm. Warmer than I'd felt indoors in almost a decade. And the smell. It still had a hint of mildew but something else too.

Paint. Fresh paint.

"I got him," the other man's voice said. Peterson released my elbow, and another hand took its place. A chill stretched up my spine. Peterson tortured me for all these years, yet his touch didn't make me shiver like that man's.

He edged me another ten or fifteen steps forward. Then he said, "Alright, put him down."

I clenched Micah closer.

He scoffed. Then he yanked my hand from his chest and lowered it to something soft. Fluffy. It rocked beneath my touch.

His voice hardened. "It's a basinet. Put him down before I make you."

My heart picked up speed in my chest. I didn't want to, but what choice did I have? Clearly, he had the high ground.

I gently lowered the little ball of warmth onto the rocker.

The man grabbed my arm and hauled me across the room. I nearly fell but caught myself. My shoulder banged against a doorframe, but he kept pulling. Then he grabbed my hand and set it on something cold. Metal.

He released my hand. "Pull it."

Had no idea what I was pulling, but again, not like I had a choice. I pulled.

Warm water splashed against my head. I jolted back.

A shower. Not a spigot in the wall, but a real shower with a handle and warm water. I'd almost forgotten what that felt like.

"You're taking care of a kid, you need to stay clean. Amy will bathe him. I don't want you to risk drowning him. But you, you clean up in here." He grabbed my hand and lifted it upward. Then my fingers touched something soft. Not as soft as the baby blanket, but softer than the scratchy scrubs against my shoulders. "Towels. And rags in case you need to clean up any spit-up. There's a toothbrush and toothpaste on the counter. Use them. Your clothes will be cleaned daily. We'll set them inside the door. Leave the ones you're wearing in their place."

What the fuck?

Why was I being treated like celebrity inmate in a state prison?

He grabbed my elbow and yanked me again. My shoulder banged against the doorframe once more. At least I could take a warm shower to relax the sore muscle now.

After about ten steps, he grasped my shoulders and pushed me downward. And my ass molded into something remotely comfortable. It wasn't a bed, but—

"This is your cot. The crib's a few feet to your left. The basinet's" — he grasped my hand and lifted it to Micah's chest— "right here. Probably best he sleeps in here 'til he's a little bigger. They used to co-sleep with him, but since you can't see, that might not be a good idea. So put him in here when you sleep. There's a rocker in the corner. We'll drop off bottles every other hour. If he shits, knock on the door. Someone will come to clean him. And your meals will be delivered twice a day. Eat them. You're no good to him dead."

What the fuck was going on? Why did I matter all of a sudden? And what did he mean? Micah was only a few days old, *who* used to co-sleep with him?

"This isn't about you, dipshit." His tone lessened in seriousness and grew slightly annoyed. "This is about him. We need him. And most of all, we need him to trust you. So be a good uncle."

AFTERSHOCKS CHAPTER 2

JUNE 27, 2019 - JEREMY

The sickly scent of cleaning agents wafted up my nose. Cold air blew from the humming register behind me. My head rested against Laila's thigh. I slid my thumb along the back of hers, trying to warm its cool feel.

For the first time in well over twenty-four hours, I started to fall asleep. My eyes were so heavy, I wasn't sure how I'd kept them open as long as I had. But the moment they started to fall, I forced them back open.

I couldn't fall asleep because what if I woke to the sound of those beeps again? What if the next time I opened my eyes, she was dead?

She looked it already.

Her long black hair was a mess of knots and matts. Hannah had tried to comb through them but only made it worse. The once plump, mauve-colored lips I'd spent the last three months dreaming of were a pale, nearly white color. Telling where they began against her paper skin was nearly impossible.

Her cheeks hollowed deep into the cave of her mouth. The collar bone beneath her flesh struggled not to rip the skin above it. The dark circles beneath her eyes were nearly black, almost as if she were punched or maybe even bludgeoned.

She looked dead.

She looked like she had no will left to live. Truthfully, I wasn't sure why she would. I wasn't sure that I did. I kept praying to whatever god was listening that she'd wake up, but if she didn't, I didn't want to keep going.

The only thing that kept me alive over the last few months was my hope for this moment, and the hope of being able to hold my son.

My stomach ached when that thought ran through my mind.

What happened to him? Why wasn't he here? What'd they do to him?

But I couldn't think about that.

I had to have hope. Her heart was beating. I felt it beneath my hand. I saw the little mountains climbing up and down on the machine. Her chest was rising and falling with breath—I had to hold myself together.

For the first time in three months, I had her back. She wasn't here, not really, but she was back. She was right in front of me. And I wasn't gonna let her go.

Hannah was the only other one who held onto hope that she was going to make it. Brody cried nonstop from the time he walked into the room until the time that he left. He couldn't even bring himself to tell me what happened back there.

Adam already gave his regards with teary eyes as he pressured me to drink water or take a nap. It wasn't something that I could do willingly at that point. My body was trying to, but my mind wouldn't let me.

Mary hadn't shown so that gave me hope. If Laila was going to die, she would've made an appearance to say her goodbyes. She must have felt the same way I did. That she was still there. Maybe locked away somewhere, but she was coming back. I knew she was coming back.

A doctor mentioned organ donation. It took everything in me not to punch him in the face, but I just turned back to her and squeezed her hand a little tighter.

As her fiancé, I had no legal right to make that call. But I was terrified that when her mom arrived, she would. Laila was an organ donor, she wanted to donate them if she died. Always said that it was the second to last way she could give back with her life upon her death. The last would be by giving a tree new life after I, and I quote, "dump her body in a hole, throw some dirt over her, and put a little maple sapling on top."

I could've seen her mom doing it. Not because she would've ever wanted Laila to die, but because she didn't look like Laila anymore. The scars alone made her look like a different person but the lack of pigment in her skin made it seem like she was already gone.

"I heard about this once." I ran my fingers along her thumb. "It was in one of those books at the library in our other hospital. The underground one, ya know?"

"Yeah." Hannah stifled a yawn. "I think I did too. Eighteenth century, right? It was a Demon though, wasn't it?"

"No, I think it was a Witch. She cast some really powerful spell. It was something to do with a war. I think she killed a bunch of people at once," I murmured. "Then she got stabbed and a Fae healed her just before she died. But her soul just didn't want to stay. Then she died of dehydration before she woke up."

Hannah fell quiet. Then she said, "She used a lot of energy. That Witch, I mean. Passing that much power through your body is physically straining. So did Laila, but she has us. And twenty-first century medical technology. She just needs some time. Leah gets really tired after she heals. Maybe this is like that. Maybe she just needs to recoup."

"Or maybe she just doesn't want to come back." I gazed up at her nearly lifeless body. "What she did back there, all the people she killed that I witnessed alone...   That's not something I can see her forgiving herself for. Even if they weren't good people."

"She's not going to die," Hannah said. "She held on when her heart stopped beating. She's coming back, Jeremy."

"I hope." I squeezed her unusually cool hand a bit tighter. "I really hope."

"Why don't you sing to her?" she asked quietly. "Laila loves your voice."

I was sure that if I attempted to sing, I'd end up sobbing. "I don't know."

"What if I tell Adam to bring your guitar?" Hannah said. "She loves music. I bet she'd like to hear that, even if she doesn't realize she's hearing it."

"Maybe."

Honestly, I wasn't sure I could do that either. I didn't want to let go of her hand. I didn't want to move. I just wanted to hold her.

Then, I heard those beeps again. The slowdown of the moving mountains before they turned to another flat plane.

My heart hammered against my chest. Not again.

Please god, not again.

"No." I stood. Hannah jumped to her feet and started toward the bed.

I screamed for help. I'm not even sure what I said. My vision blurred around the edges. Hannah gripped Laila's other hand.

Nurses rushed in a few seconds later. I stepped away, heart falling, stomach aching. A nurse touched my shoulders and began to usher me from the room.

"No, please." I struggled to see through my watery eyes. "I'll stay back, I'll let you work. Just don't make me leave. Please."

She glanced me over to make sure I was serious, then nodded. As they ripped her gown open, Hannah released her hand and joined me in the corner of the room. She placed her arms around my waist, and I put mine around her shoulders. I winced as I watched the metal touch Laila's skin before her body jolted upwards toward them.

I didn't feel it.

A shiver stretched down my spine. My lips curled down, head shaking.

Then the long beep turned back to steady, rhythmic blips on the monitor.

Relief. The mountains were climbing and falling again.

But just as I was about to let my shoulders relax with respite, an almost impossible to describe heave left Laila's lips. Her heart began to pick up speed. Her eyes remained closed, but her chest bucked forward in trying attempts to breathe air into her lungs.

My shaking hand moved to my mouth.

She couldn't breathe.

I heard someone say something about intubation. Then I watched a nurse yank her mouth open, put a long metal tool down her throat, and carefully push a tube into her writhing body.

Tears streamed past my fingers. I struggled not to scream. Once the tube was inside, they attached a large blue bag to the end and squeezed it every few seconds. Between each squeeze, the racing peaks on the monitor began to slow into small, gentle moving hills.

"She's okay." Hannah soothed her hand along my back. "She's gonna be okay."

Has *Aftershocks* left you shaking? Click the link below to read more and download now!

https://www.amazon.com/dp/B08WJXR8RX/

ALSO BY CHARLIE NOTTINGHAM

The Eluding Destiny Series

Eluding Destiny

The Horrors That Created Us

Aftershocks

The Precipice

Land of Light

The Quiet Army

Sacred Sins

Flash Back

The Shift

Lost to Time

Gods Among Us

The Cover Up

Blank Slate

Eluding Destiny Prequels

The Last Beginning

Blood Bar

Raven's Cry Series

(MMFM Paranormal Romance)

Raven's Cry

Raven's Song

Celena's Story Duology

(Completed—paranormal romance, urban fantasy)

New Normal: Celena's Story Part 1

Reprisal: Celena's Story Part 2

Origins of the Gods

(Completed Trilogy—fantasy romance, more information on the origins of the Fae and Angels, how life began on earth, where Guardians came from, and—most importantly—a badass forbidden romance)

Origins

The Thrones of Ore and Ice

Creation

Stand Alone Novels

Curse of the Gods: The Bridge Between Origins of the Gods and the Eluding Destiny Series

Sign up for Charlie's newsletter and receive a free copy of the Eluding Destiny prequel, Blood Bar:

https://liquidmind.media/eluding-destiny-prequel/

ABOUT THE AUTHOR

Charlie is a... Okay, talking about myself in third person is weird.

Nice to meet you! My name's Charlie Nottingham, and my whole world revolves around fantasy. When I'm not writing a new book, I'm either hanging out with my dogs, talking with my fans online, or reading some amazing urban fantasy, paranormal romance, or fantasy romance series (always a series, never a stand-alone, because I hate to fall for a character and never see them again). Or re-watching some Buffy or Supernatural. (They never get old!)